Feathers Of Shardaa

Books by Troy D. Wymer

Lightyears Trilogy
Lightyears
Lightyears II: Intragalactic Terrorism
Lightyears III: Ominous Intervention

Treasures From Afar

Xeno Tryst Duology
Xeno Tryst
Feathers of Shardaa

Crystal Avarice

Feathers Of Shardaa

Book Two of the Xeno Tryst Duology

Troy D. Wymer

Dedication

This novel is a dedication to my lovely wife, Robin. Not only has she been inspiring in my early writing career during the late 80s and early 90s, but she has been a wonderful help since I left my hiatus and returned to my writing career in 2016. Since the inception of WymerNovels, she has been an essential part of my brainstorming discussions. Although I have probably been somewhat persistently annoying to her throughout the writing process, she has been steadfast in her support for me during the entire writing, editing, publishing, and marketing phases.

—Troy D. Wymer
April 25, 2020

Preface

Feathers of Shardaa is the epic conclusion and book two of the *Xeno Tryst Duology*. *Xeno Tryst* ended on a cliffhanger...and for good reason. I had much more story to tell. So many questions needed to be answered and mysteries needed to be solved. My goal was to have the sequel to *Xeno Tryst* be at least the same length of approximately 75,000 words, but it surpassed the length of the first book and finished at over 91,000 words. The structure was again plotter-style. I began writing the story in April 2020 and finished exactly six months later in October 2020. The erotic space opera novel is intended for adult audiences only and has about the same amount of explicit sex scenes as the first book. The erotica in this duology is secondary to the overall story arc. The sequel certainly has much darker undertones. Throughout *Feathers of Shardaa,* I have strived to evoke emotion, leave no loose ends, include previous characters, develop rich new characters and conflicts, have detailed world building, and a fascinating story arc on a galactic scale.

Appendices are located at the end of this book with a Syrenthian Galaxy map and a terminology glossary.

—Troy D. Wymer
October 24, 2025

Chapter One

"Seriously, what the fuck?"

"Look, I know you are upset about your father, but you just can't attack the Xenolfan Government leader," Marsull said.

"I hate Siiteper Affelum. Because of him, I don't have a father," Jerex said.

Jerex and Marsull were both young adult Humolfans. There were not many Xenolfan and human mixed families in the Syrenthian Galaxy, but of the ones that existed, almost all of them lived on Olf Teruda. Humolfans had gray skin, white hair, and sapphire eyes. The warm gray skin was a mixture of the Xenolfan bluish-gray skin and the human tan skin.

"Your father died in a mining accident on Aomium Swith along with a lot of other Xenolfan men. Just because Siiteper Affelum sent the miners there to work doesn't mean he is responsible for their deaths. It was an accident," Marsull said.

"Siiteper Affelum had a contract with the Syrenthian Government to mine in their territory on Aomium Swith. Since paying a percentage to the Syrenthian Government took away from Siiteper's profits, he paid my father and the other miners less Asparell coins. I heard a rumor that it was intentionally done because the miners were protesting about their pay. Look…I know you mean well, Marsull, but even my mother has been heartbroken about this for too long," Jerex said.

"Of course she is… But it's not Siiteper Affelum's fault. Look, Jerex, it is getting late and I have a busy day tomorrow. As a fellow Humolfan, I'm asking you to give this notion a rest. I'm asking as a friend."

"I won't!" Jerex shouted.

He walked over to the corner of the room, grabbed a laser rifle into his gray hands, and headed for the door. He had recently started hunting Quillexx on Olf Teruda. It was an animal whose meat was very popular across the Syrenthian Galaxy. Jerex had purchased the laser rifle for that purpose, but was still learning to shoot accurately.

"What are you doing? No! You are going to get yourself killed. You leave me no choice but to inform your mother," Marsull said.

"Don't try to stop me!"

The night air on Olf Teruda was very humid. Xenolfans enjoyed the high humidity on their home planet. The jungle paradise planet was well populated with the indigenous Xenolfan species. The leader of the Xenolfan Government walked along the government palace grounds with his wife, Myreness Affelum.

"It was nice to give the security team the slip so that we could be alone on our anniversary. You looked absolutely stunning at the banquet this afternoon, my love. Happy anniversary," Siiteper said.

The beautiful Xenolfan woman looked up at him, her sapphire eyes sparkling in the moonlight. He stroked her bluish-gray cheek as she smiled. Her long, white hair was eloquently styled and draped over her shoulders.

"Thank you, honey," Myreness said. "Happy anniversary to you too. Those social banquets are always a joy."

It wasn't the first time they removed themselves from the protection of their security team. The palace grounds were well guarded anyway, so it was not a concern to Siiteper. As they walked along the trail, he wrapped one of his black wings around his wife, covering her set of wings.

"I love you, Myreness," he said.

"And I you," she said. "Do you remember when we were younger and we made love out here on the patio?"

Siiteper smiled at her. She noticed his smile in the moonlight. A shadow was cast over half of his bluish-gray, patterned face and white hair.

"I remember it like it was yesterday… We undressed and circled each other in flight, wrapping our wings around each other and then landing in a romantic embrace. You spread open for me and I didn't care if we were outside or not. That was so hot, Myreness."

"Mmm. Yes, it was! Perhaps when we return to the palace, we could revisit that memory," she said.

"I would love that very much," Siiteper said.

Suddenly, they noticed movement up in the tall trees along the trail. Siiteper looked up to see glowing sapphire eyes against the darkness of the night. Myreness abruptly fainted in his arms. Before Siiteper realized what had happened, a young Humolfan male flew in the air above them with a laser rifle in his hands. Siiteper realized the Humolfan made his wife faint with his glowing eyes. The Humolfan began shooting at Siiteper, but he missed due to poor aim and skill. Another Humolfan flew toward him and tried to stop him by grabbing the laser rifle from his hands. As they struggled in mid air with their wings flapping wildly, a laser shot emitted from the rifle and hit Myreness in the chest, creating a large hole of burning flesh. Neither of the young Humolfans could comprehend what Jerex just did as Marsull struggle to take the laser rifle from him. They quickly flew away. The security team that Siiteper and Myreness had ditched earlier came running. They shot at the intruders and struck one of them. Marsull fell to the ground with a terrible thud.

"Myreness! Myreness! No! No, no, no!"

Siiteper flew after the other Humolfan, but by the time he reached the airspace above the palace grounds, the Humolfan was gone. Only the silence of the night remained. He quickly returned to his wife's side as the security team split up. Half of them went toward the dead Humolfan they had shot while the other half ran to where Siiteper and Myreness were. Siiteper sat on the ground with his wife in disbelief. She was gone. The surrounding night seemed surreal. The smell of burned flesh and feathers made him nauseous. He vomited off to the side as he held her cold hand. He began to sob heavily. The loud, uncontrollable cries echoed in the night against the stone walls of the palace. When the guards reached Siiteper and saw Myreness in his arms, they gasped. His cries were heard by other palace guards and personnel near the entrance of the palace.

"They killed my wife. The Humolfans killed my wife," he said. He held her tight as he cried.

Jerex sat in his apartment, very distraught. The events of the evening replayed in his mind over and over. He didn't mean to shoot Siiteper's wife. He could not believe Marsull was dead. His mom was on her way over to his apartment. She had already been informed by Marsull of Jerex's plan before the incident.

It should have been me, not him! Jerex thought.

When Iisherth Mainter arrived at her son's apartment, Jerex explained to her what had happened. "Mom, I should have listened to Marsull!" he said.

Sunlight brightened a cemetery gathering, not far from the Xenolfan Government palace. The funeral of Myreness Affelum had just taken place. Many Xenolfans slowly dispersed from the event with heavy hearts. Siiteper Affelum was dressed in black and walked with a security detail. He had never asked for much security in the past, but times had changed. He lost the best thing that ever happened to him…all because of the Humolfans! As he was transported back to the palace, he sat in the back of the anti-gravitational transport.

Things are going to change around here. Things are going to get ugly! he thought.

Upon reaching the palace, Siiteper made his way along a secluded corridor toward the lower levels. Only the sitting leader of the Xenolfan Government had authorization to enter that area of the palace. Candles were evenly fixed along the walls of the long corridor. The flickering candlelight gave a strange shimmering effect to the corridor. A shiny, marble floor reflected the candlelight. Siiteper noticed the portrait of himself that hung on the wall, followed by portraits of all the Xenolfan leaders that ruled before him. There was room for many more portraits for future leaders. The sound of his boots echoed as he walked along. He turned left and entered a narrow corridor that was decorated with a burgundy carpet. Gothic patterns were woven into the design. Soon, Siiteper stood before a large set of double doors. After he entered the room, the pneumatic doors closed behind him. He walked across the marble floor of the dim room. Another set of doors was fixed before him. He opened them and started down a set of stairs to a landing. Continuing downward, Siiteper entered the archives. Many of the Xenolfan Government secret documents and texts were located in the archives of the palace's lower levels. After locating the documents he was searching for, he sat down at the only desk in the room. He thumbed through the pages until he reached the page he was searching for.

I will change these laws immediately! Siiteper thought.

He brought the documents back up to his palace office for major revisions and as their new location. As an autocracy form of government, he alone could change the laws.

There will be no more Humolfans born in this galaxy. The half-breeds are finished!

"According to our intelligence, there are only twenty-three interspecies couples that live off-planet. The remainder are here on Olf Teruda," Commander Darrian said.

"Well then, gathering those twenty-three mixed families up from the Syrenthian Government's territory needs to be done in a very stealthy manner. We don't need to start a war with the Syrenthian Government. Their leader, Misner Riggs, on Exandra would not be forgiving if he discovered our plan…especially since it involves humans too," Siiteper said.

"I can assure you, this operation will be extremely covert. I already have my teams en route to apprehend the interspecies families. Of the twenty-three that are off-planet, there are nine on Enax Port, seven on Red Jacket, five on Asparr Celtarious, and two on Exandra. We have extra precautions in place for the Exandra extractions since that is the capital of the Syrenthian Government. All the hundreds of interspecies families here on Olf Teruda will be much easier to gather up for this military operation," Commander Darrian said.

"As my military high-command officer, I have confidence that you can execute this operation successfully," Siiteper said.

"The prisoners are to be taken to a holding cell in our base on the satellite of Dalaa?" Darrian asked.

"That is correct. I know you have adequate room there. I can assure you, it is just temporary. They won't be in your facility too long. Unlike phase one of the operation where you gather the interspecies couples and families, phase two will be to transport them to the Shardaa Sector. I have special plans for the second phase of this operation. And phase three will not involve you so much, but military doctors and a few of our scientists," Siiteper said.

"I read the mission briefing. I understand this is quite unorthodox, but I can assure you that you have my full loyalty, sir," Darrian said.

"Your loyalty has never been in question. Keep that all the way down your chain of command and we won't have a problem," Siiteper warned.

"Yes, sir," Darrian said. "Will there be anything else?"

"Yes, there is. After an investigation, our surveillance has indicated that the Humolfan responsible for killing Myreness is Jerex Mainter. His Xenolfan father was killed in a mining incident on Aomium Swith, but his human mother, Iisherth Mainter, still lives here on Olf Teruda. Widows and widowers of the interspecies couples are included in the data for the extractions as well as adult Humolfan offspring. So, once Iisherth and her son, Jerex, are gathered on the moon of Dalaa, I want you to bring them both here before me at the palace," Siiteper said.

"Yes, sir," Darrian said.

After Darrian left the office, Siiteper looked down at a picture of his beautiful wife that sat on his desk.

"I will avenge your death, my love. I will avenge it a thousandfold."

With sudden force, the door bust inward, breaking off its hinges. Iisherth Mainter was startled as she looked up at the military officers entering her home. She was only dressed in scanty nightwear. Before she could react, one of the military officers grabbed her arm with his bluish-gray hand in a tight grip. He jabbed something sharp into her wrist.

"By the authority of the Xenolfan Government leadership, you are hereby detained," the officer said.

"What did I do?"

The officer's only response was to drag her out of her home in the middle of the night. Fear ran through Iisherth as she became extremely anxious. She was brought aboard a military shuttle that was parked outside of her home. They placed her in a cell toward the back of the ship where there were other prisoners that had already been gathered. After Iisherth entered the holding cell, the blue laser locks that crossed the door to prevent the prisoners from escaping were reactivated. Iisherth looked at the other prisoners in the cell. There were human men and women as well as Xenolfan men and women in the holding cell. There were also male and female Humolfans of all ages, including adults. What she noticed about many of the human and Xenolfan women was that they were pregnant. None of this made any sense. Iisherth began to put some of the pieces of the puzzle together when she realized they were all interspecies couples and families…and in her case, a widow.

Oh no! They're going to take Jerex too! she thought.

Iisherth had a sudden insight that this could all be a result of the actions of her son. She suddenly felt nauseated and leaned against the wall.

The military shuttle continued to stop at several locations as they gathered more prisoners. When the holding cell was full, the shuttle returned to the satellite of Dalaa.

A female voice came over the shuttle's speaker system, "Xenolfan military shuttle sixteen, you are cleared for landing on Dalaa base."

Iisherth wondered how many shuttles of interspecies families they were gathering. After the shuttle settled and came to a halt, none of the military officers came to the cell immediately. They could hear the announcement of shuttle after shuttle after shuttle arrive at the base on Dalaa. At least Iisherth knew where she was. She looked at all the people in the holding cell and figured there were approximately fifty prisoners in that shuttle alone. There were many conversations taking place among the prisoners, all wondering what was going on. Some of them came to the conclusion that the interspecies couples and families were being targeted.

Soon, several military officers arrived at the shuttle holding cell and disabled the laser lock. The prisoners were escorted off the shuttle, across the hanger bay, and through a maze of corridors into an even larger holding cell. There were many more prisoners already in the larger holding cell. After Iisherth and the others were escorted in, the blue laser locks were reactivated. There were multiple sets of laser locks in the large military base holding cell.

Iisherth tried to locate her son by looking around through the crowd. There were many people in the cell, making it very difficult to search. She walked through the crowd a short distance, embarrassed of her revealing nightwear. She noticed several of the prisoners, both human and Xenolfan, were nude. They must have taken them from their homes just as they were. Iisherth's anxiety started to become anger. Just when she was about to give up on locating her son, she heard a comforting voice.

"Mom!"

Iisherth turned to see Jerex moving through the crowd toward her.

"Mom!" he shouted.

"Oh Jerex!" she cried.

They hugged for a long moment.

"What's going on? What is the Xenolfan military doing with us?" Jerex asked.

"I don't know, Jerex. I have a feeling it has something to do with what happened," Iisherth said.

"I should just turn myself in," he whispered to his mother.

"It may be a little late for that. I think Siiteper Affelum has snapped. When his wife died, something snapped in him," Iisherth said.

"I am so sorry for what I did. I was only pissed off because of what happened to dad," Jerex said.

She looked at her son. "I wish you would have told me how you felt before all this. I miss your father too. What you did wasn't right, Jerex. But this…this also is not right."

A tall military officer walked up to the large holding cell. There were over one thousand one hundred people in the holding cell, most of them from Olf Teruda. He made an announcement over a speaker system.

"I want Jerex Mainter to step forward," the officer said.

A murmur started through the crowd as heads turned. Jerex was afraid to step forward. Finally, a large Xenolfan man stepped forward.

"I'm Jerex Mainter," he said.

"No, you are not Jerex Mainter. Jerex Mainter is a Humolfan." The officer scanned the Xenolfan before him. "When you prisoners were gathered, you were injected in the wrist with a chip. You are not Jerex. You are Bapbs. Don't make me shoot you, Bapbs. Jerex Mainter, step forward, now!"

Bapbs stepped back into the crowd and gained the attention of a human man.

"That was a brave thing you did. We need to stick together. All of us need to stick together," the human man said.

Bapbs turned toward the man. "Yes, we do. Bapbs is the name."

"Hi, Bapbs. My name is Rodes. It's nice to meet you. We need to fight this oppressive tyranny. This is absolutely ridiculous."

"Yes, it certainly is," Bapbs said.

After a short time, the tall military officer started to become visibly impatient. Jerex gave his mom a hug and then stepped forward through the crowd toward the officer, his black wings quivering with nervousness.

"I'm Jerex Mainter."

The officer scanned him and let him out of the cell. An armed officer pointed a rifle at Jerex as the first, tall officer made another announcement.

"I want Iisherth Mainter to step forward," he said.

Iisherth stepped forward toward the laser lock.

"I'm Iisherth."

The officer also scanned her and let her out of the holding cell. Another armed officer walked over toward Iisherth with a laser rifle pointed at her as well.

"You two, follow me," the tall officer said.

The two of them were led at gun point through a maze of corridors. They entered into the hanger and were prompted into a lone shuttle that sat off to the far side of the hanger bay. Once again, they found themselves in a shuttle holding cell. This time, however, it was only Iisherth and Jerex.

"What is going on?" Jerex asked.

"I don't know. They singled us out, so I'm sure they are aware of what you did."

Jerex began to cry. "I'm so stupid, Mom. I'm so stupid. Oh… Oh, why did I do that? Why?"

Iisherth shook her head and began to cry herself.

Soon, the shuttle arrived at the government palace on Olf Teruda. Iisherth and Jerex were led into the palace, up a set of stone steps, and across a mezzanine. Beyond its stone railing, the mezzanine overlooked the lobby of the palace. After some distance, they reached Siiteper Affelum's office.

"Welcome to the government palace. Have a seat," Siiteper said, gesturing toward the chairs.

They both sat down, a look of concern coming over them.

"The reason why I've brought you both here is because I have to show you something," Siiteper said.

He took a picture of Myreness from his desk and turned it around to show them.

"This was my wife, Myreness...until *you* killed her!" He shouted with such a reverberating tone that it could be heard far down the palace corridor.

"I'm sorry," Jerex cried.

"Yes! You are sorry. But it is too late for apologies. Why did you do this? Why?"

"Because you sent my father to Aomium Swith where he died in a mine. You were my target, not your wife."

Siiteper contemplated Jerex's statement. He thought about the miners on Aomium Swith and the protest that had taken place.

"So, that is what this is all about? Do you see my wife in this picture? She meant the world to me. I'm sure your father meant the world to you as well. I have an idea. Let's go for a walk, shall we?"

Siiteper stood up from his desk, followed by Iisherth and Jerex. Under armed guard, he led them down to the outdoor palace grounds. As they walked by a clear, blue pond, multiple waterfalls could be seen in the distance against a beautiful mountainous background. Natural arches crossed the river that fed the pond. Across the pond, there were several different waterfalls that also fed into the pond, flowing from different heights. Siiteper led them along the trail toward the patio. He soon stopped on the trail.

"This is the very spot where Myreness died in my arms. You took everything from me that night. Being the Xenolfan leader..." he said as we waved his arms toward the palace, "this palace...this power...it's nothing compared to Myreness. You took everything from me. And now, I'm going to take everything from you. All those one thousand plus prisoners you saw earlier. They are all going to die because of you! I'll start with your mother."

Siiteper pulled a laser pistol from his side and shot Iisherth in the chest. She fell to the stone trail, smoke rising from a crater in her chest. Jerex knelt down over his mother.

"Mom! Mom! No!" he cried.

He turned toward Siiteper, tears flowing from his eyes.

"I'm going to tell you a secret, Jerex. Your father was not killed in a mining accident. That incident was done intentionally because the miners were protesting against me for their pay and some insignificant conditions on Aomium Swith. It was made to look like an accident. I killed your father. I killed your mother. And now I am going to kill you. Afterward, all of the other prisoners..."

Siiteper pointed his laser pistol at Jerex's head and pulled the trigger.

Siiteper Affelum knew that if knowledge of his military operation of genocide reached the leader of the Syrenthian Government on Exandra, Misner Riggs, he would have several battleships on his Olf Teruda doorstep immediately. Things needed to be done very stealthily. That is why the extractions were all done at night. The second phase of his plan was to transport the prisoners to the Shardaa Sector. It was an unpopulated sector of space near the edge of the Syrenthian Galaxy. It was a well isolated and uncharted region of space. Virtually no one traveled to that territory by choice for fear of getting lost, as the star system was not programmed into the navigational systems.

Siiteper's office door sounded.

"Enter."

His military high-command officer stepped into the office.

"Good afternoon. We are ready for phase two of the operation. The prisoners have been loaded into one of our battleships, which has holding cells to accommodate all one thousand one hundred prisoners," Commander Darrian said.

"Good. I will be joining you on this phase of the mission. We will leave at once," Siiteper said.

"Many of the prisoners are complaining. The majority of the mothers are pregnant and some are even showing signs of going into labor. Many are hungry and cold. Others are complaining they have no clothes and also that there are not enough toilets in the holding cell for everyone to use," Darrian said.

"That's too damn bad! I think they're about to have a lot more things to worry about when we reach the Shardaa Sector," Siiteper said.

• • •

The military battleship *Olf Maximus* entered the Shardaa Sector. On approach toward the outer edge of the Sharasp Tharrian Asteroid Mass, they slowed to maneuver around several of the large asteroids, while blasting other smaller ones with laser cannons. The blue beams of intense light disintegrated the small asteroids with ease.

"We are one lighthour from the Shardaa Star System," Darrian said to Siiteper.

Siiteper was on the bridge of *Olf Maximus* with Darrian. They peered past Captain Nast as they both looked out the observation window at the dark and desolate area of space.

"Since the discovery of this star system, only the first planet has been named, is that correct?" Siiteper asked.

"That is correct. The first planet was named Shardaa. It does not have an atmosphere," Darrian said.

"Well, that planet will not work for our operation, then. Scan the additional planets in the system. I want their data recorded and I will name them. Let me know which ones have safe atmospheres," Siiteper said.

"You want to name them, even though this is Syrenthian Government territory?" Darrian asked.

Siiteper gave Darrian an angry look.

"Yes, sir. I will have our cartographer and planetologist get right on that," Darrian said.

After contacting other personnel, Darrian relayed the message. Soon, the data came back with promising information.

"Although some of the information on the distant planets in the Shardaa Star System is a bit sketchy, it appears there are at least five other planets in addition to Shardaa. From what we can tell, they all have atmospheres with no toxins. The first couple of planets from our proximity are a bit rough to land on, with rocky terrain, monoliths, spires, and rock outcrops. I would recommend the third or fourth planet for our operation. They seem to have adequate landing areas and at least some vegetation. What do you want to name the planets?" Darrian asked.

"Well, Shardaa is already named. Let's simply call them S2, S3, S4, S5, and S6. So, S5 and S6 have sketchy data since the outward planets are so distant?"

"That is correct. There is also a lot of interference due to the Sharasp Tharrian Asteroid Mass."

"Due to our proximity, it is logical for us to travel toward S4, the fourth planet out in the system," Siiteper said to the captain.

"Yes, sir," Captain Nast said.

The captain of the *Olf Maximus* flew the battleship toward S4. It did not take long to arrive. There was very little starlight in most of the Shardaa Sector. The stars that did shine were very bright. Siiteper knew the Shardaa Sector was the perfect place to complete the second phase of his operation. *Olf Maximus* soon entered an atmosphere of gray clouds and landed in a clearing on S4.

"Let's exit the ship and inspect the area. We need a large area for this second phase," Siiteper said.

Siiteper, Darrian, and a few other officers proceeded toward the exit of the battleship. Once Siiteper stepped out of the ship and onto the rocky terrain, he knew it would be the perfect spot for his plan. Other than an occasional tree, the area was fully open. Countless large and small stones could be seen scattered across the terrain. They walked the length of the open area toward a distant cliff. After reaching the edge, Siiteper peered down at the jagged rocks in the canyon below.

"This is perfect," Siiteper said. The group headed back toward the battleship. "Only remove fifty prisoners at a time. Start with the Xenolfan and human men. I want officers set up with laser rifles. Lead them to the cliff at the edge of the clearing. Make them jump or push them. Then we will execute the Xenolfan and human women. Save the Humolfan children and Humolfan adults for last. I will be on the bridge. Keep me posted."

"Yes, sir," Darrian said.

A short time had passed before Siiteper was contacted by Darrian. "It is done, sir. There was some resistance as some of the Xenolfan men tried to fly away, but they were shot down farther out over the canyon below. Two specific individuals were a particular nuisance. A Xenolfan named Bapbs and a human named Rodes. They were the last of the men to die."

"I see," Siiteper said. He put his finger to his mouth in thought. "Bring out fifty Xenolfan and human women at a time. Start in rows near the cliff and work your way toward the ship. Kill them all...and their babies in the womb. There will be no more half-breed Humolfans born. Once the first fifty are dead, release the next fifty Xenolfan and human mothers. When every Xenolfan and human mother has been killed, let me know. Again, leave the Humolfan monsters for last. I will be here on the bridge with Captain Nast."

Several hours later, Darrian contacted Siiteper on the bridge. "All of the pregnant Xenolfan and human women, as well as non-pregnant ones, have been killed. They are in organized rows. But we seem to have a problem."

"Problem?" Siiteper asked.

"Yes. We have run out of room in the large clearing and the bodies are lined from the cliff all the way up to the ship," Darrian said. "So, now we have no room for the Humolfan offspring... What would you like us to do with them?"

"I will be down there in a moment to make that decision," Siiteper said as he stood up from his seat on the bridge.

After a few words with Captain Nast of the *Olf Maximus,* Siiteper made his way down one of the ship's corridors and met Darrian in a corridor intersection. Darrian wore a mask.

"Before you bring out the Humolfans, I want to go outside and inspect your work," Siiteper said.

"You'll want to wear one of these," Darrian said, handing him a mask. "The smell is very unpleasant."

Siiteper looked at him for a long moment and took the mask. He put on the mask and followed Darrian toward the exit. As the two of them exited the ship, Siiteper's white hair shifted from a slight breeze that blew across the open area. Even with the mask, he could smell the strong scent of burned flesh and feathers. The scent reminded him of when his wife had been shot. The sudden emotional memory gripped him. He gazed out across the field at all the bodies. Row after row after row, he saw the bluish-gray Xenolfan women and tan human women with holes in their chests, smoke still emitting from the damage caused by the laser fire. Almost all of them had enlarged abdomens as they were pregnant with Humolfan child. The abdomens also had laser holes through the flesh. The twisted, black feathers of the Xenolfan wings and the tangled bluish-gray limbs intertwining with the tan human limbs was a morbid sight. As Siiteper walked along the edge of the field, one particular Xenolfan woman caught his eye. He paused for a moment and looked down at her. She had already begun labor and her gray Humolfan baby was partially outside of her reuleaux triangular vagina. Her mangled black wings were broken and seared. The bluish-gray skin became a translucent black near the laser wound. Her long, white hair blew in the wind. Siiteper looked at her open sapphire eyes as they stared lifelessly at the gray sky. He looked away and continued walking toward the cliff. Upon reaching the cliff, he looked over the edge at the bloody pile of bodies that landed against the jagged rocks below. He noticed several of the Xenolfan men's bodies out in the distance of the canyon. As Siiteper stared off the cliff, a single tear ran down his right cheek. He quickly turned away and strode toward the battleship at a fast pace. It took Darrian by surprise and he quickened his step to keep up with the Xenolfan leader.

"Is everything okay? Is there anything we could have done better?" Darrian asked.

"Everything is fine. Bring the Humolfans out here. I will wait."

At the entrance of *Olf Maximus*, Siiteper waited outside for Darrian to return with the remainder of the prisoners. When they began exiting the ship, Siiteper removed his mask. There were over three hundred Humolfans that exited the ship, ranging from little children to young adults.

The advent of interspecies relationships was a fairly new practice in the Syrenthian Galaxy, so the oldest Humolfan offspring was only around thirty years. Because of the stigma of being half Xenolfan and half human, none of the young adults had yet bred with anyone else.

Cries began to emit from the crowd of Humolfans as they spotted their mothers and looked back at Siiteper, Darrian, and the military officers that had exited the ship behind them. Some of the Humolfans ran and some flew toward their dead mothers once they recognized them. The sound of a multitude of sobbing cries filled Siiteper's ears.

"Shall we kill them?" Darrian asked.

There was a long pause as Siiteper looked across the scene of mass murder. He never thought he would commit genocide on his own people, or the human species for that matter. Thoughts of his wife returned to his mind.

"No. Don't kill them. Let them live here in the dark and desolate Shardaa Sector." He turned to address the crowd of Humolfans. "Listen to me, Humolfans!"

They turned and focused their attention on the Xenolfan leader. The older Humolfans were particularly tuned to his address, but there were still some murmurs and cries.

"Quiet!" Darrian shouted.

"Listen to me!" Siiteper repeated. "Your fathers and your mothers were put to death. A Xenolfan man named Bapbs and a human man named Rodes fought valiantly up until the end. They were the last of the men to die. If either of them is your father, you should be proud. It is because of you Humolfans that I no longer have my wife. But enough carnage has taken place today. I will not kill you half-breeds. But you will be banished here on S4 in the Shardaa Sector. Your exile is permanent. I will have a battleship guarding this region of space and if, somehow, you come across a way to travel away from here, you will be destroyed."

The older, adult Humolfans listened to his words, but the younger ones didn't understand. After his address, Siiteper and the rest of his military crew returned to the *Olf Maximus.* Soon, the ship lifted from the surface of S4 and departed the Shardaa Sector.

As *Olf Maximus* traveled at lightspeed toward Olf Teruda, Siiteper Affelum could not shake the images of the Humolfan children staring up at him with the sadness in their eyes. It haunted him for the remainder of the trip.

Upon returning, he began phase three of his operation. The third phase would be the most difficult. Within a short time after contacting two military doctors and three of the top Xenolfan scientists, they met in the comfort of Siiteper's office in the government palace. Soon, Darrian also joined the group and sat in one of the comfortable chairs.

The stranded Humolfans eventually discovered their fathers over the edge of the cliff. There was not much they could do to bury the bodies, so they left them. They mourned for many days. Due to the rocky terrain and no shovels, their mothers were left above ground and they covered them with stone mounds. The task of gathering enough large stones to cover hundreds of bodies with cairn burials, put gravestone markers in place, and carefully chisel their mothers' names into the gravestone markers was beyond exhausting. Harder stone was discovered and used to create tools for chiseling names into the softer gravestone markers. There were enough adult Humolfans among the group that the task was completed in several weeks. The decomposing bodies kept them motivated to work relentlessly. They put a large, flat stone at the edge of the field as a plaque with the Grave of Mothers name chiseled into it. One of the teenage Humolfans made a stone plaque that was put at the edge of the cliff to honor all of their fathers. The adult Humolfans began to organize a plan for survival. Some built shelters while others searched for food. During that time, it was essential to find a good food source to survive. They discovered various plants and animals on S4 that were used for that purpose. Despite being isolated from the rest of the galaxy, they began to make the best of their situation.

"Thank you all for coming. You have all previously been briefed on the third phase of our operation. Phase three will be to modify the DNA of all Xenolfans currently alive in the Syrenthian Galaxy. We will genetically prevent our breeding abilities with humans. Since most of us live here on Olf Teruda, the logistics of this phase should not be too difficult. How is the testing and experimentation going with the Xenolfan men and women that we are using for this phase?" Siiteper asked the doctors and scientists.

"As a top Xenolfan scientist on Olf Teruda, I can assure you that the genetic modification to eliminate Xenolfans from breeding with humans is a difficult task; however, we have made great strides. We are currently on the brink of a solution," Dr. Stratuss said.

"It hasn't been without loss, however. To date, we've lost three Xenolfan women and have permanently injured one Xenolfan man with the experimentation. He is still in our facility," Dr. Arrkid said. Dr. Arrkid was one of the two military doctors.

"Some casualties in this process are to be expected. We are on the edge of scientific achievement," Dr. Argonn said. He was the second of the three scientists.

"The Xenolfan man that has survived must be eliminated," Siiteper said. "This entire program is a stealth operation. We cannot have loose witnesses running around. Once a solution is found, we will set up an immediate follow-up program to have all the Xenolfan population come in to our regular medical facilities and have the procedure done to protect them against a 'virus.' In the meantime,

Darrian, be sure no new interspecies relationships develop. Keep surveillance on our people and stop anything like that from happening before it starts. Once phase three is complete, it will no longer matter."

"I will see to it that the Xenolfan man is taken care of," Dr. Correthell said. He was the second military doctor.

"Although the male Xenolfan DNA modification has been more challenging than the female, we are also on the brink of achievement there as well," Dr. Albriggs said. He was the third of the three scientists.

"How much time are we talking here?" Siiteper asked.

"I would say we should have a solution for both sexes within the week," Dr. Stratuss said.

"Without long-term testing of Xenolfan pregnancies between two Xenolfans, we won't know if there are any long-term side effects of this DNA modification procedure," Dr. Argonn argued.

"Early models show that there will be minimal side effects, if any," Dr. Stratuss said.

"This needs to happen now. We don't have months to wait for a Xenolfan couple's pregnancy to develop. I trust that it will work fine," Siiteper said.

"Would you care to visit the medical facility as we wrap up this testing?" Dr. Arrkid asked Siiteper.

"Yes. Darrian and I will visit the facility immediately," Siiteper said.

"Yes, that would be great," Darrian said.

The seven Xenolfan men left Siiteper's office. The secret military medical facility was not far from the government palace.

As the seven men entered the medical facility, the smell of isopropyl alcohol lingered in the air. Siiteper and Darrian were led down a series of well-illuminated corridors. They soon entered a procedure room where a Xenolfan woman lay strapped to a table. She was crying out in pain as two doctors extracted cells from her reproductive organs. Retrieving eggs from mature ovarian follicles was an essential part of the plan. A small stream of red blood drained from her and dripped into a metal pan below. Screams could be heard from another operating room beyond where they stood.

"Are these subjects not put on some type of anesthetic?" Siiteper asked.

"No. These subjects are not volunteers, but extractions from society. We have found that anesthesia interferes with some of the molecular patterns that we are monitoring," Dr. Stratuss said.

"But I have argued that the level of hormones released from the pain is also affecting the molecular patterns," Dr. Albriggs said.

"Finding a solution is the priority, not their comfort level. They won't be leaving anyway," Siiteper said.

The seven of them continued their tour of the facility. They entered the next room along the corridor where the loud screams emitted from. Another Xenolfan woman was being experimented on. She let out a deep, reverberating scream of agony that hurt their ears. Suddenly, she lay still, her bluish-gray arms falling to the sides of the table. A steady stream of red blood flowed from her reuleaux triangular vaginal opening and drained into another metal pan. One of her ovaries was completely extracted. The doctor that was performing the procedure removed a long needle and looked up at his guests with sudden embarrassment.

"Well, we lost another one…but we are so close," the doctor said as he waved at the group with a bloody, gloved hand.

As the group continued into the next operating room, they noticed a Xenolfan man on the table. His patterned face was a deep shade of purple from the agonizing pain. His breaths were shallow, yet heavy. The doctor working on him had a needle in the epididymis of his right testicle, extracting mature sperm cells.

"Why are you doing this?" he cried in a deep voice as the group passed through the room.

The next room had two humans strapped to the tables, one female and one male. Their intense cries of pain greeted the guests as they entered the room.

"I had strict orders not to experiment on the humans for phase three of the operation!" Siiteper shouted.

"We are extracting sperm and egg cells directly from them to be sure our modified Xenolfan DNA works and our species will no longer be able to breed with humans. It is necessary testing, I assure you," Dr. Stratuss said.

"If Misner Riggs of the Syrenthian Government finds out, it will start a war," Siiteper warned.

"I understand. After we are done with them, they will simply disappear, like the Xenolfan subjects," Dr. Stratuss said.

"I've seen enough. Let me know when you have a solution for both the Xenolfan men and women," Siiteper said.

"Yes, sir. It shouldn't be too much longer," Dr. Albriggs said.

"We will contact you as soon as we are there," Dr. Correthell said.

Several days later, Siiteper received a communication from Dr. Stratuss. He took the comm in his office.

"What do you have for me?" Siiteper asked.

"We are there, sir. We have developed an injectable agent that will modify existing Xenolfan DNA to achieve the solution you seek. Because of our germline gene editing, Xenolfans will no longer be able to breed with humans," Dr. Stratuss said.

"Wonderful news. I will contact Commander Darrian to start bringing in all Xenolfans to our regular medical facilities for the injections," Siiteper said.

He immediately had Darrian begin the mandatory process of Xenolfan injections.

Nine months later, Siiteper received an urgent communication from Dr. Argonn.

"This is Dr. Argonn. We just witnessed the first Xenolfan couple's baby born after the injections. It is a healthy baby, but there is one problem. It has no wings! It was born without wings. And I am hearing reports of exactly the same thing from two other hospitals here on Olf Teruda. I tried to advise the other scientists that we needed more long-term testing. We needed more research. This unintended side effect has stripped the Xenolfan species of our ability to fly! The Xenolfan baby at my hospital was a boy, but the reports from the other hospitals were of a girl and a boy."

"Oh fuck!" Siiteper managed. "I want all of you doctors and scientists in my office within the hour."

The doctors and scientists arrived in Siiteper's office. Silence filled the room and they could all tell Siiteper was extremely pissed.

"Do you know how many people have contacted the Xenolfan Government today? They are all wondering what is going on. Why are babies suddenly being born without wings? Some of them are speculating it was from the supposed virus vaccination injections. I have my public relations team trying to fix this shit. I have allowed our historian to add to our history books that we are seeing the results of microevolution. That is the official reason why this is happening. The historian believes this story and understands. He will change the texts accordingly. No one ever has to know about this mission," Siiteper said.

The doctors and scientists began to argue among themselves.

"That is enough!" Siiteper said. "Dr. Arrkid and Dr. Correthell, did you eliminate the doctors and nurses in the military medical facility?"

"Yes, sir" they both replied.

"With the testing, research, and experimentation that was done on those, now terminated, subjects to develop the DNA modification agent, and with the fact that it was flawed and has stripped our species of our wings and the ability to fly, I cannot allow you doctors and scientists to just walk around with that type of knowledge."

Darrian entered the office with a laser pistol in his hand. The five men looked up at him in surprise. He quickly fired at each of them and silence returned to the office.

"Well done, Darrian. Their arguing was getting annoying. I understand the doctors and nurses from the medical facility have been taken care of. And I take it that you have eliminated your crew that helped with phase one and phase two of the operation?"

"All of the military officers from the entire operation have recently been eliminated, including Captain Nast and the crew of the *Olf Maximus*. There was a slight incident where one of the ships with an officer aboard failed to explode after I fired on it, but I monitored it for life forms afterward and found none. So, I have mopped up the entire mess, sir," Darrian said.

"Good. I'm glad to hear everything has been covered. There is still only one loose end, however," Siiteper said.

"And what is that?" Darrian asked.

"You," Siiteper said as he pulled a trigger beneath his desk.

The laser beam from Siiteper's hidden pistol struck Darrian in the neck and he fell dead to the floor. Siiteper stared at a fixed point in the distance, his bluish-gray, patterned face motionless. The silence seemed very loud. He changed his focus from staring into nothingness to the slumped bodies in front of his desk. Then his eyes came across the picture of his wife. After all of the death and destruction he caused by avenging Myreness, he didn't feel any better about losing her. A single tear rolled down his cheek. Siiteper activated the comm.

"Can someone get to my office and clean up this mess? It seems there was an argument between the doctors, scientists, and military high-command. A firefight ensued. I don't know what motivated them to do such a thing," Siiteper said.

As leader of the autocracy, they could do nothing about him killing anyone, but he was concerned about his public image, so he altered the truth.

"I'll send a team up right away to get that cleared up. Are you all right, sir?"

"Yes, I'm fine. Thank you."

Officer Tarrias slowly crawled away from the engine cooling tanks. He was a bit frozen with ice that had formed in his white hair. Some of his black feathers were stuck to the cold tanks as he slowly pulled himself free. Tarrias could see his breath in the cold air. He could not believe the Xenolfan high-command officer, Darrian, would fire on his ship. Tarrias remembered what Commander Darrian had said over the comm just before he fired. The words echoed through his mind. Commander Darrian was ordered by Siiteper Affelum not to leave any witnesses of the operation behind. Earlier in the day, Tarrias received news of some of his other team members suddenly dying in accidents. Tarrias realized they were eliminating everyone involved in the operation that had taken place months before. So, Darrian tried to destroy his ship and presumably scanned it for life forms and found none. Since the attack knocked him into the engine cooling tank area, he must not have registered on the life scan. He limped toward the bridge. Most of the ship was automatically sealed off to protect it from the vacuum of space. As he sat down in the chair, he noticed the controls were all dead. He flicked several switches to no avail. It was only a matter of time before his air supply ran out and the temperature in the ship fell to freezing temperatures. As a Xenolfan, he was much more comfortable in warm, humid climates. His ship drifted onward in space at an odd angle. The outside of the ship was visibly damaged and scorched with laser fire. Darrian had known Tarrias was in his personal ship on furlough. Thankfully, his current location was far into Syrenthian Government territory. The Syrenthian Government controlled the entire Syrenthian Galaxy, except for Olf Teruda, which was controlled by the Xenolfan Government. So, it wasn't difficult to be in the human controlled territory. Tarrias contemplated activating the ship's distress signal. If, for some strange reason, the Xenolfan Government responded and not the Syrenthian Government, then it would mean his demise. Since he was so far into the Syrenthian Government's territory, he decided to send the signal and hope for the best. If he waited too long, he would die out in space. He pressed the button.

I cannot believe I was a part of that genocide on S4. I was just following orders, but I probably should have excused myself from the mission. That was the most fucked-up shit I've ever been a part of. The fact that Siiteper is eliminating everyone involved is even more fucked up, Tarrias thought.

"Siiteper Affelum is an insane and wicked man," he said to himself.

Within the hour, a Syrenthian Government ship appeared out Tarrias's observation window. A tractor beam was initiated and pulled his disabled ship toward a docking bay. A rescue team soon entered his ship. The humans were a welcomed sight.

"We are from the Syrenthian Government. We received your distress signal. Are you okay?" the woman asked.

"Yes. I'm just a little banged up. My ship was fired upon. I thought for sure I was going to die. Thank you for rescuing me. Tarrias is the name," he said.

"Hi, Tarrias. My name is Sharell. I can take you to the medical center for evaluation. Do you know who fired on you?" she asked.

"No. Maybe pirates…"

"Well, you're lucky the attack wasn't much worse," Sharell said.

He followed the woman out of his ship and across a large docking bay. As he limped along, he examined his feathers that were partially missing and still stuck to the cooling tanks in his ship.

"Sharell, I hope you don't mind. I need to see if I'm still capable of flight with my damaged wing."

She looked back at the Xenolfan. "Go right ahead. The docking bay gives you adequate space to fly," she said.

Tarrias began to flap his wings, but the right side was too damaged. He did not get far from the docking bay floor.

"Well, that's not good," he said. "My wing will eventually heal and get back to normal, but right now, it's useless."

Sharell led him to the medical center for evaluation. The facility was well equipped. Sharell introduced him to a nurse.

The nurse examined his wing. "I admit that I am not that familiar with Xenolfan health. But I believe your wing will eventually heal."

"Yes. It will take several months," Tarrias said.

She scanned him and found an injured knee. She examined the knee and pushed on the bluish-gray skin. He let out a yelp.

"There is no permanent damage, but you did sprain your knee. It will hurt, but eventually feel better. Try not to put a lot of pressure or strain on it. If you can, use ice packs," the nurse said. "Here, take these. They're for the pain."

"Thank you," Tarrias said.

Sharell led him from the medical center toward a conference room. They entered the room and she gestured for Tarrias to have a seat. She sat down after him.

"I need to ask you a few questions," she said.

"Okay."

"Your ship is not worth repairing, so we'll have to scrap it. The resources from recycling that metal are not worth a lot of Asparell coins, but at least we can get you something for the loss of your ship," Sharell said.

"Wow! That would be great. I wasn't even thinking that far ahead. I'm just thankful to be alive," Tarrias said.

"That's understandable. You've been through a lot. Where were you headed? Do you want us to take you to your destination? Was it Olf Teruda?" she asked.

"No! I was on my way to Salinarr Nevis. If you could drop me off there, that would be great," he said.

"Well, okay. There isn't much there but a few settlements. The planet has great potential. Perhaps someday, it will be a booming world," Sharell said.

"You never know. I have a friend there who owes me a favor," Tarrias said.

"Okay, no problem. We will take you to Salinarr Nevis. Let me inform the commander, get the paperwork for your ship, and the Asparell coins. I'll be right back," Sharell said.

She left the conference room. Tarrias sat and contemplated all that he had been through. Sharell soon returned with some paperwork for him to sign off on his ship. He signed the forms and received the Asparell coins.

"We will be at Salinarr Nevis within the hour. You are more than welcome to relax in the lounge right next to this room. There are refreshments in the refrigerator," she said.

"Thank you so much for all of your help. This was all so unexpected. Be sure to thank your commander for me as well," Tarrias said.

After Tarrias was transported via shuttle down to the surface of Salinarr Nevis, he limped toward his friend's house. The house was secluded on a large piece of property. He wished his wing hadn't been damaged so he could simply fly the distance to the house. Although the humidity on Salinarr Nevis was not as high as on Olf Teruda, it was a welcomed sensation for Tarrias. Upon arriving from the long walk, Tarrias noticed his friend in the backyard. The man was chopping wood for his fire pit. His friend's white hair was tied in a ponytail. The older Xenolfan looked well seasoned in his every mannerism. Tarrias also noticed a new spaceship parked next to his old one.

"Well, that's something I don't see everyday! Tarrias! How are you, my military friend?" the man asked. He dropped the ax and greeted Tarrias.

"I've been better, Cliven," Tarrias said.

"What happened to your wing? And why are you limping?" Cliven asked.

"It's a long story...and honestly, I'm ashamed of it. Our Xenolfan Government leader, Siiteper Affelum, recently lost his wife to an attack by a Humolfan. You know, the offspring of a Xenolfan and human... Siiteper wanted revenge on all the Humolfans and their families. They put me on this very disturbing mission, Cliven. It was a three phase operation. Phase one was to extract all interspecies couples and families from their homes under the cover of darkness as we raided at night. Phase two was to bring them to the Shardaa Sector on the planet S4 and kill them all in a mass murder genocide. Siiteper decided not to kill the Humolfans, but to leave them exiled in the Shardaa Sector. The things we did were so horrifying. It won't get out of my head. I did terrible things, Cliven. I was just following military orders from my commanding officer, Darrian. He had us kill all the Xenolfan and human men by forcing them off a cliff to their deaths. Afterward, he had our team fire on all the Xenolfan and human women, most of whom were pregnant. Apparently, months after phase two, Commander Darrian began killing off our team, one by one. I know he did. My team began to have random accidents, eliminating each of us. In a surprise attack, Darrian fired on my ship and I was thrown into the engine cooling tanks. Since the ship didn't explode, I'm sure he scanned it for life forms and found nothing since I was next to the cooling tanks. My body temperature being so low must have masked the life scan, so he thought I was dead."

Cliven looked from Tarrias's injured wing to the splinters of chopped wood that scattered the ground. Cliven stared silently at the ground, contemplating everything that Tarrias had told him. He fluttered his wings slightly.

"You should definitely be ashamed of yourself, Tarrias. There are some orders that you just don't follow. And pregnant women… How low can you get? In all my life, I have never heard of something so horrific. Tarrias…"

"I know, Cliven. I'm a monster," Tarrias said.

"And it sounds like Siiteper is covering all of his tracks to protect his image. You're lucky you survived that attack. It sounds like the rest of your team didn't get so lucky. And what was phase three?"

"I don't know. We were never told what phase three was. That's where I need your help. I want to go back to Olf Teruda and find out what the third phase was. Do you remember that favor you owe me?"

"Ha! I was just on Olf Teruda nine months ago. I had to get a vaccination for some virus. That place has certainly changed since I've been away. This is going to require more than that favor I owe you. How many Asparell coins do you have?" Cliven asked.

"Actually the Syrenthian Government that responded to my distress signal just purchased my damaged ship and paid me a decent amount to recycle. So, I have some Asparell coins. I'm going to need a lot more for the predicament I'm in. If only I could bet them in a nice card game, I could multiply the amount I have," Tarrias said.

"Well, there are no casinos on Salinarr Nevis. This is just a backwater planet," Cliven said.

"Maybe someday… So, the amount of Asparell coins I have will just have to do," Tarrias said.

"I tell you what, Tarrias… You wouldn't have come to me in the first place, if this wasn't urgent. It's not like I have a family to worry about. I will take you to Olf Teruda. I will help you find out what phase three is. You don't owe me anything," Cliven said.

"Oh, there is just one more thing…"

"With you, there always is. What is it?"

"We need to go back to S4 and help the Humolfans that are stranded there. They need food, supplies, and tools, lots of Asparell coins, if they are ever to have their own economy as they go forward, and…a ship. Siiteper has the battleship *Neothuss* guarding the Shardaa Sector, so we'll have to be careful. The crew of the ship has no clue what they are guarding against. They were just given orders to make sure no one goes in or out of that region of space. So, we will have to be very covert about it," Tarrias said.

"Lovely… You don't ask much, do you?" Cliven remarked. "I recently purchased that new ship. So, I do have a spare…although it looks like you could use it. Also, I just happen to have a large amount of Asparell coins that I would like to, let's say, get out of my possession quickly. They can have all of them. I'm doing well enough without them and I don't need to keep looking over my shoulder."

"Do I want to know where you got them?" Tarrias asked.

"No, you don't. Let's just say they were no longer needed by the previous owner," Cliven said.

"Okay…" Tarrias said. He managed a brief smile before his bluish-gray, patterned face went back to an expressionless state.

"Let me finish chopping this wood and take a shower. We'll eat something, fill up the old ship with supplies for the Humolfans, and then leave for Olf Teruda in my new ship to do a little investigating. Before we travel to the Shardaa Sector, we will come back here to Salinarr Nevis and you can pilot my old ship. We'll take both ships so we have a way back after giving the Humolfans the old ship," Cliven said.

Although Cliven was not excited to be back on his birth planet, the humidity on Olf Teruda was a welcomed sensation. Cliven and Tarrias had arrived earlier in the day and did some stealth mission work of their own. It was nice for them to be back in the safety of Cliven's ship, however. Rumor had it that Commander Darrian was dead, but the two of them wanted to confirm, so they contacted his office.

"You've reached Commander Darrian's office," a woman answered.

"Yes, I would like to speak with the military high-commander," Cliven told the woman over the comm.

"Umm…sir, you must not have heard the news. He died during a firefight with the military doctors and scientists," she said.

"Oh no! I was not aware of that alarming news. Thank you for informing me," Cliven said.

"Can someone else help you?"

"No…I'm good, but thank you," Cliven said, ending the communication.

"It's true. He's dead," Cliven said.

"I overheard. Siiteper must have also eliminated Commander Darrian and some military doctors and scientists. Doctors and scientists…" Tarrias tapped his finger on his chin in thought. "This third phase has to be some sort of medical affair."

"When we were out in public today, I overheard several women complaining that the vaccinations ruined their babies. We did have to get an injection about nine months ago because of that supposed virus. I didn't like that. We were forced to take it. Did you get one? I don't think this was ever about a virus, but something much more sinister," Cliven said.

"Yes, I did get one. Hmm… Let me check some local news sources." He fiddled with his comm and searched for the local health news. "Shit! There are reports that all Xenolfan babies are being born without wings. And they are blaming microevolution, not the vaccinations. This is it, Cliven! Siiteper has fucked with our Xenolfan DNA. I'll bet there was no virus. This was some type of DNA modification. I'm certain that Siiteper eliminated the ability for us Xenolfans to breed with humans. That would explain everything."

Cliven looked at his arm where he had received the painful shot.

"If we ever have families of our own, we better not expect our children to fly, like we can," Tarrias said.

"This is fucked up. No wonder those women I overheard today were complaining," Cliven said.

Silence filled the ship for a long moment.

"I don't even know what to think," Tarrias said.

"Tarrias, this means you can no longer find yourself a nice human woman and breed to have Humolfan offspring," Cliven said.

"Yuck! No, thank you. Nothing against humans, but I prefer Xenolfan women. It's nice to know you have a sense of humor when serious shit is happening. It also means our own Xenolfan children won't have wings."

"Well, at least we found out what phase three was," Cliven said.

"Yes. Now, if we can sneak our supplies into the Shardaa Sector to help the Humolfans there, that would be great," Tarrias said.

"They are the last of the Humolfans species…" Cliven said.

"You know what I don't understand? The very half-breed species that Siiteper hates—because one of them killed his wife—are the only ones we were not ordered to kill in that field on S4. It makes no sense to me," Tarrias said.

"The minds of the twisted…don't even try to understand and make sense of them or you'll just drive yourself crazy," Cliven said.

"Shall we go get the other ship and head to the Shardaa Sector?" Tarrias asked.

"Let's go!"

Cliven and Tarrias traveled in the two separate ships at lightspeed-plus toward the Shardaa Sector. Within hours, Cliven stopped the ship and drifted in space as he looked at the computer screen. Tarrias stopped the old ship next to Cliven's new one.

Cliven activated the comm on a private frequency. "There is the *Neothuss* that you spoke of, right on the edge of our long-range scanners. That looks like a battleship that I would not want to tangle with. We are going to have to take the scenic route. I mean, we are literally going to have to go all the way around the parameter of the Shardaa Star System to avoid being within their prohibited zone," Cliven said.

"It looks that way. That is going to bring us dangerously close to the Shaeolian Black Hole," Tarrias said over the comm.

"Damn! You're right. We need to be very careful. If we get sucked in, we could end up right up Siiteper's ass," Cliven said.

"Is that were it goes? Your humor is killing me," Tarrias said.

Cliven turned the ship to begin the long voyage around the star system. Tarrias followed in the older ship. The bridges of both ships were quiet as Cliven and Tarrias both looked out their observation windows at the darkness of space. One distant star, or perhaps a planet, caught Cliven's attention.

"We don't know much about this region of space, do we?" Cliven asked.

"No. It is Syrenthian Government territory, but it is virtually uncharted. It is so desolate and distant from the main shipping lanes that no one bothered to explore it. That is why Siiteper Affelum chose the Shardaa Sector for his genocide. The fact that he is leaving a Xenolfan battleship in Syrenthian Government territory to patrol it just shows you that even the human Syrenthian Government doesn't even patrol their own territory," Tarrias said.

Cliven changed his trajectory and continued his course toward S4. Once again, Tarrias followed. Traveling past the Shaeolian Black Hole caused their instrument panels to temporarily malfunction and they both could feel their ships shift course slightly. After some time, the systems came back online and both ships automatically made course corrections.

"Damn, that was scary!" Tarrias said over the comm.

"And I have to pass that thing on our return flight…" Cliven said.

Flying in from the backside of S4 was more stealth, but Cliven doubted the battleship *Neothuss's* scanners could pick up anything that far into the star system anyway. One battleship was not enough to effectively stop all possibilities of traveling into the Shardaa Star System. The fact that they were succeeding was proof that the attempt to block was futile.

"It's daring on Siiteper's part to occupy Syrenthian Government territory with the *Neothuss*," Cliven said.

"You know what is even more interesting? Siiteper named five of the planets that were scanned when we were here in the Shardaa Star System. When the names were passed along to the Syrenthian Government, they accepted the names as official and recorded them in their records. They never asked why we were exploring their territory or if the data was from long-range scans," Tarrias said.

"Interesting… Hey, we will be there in a little bit here. I've never personally seen a Humolfan. Is there anything I need to be aware of when we land?" Cliven asked.

"Just be careful. They can make you pass out with their glowing eyes," Tarrias said.

"And here I thought you were going to say the Humolfan women would line up to check me out as soon as I exit the ship," Cliven said.

"Not funny... Most of the older Humolfans are under thirty," Tarrias said.

"Well, shit!"

Soon, the two ships approached S4. The gray clouds could be seen from the distance of space. Cliven enabled the anti-gravitational units as he entered the planet's atmosphere. Tarrias did the same. The gray clouds whispered by their observation windows as the two ships descended. The rocky ground could be seen in the distance ahead. Cliven and Tarrias noticed several Humolfans of various ages in the area as they landed the ships.

"Here we are," Tarrias said over the comm.

"Do you think they will remember you from the killings?" Cliven asked.

"No. The Humolfans were not outside at the time to witness the actual murder of their parents. But the fact that we are Xenolfans is all it takes to associate us with what happened to their parents. We need to be very careful. We are here to help, but we don't need to run into any problems. We should both conceal a laser pistol, just in case. Do you have one on this ship?" Tarrias asked.

"Yes. There is one on the bridge in the console next to where you are sitting."

Tarrias looked down. "Got it."

Cliven and Tarrias disengaged their engines, the sound of each winding down in the background. They each carried a concealed laser pistol, just in case they were attacked. They exited the ships. Three of the Humolfans walked over to them.

"Did you Xenolfans come back to kill the rest of us?" a tall, young Humolfan man asked.

"You did enough to us already. Just finish us off and get it over with," a young Humolfan woman said.

The third, shorter man picked up a large stone. "I won't let you do it," he said.

"We're not here to hurt you. We are here to help," Cliven said.

Tarrias looked at the field were the hundreds of pregnant women had been. Every one of the bodies had been covered with stones and gravestones placed at each site with their names carved into the stone. Some stones had additional names that had been chosen for the babies, if they were known.

"How did you know we were here?" the woman asked.

"My name is Tarrias. I was part of the crew that was here before. I was asked to do horrible things in the name of duty. It was not right. They didn't even want their own team alive as witnesses. My entire team was also killed by our leader. They thought they killed me, but I survived. I immediately knew I had to help you Humolfans. So, I asked my friend Cliven, here, to help me get you some supplies, including medical supplies, tools, food, and…this ship," Tarrias said. He gestured toward the older ship.

"You killed our parents and now you want to help us?" the young man with the stone in his hands said. He tightened his grip and steadied his feet.

"Some of them…yes. What I and the others did was evil. I cannot even find the words to say how terribly sorry I am. Some orders should never be followed. It has been eating at my soul every day since then. For months, I have not been able to sleep well. I don't know if you could ever forgive me, but I am truly sorry for what I did," Tarrias said. He began to tear up when looking at the hurt written across each of their faces.

"I want to kill you so badly," the young man with the stone said. He lifted the stone in the air and held it there for a long moment. He then loosened his grip and let it fall to the ground. "But there's been enough killing."

Several more adult Humolfans flew over to where the ships had landed, their black wings extending outward. They landed near the three Humolfans that were engaged in conversation with the two Xenolfans.

"My name is Athenarr and this is Aarria and Tovels," the tall Humolfan said. He pointed to the young woman and the man who had held the stone. He turned to address the other Humolfans that flew over and landed next to them. "These Xenolfans have brought us supplies, tools, food, and this ship to help us survive."

Some of the children came out from the makeshift shelters they had built and came closer to the others.

"I have to tell you all something," Tarrias said. "Our leader, Siiteper Affelum, ordered this tragedy against you Humolfans. He then experimented on my fellow Xenolfan people so that we can no longer breed with humans. Siiteper is bitter and full of hatred. And I must say that you all are the last of the Humolfans. The sad thing is that after his experimentation on us, our own babies are now born without wings, without the ability to fly," Tarrias said.

One of the younger children flapped his wings for a moment. "That's terrible," the child said.

The young boy plucked a feather from his own wing and then walked over to Tarrias and plucked a damaged feather from his injured wing. He broke Tarrias's feather at the calamus and held the two black feathers up to form an X.

"It is a tragedy for our species," Tarrias said.

"Xenolfans are broken," the child said.

They all stared at the feather symbol the child held in his hand and realized it had significant meaning.

"As Humolfans, we have always felt like outcasts. Our parents loved each other. We are a product of that Xenolfan and human love. This…this feather symbol that he is holding up says everything. We must never, never forget where we came from," Aarria said, brushing her white hair aside.

"We will carve this feather symbol on every gravestone in our Grave of Mothers as a symbol that we must never forget," Tovels said.

"The Shardaa Sector that you have been exiled to is being guarded by one of Siiteper's battleships, *Neothuss*. There are orders not to let any ship come or go. We had to fly a long way around the Shardaa Star System to get here on S4 without being detected. They will not let you leave this star system in this ship. They will destroy you. Even for us to get here was not safe, but we're experienced pilots and we've been around long enough to know how to outsmart them. This ship is for you to get between each of the planets here in the Shardaa Star System. You should be safe doing that. If you are ever going to develop as a species, you will need to explore the other planets in this star system. If there are any among you who has had flight training while you were on Olf Teruda, that would be very beneficial. The first planet in the star system is called Shardaa. It has no atmosphere, but there are spacesuits on board. And the other planets are S2, S3, this planet of S4, S5, and S6. You can explore and discover new things out here in the Shardaa Sector. We will also be giving you all a bunch of Asparell coins. Don't ask where we got them. You can set up your own economy or trade system using those," Tarrias said.

"What about you two?" Someone from the gathering crowd asked.

"We will leave S4 the same way we came. It is a dangerous route and goes very close to the Shaeolian Black Hole. We must be extremely careful on our return trip. If the *Neothuss* detects us, they will attack. The Shardaa Sector is in the Syrenthian Government's territory. Siiteper Affelum is taking a chance on leaving the battleship in their territory. And as long as he is the leader of the Xenolfan Government, it will remain in place here for many years," Tarrias said.

A Humolfan stepped through the crowd toward the two Xenolfans. "My name is Leerial. I was trained as a pilot before we were all taken from our homes. I could easily fly this ship to check out other planets here in the Shardaa Star System," he said.

"The Humolfan future seems like a long road, but hey…at least we were able to help," Tarrias said.

"You won't be forgotten," Athenarr said.

That evening, Athenarr and Aarria stood on a hill and watched Cliven's newer ship leave S4, disappearing into the gray clouds. Athenarr had one of his black wings wrapped around Aarria and their fingers were interlaced as they held hands. Like other young adult Humolfans, they had become romantically involved after the Humolfan species was exiled to the Shardaa Sector. Their relationship was one of several couples that had developed over the months on S4.

"Well, I hope Leerial is able to safely fly this ship they gave us," Athenarr said.

"He will do fine. I'm confident of it," Aarria said.

"I hope so."

"You know what else I'm confident in?" she asked.

"What's that?"

"Your love…your sexiness…your caring spirit. You have helped our people so much…with burying the dead, building shelters, hunting, comforting the other orphaned children. I love you," Aarria said.

Athenarr leaned closer and kissed her lips with a lengthy, passionate kiss. Her tongue felt warm against his. They both opened their eyes and smiled. Her beautiful sapphire eyes contrasted her gray face. He stroked her cheek with his thumb as she stared back into his eyes.

"Let's fly to our favorite spot and make love," Aarria said.

Athenarr's sapphire eyes lit up and he smiled. He quickly flew into the air and she followed him. They soared high into the clear evening sky and chased each other in an alternating flight pattern. They hovered above a stone ledge that overlooked a green valley. Circling each other in flight, they slowly descended to the stone ledge and wrapped their wings around each other in a romantic embrace. It was an instinctive routine that both the winged Xenolfans and Humolfans were able to perform. They quickly undressed. Aarria wrapped her gray thighs around Athenarr's left leg as they both retracted their wings. He could feel the moist heat of her reuleaux triangular pussy against his thigh. As she lay down, he gently spread her legs apart and began to kiss the gray folds of her labia. His tongue slowly made its journey between each of the folds before concentrating on her clitoris. With quickening movements, he gently sucked the labia into his mouth and rubbed his tongue against them. He playfully made his way along her slit and buried his tongue deep into her creamy hole. As he brushed his hand against her white pubes, he began stroking her clit.

"Oh, Athenarr. You make me feel so good. Mmm," Aarria said, breathing heavily.

Athenarr continued to perform cunnilingus, enjoying the creamy taste of her sexy pussy. Soon, she leaned over and lowered her lips to his erect cock. The gray penis had a similar reuleaux triangular-shaped circumference. There was a section in the middle of his cock that stepped down to a smaller circumference. The tip didn't have a head, like humans, but ended at an angle with a large orifice, similar to an ovipositor. She slid her tongue from his gray balls, up the length of his shaft, and to the tip where she concentrated her lips. She took it into her mouth, slithering her tongue back and forth along the underside of the rigid member. Wrapping her mouth around the tip, she began to suck up and down. He groaned with great pleasure.

"Ahhh! Ahhh, Aarria. That's nice," Athenarr said, inhaling deeply.

Athenarr lay on his back and Aarria mounted him. She slid his gray cock into her warm pussy. Their eyes met in a lustful stare and she smiled. Using her wings to move herself up and down on his hard cock was something that she had perfected over the last several months. Her black wings flapped ever so gracefully above him. With each movement, her gray breasts bounced rhythmically. Aarria slowed her wings and she slid down fully onto his cock, pushing it deep inside of her. She rotated her hips and ground against him. The creamy, wet sounds of their coitus sent music to their ears, heightening their arousals. With each movement, she slowly massaged his gray balls against her vulva. She continued grinding and the pace of the creamy sounds quickened until Athenarr burst out with a pleasurable cry, coming deep inside of her.

"Ahhh!"

"Ohhh! I'm coming too!" Aarria shouted.

For a long moment, they lay there on the stone ledge, connected so intimately. Athenarr finally slipped out of her, his load dripping to the stone. As they lay with intertwined legs, Aarria's wings covered them both. They gazed up at the evening sky and saw a few distant stars and a couple of planets.

"That's an amazing view. We'll soon be able to travel to those planets," Aarria said.

"Yes, when Leerial is ready, we will explore the entire Shardaa Star System," Athenarr said. He smiled at her.

The most relaxed feeling of bliss overcame them as they lay together gazing at the evening sky. They slowly fell asleep.

The possibility of ongoing creation of pure Humolfans was something that never occurred to Siiteper Affelum when he decided to banish the Humolfans instead of killing them. He believed they would all just die of starvation. Eventually, Siiteper wrote a book called *Anathema Strain.* He dedicated it to his wife, Myreness. In it, he told a story of how the Xenolfans and humans would breed together, which caused a host of problems for galactic society. He went on to explain that they created monsters with their offspring. The total disdain and hatred emanating from the book was shocking. Many years later, Siiteper Affelum died in office of old age. Since the book was kept in the secret archives of the Xenolfan Government palace lower levels on Olf Teruda, only the sitting leader of the Xenolfan Government would be able to discover it among the many documents. Because the book's printing process also involved a few other individuals, the existence of the book was known by several others.

Chapter Two

Present time…

Sierra Shalinsky awoke from her unconscious state to find herself on a stretcher in a strange docking bay. She sat up and looked around at several ships. Nothing looked familiar. She noticed an IV in her arm and carefully removed it. Her long, black hair rested against the light gray jumpsuit she wore. The outfit was unfamiliar as well. In the distance, she could see several workers that all appeared human, but they all had white hair, like Xenolfans, and black wings. Wait! Did they have gray skin? She squinted her eyes to get a better look.

Suddenly, she recalled a memory of a tall woman walking up to her after the Maranadda concert on Red Jacket. The tall woman also had black wings that had extended upward as well as glowing blue eyes that somehow made her faint. Sierra recalled the woman calling herself Estrus. She remembered seeing the tattoo with the feather symbol above Estrus's reuleaux triangular pussy. The tattoo was an identical match to the feather inscription above the cave on S2 in the Shardaa Sector. She realized she had been abducted. There were other faint memories, but they were mostly a blur. How long ago was she singing at that concert on Red Jacket? It seemed as if months had passed. She did remember Estrus having conversations with her, but the details were too faint to recall.

Why can't I remember things? she asked herself.

The docking bay was quiet. There didn't seem to be anyone around the immediate vicinity. Sierra didn't know where Estrus was at that moment, but she had an opportunity to make a run for one of the small ships. She stepped down off the stretcher and took that opportunity.

She entered a small ship and ran for the controls, her long, black hair flowing behind her. They were easy enough to figure out, but the ship was quite different than her ship, *Tenebris*. She wondered where her old fighter ship was. She launched the foreign ship and maneuvered her way out of the docking bay and into a beautiful blue atmosphere.

An automated announcement came from the control panel. "You are now leaving S6 airspace."

The horizon was beautiful with white mountains against a blue sky. The scene was quickly replaced with the blackness of space. Sierra noticed her reflection in the observation window, her blue eyes showing signs of anxiety. She began to contemplate her current situation. Sierra thought her personal ship had been parked on Red Jacket, but could not remember. She had made an important sexual freedom speech with her friend Priscilla Stryderr followed by singing at Maranadda's symphonic metal concert. That seemed so long ago… She looked at the display before her and realized she was in the Shardaa Star System. It was a secluded section of space that space travelers tried to avoid at all costs.

What the hell am I doing in the Shardaa Sector? Who the hell are those people with the wings?

She suddenly recalled that she had come to the Shardaa Sector with her former unit for her employer, Galactic Emergency Medical Services (GEMS). She remembered the run clearly. They had received a distress signal from a space traveler named Dennon Cobalt. They checked out the planet Shardaa, but then discovered his ship had crashed on S2. When they found him some distance from his ship, he was unconscious. When he woke, he kept repeating that there was a woman with black wings there.

Oh fuck! He wasn't delusional after all, Sierra thought.

In her new GEMS unit, her duties as a Galactic Emergency Medical Technician (Galactic EMT) covered the territory in space that included the Shardaa Sector. Fortunately, she had not made a run into the uncharted region with her new unit. Yet, she currently found herself in the very region of space that people were afraid to travel near. Too many strange occurrences had taken place in the Shardaa Sector throughout history. Her band, Maranadda, even had a song about it.

She made her way past a few of the planets in the Shardaa Star System. S5, S4, and S3 seemed a bit more colorful than what she remembered about S2 and Shardaa. Sierra knew the Shardaa Sector had never been explored. She knew that after the two governments that existed in the Syrenthian Galaxy—the Xenolfan Government and the Syrenthian Government—had collaboratively named the first planet in the system as Shardaa, the other planets were simply named S2, S3, S4, S5, and S6 at some later date. Some people believed that there was even another planet beyond S6, but to Sierra's knowledge, it had never been discovered. Technically, that region of space was Syrenthian Government territory.

Sierra set a course for Exandra, the Syrenthian Government capital. It would be hours before she would reach Exandra. So far, there was no sign of a chase. She desperately needed to speak with her friends, Braxton and Priscilla Stryderr. Braxton was an investigator for the Syrenthian Government. Braxton and Priscilla were also lovers with Sierra. She was their unicorn. It was just one relationship Sierra had as a bisexual swinger in the Lifestyle. But sex was the last thing on her mind at that moment. She activated the comm and attempted to send a message to Exandra. Something was jamming her signal.

What the hell is wrong with this? Sierra thought.

"I only left her for a second!" Estrus exclaimed. "I was taking her to see the doctor, just like I have been every week."

"Well, isn't this just great? Just when she wakes up from her coma, she escapes!" Soltuss Yow said. "As head of the Humolfan Command, it is my responsibility to keep Sierra safe and secure. And I have failed…"

They peered out from the docking bay toward the beautiful white mountains in the distance. The sheer cliffs and tall spires of the remote mountains were breathtaking. The majestic peaks sat against a brilliant blue sky.

"It's my fault," Estrus said. "She has been in a coma for so long, I didn't think she would wake up now. I just went to retrieve my schedule."

"Well, I'm not sure how far she is by now, but go after her. Hopefully, you can find her before the Dissident Faction does," Soltuss Yow said.

Both women's white hair and sapphire eyes glistened in the sunlight at the opening of the docking bay. Estrus quickly flew up high into the docking bay and over to one of the ships, her black wings flapping ever so gracefully. She landed on her feet and entered the ship. Within seconds, she left the docking bay on S6 to pursue Sierra.

As Sierra Shalinsky approached the space near S2, a fighter ship appeared on her tail and began to fire. Intense blue laser beams penetrated the ship's deflector shields. An alarm started beeping on the control panel of the stolen ship. She was surprised it took so long before she received any resistance. She tried to outmaneuver the fighter ship to no avail. The continued laser fire weakened the deflector shields until they finally gave out. The next hit disabled her engines and she drifted on a collision course with S2.

Shit! This is not good, Sierra thought. She fastened her seat belt and braced herself for the impact.

The ship crashed and slid along the rocks on the surface of S2. The dark and desolate planet had many shards of rock and protruding stone spires and monoliths. The ship decelerated as it scraped along the jagged rocks until it finally came to a stop against a large spire of stone. Although Sierra had her seat belt on, the sudden stop flung her slightly forward against the control panel.

She recalled previously being on S2 as her team of GEMS first responders rescued Dennon Cobalt. Unlike the planet Shardaa, S2 had an atmosphere. She wondered if the reason why Dennon's ship crashed was because it was also shot down. She unfastened her seat belt and quickly exited the ship. The ship that shot her down looked like it was circling around for another pass. Sierra ran. She passed the area where Dennon's ship had once been, the stones still disturbed from the impact. Sierra remembered a cave when her team was there to rescue Dennon. They had explored the cave in search of the person that Dennon spoke of. She ran toward the same cave for shelter. Turning back, she noticed in the far distance, the ship that had shot her down settled next to the stolen, crashed ship. She made her way around the corner of a rock wall and walked along the edge of a cliff. Sierra reached the cave and stopped in front of it, looking up at the strange feather symbol that she had seen before. It was an inscription of two feathers. One leaned to the left and was unbroken. The other leaned to the right and was broken just above the intersection point, resulting in the feather on the right pointing downward. Oddly enough, it was the same feather symbol that Estrus had a tattoo of below her navel, on her mons pubis. Sierra remembered seeing the tattoo on Estrus in the warehouse on Red Jacket after the Maranadda concert. She wondered what the significance of the feather symbol was. Just like the tattoo was located above Estrus's reuleaux triangular-shaped vulva, the cave below the feather symbol was also carved into the shape of a triangular vulva.

Sierra didn't understand why these people with the black wings had pussies shaped like the Xenolfans. It was a known fact that the bluish-gray Xenolfans had genitalia that was shaped different than her tan human species. She recalled looking up at the feather symbol when she had previously been to that same spot and feeling faint. She remembered seeing blue lights in the cave at the time. She realized they were the same glowing sapphire eyes that Estrus had used to make her feel faint after the Maranadda concert. Estrus must have been in the cave and tried to make her faint then too. Sierra had fallen to the rocky ground and looked up at the starlight in the night sky. She remembered her co-worker Alex had bent down to help her and inadvertently dropped his comm down between two rocks where it had slid out of his reach. He was never able to retrieve it.

"The comm!" she said to herself.

Sierra bent down by the rocks where Alex had dropped it. She noticed the corner of the comm protruding from several stones that had covered it over time. She reach down between the rocks to grab it, but it was too far out of her reach. The loose stone shifted and the comm slid down farther.

"Shit!"

The only way she would be able to retrieve the comm would be to climb up and over a monolith of stone. The monolith rested at the edge of a cliff. If the comm slid much farther, it would fall off the cliff into the darkness below. She carefully went up and over the monolith and settled her footing on a rocky slope of loose stone. If she wasn't careful, she would slip off the cliff. She squatted down and reached for the comm, holding on to the stone monolith with one hand. The darkness below the cliff was so black that Sierra could barely see the floor of the deep chasm. To keep from becoming more frightened, she turned away from the depths and focused on the rocks immediately in front of her. The comm was almost in her grasp. She stretched her arm and finally grabbed the comm. She steadied herself and raised the comm to her lips. She blew the dust from its surface and put it into her pocket. Suddenly, she felt extreme vertigo and clenched the rocks tight as she closed her eyes for a long moment. The dizziness passed and she began to carefully climb back up and over the monolith. Sierra noticed the person that was chasing her in the ship was in the air, flying toward her with large, black wings flapping. The being had a black outfit on that blended with the black wings. Glowing blue eyes could be seen from the distance. Sierra quickly hopped down from the monolith and ran into the cave. It was dark and she did not have a flashlight. She decided it was a bad idea and turned around. Running as fast as she could, she made it to the entrance and looked for her pursuer. She did not see anyone around on the ground or in the air. She quickly ran around a rock wall on the outside of the cave and along a narrow trail that ascended upward above the cave entrance. She came to an area that was virtually enclosed with stone. The sanctuary provided a crack between the rocks where Sierra could see the front of the cave below. She quietly waited. A female, dressed in black, swiftly flew around one of the rock walls and landed on the rocky ground, her black wings folding up nicely behind her back. She drew a laser pistol and slowly walked into the cave.

Sierra reached into her pocket and retrieved the comm. She turned it on and it lit up like a star. She turned it from the Galactic Emergency Medical Services frequency to the correct frequency for the Syrenthian Government. Braxton had given her that frequency a long time ago, in case of an emergency.

"Emergency! Emergency! This is Sierra Shalinsky calling from the planet S2 in the Shardaa Sector. I have been abducted and I'm being pursued by these people. I need assistance. I repeat, I need assistance. Please help me!"

Sierra received no response.

"This is Sierra Shalinsky calling from the Shardaa Sector. This is an emergency! Please respond!"

After a brief length of silence, Sierra enabled the comm to transmit a continuous distress signal and set it up high on an elevated rock for better transmission. She did not feel well since she awoke on the stretcher. The chase activity exhausted her and she rested her head against her arms and closed her eyes for a long moment.

Estrus landed her ship on S2 next to a Dissident Faction fighter ship. She noticed the ship that Sierra had stolen had been shot down, presumably by the Dissident Faction. She grabbed a laser rifle and exited the ship. She was familiar with the area on S2 and lifted herself in flight toward the cave where she assumed they might be. She soon flew around the rock wall and saw the Dissident Faction member exiting the cave. The woman had a laser pistol in her hand and made her way around the cave toward the rock enclosure where Sierra hid. While still in flight, Estrus pointed her laser rifle at the Dissident Faction member and fired. Blue beams of intense power pierced through the pursuer and she fell dead to the rocky ground. Estrus landed next to the body as smoke from the smoldering feathers rose upward.

"Sierra! If you can hear me, come out. We need to talk. We need your help. That woman I just shot is not one of our group. Please, trust me," Estrus said.

There was only silence.

"Sierra, please! I can explain everything. Just come out. We desperately need your help."

Sierra listened to Estrus from her rocky sanctuary.

"Sierra! Sierra! Can you hear me?"

"Yes, I hear you. What do you want with me? Who is that woman that you killed? Why was she after me? What the fuck am I doing in the Shardaa Sector? Who are you people?"

"We are Humolfans and we sought you out because we need your help. Well, most of us… The woman on the ground here was part of a group that want you dead. They are known as the Dissident Faction. And I owe you a great apology. You see, when I made you faint after the concert on Red Jacket, you should have woken up by the time we arrived back here in the Shardaa Sector. Unfortunately, when you fainted, I failed to grab you and you fell off the crate that you sat on and hit your head on the concrete floor. You've been in a coma for seven months. I have felt so terrible about this. It also delayed you helping us. I am so sorry that I didn't keep you from falling. I'm also sorry that this woman almost killed you. There is so much I need to tell you. Please, come out and return to S6 with me," Estrus said.

"How can I trust you?"

"Well, I did abduct you. So, I don't blame you for not trusting me. I have taken care of you for the last seven months. Even though you were unconscious, I've talked to you on a daily basis. Just the fact that you woke up from your coma makes my heart sing. Please come back with me. There is so much I need to explain to you and to show you. If, after I reveal everything to you, you want to leave and forget about my people, I will totally understand. We'll just have to find another advocate. We've tried before on many occasions and have failed. You are really the perfect person for what we need."

Sierra left the comm in place to continue transmitting the distress signal. Stepping out from the rocky sanctuary, she noticed Estrus at the bottom of the narrow path, standing next to the dead woman. Estrus wore a blue uniform that accentuated her gray cleavage. The laser rifle was already safely slung over her shoulder. Sierra made her way down to where Estrus stood.

"Since you can't fly, I will walk with you back to my ship. I will destroy that Dissident Faction fighter ship and then we can be on our way back to S6," Estrus said.

"Just to let you know, I did send an emergency signal back to my government," Sierra said.

Estrus stopped walking for a moment and turned toward Sierra before continuing.

"I don't blame you. It is, however, going to be a shitstorm when they arrive."

"I thought the person you shot was actually you. Honestly, I don't even know what I thought. I just need some answers."

"When we get back to S6, I will explain everything."

Sierra could not help but notice the very nice ass on Estrus, partially hidden by the ends of her black wings.

"So, I was in a coma for seven months?" Sierra asked.

"Yes."

"I must have missed a lot. My bandmates, my employer, my

parents, and all my friends must be worried sick."

"I'm sure they are. You will be back with them soon enough."

"It is very interesting to know there are more than just two species in the Syrenthian Galaxy. The fact that you can fly is amazing! Wait a minute… When you walked up to me in the warehouse after the concert on Red Jacket, you had tan skin, like us humans. Now, it's gray," Sierra said.

"Yes. I had to tan my skin as a disguise to blend in with the humans when I was outside the Shardaa Sector," Estrus said.

"The Xenolfans and the humans would both freak out if they knew about you people."

"And that is why you are here…"

Chapter Three

"I really have to get these audio cables to the studio," Vincent Macenburg said to his wife.

"I know, but I told Aymreth that we'd stop by," Shaslin Macenburg said.

They stepped out of their anti-gravitational transport and onto the rusty colored stones that made up the parking area. It was a beautiful, warm day on Red Jacket. Reddish-orange, rocky mountains could be seen in the background against a sky of brilliant blue. The couple walked up a few stone steps and pressed a button on the side of the door. As they waited, they looked at the table and chair that sat on the porch. After a slight delay, the door opened to reveal a Xenolfan woman. She had white hair, sapphire eyes, and bluish-gray skin. She smiled.

"Hey, guys! Come on in. I appreciate you coming over. I see you found it okay," she said.

As they stepped into her house, she closed the door and gave them both hugs.

"Yeah, we found it with no problem," Vincent said.

"I have been anticipating this play date for a long time," Aymreth Rosenn said.

"And Vincent is concerned about getting the new audio cables that are in the anti-gravitational transport to the band studio," Shaslin said with a grin.

"As the sound technician for Maranadda, you know the cables can wait. I know we've talked about this play date for some time, but it's nice that we can finally have a threesome together. I appreciate you two stopping over," Aymreth Rosenn said.

Vincent looked over at the bluish-gray Xenolfan. The new vocalist for Maranadda stood next to Shaslin.

"Well, we wouldn't want to stop you from dropping off your cables," Shaslin said, smiling.

"I have to stop by the studio later as well," Aymreth said.

"The cables can wait. This opportunity needs my full attention," Vincent said.

Without hesitation, Aymreth led the couple up to her bedroom. It was a spacious bedroom with a large bed. The wooden floor creaked as they walked past the ivory dresser.

Aymreth undressed and looked over to the human couple. They could see the bluish-gray genetic bumps on her back that were the remainder of where wings had once been on Xenolfans a thousand years before. As they began to slowly undress, Aymreth looked at their tan bodies and became very aroused. She reached over to Vincent's cock and carefully caressed it in one of her bluish-gray hands. With the other hand, she gently massaged Shaslin's smooth pussy. The couple also were aroused by the bluish-gray sexiness in front of them. Aymreth's breasts bounced slightly as she concentrated on stroking both of the human's genitals.

"I have to admit that with us being swingers in the Lifestyle, I didn't think we'd ever be having sex with a Xenolfan. This is pretty hot," Vincent said.

"Yes, it is," Shaslin said. "There is another swinger we know from Enax Port, but we have yet to play with her. She's a Xenolfan woman named Sheena."

"Sheena... That's a sexy name. I understand the former vocalist for Maranadda was also a swinger in the Lifestyle. Sierra Shalinsky sounds like my kind of woman," Aymreth said.

The Xenolfan vocalist bent down on her knees and began

performing oral sex on Vincent and Shaslin, alternating back and forth between them. She enjoyed Vincent's nice cock as she licked up the length of it with her long tongue. Moving over to Shaslin, she flicked the long tongue wildly along the folds of Shaslin's labia and clit.

"Oh, that feels so nice," Shaslin said.

"Having you both together is such a treat," Aymreth said.

"Yes! Oh fuck!" Vincent groaned.

Aymreth pulled away and said, "I want you to fuck her and let me get in between you two so I can fucklick you."

The couple was quick to comply with Aymreth's request. Shaslin moved around and on top of Vincent, facing away from him in reverse and slid his hard cock inside of her. She leaned back toward him, exposing their genitals in full view. Aymreth leaned in and began licking his balls with her long tongue. She made her way up Vincent's shaft where it disappeared inside of Shaslin. Aymreth continued upward along the labia and then concentrated on Shaslin's clit, playfully licking side to side. She repeated the actions with her wet tongue as they slowly thrust their hips together with smooth motions.

"Ahhh, ah, Aymreth, that's so nice. Yes, right there! Oh!" Shaslin moaned.

Aymreth looked up at Shaslin with her beautiful sapphire eyes and smiled. She moved her white hair aside and continued to please them. After an incredible orgasm, Shaslin traded places with Aymreth. The bluish-gray Xenolfan squatted down onto Vincent's hard, wet cock. With two fingers, Shaslin spread Aymreth's bluish-pink labia apart and rubbed her thumb along the underside of her husband's cock. She went down and began fucklicking them. The contrast of his tan cock inside her bluish-pink pussy was quite arousing to Shaslin. The reuleaux triangular vaginal opening was filled with Vincent's cock and Shaslin was enjoying the wetness as she licked them both. They moaned as Aymreth slid down his shaft and against Shaslin's tongue. Aymreth's moan transitioned into a high-pitched, reverberating purr as she came closer to an orgasm. Suddenly, she began to pump faster until she screamed with such an intense, high-pitched cry that Shaslin and Vincent both had to cover their ears.

"Ahhh!" Aymreth screamed.

"Damn, that was loud!" Shaslin said.

"Sorry, guys. We Xenolfans do that when we have an orgasm."

"Nice to know," Shaslin said.

Vincent brushed his long, brown hair aside and quickly increased his thrusts as he approached his own orgasm. He grabbed Aymreth's hips tight and pushed up inside of her alien pussy with all of his might.

"Fuck! That feels so good," he groaned, breathing heavily.

As Aymreth slowly pulled away, his load dripped out and down onto his cock. Shaslin leaned in and took the creamy cock into her mouth, milking Vincent's last few drops of cum.

"Mmm. That's nice," Shaslin said as she reached down and stroked her own pussy. "I taste both of you and it's delicious."

It was a well established fact that humans and Xenolfans could not breed together. And since all sexually transmitted infections had virtually been eliminated from the Syrenthian Galaxy through the sex clinics that had been established, there was no need for condoms. It made sex much more pleasurable to fuck bareback.

"I know. I know. It's frustrating. Sierra has been missing for months and there is not a day that goes by that we don't miss her," Yosemite McFarlin said, putting a hand on Arvon Estivant's shoulder.

"And this new Xenolfan vocalist we have kind of sucks," Arvon said. He tightened the hardware of his drum kit. "I mean, the fans don't like her."

Yosemite set a box of guitar picks on his amp. "Aymreth Rosenn isn't that bad, but she certainly is no Sierra Shalinsky. The fact that we are loosing fans in droves is why I'm calling this meeting. We need to make a decision regarding Aymreth. We should take a vote whether she stays or not," he said.

"Yes, we should," Arvon said. He brushed his long, brown hair aside, revealing several tattoos and piercings.

"The rest of the band is taking forever to get here. I could've been riding my new quad," Yosemite said.

"You mean the one that took forever to arrive because of the terrorist attack on Shar Nefalis? That delayed the shipment from Ticrisuda Powersports for some time, if I recall correctly," Arvon said.

"Yes. I still don't understand why Xenolfan terrorists instructed by the former leader, Aaranix Tuvelless, went so far as to kill humans and Xenolfans alike in order to keep the two species from being in relationships together. I'm so glad the Xenolfan Government is now controlled by Phensiarr Charseaa. She is a wonderful Xenolfan leader,"

Yosemite said.

The symphonic metal band's studio was located on the first floor of Yosemite's house on the planet Red Jacket. The house was located near an orange, rocky trail where the band would occasionally ride ATVs along its rough terrain. Red Jacket was a rusty, orange colored planet and had many desert and rocky areas. Many years before, it was a rich copper mining community. Maranadda's studio was located in an oasis area, heavy with foliage. The other band members of Maranadda also lived on Red Jacket, including the newer, Xenolfan vocalist. Prior to the former vocalist's disappearance, Sierra Shalinsky lived on the planet Asparr Celtarious. She was the only member of the band that had lived off-planet.

Arrian Trodder, the bass player for Maranadda, entered the studio where Yosemite and Arvon sat. Like Arvon, he also had long, brown hair. He was followed by the long, blond-haired keyboardist, Kulu Avolium, and the band's other guitarist, Sanarith Raastarr.

"Hey, you're finally here. Thanks for coming over for this meeting," Yosemite said. "It is important that we address the issue of losing so many fans as of late." He locked his hands together and rested them on his head, slightly flattening his short, spiky, brown hair.

"Well, it's about time we got together for this. I think we are all in agreement that Aymreth Rosenn sucks," Arrian Trodder said. "I'm sure you all realize that even though Sierra Shalinsky and I didn't get along that well, I have come to appreciate her all the more…after all this. Our personalities might have clashed on occasion, but she was a damn good vocalist."

"At first, Aymreth was a great prospect and did very well at a couple of shows, but then it's like her appeal quickly vanished," Sanarith Raastarr said. The overhead lights glistened off his bald head.

"I think it may very well have been an act just to get in the band. Once she was accepted, her true self came out. There was no longer some fancy show to perform, just a relaxed and shitty vocalist," Kulu Avolium said.

"After all the auditions we went through, I can't believe we settled on Aymreth," Arrian said. "I think that other Xenolfan female was much better, or even that human from Exandra. But, no…we settled on Aymreth."

"So, I take it that we are all in agreement to let Aymreth Rosenn go?" Yosemite asked.

They all gave an affirmative response.

"What will we do in the interim without a vocalist?" Arvon asked.

"We have no shows coming up for a while. Let's just chill out for a bit. Maybe we can write some new material in the mean time," Kulu suggested.

Suddenly, the studio door opened and Vincent and Shaslin Macenburg walked in and noticed them all sitting around. The door was left ajar as they made their way into the studio.

"Well, how is our favorite sound tech and his lovely wife doing?" Yosemite asked.

"Oh hey, guys. We are doing fantastic. We didn't mean to interrupt you. We're just dropping off these new audio cables," Vincent said.

"You guys look pretty serious," Shaslin said. Her beautiful, long, brown hair was in a pony tail.

Vincent set the cables down near the soundboard and put his sunglasses up on his head of long, brown hair.

"Yes. We are having a discussion regarding removing Aymreth from the band," Yosemite said.

"Yeah. We were all discussing how much she sucks," Arrian said.

"We certainly do miss Sierra, but that sounds a bit extreme," Vincent said.

Silence filled the studio as they each thought about their decision and about the former vocalist that had gone missing for the better part of a year.

"Do you ever wonder if Sierra just got fed up with things and left?" Arrian asked.

"No. She was at the top of her game. She fought and won the fight for sexual freedom between humans and Xenolfans. She was so popular with our fans that they started riots when she didn't show up for a concert, due to her responsibilities as a Galactic Emergency Medical Technician. No, I don't think she was fed up at all. I think someone intentionally did something to her," Arvon said, a look of sadness in his eyes.

"I know we have all searched for her for the first few months to no avail. I mean, we looked everywhere she frequented. It's as if she just vanished from the entire galaxy," Kulu said.

"I heard the Superior Mountain Club acquired her property along Lake Serenity on Asparr Celtarious. Yeah, their Jinkins committee made some legal moves regarding property abandonment. Sierra would be so pissed," Vincent said.

"Because the members of that committee are such assholes, that is why Sierra used the term Jinkins all the time, as an insult, meaning idiot," Shaslin said.

"She was the best vocalist I've ever heard," Sanarith said.

"Well, I will contact Aymreth and have her come in to give her the news," Yosemite said.

"I can't believe you guys are doing this to her," Vincent said.

"This is not cool," Shaslin said.

The studio door, which was ajar, slowly opened farther as someone else entered the room. They all looked up to see a tall Xenolfan woman enter, her black outfit contrasting her bluish-gray skin. Her long, white hair and sapphire eyes were beautiful. The look of disbelief was written across her face.

"Aymreth! How long have you been at the door?" Yosemite asked.

"Long enough. I wasn't far behind Vincent and Shaslin." She looked over at Vincent and Shaslin. "I'm glad to hear that you guys weren't aware of this." She turned back toward Yosemite and the others. "So, you want to remove me from the band? I know how much you guys miss Sierra. I wish I would have met her. She seems like she was awesome. I'm just sorry I cannot live up to her reputation. If you think I am unaware that the fans don't like me, you're wrong. They hate me. I may not be as good as Sierra, but I have tried. I have tried too hard, I believe. I don't think I'm cut out for this anyway. I understand your decision. I'm sorry I disappointed you and could not live up to your expectations. I've always felt like an outsider anyway," Aymreth Rosenn said.

"Look, Aymreth—"

"Don't!" Aymreth shouted, raising her bluish-gray hand. "There is no need to explain. I'll be leaving now. Good luck with Maranadda."

She walked back out the studio door. The room was quiet for some time as they all just looked at each other. Shaslin and Vincent had a look of shock on their faces.

"Well, that kind of sucked," Arvon finally said.

"It had to be done. Aymreth is a nice person, but not a good fit for Maranadda," Yosemite said.

"Sierra would probably think you are all assholes for doing that," Shaslin said.

"Yes, she would. Someday, maybe, we will find out what happened to Sierra," Arrian said.

"Perhaps… We have looked everywhere. Sierra's friends Priscilla and Braxton Stryderr, along with the Syrenthian Government, did an extensive search as well. I know that Sierra didn't talk about her parents much, but Ralger and Cathin Shalinsky spent a lot of time and credits devoted to searching for their daughter too. They are such wonderful people. Even Sierra's work director at GEMS, Sethain Absoneth, and Sierra's co-worker, Rasmond Echeon, did some searching on their own to no avail. But still, this thing you guys just did to Aymreth is not cool. I'm going to go talk to her," Shaslin said, leaving the studio.

"Sir, we just received a disturbing message and a very weak distress signal emitting from…the Shardaa Sector." The Syrenthian Government communications technician looked over to her superior officer.

"What is the message, Tanorra?" he asked.

"I'll play it for you," she said.

A very staticky signal emitted from the speaker. "Emergency! Emergency! This is Sierra Shalinsky calling from the planet S2 in the Shardaa Sector. I have been abducted and I'm being pursued by these people. I need assistance. I repeat, I need assistance. Please help me!"

"It continues after a pause," the technician said.

"This is Sierra Shalinsky calling from the Shardaa Sector. This is an emergency! Please respond!"

"And then it switched to the weak distress signal that we are currently receiving."

Parker was the senior officer for the Communications Department. He put his finger on his upper lip in thought for a long moment.

"Have you responded?"

"I have, but our signal does not seem to be reaching her location. There is a lot of interference. It seems to be caused from the Sharasp Tharrian Asteroid Mass, a small asteroid mass in the Shardaa Star System's outer region that is currently directly in the path of our signal. Once it has moved along in its orbit, our signal should have no problem reaching her comm," Tanorra said.

"I will inform Edward Sirlain of this. Was this signal relayed to us from Galactic Emergency Medical Services?" Parker asked.

"No. She must have known our direct frequency," Tanorra said.

"Odd. I will be back shortly."

The senior officer left the Communications Department and made his way through the government building on Exandra. Soon, he entered the executive offices of Edward Sirlain, leader of the Syrenthian Government. The elegant offices were decorated with a brown carpeting and light caramel colored wall accents. The secretary that sat at the desk in the center of the main entry looked up at the senior officer who entered.

"I need to see Edward Sirlain."

"I will see if he is available," she said, reaching for the comm. "Parker is here to see you, sir."

"Send him in, Jareen," Edward Sirlain said.

Parker left the reception area and entered into Edward Sirlain's spacious office as the door swiftly slid aside. A few tall bookshelves could be seen to the right of the entry. On the left of the office, there was an elegant couch and chair, both upholstered with a fine beige leather. Edward Sirlain sat at a wide desk toward the back of the office. He wore his long, grayish-blond hair in a ponytail. Beyond his desk, a large window displayed a beautiful courtyard, sunlight brightening its greenery. Several small trees in the courtyard had blossomed with vibrant, pink petals.

"Hey, Parker. What can I do for you?" Edward asked.

"We just received an emergency communication and distress signal from Sierra Shalinsky. It's emitting from the Shardaa Sector."

"Seriously?" Edward Sirlain straightened his posture and stared at Parker with a sudden questioning look. "Sierra Shalinsky? We gave up searching for her months ago. Braxton Stryderr was lead on that team. And she is in the Shardaa Sector of all places? That's probably why we didn't find her. We never searched there. It is very odd that she is there. Over the years, there has been nothing but odd stories surrounding that region of space…including other distress signals in the past."

"She sounds like she's in trouble and needs assistance. According to the message, she was abducted and is being pursued by 'these people,' as she stated," Parker said.

"'These people?' What people?" Edward asked.

"That's a good question. The only thing I can think of is there may be pirates in the area."

"Parker, I want you to inform Braxton Stryderr to pick up this investigation and search where he left off months ago. We need to get on this right away," Edward said.

"I believe Braxton is on vacation, sir."

"Shit, that's right. Braxton and Priscilla are on vacation at The Avalanche Resort on Aamaress. Well, you'll just have to interrupt their vacation for this assignment…if they haven't froze to death on that snow planet," Edward said, sarcastically.

"I will contact Braxton right away, sir," Parker said.

After Parker left Edward Sirlain's office, the Syrenthian Government leader swiveled his chair to face the courtyard window and gazed at the scenery in deep contemplation.

The Shardaa Sector? The thought astonished him.

Chapter Four

After Estrus destroyed the Dissident Faction fighter ship, they flew back to S6 in her ship, *Aileron.* Leaving behind the damaged ship that Sierra had taken was a minor setback. It did not take long for them to reach S6. Maneuvering through the blue atmosphere and over the majestic, white mountains, Estrus flew the *Aileron* toward the docking bay of the Humolfan Command facility. As the ship settled to the floor, Sierra found herself in the familiar docking bay that she had left earlier. They both stepped out of the ship and onto the shiny floor. Soltuss Yow flew over to where they stood, her wings making a heavy, flapping sound above them. Her boots scuffed the floor as she landed and tucked in her wings.

"I am relieved that you have found Sierra," Soltuss said. An optimistic smile covered her face.

"Me too. A Dissident Faction fighter ship shot her down on S2 and she was about to be killed. Sierra, this is Soltuss Yow. She is head of the Humolfan Command as well as this facility on S6. Your safety is her number one concern, especially in the face of the Dissident Faction," Estrus said.

Sierra looked back and forth between the two winged women.

"It is nice to formally meet you in a conscious state, Sierra. Estrus, do you still need to bring her to see the doctor? After all, that is where you were heading before all this," Soltuss said.

"No. Now that she is out of her coma, I don't think a visit to the doctor is a priority. She can see the doctor later," Estrus said.

"Well, I've been a little lightheaded since I woke up. Although I need a lot of shit explained to me, it is nice to meet you as well," Sierra said to Soltuss.

"Okay, Sierra, let's head to my quarters and I will explain why you are here," Estrus said.

Sierra followed Estrus to the far side of the docking bay, toward a corridor that led deeper into the facility.

"If you could wait here for just a moment, I forgot to tell Soltuss Yow something," Estrus said.

Estrus lifted herself in flight back to the other end of the docking bay where Soltuss Yow stood speaking with another officer. Estrus landed next to them. Soltuss finished her conversation with the officer and dismissed her. She turned toward Estrus.

"There is an emergency distress signal currently being transmitted from S2, in the rocks just above the cave entrance there. You may want to end that transmission before we have a shitstorm on our hands," Estrus said. "Also, have a salvage team retrieve our ship from the surface."

"Oh… I will send a team there to do just that. Thanks for the info," Soltuss said.

As Sierra waited, she noticed two men walking along the far side of the docking bay. They were dressed in all black with an insignia embroidered on the back of their jackets. Unlike all the other people Sierra had seen, these two men had no wings and their hair was black, not white. They looked very familiar, but she could not put her finger on it.

Estrus flew back toward Sierra, her large, black wings flapping ever so gracefully in the heights of the docking bay. She landed next to Sierra, who had watched her approach.

"That's amazing," Sierra said.

"Yeah, I guess flying is…" Estrus said.

As they left the docking bay and walked along the corridor, Sierra looked at the art that was on display along the white walls. There was a variety of abstract paintings. The height of the corridor did not lend itself to Humolfan flight. Other Humolfans stared at Sierra as they passed by in the opposite direction. After several turns, they came to a stop in front of Estrus's quarters. She pressed a button on the wall and the door slid aside. The illuminators automatically activated as they entered the room.

Suddenly, a small dog ran up to Estrus, wagging its tail and barking. He had white fur with hints of brown and black. He looked up at the two of them with his curious brown eyes as they entered.

"Aww! He is the cutest little dog I've ever seen," Sierra said.

"This is Thepsi. He is my little buddy," Estrus said. "How are you doing, little guy?"

The dog took interest in the new person that entered his home. Sierra knelt down and petted his soft fur as he wagged his curly tail.

"So, would you like something to drink? Perhaps you would like to try some Ginger Alquinola. I have plenty of it," Estrus suggested. "Or I have ale."

"I'll try the Ginger Alquinola. It sounds good," Sierra said as she stood back up from petting the dog.

Estrus went into the kitchen and grabbed two Ginger Alquinolas from the refrigerator. As she returned to the living room area, she handed Sierra a bottle, adjusted her wings slightly, and sat down in a chair.

"Sit down and make yourself comfortable," Estrus said.

Sierra sat down on a soft couch and took a long drink of the beverage. As she set the bottle down on a table next to the couch, she gazed around the room and then looked at Estrus.

"This is delicious. It reminds me of Sevis, yet with alcohol and even more effervescence. The ginger is very spicy and has a hint of lemon. So...tell me why I'm here."

There was a pause and Estrus took a drink of her own beverage. Setting the bottle down, Estrus stared a Sierra for a long moment.

"First of all, I am so very grateful that you are here. We've waited for this opportunity for so many years. We are Humolfans. We have gray skin, a mixture between the bluish-gray Xenolfans and the tan humans. We have white hair and sapphire eyes, like Xenolfans. Our genitalia are shaped like Xenolfans...well except in rare cases where they are like the humans. We have black wings and can fly and soar in the sky, just like the Xenolfans could do one millennium ago. Unlike the Xenolfans, our sapphire eyes can glow and make people faint. Our species is a hybrid of humans and Xenolfans."

"How do you make people faint with your eyes? Xenolfans can't even do that," Sierra said.

"It is an unknown genetic anomaly that all Humolfans have. To this day it remains a mystery that our scientists cannot fully solve," Estrus said.

"Wait a minute. It is a known fact that humans and Xenolfans cannot breed," Sierra said.

"Yes, you are correct in that the two species cannot currently breed together. However, one thousand years ago, that was not the case. You see, back then, humans and Xenolfans could breed and did breed. We are the results of those unions," Estrus said.

"I do remember hearing that Xenolfans used to have wings a thousand years ago, but through microevolution, their wings had eventually disappeared. They just have bumps on their backs of what used to genetically be there," Sierra said.

"Yes, except it was not through microevolution that Xenolfans had their wings stripped from them. It was a side effect of intentional genetic manipulation. You see, one thousand years ago, a very evil Xenolfan, named Siiteper Affelum, hated human and Xenolfan unions so much that he began a crusade against them. He did such horrible things...such horrible things." Estrus stared into the distance, tears forming in her beautiful sapphire eyes.

"That sounds a lot like Aaranix Tuvelless. What horrible things did this Siiteper Affelum do?" Sierra asked.

"Oh... Well, first of all, Aaranix Tuvelless is a terrible Xenolfan and deserves the death penalty that he is scheduled to receive, but he has nothing on Siiteper Affelum. Siiteper's hatred was so intense that he began a genocide campaign against all interspecies couples. At first, he located every one of them and kept them under surveillance. And later he had them tracked down, brought to S4, and killed. Their offspring—us Humolfans—were banished to the Shardaa Sector by Siiteper's authoritative decree. Our exile was kept secret from galactic society. There were adult Humolfans at the time. They were responsible for our survival out here in this region of the galaxy. The adults helped build a new life for our species. Any human and Xenolfan mothers who were pregnant with a hybrid Humolfan were killed by Siiteper Affelum and buried on S4. Later, I will bring you to

S4 and show you the Grave of Mothers. You must know our story. You must know the truth."

Sierra stared at Estrus for a long time before she found the words to speak. "I have so many questions, Estrus," she finally said.

"While Siiteper Affelum was alive as leader of the Xenolfan Government, he prohibited anyone from leaving the Shardaa Sector. He had a military battleship patrolling the star system, ready to destroy any ship that entered or left here. We have been secluded in isolation for one thousand years."

"Surely, you must have had your people come out from time to time. After all, you found me on Red Jacket," Sierra said.

"Many generations after Siiteper Affelum's reign, we did send out our people on missions from time to time. By then, most of the galaxy had forgotten about the intermixed breeding that previously occurred. Generations later, they had never seen a winged Xenolfan let alone a Humolfan. Our seclusion kept us in secrecy. We have sent our people out on missions in the past. For many years, we have been searching for someone like you to advocate for our species so we can return and have repatriation back into galactic society. We have tried and every time the person we chose, whether it was a human or a Xenolfan, never worked out. We were so close with Dennon Cobalt, but the damn Dissident Faction had to fuck that up. Oh, they are an evil lot!" Estrus said.

"What happened to Xenolfan wings? Why can't we breed with Xenolfans anymore?" Sierra asked.

"Siiteper Affelum did so many horrible things to his own people. He did genetic experiments and testing on Xenolfan men and woman until he was able to change the DNA and make it impossible for them to breed with humans. An unintended result of his experiments was that Xenolfans lost their ability to fly. Their wings no longer developed in Xenolfan children. It was not microevolution. Siiteper forced the education system to teach microevolution as a fact," Estrus said. She took a long drink of her Ginger Alquinola.

Sierra took another drink as well. "So, what were you doing with Dennon Cobalt?"

"Dennon was a great prospect to advocate for us because he is an expert at marketing. The Dissident Faction shot his ship down on S2, just like they did to you. When I heard that he had been shot down on S2, I tried to get there as fast as I could. He had already activated his distress signal and your Galactic Emergency Medical Services team had arrived soon after I did. He was supposed to meet me on S6 for a meeting. When I first arrived on S2, I was going to make him faint with my eyes. But he was in and out of consciousness from the crash, so I decided not to. I tried to wake him, but I had to find shelter in the cave when your team arrived. Can you imagine if your GEMS team would have seen a winged creature? Anyway, your team took him away and with that, we lost hope in Dennon as a prospect to advocate for us. Of course, he was not here for seven months in a coma, like you," Estrus said.

"You are that woman with black wings and blue eyes that Dennon Cobalt spoke of. He kept saying 'She's here.' You were in the cave when Alex and I went searching for the woman that Dennon spoke of. The blue lights I saw in the cave were your glowing eyes. You made me faint with your eyes, didn't you?" Sierra asked.

"I did. I knew I had lost Dennon and I was so desperate to replace him with you. It was so ironic that you were on the team of first responders for Dennon's distress signal. You see, we already knew who you were and our sources kept tabs on you. You were actually our next prospect anyway."

"So, you want me to advocate for the Humolfans to be introduced back into galactic society? And you needed to abduct me to do this?"

"Yes and yes. You would have never agreed to come on your own if you knew there was a strange winged species in the mysterious and dark regions of the Shardaa Sector. You were chosen because you have advocated for sexual freedom between humans and Xenolfans with galactic success. You helped establish both human and Xenolfan sex clinics throughout the galaxy. You are okay with interspecies sex. You are very sexually active and a bisexual swinger in the Lifestyle. You are a self-spoken leader in a band. You help people as a Galactic Emergency Medical Technician. You seem to be the perfect person to help us Humolfans."

"You seem to know a lot about me, including my personal sex life. How do you know all this?" Sierra asked.

"I was assigned to track you after the Dennon Cobalt incident. I was there at times when you didn't even know it. There are other—"

"You were in the cave on Aamaress!"

"Yes. When I flew through that snow storm, I about froze my wings off. I was trying to abduct you then, but it just didn't work out," Estrus said.

"Then, you saw me having sex with the Xenolfan man, Garrious?"

"I did."

"He turned out to be the murderer that flew the missiloid into Winterfest and killed all those innocent people," Sierra said.

"I know. But... Sierra, the sex you had in that cave turned me on so much, you can't even imagine. It was on a level deeper than you even realize. You see, it was as if I witnessed firsthand the desires that my human and Xenolfan ancestors had for each other. We Humolfans are very sexual creatures. I may sound like a sexual deviant, but seeing you two had a very special meaning for me. Taking care of you everyday for the last seven months has brought me very close to you in a lot of intimate ways."

"What do you mean?"

"Well, I've bathed you, I've helped the doctors with catheters, I've read to you, I've had so many one-way conversations with you. I've come to know you in a very different way. And you are the sexiest human I've ever seen. I often fantasize about you and I together. I am so very grateful that you woke up. I thought I had killed you for sure when you hit your head on the concrete after that concert on Red Jacket."

Sierra smiled at Estrus, suddenly realizing she somehow had an attraction to Estrus that she could not explain.

"I cut you off earlier. You said, 'There are other...'" Sierra said.

"Yes... There are other Humolfans that have a secret presence in the galaxy. Sometimes they were also assigned to watch you. Have you ever heard of the Syrenthian Brotherhood Knights of Darkness?"

"Yeah. They are a badass gang that you don't want to mess with. In fact, one time, I saw a Syrenthian Brotherhood Knights of Darkness member kill an identity thief right in front of me for stealing his identity. I remembered he gave the bartender, Remywian Yort, an Asparell coin to compensate for the mess. That identity thief had also stolen my identity. I say the badass guy was a hero for cleaning up the galactic trash," Sierra said.

"I know the rest of the Syrenthian Galaxy hasn't used Asparell coins for a thousand years, since back during Siiteper Affelum's time. We actually still use Asparell coins here in the Shardaa Sector. You see, the Syrenthian Brotherhood Knights of Darkness are actually a gang of Humolfans that have dedicated their entire lives to protect us and stand up for justice and righteousness. They take an oath to permanently clip their wings off, tan their skin, dye their hair from white to black, and to use special contact lenses to conceal their sapphire eyes. The term 'Darkness' used in their name comes from the Shardaa Sector being a dark and desolate region of space. They became greater in number out in the galaxy after the Syrenthian War between the humans and Xenolfans one hundred years ago. If the one you speak of killed an identity thief for stealing his identity, it was only a pseudo identity anyway since no one had his real identity as a Humolfan."

"Oh my! Those two men I just saw in the docking bay were Syrenthian Brotherhood Knights of Darkness members."

"Oh, did you see a couple of them? Yes, you are correct. They are really Humolfans from here in the Shardaa Sector."

"How many Humolfans are there?" Sierra asked.

"There are about seventeen million Humolfans, mostly on Shardia and S6, but some on S5 and the Dissident Faction on S3. No one lives on Shardaa because it has no atmosphere, no one lives on S2 because it's so desolate, and no one lives on S4 because it is set aside only for the Grave of Mothers," Estrus said.

"Okay."

Sierra sat for a long time absorbing everything about this new revelation. After taking another drink of her beverage, she gave Estrus a puzzling look.

"What?" Estrus asked.

"Were you also on the planet Shardaa when our GEMS team first searched for Dennon Cobalt's distress signal? Something made me feel faint there too."

"No. That was a Dissident Faction member that was all suited up in a spacesuit and ready to kill you and your entire team. They must have decided not to. You see, the Dissident Faction is a group of people within our Humolfan species here in the Shardaa Sector that do not want to assimilate back into galactic society. They have known about our plan and they have been attacking us for years to stop us. You should see the destruction they've caused. They have also tried to kill you because they don't want you to advocate for us. We can never underestimate their surveillance technology. They never want us to leave the Shardaa Sector. They tried to kill Dennon Cobalt as well. They've been attacking ships for a hundred years in the Shardaa Star

System. Many of your missing ships and strange encounters in this region of space has been because of the Dissident Faction's activities. The Dissident Faction's current leader is Gramer Moss. She is a ruthless killer. But their days are numbered. We are currently working on a military campaign that will finally wipe them out for good. Anyway, I digress…"

"Please explain the mysterious feather symbols that I saw above the caves and the same feather symbol tattoo that I briefly saw on your mons pubis that day on Red Jacket before you abducted me."

"Ah yes. The Feathers of Shardaa… You see, there is a great significant meaning in that feather symbol. In the early centuries of the Humolfans being exiled to the Shardaa Sector, they would inscribe them above caves and on mountain rock walls. They would carve the surface below to look like our vulvas. You see, as you're looking at the symbol, the feather that leans to the left represents the Humolfans ability to fly, while the broken feather on the right represents the Xenolfans being stripped of their ability to fly. Around the time the first Xenolfans were born without wings, they also could no longer breed with humans. It all revolved around the womb. So, you will always see the Feathers of Shardaa symbol directly above a vulva. Every Humolfan female has a Feathers of Shardaa tattoo on her mons pubis. When we reach a certain age and understand the significance of what the feathers symbolize and what was lost a thousand years ago, we are ready for the tattoo. I received mine when I was seventeen. Do you understand why seeing you and that Xenolfan having sex in the cave on Aamaress had a deeper meaning for me?" Estrus asked.

"Why are humans not involved in the feather symbology, if they were a part of the Humolfan creation process?" Sierra asked.

"Human DNA was not modified. Siiteper didn't dare mess with too many humans because, if the Syrenthian Government would have found out, it would have led to war. I know pure Humolfan DNA was not modified either, but it is more of a comparison of our flight abilities to what was stolen from the Xenolfans. However, Siiteper did kill many humans as well, most of whom were in relationships with Xenolfans. The human element is not forgotten by any means. So, the Feathers of Shardaa symbol is more representative of the results of the experimentation that was done. Mazniriatt is one of the best tattoo artists when it comes to the feather symbol," Estrus said.

"That tattoo ritual is fascinating. Mazniriatt?" Sierra looked down at Estrus's lower section where her feather symbol tattoo was covered by her uniform.

"My tattoo is the work of Mazniriatt. Would you like to see it again?" Estrus asked.

Sierra remembered seeing the tattoo briefly in the backstage warehouse after the concert on Red Jacket, before her comatose state. The invitation to see the tattoo again suddenly aroused Sierra and she could feel the warmth build in her pussy.

"Yes. I would like that very much," Sierra said. She found herself breathing heavily.

Estrus stood up from the chair and walked over to the couch where Sierra sat. Sitting down on the couch, Estrus slowly removed her blue uniform. Pulling down the uniform from the top revealed her large, gray breasts as they protruded outward from the fabric. Her long, white hair draped over her left nipple. She carefully pulled her large, black, feathery wings from their openings and slid the uniform down farther to reveal the feather symbol tattoo.

Sierra studied the intricate ink patterns of the feather tattoo. The unbroken feather that pointed to the left was an asymmetrical black, flight feather. The detail in the rachis, barbs, and barbules was amazing. At the bottom of the feather, the calamus crossed the other feather, forming an X. The calamus of the feather that pointed to the right was broken just above the X intersection and, unlike the left side, the feather pointed downward. The broken feather displayed barbs that had been damaged and barbules that were roughed up. Sierra thought about the meaning that Estrus had explained and realized how very sad it was and how significant the feather symbol was to the Humolfans. She felt moved by the story that Estrus had shared. As she looked closely at the tattoo, Estrus pulled her uniform farther down to reveal her vulva. Sierra looked up into her sapphire eyes for a long moment and then back down past the feather symbol tattoo at Estrus's pussy. The vaginal opening was in the shape of a rounded, reuleaux triangle. Sierra had seen this vulvar shape before on Xenolfan women, except their skin was bluish-gray. She thought it strange to see such a pussy shape on someone with gray skin. She had also seen and been with both male and female Xenolfans, whose males had reuleaux-shaped cocks that were a perfect fit into the same-shaped pussy. The bluish-gray Xenolfan male cocks were also stepped down in the center with a smaller girth toward the tip. The tips did not have a head, like humans, but were angled and had large urethral openings. Sierra's thoughts shifted from Xenolfan cock back to the alien pussy before her.

"May I kiss it?" Sierra asked.

"Most definitely. I've enjoyed both male and female Humolfans, but you're going to be a treat," Estrus said. She adjusted her hips on the couch.

Sierra gently kissed along the top of the vulva and then down each labia. Using her tongue, she parted the inner labia folds and began to slide her tongue up and down the wet grooves. She flicked at Estrus's clit and gently sucked on it. She paused slightly as Estrus completely removed her uniform. The gray thighs that were spread before Sierra were most beautiful. She could feel her own wetness begin to dampen her panties. Sierra returned her tongue to the folds of Estrus's pussy, licking up her pleasant taste. Estrus moaned loudly and placed a hand on Sierra's head. Sierra stopped for a moment and looked up.

"What is it?" Estrus asked.

"You don't have a high-pitched, reverberating purr, do you?" Sierra asked.

"Ah…no. What are you talking about?"

"Xenolfans let out loud, high-pitched, reverberating moans when they reach orgasm."

"Really? Wow! No, Humolfans just have a normal moan."

"Sorry for the distraction," Sierra said as she continued.

Sierra's tongue danced around with fast and then slow movements. She enjoyed her bisexual side from time to time, but it certainly was no replacement for cock in her life. Estrus pushed her hips up against Sierra's mouth and let out a loud moan.

"Ahhh!"

Sierra turned it up a notch and quickly moved her head side to side, pushing against Estrus's pussy lips. She then returned to focus on Estrus's swollen clit. With every wet stroke, Estrus quivered with bliss. Her heavy breathing became quicker and quicker until she shouted loudly and pushed Sierra away.

"Oh, oh… Sierra, you are amazing."

"Did you like that? I think I may be a bit overdressed for the occasion."

Sierra stood up and quickly removed her light gray jumpsuit. Her black hair partially covered her firm breasts. As with Estrus, Sierra too had a smoothly shaved pussy. As Sierra stood before Estrus, the

Humolfan looked up from where she sat on the couch toward Sierra's pussy. She studied it for a long moment.

"I've shaved your pussy while you've been in a coma. Until you came along, I've never seen a human vulva before. Like I mentioned before, in rare cases, Humolfans are born with human-shaped genitalia. It occurs with one in every thirty-five thousand Humolfans. Sometimes they aren't treated the best by others because of their difference, but it is so rare to find someone like that. If they have human-shaped genitalia, it is not something they announce to everyone. It is difficult for most of them to find partners because they are afraid they will be judged, not accepted, and then ousted," Estrus said.

"That is sad. I feel that the differences are more sexually exciting and erotic," Sierra said.

"Yes. And you certainly look sexy," Estrus said.

Estrus moved forward and planted her mouth against Sierra's pussy. The warmth that Sierra felt was so intense, its wave radiated outward to each extremity. Sierra stood in front of the couch and put one foot up on the cushion, being careful not to step on the bottom of Estrus's wing. Sierra closed her eyes as Estrus worked magically. The pressure of Estrus's wet tongue sent surges of ecstasy pulsating outward from Sierra's pussy. Sierra moaned with little, sharp breaths. Estrus licked at Sierra's clit and then back between the folds before burying her tongue inside Sierra's hole.

"Ah, ah, ah…Estrus don't stop. Ahhh!" Sierra screamed as she came to an incredible orgasm.

As Sierra's breathing slowed and she caught her breath, she looked down at Estrus and smiled, her eyes half shut.

"So, Humolfans don't have long tongues like Xenolfans, then?" Sierra asked.

Estrus looked up at her with an odd expression. "Apparently not. Do they have long tongues?"

"Yes, much different than humans…or Humolfans for that matter. But there is certainly nothing wrong with your tongue at all. That was so amazing. I needed that so badly, I can't even tell you," Sierra said.

"You and me both. Taking care of you for the last seven months has really made me fantasize about you a lot. Normally, I date men, but I have been with a couple of Humolfan women. But with you…and how different you are, it was a huge turn-on for me."

"Well, I hope I didn't disappoint you," Sierra said.

"Not in the slightest," Estrus said, smiling with her bright, sapphire eyes.

As they each put their outfits back on, Sierra paused and looked at Estrus. "So, how do you do that thing with your eyes, like in the cave?"

"We just focus our attention on our eyes and look at the person we want to faint and then just think about it. They start glowing and emit a melatonin wave through the air that envelopes the other person's mind. It is my understanding that neither humans nor Xenolfans have that power. But the hybrid of the species does. Like I said before, our scientists still can't completely figure it out. When we are children, we are taught early on not to use that power unless absolutely necessary. You'll sometimes see two Humolfan children both on the ground who were in a battle of the eyes. Of course, when they wake up, they get in big trouble." She laughed. "I remember doing that a couple of times as a child."

After she zipped up her light gray jumpsuit, Sierra finished her Ginger Alquinola. Estrus finished her beverage as well. As she brought the bottles back into the kitchen, she looked down at her dog in the corner.

"Do you want some fresh water, Thepsi?"

The dog lifted his head and looked up at her, his brown eyes slightly covered with the fur along his face. She filled up his water dish and food bowl.

"He's such a cutie," Sierra said. "The fact that Humolfans even exist is incredible. I feel honored that you chose me to represent your repatriation," Sierra said.

"I'm sure it is quite a shock for you. Humans and Xenolfans don't know we exist, but we know that you both exist. That's because we are taught our history that explains both of your species. We have an extensive atheneum, which is absolutely impressive. There are a ton of books on the subjects. If I had studied more, I may have known about our genital differences when I was much younger," Estrus said.

"Nothing like a first-hand lesson," Sierra said, smiling.

"Mmm, yes," Estrus said.

"I would like to see this extensive atheneum you speak of," Sierra said.

"I'll show you that. I still have so much to tell you and to show you..."

"I'm looking forward to it."

Deep inside, Sierra had doubts about helping the Humolfans, but she had to admit that the Humolfans seemed to be in a desperate situation.

"If you're up to it, the first thing I want to show you is the Grave of Mothers on S4. You'll want to bring these," Estrus said, handing Sierra a box of tissues as she headed toward the door.

Chapter Five

The *Aileron* flight was fairly quiet. Sierra and Estrus sat on the small bridge and gazed at the sparse stars stream by as the ship traveled at lightspeed-plus.

"So, the Humolfans have been in isolation, but you have ships that can travel lightspeed?"

"Oh yes. We have been out here for a thousand years. During that time, we have developed many things."

"Tell me more about the Shardaa Sector. Tell me about each planet. I've been on a couple of them, but they seem fairly desolate," Sierra said.

Sierra brushed her long, black hair aside and looked over at Estrus who made an adjustment on the control panel.

"Most of the Shardaa Sector is quite dark and desolate. This region of space sits on the edge of the Syrenthian Galaxy. People are afraid to come here, mostly because of the Dissident Faction's attacks over many, many years. We have received a very mysterious and bad reputation. The Shardaa Sector consists of the Shardaa Star System, the Sharasp Tharrian Asteroid Mass, and a mysterious space object called Shaeolian Black Hole. The first planet in the system is called Shardaa. It is the only planet in the Shardaa Star System that does not have an atmosphere. Centuries ago, my people carved the feather symbol on a rock wall there as well as every planet in the star system. I know you were there with your GEMS team. That is where a member of the Dissident Faction was about to kill your whole team. Next, we have S2, which has an atmosphere, but is very desolate. The cave there, with the feather symbol chiseled in stone, is where I found you after the Dissident Faction shot you down. It is also where your GEMS team found Dennon Cobalt. S3 is also a desolate planet. It is where the Dissident Faction operates from. There aren't many of them, but they are a thorn in our side. Any ship that passes near S3 will become a target for the Dissident Faction. Their current leader, Gramer Moss, has organized their little faction into a force to be reckoned with. The rest of us are not overly concerned about the Dissident Faction since we are more powerful than they are. S4 is where we are headed to see the Grave of Mothers. It is a desolate planet…a sad planet. S5 has some of my people on it, but not many. It is not as desolate as the other planets that I previously mentioned. S6 is where I live. We have beautiful mountains. It is a lovely place. And finally, there is Shardia…"

"Shardia? So, there *is* another planet beyond S6 in the Shardaa Star System," Sierra said.

"Yes. There are seven total. We discovered Shardia long after Siiteper Affelum was gone. The region of space near Shardia is not dark and desolate at all, but sits against a beautiful light blue constellation. In fact, that is where the seat of the Humolfan Government is located. It is also the most beautiful of all the planets in this system. It is green with life and blue with water. Our leader, Yilran Taw, lives there in the government palace."

"Wow, Shardia sounds interesting. Anyway, I believe that is the same light blue space you can see in the Aamaress Star System, which is not far from the Shardaa Sector," Sierra said.

"Yes. It is actually called Blue Space. I will take you to Shardia and show you the extensive atheneum there. There are so many books there, the shelving goes as far as the eye can see. There is one book in particular that I want to show you."

"Okay."

"Every planet in this star system beyond Shardaa was named by

Siiteper Affelum, except Shardia, which they did not know about at the time."

"I wonder why recent astronomers have not discovered its existence," Sierra said.

"It is the farthest planet out here. Perhaps your astronomers weren't looking," Estrus suggested.

A beeping sound began to emit from the control panel as S4 came into view. Estrus slowed the ship down, exiting from lightspeed-plus and programmed the coordinates for their destination.

"We are approaching S4," Estrus said.

The *Aileron* flew through the thick, dark clouds of S4's atmosphere. Estrus maneuvered the ship toward the Grave of Mothers. The terrain was somewhat different than S2. A desolate ambiance resonated with the rocky terrain on S4. There were leafless trees scattered sparsely about the area, evidence of at least some life. In the distance, Sierra saw endless rows of gray stones. As they advanced closer, she could see they were all gravestones. Estrus settled the ship in a landing area and disengaged the engines. She stood up and grabbed a few tissues from the box they had brought. Sierra stood up and followed suit by taking a few tissues as they exited the ship. The temperature outside was a bit chilly. Sierra could immediately feel a cool breeze blowing at them that sent shivers up her arms. The landing pad was just one of many that were located around the Grave of Mothers. Sierra followed Estrus past the original memorial plaque that was placed at the edge of the field with the name of the cemetery, Grave of Mothers. Next to the memorial plaque sat a newer plaque that was added by the Humolfans many years later, which explained what had happened on S4. They proceeded toward the first row of stone cairn burials. Each of the dead were covered with stones that were piled above ground. To Sierra's amazement, every gravestone marker had the feather symbol engraved into the upper corner, above the names.

"Every gravestone was painstakingly added by us Humolfans after the genocide and mass killings that Siiteper Affelum had executed. There are so many human mothers here that were pregnant with Humolfans, that it just aches my heart. Their male Xenolfan partners were also killed. There are even more Xenolfan mothers buried here, also pregnant with Humolfans. Their male human partners killed in the same brutal way. These mothers were at varying stages of pregnancy. Some had just conceived, others were in their last trimester. Some were even killed while giving birth and both mother and child left for dead. Siiteper Affelum had all the interspecies families shipped here to S4 a thousand years ago," Estrus said.

They slowly made their way along the countless gravestones. Between each stone cairn mound, the ground was littered with dark, loose rocks. There were strands of grass struggling to grow between many of the rocks. Passing a large, leafless tree, Sierra carefully studied the inscriptions on many of the gravestones as she walked along.

"These women did nothing wrong...nor did their partners. They simply loved someone from a different species and they were murdered for it. All these lives...all these baby Humolfans...just tragically lost. I couldn't even imagine the pain and suffering they went through," Estrus said.

"Where are the men buried?" Sierra asked.

Estrus stopped and looked at Sierra for a long moment. "They were all thrown off a cliff to the jagged rocks below, just over there beyond the Grave of Mothers. I will show you that as well."

Sierra's expression became a bit grim. As they quietly walked through the cemetery, something caught Sierra's eye. She walked closer to one of the gravestones.

"What is it?" Estrus asked.

"This woman had the same last name as mine."

"You may have had a distant ancestor that was in love with a Xenolfan. My 38th great grandmother is over there. She was a Xenolfan. She already had another Humolfan daughter, which was my 37th great grandmother. The Humolfans that were alive at the time were not killed, but banished...exiled here in the Shardaa Sector."

Was the person that shared her last name truly an ancient relative of hers? Sierra imagined the horrible things those mothers went through. It was a tragic end to what could have been so many beautiful lives.

Sierra looked up at Estrus. "All this," she motioned around the cemetery with her hand, "could have been prevented. It is such a tragedy. I don't understand why someone didn't stand up to Siiteper Affelum and stop this genocide."

Only silence filled the air.

"Much of what Siiteper Affelum did here was in secrecy. My heart aches every time I visit this place. The dead...they haunt my thoughts. I want nothing more than to fix what happened a thousand years ago, but I cannot," Estrus said.

Estrus led Sierra through a section of crooked gravestones, some of which were cracked and broken. She stopped at a particular gravestone and stared at the name for a long moment. Light black lines of weathering were present below the inscription. A slight breeze tousled their hair, carrying a musty scent from across the cemetery.

"This is where my 38th great grandmother lies."

Sierra looked below the feather symbol and read the inscription on the gravestone. "*Here lies Destiny and her unborn son...* What a tragedy," Sierra said.

"I remember visiting the Grave of Mothers when I was a child. My mother taught me the precious value of life inside the womb. Although I don't yet have children of my own, I know the values that my mother instilled in me. I miss my own mother so much. I miss her loving care. I miss her voice. I've felt so alone with her gone. I miss her holding me with long hugs. Of course, she is not buried here, but on S6 where I live. I hold the memories I have of my mother close to my heart. Sometimes, I cry out to the wind for her to please come back to me... Only silence returns my call," Estrus said.

Estrus brushed back her white hair and fluttered her wings slightly as she silently shed tears. She wiped her eyes with the tissue she had brought.

I hate the Dissident Faction! Estrus thought.

Sierra stood frozen and thought about her own mother for a long moment. Even before her abduction by the Humolfans, she hadn't seen her parents in a very long time. She knew they must be worried sick about her. She could still hear her mother call after her with love the last time she saw her.

"I should have visited my parents more..." Sierra said.

"Aren't they both alive?"

"Yes, they are both alive...at least they were seven months ago. I plan to make some positive changes in my life when I return from the Shardaa Sector. The Grave of Mothers here is really pulling at my heartstrings. I could write a song about this."

Sierra fought back tears of her own as she gazed across the cemetery at all the gravestones and her own precious memories flowed through her mind. As the salty tears reached her lips, she took one of the tissues from her pocket and dabbed her eyes.

"Do you ever wonder what it would have been like if things had turned out different for these mothers…for these families?" Sierra asked.

"If this would have been a different scenario, the galaxy would be a much different place today. My people would be free with yours. There would be hybrids of Humolfans and humans and Humolfans and Xenolfans. And there would be nothing wrong with the mix at all. It's all about the love. Yes, if Siiteper Affelum had not been an evil person, none of this would be," Estrus said.

They made their way from Destiny's grave and slowly walked farther into the cemetery. There was a slight dip in the terrain and they went down and back up the slopes. A particularly large tomb was at the bottom of the hill with a fancy stone border around it. Sierra looked at Estrus questioningly.

"A few of the older Humolfans created exceptional resting places for their mothers. That is one of them," Estrus said.

A dimness overcame the cemetery as daylight began to fade. In the distance, Sierra could see the edge of a cliff beyond where the cemetery ended. A remote plain of rocks and vegetation lay far below the cliff for a long distance before fading into a forest. They made their way to the edge of the cliff.

"This is the cliff where Siiteper Affelum ordered the fathers to be pushed off to their deaths," Estrus said.

Sierra peered over the edge to the rocky ground far below. She stared in disbelief at what she saw. A tangled mound of skeletons lay below the cliff, broken and shattered against the rocks. She looked up at Estrus in horror.

"Oh my…that is beyond words. How awful. This is just absolutely terrible," Sierra said.

Sierra noticed several skeletons that were much farther out beyond the bottom of the cliff. Estrus noticed her gaze.

"The skeletons that you see farther out were Xenolfan men trying to fly away from the madness. They were shot down to their deaths. That was back when Xenolfans had wings, before Siiteper Affelum experimented on his own people," Estrus said.

"I thought Aaranix Tuvelless was bad, but this Siiteper Affelum was much worse," Sierra said.

"They were both evil men," Estrus said.

"Aaranix is actually still alive. He is scheduled for execution soon…well, a lot sooner now that I've been out of the loop for seven months," Sierra said.

"Yes. I know he is. I've been following the situation from afar. I would like to be there at the execution," Estrus said.

"That would be poetic…" Sierra said.

"Do you trust me, Sierra?"

"Umm…what do you mean?"

"I can pick you up and fly down to the bottom of the canyon."

"Oh. Umm… Be careful."

Estrus picked Sierra up in her arms and held her tight. She lifted her black wings in flight and soared off the edge of the cliff. Sierra's sense of gravity disappeared as the sensation of controlled free fall overcame her. Estrus expanded her wings in graceful motions and slowed down to a gentle landing at the bottom of the cliff. She set Sierra down and they turned toward the pile of skeletons. The remains of countless human and Xenolfan fathers lay as a twisted pile of broken bones.

"We call this place Bapbs & Rodes Last Stand. Bapbs was a Xenolfan man and Rodes was a human man. They fought Siiteper's officers to the very end and were the last of the men to die," Estrus said.

"You know, Estrus, I have seen enough tragedy that was committed by Siiteper Affelum that it makes my stomach turn. The pure hatred he had for his Xenolfan people having relationships and families with my people is just unforgivable. I have fought for sexual freedom for years against Aaranix Tuvelless so Xenolfans and humans could be together. I was trying to decide if I even want to help you Humolfans after how you abducted me, but I've come to the realization that you Humolfans desperately need my help to advocate for you. So, I am committed to help. I can sympathize with your need to be free from the Shardaa Sector," Sierra said. "So, the pregnant mothers were killed along with the fathers, but the children that were already alive were exiled as orphans?"

"Yes. The ages of the existing Humolfans ranged from very young children to adults under thirty years of age. It is the adults that had a very heavy burden on their shoulders. Not only did they need to take care of the younger children, but they also had to organize the cemetery up there so each of their mothers could be properly buried. For the fathers, they were unable to identify them due to their brutal condition after hitting the rocks down here. So, at the edge of the cliff up there, there is a plaque dedicated to all of the fathers and lists all their names. It also tells the story of Bapbs & Rodes Last Stand. The adult Humolfans managed to travel to each of the planets in the system with a spaceship that was given to them by Cliven and Tarrias, two Xenolfans that helped our people here on S4. I'm not sure where they came from. Perhaps they were wayward space travelers… As time went on, we became more advanced and at some point developed our own spaceships."

"What a difficult road. All that time, the rest of the galaxy was free with our technology and conveniences…"

"Yes. It doesn't seem quite fair, does it?"

"Not at all, because of Siiteper…the fucking Jinkins! Why didn't you all just leave here and go back into the rest of the galaxy?" Sierra asked.

"My ancestors that were exiled here were threatened by Siiteper Affelum that if they ever tried to leave, a battleship would be waiting for them. By the time Siiteper had died of old age and the battleship crew was ordered to leave, the opportunity for Humolfans to leave was gone. There was no more threat of military action, but it was many years later. In fact, it was a couple of generations later and the rest of the galaxy had forgotten about the rare occurrences when Xenolfan and human people had families together. The Xenolfans no longer had wings and our introduction would have been far too alarming for people to accept it."

"So, all Humolfans here are a pure, non-mixed species?" Sierra asked.

"That is correct. However, we know where we came from and could care less about mixed breeding. I assume Humolfans can breed with Xenolfans as well as humans. But after the DNA modification, who knows? It is the Dissident Faction that wants to stay in isolation. It would be unfair for me to say that remaining as pure Humolfans is the only reason the Dissident Faction has. They also value their seclusion from the outside. But we never said they had to leave here. I think it is really a fear of disdain and rejection from the outsiders," Estrus said.

"Don't you think they should have the right and freedom to stay in isolation here in the Shardaa Sector? If they are okay with exile, what does it matter?" Sierra asked.

"Yes, they do have the right. But they want to stop us from having our right to repatriation back into galactic society. They may fear outsiders invading their sovereign planet of S3."

"Can't you guys come to a compromise?" Sierra asked.

"We would love to, but they only want things their way. The hypocrites have caused so much destruction to us, it is unbelievable. I will show you some of the things they have done when we arrive on Shardia," Estrus said.

"That is where the atheneum is located?"

"Yes. The Humolfan Government palace is also there. Night is setting in. So, are you ready to leave this depressing place?"

"Yes."

Estrus picked Sierra up in her arms once more and held her tight as she extended her large, black wings. She flew over the top of the cliff, leaving the mound of bones far behind. Sierra looked down and noticed the plaque that Estrus had mentioned with all the fathers names listed. It sat off to one side, near the edge of the cliff. Estrus continued to fly over the cemetery toward the *Aileron.* Soon, she landed and gently set Sierra down on the ground.

"Flying through the air with you is quite amazing," Sierra said.

"Thank you," Estrus said. "Now, I will show you the great atheneum on Shardia."

They entered the ship and soon departed from the surface of S4, leaving behind the constant ominous and eerie ambiance the Grave of Mothers emitted.

As the *Aileron* approached Shardia, Sierra stared out the observation window in awe at the planet. Unlike most of the other planets in the Shardaa Star System, Shardia was indeed lush and full of life. Its green and blue colors brightened the light Blue Space beyond. White clouds were scattered in the atmosphere. A gray natural satellite orbited Shardia, casting a shadow on a portion of the planet.

"It *is* beautiful. And what is the moon called?" Sierra asked.

"Oh, Shardia's satellite is called Sharsia," Estrus said.

Sierra could feel slight turbulence as the *Aileron* descended through the atmosphere. As the clouds dissipated, Sierra could see many towns across the land. Eventually, they entered a large, beautiful city that sat near the edge of an ocean. In the distance, an immense palace could be seen with alluring details of beauty.

"This is the city of Naantress. That beautiful palace over there, near the ocean…that is the Humolfan Government palace where our leader, Yilran Taw, lives and governs from," Estrus said.

"It is absolutely beautiful. The intricate details in the spires are stunning," Sierra said.

"Yes. It is quite an amazing work of architecture. The atheneum is as well," Estrus said.

Estrus flew the *Aileron* along the city route toward the great atheneum. Sierra could see several Humolfans flying through the air down farther, near a neighborhood.

"This is the largest settlement of Humolfans that exists," Estrus said.

Estrus settled the *Aileron* on the landing pad and disengaged the engines. Sierra followed her as she exited the ship. Sierra took a deep breath of fresh air and gazed up at the building in awe. The extensive Humolfan atheneum had multiple levels. Arches and pillars decorated the front of the building. They made their way toward the entrance. The double doors swiftly slid aside as they approached, revealing a large foyer with marble flooring. They passed through a second set of doors and into the main atheneum. Sierra looked at the vast array of books that filled the endless shelves. The shelves went on for a great distance. She looked up toward the cathedral ceiling at the mezzanine and the upper wooden balconies in the higher levels. The bookshelves from the upper levels looked so distant from where she stood. An information center was close to the entrance.

"This library is fucking huge!" Sierra finally said.

"Yes. It is collectively a tome of knowledge far beyond anything you could imagine. There is one section in particular that I want to show you. It is up on the third level," Estrus said.

"Okay. After you..."

Estrus led Sierra toward a wooden stairway that was carpeted with a blue and silver pattern. The staircase curved in an S shape and ended at the mezzanine between floors where a couple of reading chairs and a small table were located. On either side of the mezzanine, steps continued upward. The steps on the left led to the second level, while the steps on the right led to the third level. Estrus turned to the right and led Sierra up the steps toward the third level. They could see the balcony of the second level as they passed. The stairway had no exit for the second level, but continued upward toward the third level. Upon reaching the third level, they turned right onto the narrow aisle. Like the second level, the third level also had a wooden railing that overlooked the main floor far below. Opposite of the wooden railing, shelves of books expanded along the wall. The carpeted aisle had the same blue and silver pattern that decorated the steps. Sierra followed Estrus down the aisle. They passed a woman who was reaching for a book. The woman looked at them as they approached, her jaw dropping when she noticed Sierra was not a Humolfan.

After some distance, Sierra asked, "Can't you guys just fly up here?"

"No. It is against the atheneum rules because it would be too distracting," Estrus said.

Sierra noticed the aisle and bookshelves ended at a wall ahead of them. The bookshelves ended slightly before the wall to accommodate an electronic, wooden-paneled door that matched the wooden railing. Estrus turned left and led Sierra through the door as it slid inside the wall to the left. The room beyond was empty, except for a control panel on the far wall and a security officer. The officer stood between the control panel and another door on the far side of the room. A laser rifle was slung over his shoulder.

"The archive we are about to enter is environmentally controlled. The temperature and humidity must be maintained to preserve the ancient books," Estrus said.

The security officer nodded at Estrus as they passed him and entered the archive. As the door shut behind them, the overhead illuminators lit up the small archive to reveal several bookshelves. To the right sat two reading chairs and a small table identical to the set down on the mezzanine. Estrus led Sierra over to one of the shelves and slid her finger along the shelf, searching for a specific title. She stopped and carefully removed a particular book from the shelf. She turned toward Sierra and showed her the book.

"This is the original copy of *Anathema Strain* by Siiteper Affelum. The book the Xenolfan Government had for years in their inadequately controlled environment of the palace lower levels was just a copy. Word had eventually made its way from the publisher of the book to a Syrenthian Brotherhood Knights of Darkness member. The original was secretly taken and later swapped out for an identical copy by the Syrenthian Brotherhood Knights of Darkness. We've monitored many happenings over the years. We know that Aaranix Tuvelless read the copy of this book and formulated his opinion about Xenolfan and human interspecies relationships. We know their inadequately controlled archives were destroyed when the lower levels of the Xenolfan palace on Olf Teruda were flooded by the nearby pond.

Only sitting leaders in the Xenolfan Government are permitted to enter the palace archives. Aaranix Tuvelless was the only leader of the Xenolfan Government to ever discover the book since the time Siiteper Affelum published it one thousand years before. Had the Syrenthian Brotherhood Knights of Darkness knew what Aaranix Tuvelless was going to do after reading the copy they stealthily returned, they would have never returned it. Siiteper Affelum wrote this book about us Humolfans being the product of the human and Xenolfan relationships that he had so much contempt for. Let me show you something in this book," Estrus said, turning to a specific page. "Here is the part that Aaranix Tuvelless interpreted as the two species producing monsters."

Estrus showed Sierra the paragraph in the book. Sierra carefully read the words and looked up at Estrus.

"Siiteper Affelum was such a damn Jinkins! He had such a hatred for human and Xenolfan interspecies relationships, it is beyond disturbing. The disdain he had for them and their Humolfan offspring is just…fucked up. He did refer to Humolfans as monsters in this paragraph. And Aaranix Tuvelless believes that hatred as the truth and caused all the hate and murders all these years later. It pisses me off to no end, Estrus."

"I know. 'Breeding monsters…' *He* was the fucking monster. The only thing we Humolfans have that is any different is our ability to make people faint with our glowing eyes. He probably couldn't accept that oddity. *Anathema Strain* is nothing more than a book of Siiteper Affelum's hatred," Estrus said.

She closed the book and returned it to the shelf.

"So, I take it that all of these books in this room are fairly old," Sierra said.

"Yes. Some of the other books of interest are early Xenolfan history books that lied to students stating that their wings were lost to microevolution instead of Siiteper's genetic engineering and DNA modifications. We even have notes on that very experimentation and testing on these shelves. That is why this room is guarded. These ancient texts are proof of what really happened one thousand years ago. Down in the main history section on the first level of the atheneum, we have history books with the correct account of our history. That truth needs to be distributed into the whole Syrenthian Galaxy after you reintroduce us. It is vital that people awaken to the truth," Estrus said.

The door opened and an older woman walked into the archive. She wore a dark gray outfit that matched her gray skin and complemented her black wings, white hair, and sapphire eyes.

"Hi, Whitney!" Estrus said.

"Hello, Estrus. I understand we have a human among us. I had to come up here and see for myself."

"Yes! Whitney, this is Sierra Shalinsky. Sierra, this is Whitney Motevell. She is the head librarian," Estrus said.

"Hi, Whitney. It is nice to meet you. I really love the atheneum here on Shardia," Sierra said.

"Well, thank you. I am so excited to meet you. Our people have been waiting for so many centuries to return back into galactic society. We've tried, and tried, and tried over the years. Every attempt failed. You are the hope that we have been waiting for. You may not know how much it means to us, but let me tell you. What you are doing for the Humolfans is worthy of galactic recognition in the history books. Seriously!" Whitney Motevell said.

"I'm speechless. Thank you," Sierra said.

"I'm happy to see that you came out of your coma. I'm sorry this had to be done through abduction." Whitney turned toward Estrus. "Don't you let the Dissident Faction hurt her. We've never been this close to our freedom from the Shardaa Sector before. Don't let them ruin it."

"Yes. We are keeping our guard up," Estrus said.

"Did you show Sierra the destruction the Dissident Faction has caused here on Shardia?"

"Not yet. I was planning on doing that next," Estrus said.

Estrus flew the *Aileron* from the atheneum, past the Humolfan Government palace, and toward the ocean. Buildings were sparse in the area. As they flew closer, Sierra could see many of the buildings were destroyed and only bombed-out shells remained. Estrus flew the ship beyond the barricades that served as a warning to keep people out of the area. Although people could simply use their wings to fly over the barricades, it was generally not done because the area was too dangerous. Estrus landed the ship on the old road that ran between the destroyed buildings. The road led toward the ocean ahead. The road itself had deep craters sporadically littered along its surface. Parts of the road were buckled upward, the concrete totally destroyed. After exiting the ship, Estrus walked with Sierra along the war-torn road. Soon, the road became a bridge when the land beneath fell away along a steep slope. The destruction on the bridge section of the road was no different. Craters from bombs could also be seen along its surface.

"This was the Ocean Port Bridge. Hey, watch your step here, Sierra," Estrus said.

"Damn, this destruction is brutal," Sierra said.

They paused for a moment and looked down through a hole in the concrete to the ground far below. Even the metal railings of the bridge were mangled and twisted, their tangled remains hanging far below. Sierra became disoriented and sat down on a chunk of concrete and closed her eyes.

"Are you okay?" Estrus asked.

"I have vertigo again, I'm lightheaded, and I feel like blacking out," Sierra said.

"I'm sure you are having post-coma symptoms. We'll get you to the doctor after this," Estrus said.

After a brief rest, Sierra stood up. They continued along the road toward the ocean, avoiding the dangerous areas. When the bridge was entirely over the water, Sierra could see where it ended ahead of them. They walked way around a hole in the concrete where they saw the ocean water splashing up against the pylons far below. Twisted rebar mesh protruded from the edge of the hole, its jagged edges ready to stab an unexpected victim. The two women slowed to a stop where the road abruptly ended at a drop-off. The vast blue ocean could be seen far below. In the distance, there was a small island where the remainder of a bridge pylon was located, the broken pieces of concrete hanging down to the island beneath it. Farther out across the ocean inlet, Sierra could see where the road continued onto the mainland again. That section was also destroyed. Against the backdrop of a mountainous tapestry, the crescent moon of Sharsia could be seen peeking over the horizon.

"This was once a busy road for us Humolfans. We would travel from Naantress to another smaller city farther away. This bridge across the ocean inlet was a convenient way to travel there. The Dissident Faction came one day and destroyed the entire bridge and many businesses back there. There were a lot of people in those buildings when it happened. There were a lot of people on this bridge when it happened," Estrus said.

Suddenly, tears began to flow down Estrus's face in steady streams.

"Are you okay?" Sierra asked.

"My mom was on this bridge when they attacked!"

She began to sob. Sierra leaned in and hugged her tight, the back of her hand brushing against Estrus's feathers. Estrus continued to breathe heavily and cry on Sierra's shoulder.

"Oh Estrus. I'm so sorry. The Dissident Faction did all this? It must be really hard for you to show me this place."

"They did more than this. They also destroyed many of our monuments and memorials here on Shardia. The statues represented our history...our legacy. They destroyed a monument of Cliven and Tarrias, the two Xenolfans that helped our people on S4. They destroyed a memorial statue of Athenarr and Aarria, the first Humolfan couple to advance our race. I cannot fathom the Dissident Faction's rationale. I just have no words... This is the first time I've been back to this bridge since it happened. But I had to show you what they did. I hate the Dissident Faction. My mom wanted to go out into the rest of the galaxy so badly. She never had the chance. I just want to thank you for your help, Sierra. It means everything to me. My mom would have loved to meet you."

"I will do my best to advocate for your people."

Sierra gave Estrus an extra tissue she had in her pocket.

Chapter Six

The Avalanche Resort on the snow planet of Aamaress was once the secret location for interspecies couples to express their feelings of love, sex, and intimacy toward each other. It was a place to escape the Xenolfan Government's law against interspecies relationships. Since sexual freedom was granted by the current leader of the Xenolfan Government, Phensiarr Charseaa, Aamaress was converted to a prime vacation destination for all. Business had declined slightly, but not enough to affect The Avalanche Resort significantly. Sierra Shalinsky and Priscilla Stryderr both played a role in the current sexual freedom by gathering petitions from all over the Syrenthian Galaxy that had been delivered to the Xenolfan Government leader at the time, Aaranix Tuvelless. Although he threw all the petitions away, one of his officials, Phensiarr Charseaa, had seen them and knew how important the sexual freedom movement was to the people of the galaxy. Phensiarr had also studied Sierra's sexual freedom advocating and how she had set up the sexual health clinics for both the Xenolfans and the humans throughout the galaxy. Phensiarr had read articles from both Sierra and Priscilla regarding the important subject. She even read

Sierra's sexual freedom speech and Priscilla's sexual health speech that they both had given on Red Jacket. Knowing that Aaranix Tuvelless had sent a missiloid to Aamaress and killed many Xenolfans and humans who disobeyed his unjust law, Phensiarr had recently sent a plaque to The Avalanche Resort on Aamaress with an official apology. The plaque came with a very large amount of credits to compensate for damages. Credits were also sent to the surviving victims of the assault and the families of the deceased victims of the assault. With the funds The Avalanche Resort received, they were able to pay for the repair of their docking bay at the main lodge as well as rebuild and create the New Winterfest Memorial Lodge. Gathin and Eslarr were the interspecies couple that were asked to manage the project. Since they already lived on Aamaress, it was an honor for them to do so.

The construction of the lodge in New Winterfest was breathtaking. It was modeled after the main lodge to the south, but much smaller. There was no docking bay at the smaller lodge, only a landing pad. Gathin and Eslarr managed the new lodge, while Max and Mauve managed the main lodge. Staring up at the plaque from Phensiarr Charseaa that hung above the stone fireplace in the grand foyer, Gathin read the letter. Each time he read it over the last several months, he felt grateful there was a wonderful new Xenolfan Government leader.

Gathin and Eslarr's adopted wolfdog, Stormy, was sleeping in the corner of the grand foyer. The wolfdog had belonged to the previous owner of The Avalanche Resort. When the owner died in the missiloid assault, Gathin and Eslarr adopted the wolfdog at the suggestion of Max and Mauve.

Eslarr walked up beside Gathin. "What are you looking at?" she asked.

"Oh, I'm just reading the plaque again," Gathin said.

"Things have been really slow here for a while. Since sexual freedom is no longer an issue in the galaxy, we have lost a lot of business. I know our marketing team has tried several campaigns to get visitors, but the numbers are still low," Eslarr said.

"Yes, but at least we have several vacationers up here in the Northern Territories," Gathin said.

Eslarr smiled at Gathin and stared into his eyes for a long moment. He knew exactly what that stare meant.

"We're slow enough that we can disappear for a little while and no one would know we were missing," Eslarr said.

"We'll be right back, Stormy," Gathin said.

Eslarr reached out with her bluish-gray hand and grabbed Gathin's tan hand. She led him from the grand foyer toward their personal suite along a side corridor adjacent from the office counter. When they entered the living room and shut the door, they quickly undressed.

"You know, seeing your beautiful wolf tattoo never gets old," Eslarr said.

She was referring to the wolf tattoo on his left side.

"Seeing your gorgeous sapphire eyes, elegant white hair, and beautiful blue face never gets old either," Gathin said.

She lightly stroked her bluish-gray hands down his tan chest and squatted before him. She began to massage his genitals with smooth motions. The sensation he felt was very arousing. He soon became fully erect and Eslarr began sucking his cock. The warmth of her moist mouth sent a surge of pleasure through his body. Her long tongue wrapped around his cock and she bobbed her head up and down with smooth motions. She continued sucking for some time before removing his member from her mouth and licking from his smooth balls up the underside of his cock to the tip. Eslarr concentrated flicking her tongue on his frenulum, sending waves of bliss radiating through him. She returned his cock to her mouth and he moaned with excitement. They soon switched and she sat on the couch with her thighs spread apart. Gathin knelt down and rubbed her beautiful bluish-gray thighs. He began kissing her bluish-gray outer pussy lips and then made his way to her bluish-pink inner lips. He licked her pussy and buried his tongue deep into her reuleaux triangular vagina. Making his way back up to her clit, he increased the pressure of his tongue. He remained at her clit, swirling his tongue around his circular motions. A high-pitched, reverberating purr escaped her as she cried out.

"Ahhh!"

Gathin smiled as he continued to perform cunnilingus. He had become accustomed to the high-pitched sound that she made during sex. All Xenolfans made the sound, but it was especially prominent with Xenolfan women. As she became more aroused, a significant amount of arousal fluid secreted from her pussy and Gathin licked it up.

"Mmm," he said.

Eslarr moved from the couch over to the carpeted floor and

positioned herself on all fours. Gathin entered her pussy from behind. The creamy warmth felt so nice. Gathin closed his eyes and breathed in deep, a dreamy smile expressed across his face. His shoulder-length, curly, brown hair bounced slightly as he slowly pumped her. He rubbed her asscheeks and the small of her back. His hands made their way up her back to the two genetic bumps that protruded slightly. They were the genetic remains of what once were wings on their species a thousand years before. He lightly rubbed them and then reached under her rib cage and massaged her bouncing breasts. Gathin gently cupped and massaged them in his hands as he slowly fucked her. Her eloquently braided, white hair hung down on the right side of her neck as she glanced back at her husband.

"Let's switch it up. I want you on top of me," she said.

Gathin withdrew his cock and she turned over onto her back. He entered her again and leaned forward onto his elbows. Gathin smiled and looked at her beautiful sapphire eyes.

"I love you, Eslarr," he said.

"Oh Gathin, fuck me."

With his cock buried deep inside of her, he moved forward slightly and rode her pelvis high. Rubbing against her clit with a coital alignment technique, he began to rotate his hips in a circular motion. Eslarr's toes pointed forward and she screamed. The resulting orgasm caused a gush of her cum to surround his cock. The high-pitched, reverberating purr that escaped her was extremely loud. Gathin could smell the sexy muskiness of her cream. The feeling of ecstasy overcame him as he reached his own orgasm, sliding his wet cock in and out of her alluring pussy. She could feel his hot load squirt deep inside of her. His heavy breathing began to subside as he pulled out and sighed deeply.

"That was amazing, my love," Eslarr said.

"That was *very* amazing," Gathin said.

"Well, we better get cleaned up and back to the office in case someone shows up," she said.

"I suppose…"

Braxton and Priscilla Stryderr sat in the back of a sleigh. She smiled at her husband, a sparkle in her eyes. The warm clothes they were bundled in kept them comfortable from the chilly air on Aamaress.

Flakes of snow blew at them as they made their way along a trail in the rugged wilderness. The driver in front drove the two horses carefully along the dangerous curves of the mountain trail. The horses trotted through the deep snow with ease, their black fur blowing slightly in the wind. This was one of the best vacations Priscilla could remember. Her smile didn't fade as Braxton smiled back, their eyes meeting for a long moment. He held her gloved hand tight.

"I love you, Priscilla."

"I love you too. Thank you for this."

The sleigh wobbled slightly as the trail dipped near a large boulder. The movement slid Priscilla against her husband. Braxton put his arm around her to steady her movement. Their cold lips touched and their tongues came together with great affection. Time seemed to stand still as the passionate kiss continued for some time. When their lips finally broke free, steam escaped into the brisk air. They each wiped the excessive moisture from their lips and continued smiling at each other. Priscilla sighed deeply. Their focus was drawn toward a valley below the edge of the trail. Far below, a forest of snow-covered pine trees decorated the valley. The far edge of the mountain revealed sheer cliffs of brown rock, speckled with snowy inlets. It was truly a breathtaking experience. The horses both began neighing as the sleigh driver made as sharp turn along the snowy trail.

"Sorry, guys. This trail is a bit rough," the driver yelled back.

"No problem," Braxton said.

As Priscilla gazed at the snowy mountains, Braxton stared at her beautiful face and the long, blond hair that trailed down from her hat and scarf.

I'm so lucky, he thought.

She noticed him smiling at her and she reached over and rested her gloved hand on his leg.

"What?"

"You. You are so beautiful," he said.

"As frosty as it is out here, my face is going to freeze in this smiling position. You are truly an amazing husband, Braxton Stryderr."

Snow fell from the white sky, its crystal patterns accumulating on the powdery ground. White pines stretched as far as the eye could see. The pines sat below the snowy mountains that decorated the Northern

Territories region of Aamaress. Some distance from the town of New Winterfest, a small cabin sat off from the main trail. The cabin was located in a grove of white pine trees, their boughs blanketed with snow. Two newer model Ticrisuda Powersports snowmobiles were parked in front of the cabin. Braxton and Priscilla had just arrived back to their cabin after an amazing sleigh ride along a mountainous trail. Smoke emitted from a metal chimney on the roof of the cabin, the smell of burning wood filling the air. Steamy ice formed on the cabin windows.

Inside, moans of pleasure escaped from Priscilla as Braxton pounded her hard from behind. He slapped her right asscheek with his hand and she moaned again. Braxton's heavy breathing aroused Priscilla and her moans aroused him. They both enjoyed the creamy, wet sounds of their genitals colliding together with each of Braxton's thrusts. His smooth balls continuously slapped against her clit. She pushed back against him in a rocking motion, her tits bouncing wildly. Moments before, he had spent an extensive amount of time down on her as she enjoyed her absolutely favorite sexual desire of cunnilingus.

"Oh Braxton! Fuck me! Ahhh… Fuck me!" she cried.

Braxton increased his speed and Priscilla let out a loud scream of orgasmic bliss. He continued to fuck her hard until he reached an epic orgasm himself, his cock pulsating inside of her. She could feel his warm load deep in her pussy. His grunts subsided as he pulled free. She turn back and smiled at him.

"I needed that so badly," she said.

"Yes. Me too… But I think we steamed up the window in here."

Priscilla looked over to the bedroom window. "Yup, we sure did."

"This is one of the best vacations we've had in years," Braxton said.

"A much needed one…" Priscilla said.

"The Avalanche Resort here on Aamaress was the best getaway that I could think of for our vacation," Braxton said.

They stood up from the bed and made their way to the small bathroom to get cleaned up. The cabin had a rustic theme and was fairly small and cozy. Adjacent to the bedroom and bathroom was a living room and kitchen combination. After cleaning up, they began to get dressed. Suddenly, there was a knock at the door.

"Just a minute!" Braxton yelled.

"Who the hell could that be? We're in the middle of a forest after a snowstorm," Priscilla said.

They finished dressing and Braxton walked over to the cabin's wooden door and unlocked it. He quickly slicked back his short, brown and gray hair and opened the door. The door's hinges made a creaking noise when he opened it. A man stood outside the door, a bit frozen. A cool breeze blew snowflakes inside the cabin. Braxton recognized him from when they signed in at the New Winterfest Memorial Lodge. They had met him and his Xenolfan wife, Eslarr, when they arrived.

"Gathin! Come in out of the cold," Braxton said.

"I hope I'm not interrupting anything. Eslarr and I just got back to the office in time to receive a message for you," Gathin said.

Stepping into the cabin, he immediately felt the warm and comfort of the wood stove located in the corner.

"Interrupting? No, but any sooner and you would have," Braxton said, laughing.

"Since you two elected to leave your comms with us at the lodge office, I am here to bring you an urgent message that we received," Gathin said.

"Urgent message?" Priscilla inquired.

"Apparently, there is a Parker from the Syrenthian Government trying to contact you regarding a distress signal they received from Sierra Shalinsky," Gathin said. "Eslarr and I met Sierra back when the missiloid struck Winterfest and killed all those people. She invited us to her Maranadda concert and sexual freedom speech. She is an amazing woman. When we found out she was missing, we were devastated. She advocated for interspecies relationships, like Eslarr and I enjoy, long before it was legal. She is like a hero to us. She even wrote a song for us. Please let Eslarr and I know what you find out about Sierra," Gathin said. He adjusted the hat that covered his curly, brown hair.

"Sierra?" Priscilla gasped.

Sierra was a great friend and lover to Braxton and Priscilla. They often had threesomes together, with Sierra being a swinger in the Lifestyle. Although Braxton and Priscilla were exclusive to her, she was not exclusive to them, which they were fine with. The fact that Sierra had sent a distress signal was shocking. They had pretty much given up on any hope of ever finding her.

"Oh my! Sierra's alive? This is so good to hear. Let's get to the lodge and contact Parker right away," Braxton said.

Braxton and Priscilla quickly bundled up in some warm clothes and followed Gathin out the cabin door. Gathin sat on his snowmobile and the Stryderrs sat on the other two snowmobiles. The three of them put on their helmets and began their journey along the snowy trail toward New Winterfest. As the pines rushed by, Priscilla thought about how much she missed her friend.

I hope she's okay, Priscilla thought.

After traveling several kilometers along the snowy trail, they came to a stop in front of the New Winterfest Memorial Lodge. The two story lodge was newly built and featured a rustic theme with logs and stones as part of its design. Gathin and Eslarr made it their mission to create a memorial in what used to be Winterfest after the missiloid attack orchestrated by the former leader of the Xenolfan Government, Aaranix Tuvelless. The memorial inside the grand foyer of the New Winterfest Memorial Lodge had become a featured attraction. The memorial was separate from the plaque with the letter from Phensiarr Charseaa. The memorial displayed a list of all the names of those Xenolfans and humans that died on that dreadful day about a year before. The large slab of asteroid that had protruded from the ground on an angle at the impact site was removed and the new facility built immediately afterward. Many people came from around the Syrenthian Galaxy to visit the memorial in honor of those who had died. Gathin and Eslarr were well known for creating the memorial.

As the three of them arrived at the facility, Eslarr looked up from the counter where she stood.

"Hi, Braxton. Hi, Priscilla. Come on in out of the cold. How are you two?" Eslarr asked.

Eslarr's long, white hair was braided with intricate patterns and looked absolutely stunning against her bluish-gray face. Her sapphire eyes sparkled as the three of them walked up to the lodge counter where she stood. She had already set their comms up on the counter for them to grab.

"Eslarr! You are looking lovely, as usual," Braxton said.

"Thank you," Eslarr said.

"Let's find out what Parker is referring to," Braxton said.

Both Braxton and Priscilla retrieved their comms from the counter.

"Parker, this is Braxton. I understand you are trying to contact me regarding Sierra. What's going on?"

After a brief pause, Parker answered. "Hey, Braxton. Sorry I had to disturb you and Priscilla on your vacation, but I thought you might want to know about this. We have received a distress signal from Sierra Shalinsky, emitting from the Shardaa Sector. There was a bit of interference from the Sharasp Tharrian Asteroid Mass, but she said she was on S2. She said she was abducted and pursued by some people, but she didn't explain who they were. Edward Sirlain wants you to pick up your investigation from where you left off several months ago with this new information," Parker said.

"Damn! Yes, we will get right on that. Thank you, Parker," Braxton said.

"Gook luck, sir," Parker said, ending the communication.

Braxton looked over at Priscilla. "This news has me all wound up. We need to get back to Exandra and get this investigation rolling again. If she's in trouble, we're going in with a battleship," Braxton said.

Suddenly, Priscilla's face went pale and she stood frozen with a blank stare. A strange epiphany overcame her. She walked over to a couch located near the stone fireplace and sat down. She stared into the flames of the crackling fire. Braxton, Gathin, and Eslarr followed her over to the lounge area of the grand foyer.

"What's wrong?" Braxton asked.

"There's something that Sierra said to me once regarding the Shardaa Sector. I'm trying to remember what it was. She told me about one of her runs with the Galactic Emergency Medical Services where they went into the Shardaa Sector. I'm trying to remember what she said…" Priscilla said.

They each looked at each other and also sat down near the fireplace. Priscilla squinted her eyes and stared into the fire.

"Well?" Eslarr asked.

"I got it! I recall the conversation vividly. Some time ago, Sierra was over visiting. She came over so we could go over our sexual freedom and health speeches together. She mentioned one of her runs to the Shardaa Sector with GEMS. She said they were responding to a delusional space traveler named Dennon Cobalt on S2. That is the same planet that she sent the distress signal from. She had said this Dennon Cobalt mentioned seeing a woman there. Sierra said she saw caves shaped like Xenolfan pussies with odd feather symbols above them. She also told me she saw glowing eyes or lights in a cave there. She thought that perhaps this Dennon Cobalt also saw the glowing lights," Priscilla said.

Braxton soaked in the information for a long moment. Gathin and Eslarr looked at each other.

"Why didn't you mention this before, during our investigation into Sierra's disappearance?"

"It was the Shardaa Sector, so I didn't even think it was relevant. I guess I was wrong," Priscilla said.

"While we are on Exandra preparing the battleship, I will do some research on this Dennon Cobalt. We need to pay him a visit. Perhaps we can get more information about why he was in the Shardaa Sector and what he saw out there. That region of uncharted space is the last place in the galaxy that I would expect Sierra to be in, so I understand why you didn't mention this Dennon Cobalt before, Priscilla," Braxton said.

"Exactly," Priscilla said.

Braxton looked over at Gathin and Eslarr. "How would you two like to come with us to find Sierra?" he asked.

Gathin and Eslarr looked at each other.

"We would love to," Gathin said.

"Definitely! I will contact Max and Mauve at the main lodge and have them cover for us while we are gone. We'll have to drop Stormy off at the main lodge so they can watch him," Eslarr said.

Chapter Seven

Within a large medical facility on Shardia, Sierra waited to see the doctor that had been helping her during her seven months in a coma. Estrus sat with her. The lighting in the waiting room was fairly bright. The two of them were the only ones in the waiting room.

"So, tell me more about the strange occurrences that have been reported to my government over the years. I mean, there has been strange sightings, ships disappearing, and lost space travelers. Maranadda has a song called Tales of Shardaa that refers to all those odd things," Sierra said.

"Well, like I said before, the Dissident Faction is responsible for most of the disappearances and missing space travelers. They simply destroyed the ships and killed the crew. Those of them that have escaped the Shardaa Sector are fortunate, but no one generally believes their stories. I mean, who is going to believe they've seen a gray creature with wings?" Estrus explained.

"You said before that they've been doing this for a hundred years. Have you guys been trying to reconnect with the rest of the galaxy for that long?" Sierra asked.

"Yes. Actually, we've been trying off and on for longer than that. The Dissident Faction formed about the same time the rest of the galaxy were experiencing the Syrenthian War that occurred about a hundred years ago. We believe it is the Syrenthian War between the Xenolfans and humans that caused the Dissident Faction to form their current ideology against our repatriation back into galactic society. It was a very sad war of prejudice on both sides. It really affected us Humolfans, seeing both of our ancestor species fighting each other. I've read that account in our history books many times. It always makes me sad, especially all the missiloids that were used to assault the various human planets. And even though the war ended and both the Xenolfans and humans made peace, the Dissident Faction never changed their position," Estrus said.

"I own an old fighter ship from the Syrenthian War. When I found it, it had been striped of its original weaponry systems. It's black and I had it modified with laser weapons. It's called the *Tenebris*... I miss my ship," Sierra said.

"You own a Syrenthian War fighter ship? Wow! That's cool," Estrus said.

At that moment, the door opened and a nurse had them follow her in to see the doctor. She led them down a corridor to an exam room. Soon, an older male Humolfan doctor entered the room.

"Sierra Shalinsky, I am happy to see you awake. I'm Dr. Graluss. Between Estrus and I, we have been taking care of you over the last seven months," he said.

"It's nice to meet you, Dr. Graluss. Thank you for your care," Sierra said.

"How are you feeling?"

"It's funny you ask. I'm the one that is usually asking that question. I'm a Galactic Emergency Medical Technician. But yeah, I've been experiencing vertigo, dizziness, and lightheadedness since I woke up."

"Are you having any speech problems or balance and coordination issues?" Dr. Graluss asked.

"Maybe a little," Sierra said.

The doctor looked into her eyes and then put his head down.

"Is there something wrong?" Sierra asked.

"I wish I had more human medical knowledge. Have you been able to think clearly?"

"For the most part, yes," Sierra said.

"Well, I think you should consider yourself fortunate. If humans are anything like Humolfans, there are usually coordination and cognitive issues after waking from a coma…as you probably know from your line of work," Dr. Graluss said.

"I'm sure my symptoms will subside," Sierra said.

"I hope so because we have work to do," Estrus said.

"Don't push her too hard. She needs to rest when she feels faint," Dr. Graluss said.

"I won't. She can rest at my place as long as she needs to," Estrus said.

"Okay, you two. I'll be fine. I appreciate you both taking good care of me. And if we are heading back to your quarters, I could seriously use a nap," Sierra said.

Sierra lay asleep on the couch in Estrus's quarters, still wearing her clothes from that afternoon. She made an indistinguishable sound and her arms twitched as she dreamed. With her eyes shut, a frown was suddenly expressed on her face. She shouted in her sleep and woke herself up. Estrus's dog, Thepsi, woke up and barked several times.

Damn! I dreamed about all the horrible things Siiteper Affelum did. That was a fucked-up dream, Sierra thought.

She sat up on the couch and focused her eyes on the dim living room. Thepsi stopped barking and fell back asleep, silence returning to the room. The dream replayed in her mind over and over as the vertigo she experienced earlier returned. Sierra stood up and made her way to the refrigerator. Squinting at the bright light inside, she grabbed a Ginger Alquinola and made her way back to the couch. The bottle opened with a distinct pop. She sat in the dark and drank.

Damn, this is good stuff!

Sierra felt great empathy for the Humolfan people. She had to advocate for them. It was the right thing to do. She finished the Ginger Alquinola and returned to the refrigerator for another bottle. The second bottle when down smooth. It led to a third and a fourth. Before too long, Sierra had the small end table next to the couch full of empty bottles.

"I gotta help 'em out… I'm gonna go." Sierra slurred her words in the dark living room.

She stood up from the couch and made her way toward the entry door.

• • •

When morning arrived, Thepsi began barking again.

"What the hell are you barking at, Thepsi?"

Estrus made her way through her quarters toward where the dog slept in the corner of the living room. She turned on the light and noticed Thepsi barking at the entry door.

"Where is Sierra? What are you barking at? Did Sierra get locked out?" Estrus asked.

Noticing the power on the comm was turned off, Estrus walked over and powered it on. She saw many empty bottles on the end table. Estrus opened the entry door to reveal a vacant corridor. Thepsi stopped barking and looked up at Estrus.

"That's odd."

Suddenly, the comm sounded.

"This is Estrus."

"Hi, Estrus. This is Flight Control. We've been trying to contact you to inform you that your ship has taken off from the docking bay several hours ago, piloted by the human woman that you've been taking care of," the flight controller said.

Estrus didn't bother to respond. She ran out the door toward the docking bay. The officer from Flight Control was standing in the middle of the docking bay when Estrus arrived.

"Where the fuck is my ship? Where's my fucking ship?"

She ran toward the edge of the docking bay opening and jumped into the air, spreading her wings. She soared high into the air, feathers from her long, black wings blowing in the wind. She scanned the horizon, but there was no sign of Sierra. Estrus flew back down into the docking bay and landed next to the flight controller.

"Contact Soltuss Yow from Humolfan Command. And get the tracing information for my ship!" Estrus said.

"I'm on it," the woman said, flying toward an office on the upper balcony that overlooked the docking bay.

After what seemed like eternity, Soltuss Yow entered the docking bay and flew toward Estrus, landing next to her.

"After everything I told her and showed her... I thought she was going to help us," Estrus said.

"I understand you're angry. Just calm down," Soltuss said.

The flight controller yelled from the upper balcony. "Your ship has been traced to Shardia," she said.

Estrus and Soltuss looked at each other.

"Shardia? What the hell is she doing on Shardia?" Estrus asked

"Well, apparently she's not leaving the Shardaa Sector after all," Soltuss said.

"Apparently not. I'm going to change out of this nightwear, then we can head over to Shardia and see what Sierra's up to," Estrus said.

"I'll get my ship ready," Soltuss Yow said.

The colorful city lights of Naantress brightened the evening sky as Sierra walked along a main thoroughfare. Some Humolfans could also be seen walking along the streets, going to and from the various establishments. Several of them stared at Sierra. She looked back at them.

"Sa matter, ya never saw human 'fore?" Sierra slurred.

The vertigo she felt in the last several days after waking from the coma slightly crept back into her senses for a brief moment. She stopped and leaned against a brick wall, feeling very nauseated.

Perhaps it's the alcohol, she thought.

Sierra tried to remember where she landed Estrus's ship, *Aileron*. She dismissed the thought and continued to walk down the street.

"Ha! There's the shop!" she said.

Sierra stumbled her way toward a tattoo shop with the name Mazniriatt lit up. The colorful sign brightened the front window display. She entered the building and made her way along a counter of endless designs that were displayed. The walls were covered with awesome examples of the work that had been done on clients. A complete portfolio book was on the counter as well. One particular image on the wall caught Sierra's attention. It was a beautiful Humolfan woman, totally nude. Her gray skin was decorated with a Feathers of Shardaa tattoo, intricately inked above her mons pubis.

"Well, hello!" a Humolfan man said as he came from a back room.

"Hey," Sierra said.

"Look at you! You're not a Humolfan. You are human! It certainly isn't everyday that I see a human walk into my shop…and a beautiful one at that. You must be the advocate they found," he said.

"I'm lookin' for Mazniriatt. Estrus said ya do the best feather symbol tattoo…like the one on the wall," Sierra said.

"Yes, the Feathers of Shardaa is my specialty. And it is complementary. No Asparell coins needed for *that* tattoo. I've never met a human, let alone given one a tattoo. My name is Mazniriatt," he said.

His short, spiky, white hair had some product in it. Both of his gray arms were covered with tattoo sleeves in very intricate and colorful designs.

"I'm Sierra Shalinsky. I'm a little drunk," she said.

"Nice to meet you," Mazniriatt said. "You do need to sober up a bit before I ink you, however. It's my policy," Mazniriatt said. "There's a love seat up front you can rest on for a while."

"Gotcha. I'll do that," Sierra said.

Sierra made her way to the front of the shop and found the love seat. Lying down, she closed her eyes and rested for a while. Mazniriatt grabbed a blanket from the back and covered her up. He also brought her a bottle of water. Keeping himself busy for about an hour, he organized some of his equipment and supplies in the back. When he finished, he went back up front to check on Sierra. He was surprised to find her eyes open. She sat up and set the blanket aside.

"Are you sobered up now?" Mazniriatt asked.

Sierra opened the bottle of water and took a long drink.

"Good enough," she said.

"Well, you lucked out tonight since I'm open late. If you want to follow me into the back studio, we can get started," he said.

Sierra stood up and followed Mazniriatt to the back of the shop and through a doorway with a black, cloth curtain hanging from it. The back studio was fairly small with a chair in the middle. There were several shelves above the work counter with equipment and various ink colors stored.

"I want the Feathers of Shardaa tattoo, just like the example on the wall with the picture of that sexy Humolfan woman. So, are all the pics out there on the wall your work?" Sierra asked.

Sierra sat down in the chair and made herself comfortable.

"Yes. I run this shop by myself. Hey, I have a lot of questions for you. You said Estrus referred you to me?" he asked.

"Well, she mentioned that you are the best tattoo artist to get a Feathers of Shardaa tattoo. I remember she mentioned your name. She doesn't know I'm here. I've been in a coma for seven months here in the Shardaa Sector. Estrus has been taking care of me," Sierra said.

"Oh, I'm all aware of us Humolfans trying to get an advocate. So, as our advocate, you decided you want a Feathers of Shardaa tattoo. I see. So, tell me a little about yourself. What's it like out in the rest of the galaxy?" Mazniriatt asked.

"I'm a Galactic Emergency Medical Technician, I'm a vocalist for the symphonic metal band Maranadda, and I was formerly a sexual freedom advocate. Now that sexual freedom between humans and Xenolfans has been granted, it is no longer necessary for me to lead that charge. Now, I will be advocating for you Humolfans. And you asked what it's like on the outside. Well, just normal stuff. I don't know how to put it. Of course, there are assholes. No matter where you are, there will always be assholes," Sierra said.

"Well, I appreciate you advocating for us. I still cannot believe you are here in my studio," Mazniriatt said.

Sierra stared into his eyes for a long moment. "I love the sapphire eyes of your people," she said. "They are just like the Xenolfans."

"Although your blue eyes are not exactly sapphire, they are beautiful as well. Seeing black hair on a woman instead of white is so strange…in a good way. So, you know Xenolfans as well?" Mazniriatt asked.

"Yes…some."

"You were a sexual freedom advocate? Like, what do you mean?" he asked.

"The former Xenolfan Government leader created a law that forbid Xenolfans and humans to have sexual relations. I did my best to help fight that. The new leader repealed that law. I also helped to set up sexual health clinics across the galaxy for both Xenolfans and humans," Sierra said.

"So, have *you* been with a Xenolfan?" Mazniriatt asked.

"Yes. I swing both ways, so I am familiar with the anatomy of both Xenolfan males and females. I am a unicorn swinger in the Lifestyle."

"What does that mean exactly?" he asked.

"Well, a bisexual unicorn swinger in the Lifestyle means I basically have sex with other married swingers or singles of either gender…or species for that matter," she said.

Suddenly, Mazniriatt became aroused at the thought.

"Our ancestry comes from the relationships between Xenolfans and humans. That's exciting. So, are Xenolfans much different than humans?" he asked.

"Yes. And from what I understand about Humolfans from Estrus, your genitals are just like the Xenolfans, except for the rare occasion when a Humolfan has human genitalia, which is one in every thirty-five thousand people, according to Estrus," Sierra said.

"True. Mine is the normal reuleaux triangular shape, not the odd one," Mazniriatt said.

Sierra smiled, entertaining the idea of having sex with Mazniriatt. He could tell she was becoming aroused as well.

"Except yours is gray…"

"It is." He smiled.

"Well, my pussy may look a little odd to you, then. It's not triangular," she said.

"Curiosity has got me now," Mazniriatt said.

Sierra undressed and threw her clothes onto the floor. She removed her panties and spread her thighs. Mazniriatt looked at Sierra's vulva with awe. He removed his shirt, exposing his full gray chest.

"Freshly shaved pussy, courtesy of the extra razor Estrus gave me," Sierra said, stroking her finger upward along her slit.

"Wow, that's…different. You have me aroused," Mazniriatt said.

Sierra reached over and caressed Mazniriatt's genitals through his pants. She could feel his cock becoming erect. Mazniriatt finished undressing, his gray member flopping out. Its reuleaux triangular circumference was fairly thick.

"Damn, that looks nice," she said.

She leaned forward in the chair and kissed his lips. He returned the kiss and began to massage her nice breasts. He delicately squeezed her left breast as he moved down and attached his mouth to her nipple. As he gently sucked, he continued massaging. He kissed along her sideboob and underneath before making his way back to her sensitive nipple.

"That feels great," Sierra said.

Mazniriatt switched to her right breast. Sierra ran her fingers through his white hair. She pushed his head down toward her pussy. Moving downward, he peered at her vulva for a long moment, then began kissing along her labia. The kisses slowly became wetter as he began sliding his tongue along her slit. Sierra squirmed in the chair as the wet blissful feeling radiated outward from her pussy.

"Mmm. That feels so nice."

Sierra rubbed her hands along her tan, inner thighs. Mazniriatt concentrated on her clit, the pink pleasure center that emanated surges of ecstasy. His tongue danced around her pussy with such precision. He continued for a long time until she moaned loudly, arching her back in the chair with an epic orgasm.

"Oh fuck!"

Sierra's chest raised and lowered as she panted, exposing her ribs slightly with each inhale.

"I enjoy human pussy," Mazniriatt said, smiling.

Sierra stood up from the chair and squatted down in front of his erect, gray, alien cock. She took it into her mouth. She, once again, explored the familiar shape that she had previously experienced with a Xenolfan man. Sliding her mouth over it, she gently sucked, her lips flowing over the stepped-down section that divided the thicker reuleaux triangular circumference from the thinner circumference. She flicked her tongue along his sensitive underside and around the angled end of his cock.

"You are so good at that, Sierra. Would you like me to slide it inside of you?" he asked.

"Very much so," she said. "But…since I've been in a coma for months, I am not on birth control right now. Unlike the Xenolfans, who were genetically modified so they can't breed with humans, I don't know if I can get pregnant by a Humolfan. So, do you have a condom?"

"Yes."

He walked over to the corner of the room and reached into his backpack. He returned to the chair and opened the package. Sliding on the reuleaux triangular-shaped condom, he moved in closer.

She sat back up on the edge of the chair and leaned back with her pussy at the edge. She pulled her legs back. Mazniriatt stood at the edge of the chair, holding either of her ankles as he slid his cock deep into her warm pussy. The sensation was absolutely incredible. He slowly pumped between her sensual pink folds. She looked down at his gray cock disappearing inside of her, her inner labia brushing on either side of the clear condom. The feeling of being filled with his nice cock was amazing. It had been so long since she had any cock that it was a welcomed delight.

Mazniriatt grunted loudly and quickened his thrusts. She could feel him pulsate deep inside of her. Suddenly, he burst, filling the condom with his hot load.

"I'm so sorry. I didn't mean to come that quickly," he said, noticeably embarrassed.

"Hey, don't worry about it, Mazniriatt," Sierra said. "I already had an amazing orgasm."

He withdrew his penis and removed the cum-filled condom. Wrapping it into a paper towel, he discarded it.

"Let me get cleaned up here a minute and I'll be right back," Mazniriatt said.

He went into a small bathroom toward the back of the studio. She looked down.

It's kind of nice not to deal with a load of cum. I am going to have to get checked for STIs after being with Humolfans. None of the Humolfans have ever been tested at the clinics that I helped develop. That is one thing I'm going to have to demand in my advocating. Their entire population needs to go through that procedure as part of their repatriation back into galactic society, Sierra thought.

Mazniriatt returned and got dressed. Sierra then used the bathroom to clean herself up as well. She returned to the chair.

"My clients aren't normally nude in my chair, so at least there's no need to protect your clothes from the ink. I'll just grab a Feathers of Shardaa stencil and start my line work," Mazniriatt said.

Sierra smiled at Mazniriatt. "How many times have you done the Feathers of Shardaa tattoo?"

"Oh wow... Too many to count. It is my number one tattoo. I have preprinted stencils so every tattoo is exactly the same. As you may know, it is a rite of passage for Humolfan women to get the Feathers of Shardaa tattoo. And it is always in the same spot, slightly above the mons pubis. It has great significance to our people. It is a nice gesture that you are getting one, Sierra," he said.

Mazniriatt put on a pair of gloves and cleaned her skin. He carefully stretched the skin along her mons pubis by applying pressure and pulling outward with his palms. He then moistened Sierra's skin using a solution. Grabbing the preprinted Feathers of Shardaa stencil, he applied it slightly above Sierra's smoothly shaved mons pubis. With delicate motions, he rubbed the stencil against her skin until it was adhered well. After a short time, Mazniriatt slowly pulled the stencil free, revealing the intricate line art of the two feathers.

"How bad is this going to hurt?"

"Umm... Well, you do have some alcohol in you, but yeah...it will hurt like a bitch," he said.

He reached over to the work counter and filled a few ink caps from color tubes of black, a couple of gray shades, and tan. Grabbing his tattoo machine, he dipped it into the black ink cap, the liquid drawing up with capillary action. Sierra looked down and saw the needle as he began tattooing the line art. She immediately closed her eyes and clenched her fists. Alcohol or not, the pain was intense. Mazniriatt inked over the feather outlines in intricate detail. He darkened in the lines along the calamus of each feather. He then worked on the broken feather barbs to give them a damaged look. The roughed-up barbules were next. Soon, Mazniriatt began to blend colors in the feathers with black, two shades of gray, and tan using magnums needles. Afterward, he began shading to provide a slight shadow effect. It took almost three hours to complete the entire tattoo.

"Okay, I'm finished. Let me just clean up the area a bit and then get some ointment and a bandage to apply," Mazniriatt said.

Sierra looked down at the area and then her eyes followed him across the room.

"Well, that was most unpleasant," she said.

Mazniriatt came back, cleaned up the area, and applied a clear bandage.

"Tomorrow, take off the dressing, clean up the area with hot water, and apply this ointment. You'll want to reapply it as needed," he said. He set two packets next to her.

Sierra stood up from the chair, found her clothes on the floor from earlier, and proceeded to get dressed. She took the two packets of ointment and put them into her pocket. Sierra followed Mazniriatt through the black curtain that hung in the doorway and to the front of his shop.

"Well, I have to say this was the most unusual interaction I've ever had. Sierra, it was an absolute pleasure to meet you, get intimate with you, and a privilege to ink you," Mazniriatt said.

"I thoroughly enjoyed you as well…maybe not the tattoo pain, however," Sierra said.

They both laughed. She leaned in and kissed him.

"You take care of yourself, Mazniriatt," Sierra said.

She turned around and walked out the shop door and into the darkness of the Shardia night.

• • •

Several blocks from Mazniriatt's tattoo shop, Sierra began to wonder where she had landed the *Aileron*. The darkness of night did not help her in trying to locate Estrus's ship. She walked along a side street, the illuminators from the main street casting shadows along the brick buildings.

They seriously need to put more street illuminators here, she thought.

After several blocks, Sierra stopped in front of what looked like a factory office. She looked inside the dark windows. Everything in the immediate vicinity was closed. The side streets were desolate at that hour. She remembered landing the ship next to a park. If only she had a comm… As she walked along the buildings, the distinct sound of a metal bar dropping onto the cement sidewalk broke the silence of the night. Sierra turned around to see where the noise came from. She only saw a dark, empty street. Wait! Someone's shadow moved near a distant street sign.

Is someone following me? Sierra thought.

She began walking back toward the main street, which was a few blocks away. She could see the distant lights and traffic on the main street ahead of her. She quickened her pace. Suddenly, a Humolfan man jumped out in front of her. He wore a black outfit that blended with the night. His white hair contrasted the darkness. Another Humolfan landed behind Sierra, her black wings retracting. Sierra turned around and saw the woman that landed. A third Humolfan swooped down and hovered in the air before landing in the street. The last arrival of the trio was very tall. She walked toward Sierra. They each wore matching black outfits. Sierra turned to the newest threat.

"What do you people want?" Sierra asked.

The tall woman who landed last walked up to Sierra. "So, you are the human Estrus has found to advocate for them. They have kept trying over the years and we have stopped them every time. But *you*…you managed to get past where all the others have not. The Dissident Faction tried to stop you on S2, but our member was killed and our fighter ship was destroyed. If you think you are going to advocate for them, you are sadly mistaken."

The other woman flicked out a knife and swung her arm at Sierra. As Sierra tried to back away, the Humolfan man grabbed her from behind, holding her in place. The tension on her shirt lifted it up slightly, exposing the clear bandage that revealed her fresh Feathers of Shardaa tattoo. The woman with the knife came closer. Both fear and anger ran through Sierra. She tried pulling from her captor's grip to no avail. The woman put the knife up to Sierra's neck.

"You got a Feathers of Shardaa tattoo? That's a disgrace! You're not even Humolfan. It's too bad we couldn't get laser weapons past security here on Shardia. You would have already been dead," the woman with the knife said.

"They will find your body tomorrow and Estrus will need to start her search for a new advocate all over again," the tall woman said, laughing.

"Don't you people realize that arrangements can be made so S3 isn't disturbed by the rest of the galaxy when the other Humolfans return to galactic society?" Sierra asked.

"That won't be happening," the man said.

"You people are so fucking pathetic! You destroyed that bridge, killed innocent people, damaged the businesses along the area here on Shardia. You don't care about the Humolfan species, your very own people… Your agenda is flawed and you're blind," Sierra said.

The woman with the knife moved it away from Sierra's neck. Her eyes began to glow as she stared at Sierra. Sierra suddenly felt faint in the man's arms.

"Don't you do that shit to me, bitch!" Sierra said.

"Gramer Moss wants us to kill her. Let's get it over with," the tall woman said.

In a brutal assault, the woman with the knife abruptly shoved it into Sierra's neck and pulled it back out. Blood gushed onto the man's arms. Sierra felt the sharp pain in her neck as blood drained down her throat. The man dropped her to the ground. Being a Galactic Emergency Medical Technician, she knew the wound was bad…very bad. The strangest memory filled her mind. She recalled the time she sat at an intoxication joint on Volum and witnessed a Syrenthian Brotherhood Knights of Darkness member stab an identity thief in the neck. He had bled out onto the floor and died.

"No!" Sierra cried.

The tall woman removed a black spray paint can from a pouch and sprayed the letters DF on the brick wall next to Sierra.

"Let's get out of here," the man said.

They each spread their wings and lifted from the ground. Moments later, quick bursts of intense blue laser fire brightened the darkness of the night. Two of the Dissident Faction members fell dead to the ground. The tall woman managed to fly away. A team of Humolfan Government security agents quickly ran toward Sierra. There was a tall man among the agents that wore his white hair long. He had a special uniform on that was far different than the others in his team. He knelt down to where Sierra lay on the cement and quickly covered her wound with his hand. Her eyes opened slightly to see the man staring down at her. He was very handsome and alluring. She knew he wasn't from the Dissident Faction. These people were different Humolfans. Everything seemed to be happening in slow motion. Tears formed in Sierra's eyes and the mysterious man became blurred. As she faded into unconsciousness, she could hear the man bark orders at the others as he held her neck tight.

CHAPTER EIGHT

GOING THROUGH THE security at the Syrenthian Government administrative center on Exandra made Eslarr a bit nervous. After entering the building, Gathin, Eslarr, and Priscilla followed Braxton down a long corridor. They turned a corner and Braxton came to a stop.

"This is the lounge. You three can wait here while I do some research on this Dennon Cobalt," Braxton said.

"Thanks," Gathin said.

Braxton left the room as the three of them made themselves comfortable in the soft chairs.

"Do you two want a Sevis to drink or perhaps a snack?" Priscilla asked.

"That would be great," Eslarr said.

"Yes. Thank you. A snack would be great as well," Gathin said.

Priscilla stood up, walked over to the refrigerator, and grabbed three bottles of Sevis. She then found some salty snacks in the cupboard. Bringing them over to where Gathin and Eslarr sat, Priscilla once again made herself comfortable in the chair. They each opened their beverage with a distinct pop sound. Gathin took a long drink.

"This is quite a facility," Gathin said.

"Yeah… And it's very secure," Eslarr said.

"Yup. This is where Braxton works as a government investigator and administrative clerk," Priscilla said.

"And where do you work?" Eslarr asked.

"I work at the hospital here on Exandra," Priscilla said. "It was nice of you two to join us on this journey. We understand that you both know Sierra as well. It's a nice gesture. That doesn't mean there won't be danger, however. We will be heading into uncharted space where a lot of strange things have been reported over the years."

"I just hope Sierra is all right and I hope we find her. She is such an amazing person," Eslarr said.

"I hope we can too," Priscilla said.

Two people sat at the console in the Communications Department. They looked up at Braxton as he entered the room.

"Parker… Tanorra… How are you two doing?" Braxton asked.

"Ah! You're back from your vacation. I'm glad you were able to contact me from Aamaress," Parker said.

"Yes. Although we were not finished with our vacation by any means, Sierra is much more important. So, I need you to search for the location of Dennon Cobalt," Braxton said.

"Yes, I can see how Sierra would take the priority over vacation. Receiving Sierra's message was certainly a surprise. And just to let you know, the distress signal has stopped. So, we are unable to pinpoint the exact location on S2 it was generated from," Parker said.

"Well, that's great," Braxton said.

"So, Dennon Cobalt… Let me see what I can find," Parker said.

He began searching through the Syrenthian Government records. After switching to several different screens, he leaned in toward the display.

"Dennon Cobalt is a marketing specialist for the StellularNav Corporation on Shar Nefalis. They manufacture parts for our SG302 fighter ships," Parker said.

"Nice. Well, he may have some info about the Shardaa Sector that will be helpful," Braxton said.

"I understand that you sent a message ahead to Edward Sirlain. They have prepared a battleship for you with a small crew. Also, you may want to consult with Captain Linex Railler of the *Deliverance*. Galactic Emergency Medical Services made a run to the Shardaa Sector in that hospital ship to rescue Dennon Cobalt," Parker said.

"I know Sierra was part of the team that went in, but I will get specifics from Captain Railler. Thanks, Parker."

"Good luck," Parker said.

Braxton, Priscilla, Gathin, and Eslarr stood on the bridge of the *Dignity*. The Syrenthian Government battleship had just departed Exandra and was en route to the Shar Nefalis Star System in the Industrial Sector. There were several other government officials on the bridge. The small crew that was assigned to the *Dignity* went about their tasks with great proficiency. Braxton stepped up next to the captain's chair.

"So, Captain Xaanoss, wasn't the *Dignity* one of the five battleships that fought in the brief New Syrenthian War with the Xenolfan Government?" Braxton asked, looking at the older gentleman.

"Yes. The other four battleships that were sent with us to Olf Teruda were *Godspeed*, *GrayMar*, *Sanctuary Star*, and *Syrenth*. Our ships took some damage, but we destroyed the Xenolfan Government battleships *Oldstaff* and *Deltarr*. We also sent three other battleships to Salinarr Nevis, but they did not engage. They were the *Linerston*, *Patriot*, and *Truliniot*. That very brief war was the last devious act of Aaranix Tuvelless. As you know, after the New Syrenthian War, he was forced to step down as the leader of the Xenolfan Government," Captain Arbin Xaanoss said.

"That is fascinating... Before we boarded the *Dignity*, I contacted Captain Linex Railler of the *Deliverance*. Apparently when GEMS was sent on the run to the Shardaa Sector to rescue Dennon Cobalt, the hospital ship remained at the edge of the Shardaa Sector. Captain Railler didn't feel comfortable going into that sector, so they sent in a medical shuttle the remainder of the way. He said the Sharasp Tharrian Asteroid Mass was not an issue for the medical shuttle because it was at a different area along the system's plane at the time," Braxton said.

"Well, we will be taking the *Dignity* in all the way and the Sharasp

Tharrian Asteroid Mass is currently in a position that we will need to navigate," Captain Arbin Xaanoss said. "We may not be the *Deliverance,* but we do have a great medical facility on this ship."

"Well, hopefully Sierra doesn't need any medical help," Braxton said.

One of the other officers on the bridge turned toward Captain Arbin Xaanoss.

"We will arrive on Shar Nefalis in ten lightminutes, sir," the navigator said.

"Thank you for the update," the captain said.

"Parker gave you the coordinates to the StellularNav Corporation?" Braxton asked.

"Yes. Since they are one of our suppliers for ship parts, they have a large landing pad where we can set the *Dignity* down with ease," Captain Arbin Xaanoss said.

Soon, the *Dignity* descended through the clouds of the Shar Nefalis atmosphere and landed at the StellularNav Corporation. Braxton, Priscilla, Gathin, and Eslarr exited the ship and walked across the landing pad toward the building entrance. The battleship's crew remained aboard the *Dignity.* Inside the building, the light gray corridors were well illuminated and had very little traffic.

"Is he expecting us?" Priscilla asked.

"No. I didn't want to alarm him. We need answers, not a chase. From what I was told by GEMS, his ordeal in the Shardaa Sector messed him up psychologically and we cannot afford for him to get freaked out and run," Braxton said.

They soon entered the offices of the StellularNav Corporation. It was decorated with a clean, modern theme and it was very spacious.

"May I help you?" the receptionist asked.

"I'm here on Syrenthian Government business," Braxton said, presenting his credentials. "Can you tell me where Dennon Cobalt is located?" Braxton asked.

"I'll let him know you're here," the receptionist said.

"It would be best if you don't. Just point me in his direction," Braxton said.

"Ahhh… Through the door, turn left. It's the last cubical on the right," she said.

The four of them proceeded through a door and into more offices. Braxton led the way, following the receptionist's instructions. Upon reaching Dennon Cobalt's cubical, they stopped and looked at the man who sat if front of a computer. He looked up at them and recoiled in surprise.

"Who are you?"

"My name is Braxton Stryderr, this is my wife, Priscilla, and these are our friends, Gathin and Eslarr. I work as an investigative agent for the Syrenthian Government and I need your help. May I have a seat?"

Dennon Cobalt stared at Braxton for a moment and then looked at the others.

"Um…of course. Let's go into the conference room," he said.

He led them around a corner and into a room with a large table in the center. They each sat down and Dennon Cobalt gave Braxton a questioning look.

"So, what is it that you need help with?" Dennon asked.

"We are searching for a very good friend of ours. She has been missing for months. The Syrenthian Government has recently received a distress signal from her. It was emitting from the Shardaa Sector," Braxton said.

Suddenly, Dennon froze, a frightening expression revealed across his face. He became visibly nervous and began to shake.

"What? What? No! Why are you here?"

"Dennon, I know this is a difficult subject for you to talk about, but we desperately need your help. Please… Our friend's life may depend on it," Braxton said.

"Okay. I will do my best to help, but the Shardaa Sector is one place I try to forget. It is very stressful for me to talk about," Dennon said.

"I understand. Just do your best. So, I was given the details about your rescue by GEMS, but I need to know why you were there in the first place. I need to know the things you saw there. I need a description of the person you are reported to have seen there," Braxton said.

For a long moment, it looked as if Dennon's focus had shifted to a distant world as he stared into nothingness.

"Dennon?" Priscilla called.

Dennon Cobalt shook his head. "I'm sorry. It's just… I've gone through therapy regarding this very subject and it frightens me to the core to be reminded of it."

"Please…" Braxton said.

"I was contacted by a woman who said she needed my help with a very large marketing campaign. She explained that my experience in marketing would help tremendously with the project and that it was a perfect fit with StellularNav Corporation. It sounded like a great opportunity, although the request was a bit odd. She gave me coordinates to a location on S6 in the Shardaa Sector. At first, I thought this was some big marketing campaign, using the uncharted Shardaa Sector. I thought it was a brilliant idea. …The untapped resources of new worlds, etc. But as I passed a planet called S2, on my way to S6, a fighter ship suddenly appeared out of nowhere and shot me down. My ship crashed on S2. It was damaged pretty badly. I hit my head on the ship's control panel from the impact. I sent out a distress signal and then left the ship. Thankfully, the atmosphere of S2 was not toxic. I saw another ship blow that fighter ship out of the sky. The second ship landed and a woman stepped out. She was not human…nor was she Xenolfan. I don't know what she was. She was very sexy and had gray skin. I have never seen anyone like her before. She had black wings and flew toward me, her eyes glowing blue. I ran toward some rocky monoliths. My head hurt badly from the impact. Then I blacked out for a moment. I hurt my arm on the sharp rocks, but I got up and kept running. At some point, I must have blacked out again. The next thing I know, I woke up in a hospital bed aboard the *Deliverance*. They said I was a delusional space traveler. That's a fucking lie! I know what I saw. You don't have to believe me. They think I have mental issues. My therapist said she believes me," Dennon said.

Braxton and the others soaked in all the information.

"So, someone communicated with you and led you to the Shardaa Sector where you were attacked?" Braxton asked.

"Yes…exactly. But there seemed to be two different players involved that were against each other. I really don't know much beyond that. I was not contacted by the individual again. It was the strangest thing that ever happened to me in all my life," Dennon said.

"I believe you. It is virtually uncharted space. There could be anything there. We just don't know. We are traveling to the Shardaa Sector in a Syrenthian Government battleship, the *Dignity*. So, we are well prepared for anything. Sierra Shalinsky was one of the Galactic Emergency Medical Technicians that actually helped you on S2. It would be nice to know first-hand what we are heading into," Braxton said.

"I don't remember Sierra or any of the first responders. I remember bits and pieces and then waking up on the hospital ship. It's all a bit foggy," Dennon said.

"Would you like to come with us as a consultant?" Braxton asked.

"No! That is one place I will never return to. Please don't ask me to do that," Dennon said.

Dennon Cobalt looked physically sick.

"Take it easy. It was just a suggestion. No one is forcing you to go. I understand why you would not want to return. You have been very helpful and we appreciate it," Braxton said, standing up from the conference room chair.

Priscilla, Gathin, and Eslarr stood up as well.

"Thank you for your time, Dennon," Braxton said.

Dennon remained quiet as the group walked toward the door.

"Good luck on finding your friend. I hope she's okay," Dennon said.

"Me too," Braxton said.

The *Dignity* maneuvered around several asteroids in the Sharasp Tharrian Asteroid Mass. The ship's laser cannons disintegrated several smaller asteroids. The battleship proceeded through the outer perimeter of the gray, icy rocks. The path through the crowded asteroids soon opened up to the empty blackness of space beyond. The Shardaa Star System was not far from their location.

"Parker said the distress signal had stopped, but it was generated from S2. So, let's travel there and see what we can find," Braxton instructed the captain.

Captain Xaanoss addressed a few crew members on the bridge. "I need you laser cannon operators on high alert. Be sure the deflector shields are at full capacity."

They each gave an affirmative response and began making adjustments on the control panels.

The captain activated the ship's internal comm to address the crew. "This is Captain Arbin Xaanoss. We are about to enter the Shardaa Star System. There have been reports of attacks and disappearances in this sector over the years. I want everyone on alert," he said.

Soon, S2 could be seen in the distance of space through the observation window. As they traveled closer, its desolate gray landscape became clearly visible.

"Scan the planet for life forms," the captain instructed a crew member.

"No life forms found, sir," the woman said.

Captain Xaanoss turned to Braxton with a puzzled look and sighed.

"You are certain the distress signal was generated from S2?" Captain Xaanoss asked.

"That is what I was told from Parker. Since the signal had stopped, the Communications Department was unable to determine where on S2 it had come from," Braxton said.

"Do you think we should send down a team to investigate?" Gathin asked.

"I don't think it would do any good if there are no life forms. But we will keep that option on the table. Captain Xaanoss, let's check the other planets for life forms. Shardaa has no atmosphere, so let's skip that one," Braxton said.

"S3's orbit is currently farther than S4, so let's head to S4 first," Captain Xaanoss said.

The star system was not conveniently programmed into the ship's navigation system. The ship's pilot and navigator worked together to make the calculations and adjustments needed.

"We will—"

Captain Arbin Xaanoss was cut short from an emergency alarm that began blaring loudly on the bridge of the *Dignity.*

"We have two incoming fighter ships, sir!" one of the crew members said.

Captain Arbin Xaanoss jolted in his seat and looked at the screen. The others followed his gaze. The two fighter ships could be seen on the screen as they began to fire their lasers at the *Dignity.* The blue beams of energy were absorbed by the *Dignity's* deflector shields in a brief fiery eruption. The two fighter ships maneuvered under the battleship's belly toward the starboard side. They opened fire again, aiming for the docking bay entrance. Once again, the deflector shields blocked their laser fire, the shots ending abruptly in space around the battleship.

"Fire on those ships," the captain ordered.

The laser cannon operators locked the battleship's weapons onto the targets and fired. Large blue beams of energy projected outward from the *Dignity* and struck one of the two fighter ships. It exploded with a blinding light and disappeared into space dust and energy. The remaining fighter ship escaped the laser cannons and flew around toward the bridge. It opened fire with a relentless barrage of lasers. An emergency shield immediately covered the observation window on the bridge. The crew quickly turned to the digital screen. They could hear and feel the attack, as the bridge vibrated with the assault. As the fighter ship swooped around for a second pass, one of the laser cannons sliced through it, destroying it with a silent explosion. The observation window shield retracted, revealing the calm blackness of space. Everyone on the bridge breathed a sigh of relief.

"Well, that was certainly unexpected. I've never seen that type of fighter ship before. There is more out here in the Shardaa Sector than meets the eye," Captain Xaanoss said.

"That's for sure. I wonder where they came from," Priscilla said.

"According to our scanners, I believe they came from S3," the navigator said.

"S3? Well, that is out of our way, but we will have to check it out after we scan S4 for life forms," Captain Xaanoss said.

"This attack is very concerning. I certainly hope Sierra is all right," Eslarr said.

"They may have been pirates. Rumors circulate regarding pirates in the Shardaa Sector, but nothing has been confirmed," Captain Xaanoss said.

Priscilla and Braxton looked at each other with grim expressions.

"Why don't we know much about the Shardaa Sector?" Gathin asked.

"Well, it's an uncharted region of space because it's so distant from the rest of the Syrenthian Galaxy and, to our knowledge, there isn't much here. It sits on the edge of the galaxy. I believe the planets were named by some Xenolfan Government explorers back in the day, but our Syrenthian Government that owns the territory never explored it further," Captain Xaanoss said.

"Eslarr, I'm wondering why the Xenolfan Government only owns two planets in the entire galaxy. Do you know why?" Priscilla asked.

"We prefer humid planets. My home planet of Olf Teruda, where our people originated from, is very humid. I miss that sensation. Aamaress is so frigid and cold compared to Olf Teruda, you would think I'd freeze to death there. But I do enjoy Aamaress, nonetheless. As far as Salinarr Nevis, Xenolfans acquired that planet about one hundred years ago, after the Syrenthian War, as a type of settlement or reparation for the mistreatment of my people back then. Since the planet is also very humid, it was a great acquisition. The amount of credits that our government brings in from all the casinos on Salinarr Nevis is shocking. I guess the Xenolfans were never really interested in acquiring a lot of territory because there are not many planets where we are fully comfortable. Of course, Xenolfans currently live on many planets throughout the Syrenthian Government's territory as well, but they are certainly not as comfortable as the humid conditions on the two planets that we do possess," Eslarr said.

"Very interesting," Priscilla said.

Almost every ship in the galaxy had lightspeed-plus capabilities, which enabled ships to travel much faster than the speed of light. With those capabilities, it didn't take long for ships to reach their destinations. As the *Dignity* reached S4, the planet loomed ahead of them in the observation window. One of the crew members on the bridge scanned the planet.

"I'm not detecting any intelligent life forms, Captain. Only vegetation and a few animal species can be found," he said.

"Well, I certainly hope we find Sierra," Braxton said.

"So, on to S3, then," Captain Xaanoss said.

"Wait a minute, sir. Check this out. The information we scanned from S4 does show what appears to be a cemetery," the crew member said.

"A cemetery...out here in the middle of the Shardaa Sector?" Captain Xaanoss inquired.

"That is correct. There are over three hundred gravestones down there and...a pile of hundreds of skeletons. There are some landing pads at the cemetery as well," the crew member said.

"What?" Captain Xaanoss looked at the screen. "Okay, let's set down on the surface and investigate this cemetery," he said.

"My thoughts exactly," Braxton said.

They landed the *Dignity* next to the cemetery on the largest landing pad available. Captain Arbin Xaanoss, Braxton, Priscilla, Gathin, and Eslarr exited the battleship and walked toward the stone cairn burial sites.

"This is the most bazaar thing I think I've ever come across in all my years of space travel," Captain Xaanoss said.

"Look! This is called Grave of Mothers. There is a plaque over here that tells about it," Priscilla said.

She proceeded to read the description on the memorial.

"Oh my… You guys have to see this!" Priscilla said.

The others walked over to the memorial plaque.

"These graves are all Xenolfan and human women, most of whom were pregnant at the time they were murdered by Siiteper Affelum," Priscilla said.

"Siiteper Affelum? He was a Xenolfan Government leader a thousand years ago," Eslarr said.

They all looked at each other with confusion.

"What the hell happened here?" Braxton wondered.

"Something terrible, apparently," Gathin said.

They made their way through the gravestones and read many names of the women and babies listed.

"There is a feather symbol on each of these gravestones. They are all the same symbol," Eslarr said, a breeze slightly blowing her white hair.

"The feathers! Like I mentioned back on Aamaress, Sierra once told me on her GEMS run out here in the Shardaa Sector that she saw these strange feather symbols above caves that were shaped like Xenolfan vulvas. I wonder if the feather symbols on these gravestones are the same thing," Priscilla said.

Eslarr became slightly embarrassed and looked down at her crotch. Being the only Xenolfan among the group, she felt a bit awkward after the statement. Priscilla noticed her reaction.

"Oh, Eslarr… I didn't mean to embarrass you. That is something that Sierra had told me once. I'm not exactly sure what she saw, but these feather symbols fit that description," Priscilla said.

"No problem. I heard you mention that back on Aamaress, but I didn't say anything. It's just a little strange," Eslarr said.

The cliff at the edge of the cemetery became a curious destination for the group. They proceeded beyond the last row of gravestones and stopped at the cliff. Captain Arbin Xaanoss gasped when he looked over the edge.

"Oh no! Look at all the bones down there. That must be what the scanners picked up. What the hell is this place? There is another memorial plaque over there," Captain Xaanoss said.

They each peered over the cliff and then proceeded toward the plaque.

"It appears to be all male names of Xenolfans and humans and tells the story of Bapbs & Rodes Last Stand. Whatever happened here is something that has never been talked about in our history books," Braxton said. "We need to investigate this further."

"Well, right now, we need to find Sierra," Priscilla said.

"Yeah, you're right. Let's go check out S3," Braxton said.

They made their way back to the *Dignity.*

Chapter Nine

S3 was very similar to S4 with a mix of rocky terrain and vegetation. The sky was dark with overcast clouds of gray. It was the usual semblance of S3's atmosphere. The military base on S3 was swarming with Dissident Faction members hastily performing emergency tasks. Two of their fighter ships were destroyed by an unknown battleship and it was heading in their direction.

"I want every fighter ship we have prepared to launch. Ready the ground laser cannon!" Gramer Moss shouted.

The Dissident Faction leader had long, white hair that was braided on the sides. A feather puffed out into the air as she adjusted her large, black wings. Her black uniform complemented her gray skin. An angry look could be seen in her sapphire eyes.

A young male Humolfan ran into the war room where she stood. "Gramer, the battleship is approaching!" he said.

Gramer Moss enabled the comm. "Launch the fighter ships. Stand by with the ground laser cannon. I will give you confirmation on when to fire," she said.

A fury of fighter ships launched from the Dissident Faction base on

S3. They continued to exit the hanger bay, one after another. There were twenty fighter ships in all, heading through the gray clouds toward space. Despite the timely launch, Gramer knew the Dissident Faction needed to be better organized. They had lost several fighter ships recently. Their attempt to kill the human advocate on Shardia was a disaster, leaving two of their members dead. Gramer did not know the status of the human advocate's medical condition because she was too well guarded for their surveillance team to get in.

This unknown battleship is the last thing we need right now, Gramer Moss thought.

A female Humolfan ran into the war room and paused for a moment when she saw the disgusted look on Gramer's face.

"They are having issues getting the ground laser cannon online for targeting," the woman said.

"Fuck!" Gramer shouted. She activated the comm. "Use the manual override and aim the best you can."

"We will do our best, Gramer," the member said.

"When there is a clear shot at the battleship, take it. Make sure our fighter ships are not in the way," Gramer said.

The *Dignity* approached S3 with caution. Captain Arbin Xaanoss gave the order to stand by with laser cannons.

"Unfortunately, with the small crew, we don't have enough officers to man the SG302 fighter ships. So, hopefully, we don't get any surprises," Captain Xaanoss said.

"We have surprises!" one of the officers on the bridge said. "There are twenty of those same fighter ships advancing on the *Dignity*. We have deflector shields at full capacity."

"Fire at will," Captain Xaanoss said.

The officers fired the *Dignity's* laser cannons. Intense blue beams of destruction sliced through the darkness of space. One of the beams nicked a fighter ship, but it was not severely damaged. As the fighter ships swarmed the *Dignity*, they fired along the surface of the hull in various locations. The deflector shields held their strength as they were bombarded with laser fire. One of the battleship's laser cannons came into direct contact with a fighter ship, causing it to explode. The rest of the fighter ships flew under the battleship and around to the port side, firing once again. As they came around, another one was caught in the path of the battleship's laser cannons. It was destroyed. The remaining fighter ships once again swooped under the battleship and around to the port side. When the starboard side of the *Dignity* was clear, the crew manning the ground laser cannon on S3 fired the massive laser at the battleship. It struck the starboard aft section of the deflector shield, which immediately failed and the *Dignity's* internal illuminators flickered for a brief moment.

"Shit! Watch out for that ground laser cannon. It's intense! We lost part of our rear deflector shield. One more direct hit at the starboard aft section of the *Dignity* and it's game over. Turn the ship around!" Captain Xaanoss shouted.

The *Dignity* rotated 180 degrees. The fighter ships relentlessly swarmed the battleship, firing lasers at the exposed starboard aft section. Some damage occurred, resulting in internal fires and explosions. The group on the bridge held onto whatever they could grab as the ship shook violently. As the fighter ships cleared another path for the ground laser cannon, another intense blast came from S3. It missed the *Dignity* by meters. The next ground laser cannon shot was another direct hit, this time on the port side of the aft section. The ship shook violently.

"Now, we have no protection at all in the aft section, sir," an officer reported.

"Jump to lightspeed. Let's get out of here and back to Exandra. We will return with an armada of battleships, fully crewed with SG302 fighter ship pilots," Captain Xaanoss said. "I'm sorry we couldn't locate your friend."

"That's totally understandable in these circumstances," Braxton said. "I just hope she's alive out here somewhere. Perhaps after we return with the armada, we will be able to locate her."

Sierra opened her eyes and looked around the hospital room that she found herself in. There were no other people in the room at that moment. She remembered being attacked by a group of idiots. Sierra remembered seeing the most handsome man she ever saw in her entire life…and then everything got blurry and faded to black. She looked at the IV in her arm and a sense of deja vu came over her as she recalled when she woke up from her coma in the docking bay on S6. She wondered what planet she was currently on. Her neck and throat were sore. Sierra recalled the blade going into her neck and then blood gushing out as she fell to the ground. She reached up and felt her neck. Her fingers came across a bandage. She swallowed with a slight pain and squinted her eyes. Sierra then vaguely remembered getting a tattoo. She looked down and moved her hospital gown aside to look at her mons pubis. Sure enough…there was a Feathers of Shardaa tattoo above her vulva. She covered herself back up and rested her head against the pillow, staring at the monitors next to her. Her mind wondered back to the handsome man that knelt down to help her after the attack. Never in her life had she seen someone as handsome as him. Sierra recalled him barking commands at some others.

Who was *he?* she wondered.

As Sierra looked toward the door, she saw Estrus enter the room.

"Well, someone's awake. How are you feeling, Sierra?" Estrus asked.

"Hi, Estrus. My neck and throat are a bit sore. It hurts to swallow. But other than that, I feel fine," Sierra said.

"You should be out of here soon. Dr. Graluss has been assigned to you here since he is already familiar with you as a patient. He said the surgery they did on your neck went well and they did their best to minimize the scar."

"I'm sorry I took your ship to Shardia. I don't even know where I landed it."

"Soltuss Yow and I found the *Aileron*. The ship is fine."

"Oh good. I was concerned about it."

"Why exactly did you fly to Shardia?"

Sierra opened her gown to show Estrus the tattoo. Estrus's jaw dropped as she gasped.

"You went to Mazniriatt and had a Feathers of Shardaa tattoo inked. Oh my… Sierra, I love that. You are so empathetic to our people and our cause." Estrus smiled. "You're awesome. But don't drink and fly, okay?"

"Yes. I'm such a Jinkins."

"Jinkins?"

"Idiot."

"Oh."

"So, I saw the most gorgeous, handsomest man I think I've ever seen in my life. He came to my rescue when I was stabbed in the neck. He seemed to be in charge of the others. Do you know who that was?"

Estrus smiled at Sierra. "Yes, I do. After the Dissident Faction members tried to murder you, Yilran Taw and a highly-skilled security team came to your rescue. They had been tracking the Dissident Faction members before the attack. You may remember me speaking of Yilran Taw when I first brought you here to Shardia."

"I'm still on Shardia?"

"Yes. You are in the Naantress Hospital. We have security guarding you from any further attacks."

"Yilran Taw," Sierra repeated as she smiled. "He is hot! Remind me who he is again."

"Yilran Taw is the Humolfan Government leader who lives in the palace here in Naantress."

Sierra's jaw dropped this time, a look of disbelief displayed in her expression.

"You're shitting me. He's the man who came to my rescue? Wow! Can I meet him?"

"Oh, don't you worry about that, Sierra. He has made it quite clear that he wants to meet you. Since you are the human that is advocating for our people, he is even more interested in you. In fact, he personally told me very similar things about you. He thinks you are very beautiful and unique. Yilran instructed Dr. Graluss to inform him when you are discharged from the hospital. So, in the next day or so, you will get to meet Yilran Taw in person."

The comm sounded in the spacious great room of the Humolfan Government palace on Shardia. Yilran Taw walked over and answered the communication.

"This is Dr. Graluss. You wanted me to inform you before Sierra Shalinsky is discharged from the hospital."

"Yes. Thank you Dr. Graluss. I will leave for the hospital immediately," Yilran said.

Yilran Taw turned off the comm and walked down a corridor to a bathroom. He looked at himself in a wide mirror. He adjusted the ponytail that held his long, white hair. Wetting his hand under water, he carefully groomed the top of his black wings. His blue uniform looked very stylish. Yilran held up his gray hands and touched his gray face, wondering what Sierra would think of his Humolfan differences. After spraying a mist of cologne onto his chest, the air was filled with an incredible scent. It was an aroma of citrus top notes, green, floral, and spicy center notes, and musky and woodsy base notes. He made his way back down the corridor toward the palace exit.

As Yilran made his way along the stone walkway on the side of the palace, he stopped to pick a fuchsia flower from the floral garden that grew below the stone wall. He informed his driver that he was ready and they both adjusted their wings as they stepped into the confined space of the anti-gravitational transport.

The ride from the palace to the hospital was a short one. The driver stopped at the hospital entrance to drop off Yilran Taw.

"I will wait for you in the parking area," the driver said.

"Okay. Thank you," Yilran said as he stepped out of the vehicle.

He stood at the entrance of the hospital with the fuchsia flower in his hand and looked up at the tall building.

Why do I feel so anxious? he asked himself.

After making his way to the secure waiting lounge on the second level where Sierra was located, he paused just before entering the room and exhaled a deep breath. Passing two security guards, Yilran knocked on the door and entered the room.

After Sierra was released from her hospital room, she relaxed in a secure lounge on the second level of the Naantress Hospital. The cushioned chair she sat in was very comfortable. She was *so* ready to depart the hospital. Three guards were present in the room with her and two outside the door. She understood the need for protection with extra security after what had happened to her with the Dissident Faction.

There was a slight knock at the door and it opened. The three guards quickly pointed their laser rifles at the door, prepared for anything. They relaxed when they saw it was Yilran Taw. Sierra looked up at the new arrival. He was even more handsome than she recalled from that horrible night. She smiled.

"So, you are the famous Sierra Shalinsky, the chosen advocator for our people," Yilran said.

"I am. And you must be Yilran Taw, leader of the Humolfan Government," Sierra said.

"I am."

There was a slight awkward pause. Sierra found the scent of his cologne to be most pleasant. Yilran handed Sierra the fuchsia flower that he held. She smiled at the surprise and reached out to hold it by its stem. She held it up to her nose, its aromatic floral fragrance filling her with a certain joy.

"The Dissident Faction almost killed you. I'm glad we were in the area tracking them. I have to admit, you are the most beautiful and unique woman I've ever seen in my entire life. I held your neck to stop the bleeding until the emergency medical technicians arrived. If the knife would have been a few millimeters over, we would have lost you that night. That, Sierra, would have been the most tragic day of my life. I stayed with you until they brought you here for emergency surgery. I don't know what it is about you, but I didn't want to lose you and I feel this…this connection with you. I cannot explain it."

"When I saw you coming to my rescue, I witnessed the most handsome man in the galaxy. It was like a dream. But it's not a dream. You really are the most handsome man I've ever seen. I feel a similar connection."

"Even though I'm so different than you?" he asked, referring to his gray skin and black wings.

"Diversity doesn't bother me. I've been with humans, Xenolfans, and…Humolfans, both male and female. I am a tan human, I have no wings, my hair is black, and—although they are blue—my eyes are not sapphire, like Xenolfans and Humolfans. I hope all those differences don't bother *you*."

Yilran smiled. "Nothing about you bothers me, Sierra," he said.

He leaned in and looked at her neck where the bandage had been. There was only a slight scar after her surgery. Yilran moved closer and kissed her lips. The warmth felt wonderful against her mouth as she opened to playfully dance her tongue against his. Of all the times she had been with others, she had never felt passion as strong as that before. Of all the sexual situations in the swinger Lifestyle and all the partners she's had, nothing felt like the magic that she currently found herself immersed in. Her heart felt like it was free falling in a wonderful spin. Sierra could not explain her emotions as they kissed. The exhilarating experience was like nothing she had ever felt with anyone else before. Yilran felt a similar passion for Sierra as they kissed. He felt as if the loneliness that he had experienced over the years in the palace was quickly vanquished with this person that suddenly came into his life. When the kiss finally ended, Sierra stared at him with her beautiful blue eyes. She could not explain what she was feeling as she hugged him tight.

I think I'm lovesick, she thought.

"You know, the Humolfans have accomplished a lot in the thousand years you've been here in the Shardaa Sector," Sierra said.

"Thank you. We have been pretty innovative for being isolated from the rest of the galaxy. So, tell me all about yourself, the humans, the Xenolfans, and the outside galaxy," Yilran said.

"Only if you tell me all about yourself and the Humolfans," Sierra said.

"Fair enough. You go first," he said.

"Wow. Where do I start?" she asked.

Staring into the distance, she began to tell Yilran her story in great detail. Everything from the name of her ship to her favorite microphones was mentioned. She mentioned her career as a Galactic Emergency Medical Technician, her job as a vocalist for Maranadda, her advocacy for sexual freedom, and even that she was a bisexual swinger in the Lifestyle. Yilran Taw shared his life story with her from when he first learned to fly to the tragic death of his people by the Dissident Faction. He spoke of the Syrenthian Brotherhood Knights of Darkness campaign that was in the works to wipe out the Dissident Faction. He also mentioned adventures from his flight academy days, his rise to power, and his interest in literature and music. They talked for hours. As details became more intimate and personal boundaries were lowered, he revealed how lonely he had been over the years. She certainly did not understand why, since he was so gorgeous.

"But I don't understand. You can literally have any Humolfan woman you want. There is something that you are not telling me. I can tell that something deep down is troubling you," Sierra said.

After some hesitation, he leaned in and whispered into her ear, "There are things that I'm just not ready to share yet."

Knowing there were guards in the room, Sierra was discreet. "Whatever serious things are bothering you, I am here when you are ready to talk," she whispered back.

For another half hour, they discussed more about each other's likes and interests.

"How would you like to have a personal tour of the palace?" Yilran asked.

"Oh my! I would love that," Sierra said.

"Well then, let me contact my driver and we'll get started," Yilran said.

• • •

The Humolfan Government palace was breathtaking. Yilran led Sierra through the beautiful interior of the palace. As they walked through the great room, she gazed up at the stone fireplace. Intriguing paintings of art were fixed on the walls. A wooden staircase curved upward toward the second floor. The areas that she had seen on the lengthy tour were fabulous. She could not believe Yilran was a bachelor. As they made there way up the curved stairs, Sierra looked down at the elegant great room. A wooden railing ran along the top of a mezzanine, its rich brown wood matching the steps. Yilran continued to show Sierra the different rooms. At the end of the mezzanine, a harpsichord sat just outside of his large office. After viewing his office, she soon found herself following him to the third floor. There were guest accommodations with the finest amenities on the third floor. The fourth floor was where Yilran's master bedroom was located. Sierra had never seen a more luxurious bedroom. For a brief moment, her mind drifted to her own bedroom back on Asparr Celtarious. She missed her bed.

"You are staring at the wall. Are you okay?" Yilran asked.

"Oh…sorry. I was just thinking of my own home. I haven't seen it in forever and I miss it," she said.

"I understand," Yilran said.

He sat down in a soft chair next to the large dresser. As Sierra walked past a mirror to another chair, she paused and looked at her neck in the mirror. The knife wound was almost invisible. She continued to the chair and also sat down.

"They did a phenomenal job on my neck," she said.

"Yes, they did. We have some of the best surgeons here on Shardia," Yilran said.

Sierra looked at some of the art on the walls. Yilran followed her gaze.

"That piece is of a Humolfan mating ritual where two lovers circle each other in flight, then land together, and wrap their wings around each other. The two in that piece represent Athenarr and Aarria. They were two of the original Humolfans from S4 that created the first Humolfan baby by two Humolfans. There was also a statue of them down at the park, but the Dissident Faction destroyed it. We are in the process of having it resculptured," Yilran said.

"The Xenolfans used to perform the exact same mating ritual back when they had wings," Sierra said.

"Yes. It's a little sad that humans cannot fly," Yilran said.

Sierra looked over to Yilran, his sexy white hair still in a ponytail. He smiled at her.

"Sad because you and I cannot perform the mating ritual together?" she asked, tilting her head.

Yilran hesitated. "Yes," he said.

"Oh, Yilran... Us humans are very different than Humolfans, and Xenolfans for that matter. You see, we don't have reuleaux triangular vulvas, like Humolfan women."

Suddenly, Yilran had an astonished look on his face as he gazed at her with a frozen stare.

"What's wrong?"

"At the hospital, I told you I wasn't ready to share some things. With you, I feel that I can finally lift this burden from my shoulders. It's strange how I'm comfortable enough to confide in you, Sierra, but I don't feel comfortable enough with most of my own people."

"And I don't take that lightly," she said.

"There are two things that have weighed heavy on me for a long time. The first thing is that I'm not like most other Humolfan men. I don't have a reuleaux triangular penis. One in every thirty-five thousand Humolfans is born with a human penis. That is why I am not married. Humolfan women have not been very understanding about my difference. It's been...lonely," he said.

"So, we are very much alike in that regard. I've always been a very sexual person," Sierra said.

"I did have a serious relationship once, but it was short-lived due to me being different. We were never married," Yilran said.

Sierra smiled at him. "Any Humolfan woman that has rejected you because of your difference is a fool."

"Being similar in that regard is another great reason to connect with you," he said.

"And here we are in your bedroom..."

Sierra looked at him with a very seductive stare.

"No...I can't. I am the leader of the Humolfan Government. I cannot take advantage of you like that. My people would not think very highly of me," he said.

"You know what? Sometimes you need to make yourself happy.

There is something about you that is irresistible."

"I would like to get to know you more before we get sexually involved," Yilran said.

"Okay. This revelation brings a certain intimate connection for me as well. And I can appreciate you wanting to wait. So, what is the second thing that is weighing heavy on you?" Sierra asked.

"Of the short-lived relationship that I did have many years ago, a child was produced. We had a son. He was such a good boy…"

"And?"

"He grew up and kept his distance. He… Damn it, Sierra, I feel guilty for what the Dissident Faction did to you."

"What are you talking about?"

"My son is part of the Dissident Faction."

Sierra moved back in the chair slightly with surprise.

"How?"

"I don't really know. He just kept his distance from me and also from his mother. We may be the only two Humolfans that know about his involvement in that organization. If others found out, things would get ugly for me. He must not want our people to be free from the isolation of the Shardaa Sector. We keep trying to tell Gramer Moss and the Dissident Faction that they don't have to be a part of the repatriation and that S3 can stay isolated, but they choose to keep attacking us instead."

"Thank you for sharing that with me. Just because he's your son, doesn't mean you need to feel guilty for what they did to me. It's not your fault. He may not even know about the incident. I can see how that burden has weighed you down. What's his name?"

"His name is Inatharr. Although I have not seen her in years, his mother, Arrvia, lives here on Shardia as well. The end of the Dissident Faction is coming soon. I just don't want to lose my son. Perhaps I already have…"

"There is always hope. Hopefully, he is not so entrenched in the group that he cannot get himself out."

"I hope you're right." Yilran sighed heavily. "Hey, would you like to go out to dinner? You can order soft food for your healing throat."

"That would be wonderful."

"It's a date, then."

• • •

Upon the return of the *Dignity* to Exandra, Edward Sirlain was informed of the attack from S3. The leader ordered an armada of Syrenthian Government battleships back out to respond to the attack. This time, they were fully crewed with an adequate amount of fighter pilots to fly the SG302 fighter ships. Braxton, Priscilla, Gathin, and Eslarr were standing at the entrance to an extremely large docking bay on Exandra, near the government administrative center.

"It's a shame we could not finish searching for Sierra out there," Gathin said.

"Yes, I agree. Being chased out of that region of space was not something that we anticipated," Braxton said.

"When you go back there with the armada, please be careful," Priscilla said.

"Don't worry, honey. We will be prepared for them this time," Braxton said.

"I'll miss you. Please be safe," Priscilla said.

"Perhaps you'll still find her," Eslarr said.

"I hope so," Braxton said. "Gathin and Eslarr, we appreciate you coming with us on that first run to the Shardaa Sector to search for Sierra."

"We appreciate the opportunity that we had to be a part of the search," Gathin said.

"I can take you two back to Aamaress in my ship. But as far as our vacation goes, it's pretty much over. I'll pay you the credits due when we arrive back on Aamaress," Priscilla said.

"Hey, we appreciate the ride," Gathin said.

Priscilla kissed Braxton and they parted ways. Braxton turned toward the docking bay and quickened his pace to help prepare the fleet. There were ten battleships being prepared for the voyage back to the Shardaa Sector. They were *Blue Star, Celestial, Dignity, Godspeed, GrayMar, Linerston, Patriot, Sanctuary Star, Syrenth,* and *Truliniot.* The Galactic Emergency Medical Services was also contacted to schedule the hospital ship, *Deliverance,* to remain nearby at the edge of the Shardaa Sector as a precautionary measure. It would take several days to complete the logistics of the operation. Each battleship contained ten SG302 fighter ships in their docking bays. They wanted to be prepared for anything from S3 that could be thrown at them. When the armada was ready for flight, Braxton was again aboard the *Dignity* with Captain Arbin Xaanoss. Investigating the military force behind the attack was also part of Braxton's mission. Assigned to the fleet was Admiral Lytria Foss. She was stationed aboard the *Syrenth.*

Chapter Ten

"It is time," Yilran Taw said.

"Roger that," Argenniss replied. "As you had requested, we tried one last time to reason with them and assure them they can stay on S3 in isolation while we reconnect with the rest of the Syrenthian Galaxy. We were told there would be no compromise."

"You know what the Syrenthian Brotherhood Knights of Darkness and the Humolfan Command must do according to our plans. As I discussed with you previously, do not destroy stronghold number nine," Yilran said.

"Stronghold number nine will be left alone, per your request, sir," Argenniss said.

"Good luck."

Argenniss was the leader of the Syrenthian Brotherhood Knights of Darkness. He changed frequencies on the comm.

"We have just received authorization from Yilran Taw to commence Operation Reprisal," Argenniss said. "Do not attack stronghold number nine."

The communication was addressed to all members of the

Syrenthian Brotherhood Knights of Darkness. As their leader, Argenniss had been waiting a long time for this approval. His members were very well trained and prepared for the forthcoming operation.

"It is time we avenge our loved ones who have been murdered by the Dissident Faction. It is time to seek vengeance for every advocate we have ever tried to recruit who has been injured or killed by these terrorists. It is time we repay the Dissident Faction for the destruction of our city, our monuments and statues, and our Ocean Port Bridge, where many of our people were murdered. We didn't rebuild the bridge because we wanted it as a reminder of what our enemies have done. We stood down after that to negotiate. We gave them the benefit of the doubt. They never wanted negotiations. They were offered to be left alone during our introduction back into galactic society. Instead, they chose to destroy. We are done! You all have your specific instructions and targets. We will head out as the second strike unit to S3 in ten minutes. Humolfan Command has also received approval from Yilran Taw and just left with the first strike unit. The ground laser cannon is our primary target. After that is destroyed, we will be on the ground. You all have your target lists. Let's move out!" Argenniss said.

He turned off the comm, put on a pair of black leather gauntlets, and quickly made his way across a docking bay to his fighter ship.

The Syrenthian Brotherhood Knights of Darkness was primarily used for data collection and influence outside of the Shardaa Sector. Their commitment and self-sacrifice of personal changes for that cause was commendable. There was an extra vigor that ran throughout all the members because they knew if Operation Reprisal was not successful, then their sacrifice through the years would have been in vein. As another front of Operation Reprisal, Soltuss Yow and the entire Humolfan Command from S6 and Shardia was en route to S3 in a battleship containing many skilled fighter pilots. It was the first time the Humolfan Command and the Syrenthian Brotherhood Knights of Darkness worked together on a military operation of that magnitude. Since they had trained together for the campaign, it was expected to go very smoothly.

Wings of Shardaa exited lightspeed upon arrival at S3. The one and only Humolfan Command battleship was commanded by Soltuss Yow. She knew where to position the battleship to keep it from becoming a target of the Dissident Faction's ground laser cannon. It was a large ship with plenty of weaponry. Its deflector shields were already engaged when they arrived. With a docking bay on either side of the battleship, it was able to accommodate twenty fighter ships, with ten in each bay. All twenty fighter ships launched from the docking bays as soon as *Wings of Shardaa* exited lightspeed, each with their own target list. Although the Dissident Faction was taken by surprise, Gramer Moss quickly launched their fighter ships in response. Speeding from the surface of S3, they met the incoming opposition. Several of the Humolfan Command fighter ships were en route to a power station to destroy it. A few more were approaching a weapons factory on their target list. The remaining Humolfan Command fighters engaged the ten Dissident Faction fighters in an intense exchange of laser fire. Every chance the gunners aboard *Wings of Shardaa* could get, they would fire the battleship's laser cannons at the enemy fighters, picking off several. The darkness of space was lit up with intense blue laser fire as a barrage of beams struck several of the Dissident Faction ships. Two exploded with an extremely bright burst of energy and disintegrated into space dust. Three of the Dissident Faction fighters engaged with the Humolfan Command fighters and destroyed them with clean shots. The space battle raged on between the two groups as several of the Humolfan Command fighters moved toward their specific targets at the power station and the weapons factory.

Suddenly, the Syrenthian Brotherhood Knights of Darkness group exited from lightspeed at S3 in twenty distinctly different fighter ships. The ground laser cannon was fired and immediately took out two of them before they could react. They quickly maneuvered away from the path of the laser cannon. Ironically, the cannon itself was their primary target. The remaining eighteen fighter ships quickly flew toward the surface of the planet and began their attack against the weapon. After several passes of blasting their lasers at the cannon, it exploded with a cloud of fire that spread high into the sky. Shrapnel from the explosion flew in every direction. One sharp, metal panel lodged itself in the underbelly of a Syrenthian Brotherhood Knights of Darkness fighter ship. The pilot looked down at the sharp, jagged piece of metal that suddenly appeared between his legs, just missing him. The pilot knew landing the ship would be a death sentence because it would push the jagged piece of metal farther up into his ship, slicing right into him. Once the large ground laser cannon was destroyed, their targets were the Dissident Faction strongholds on the ground. Along with half of his fellow pilots, he began to fire directly into the armored gates of the Dissident Faction strongholds. The other half of the fighter ships landed to begin a ground assault against the forces of the strongholds. Of the ten strongholds, they were specifically told not to destroy stronghold number nine. As the last of the gates were destroyed, the shrapnel embedded in the fighter ship suddenly fell out and landed on the ground far below. The pilot looked down with a sense of extreme relief. The remaining ships landed to help in the ground assault.

The concussions of the assault continued to shake the strongholds next to number nine where Inatharr Taw was located. He sat with a few of the other Dissident Faction members, looking at the computer display. He suddenly picked up a comm and quickly changed frequencies.

"Mom… This is Inatharr. We are under attack by Dad's forces. I don't think I'm going to make it. Please know that I love you and that I'm sorry for everything."

Before she could respond the power died and the comm went dead. "Mom? *Mom?*"

Emergency illumination brightened the room Inatharr was in. The other members looked at him in a strange manner.

"Your dad did this? You mean, your dad is Yilran Taw? You're a traitor to our movement!" one of them said.

They immediately ran over to him in the dimly lit room and began to beat him profusely. After several blows to the face, he fell to the floor. They continued to attack him while he was down, repeatedly kicking him. His black wings became mangled and broken. Blood drained from his nose and mouth. The attackers quickly left the stronghold to escape a potential assault.

In space, the battle raged on. The remaining Humolfan Command fighter ships methodically destroyed each of the Dissident Faction fighters. After the last of the Dissident Faction fighter ships was destroyed, they returned to the docking bays on the *Wings of Shardaa*. The fighter ships that had destroyed the power station and the weapons factory joined the others in the docking bays soon afterward. The battleship personnel were ready to join the forces on the ground. Soltuss Yow began the descent through the atmosphere of S3. She landed the battleship in a clearing at the edge of the fortress structures. The military personnel exited the ship, spread their wings, and flew to help the Syrenthian Brotherhood Knights of Darkness members against the occupants of the strongholds. The Humolfan Command officers could see far ahead of them that the entire group of Syrenthian Brotherhood Knights of Darkness had come under attack. A Dissident Faction member was shooting at them with a laser rifle from an upper level of a stronghold building. The Syrenthian Brotherhood Knights of Darkness members quickly returned fire and struck the individual. He fell from the upper level to the concrete below with a thud. A few more of the Dissident Faction members leaped from a roof, spreading their black wings in flight and targeting the ground forces with laser rifles. They were met with much greater laser fire and shot down from the sky. The three Dissident Faction members fell to the concrete with a splat, smoke pouring up from their wings.

A medium-sized, sleek ship with the name *Sharlexx* displayed on the side could be seen landing in the background. A group of Dissident Faction members moved out from various structures and began to encroach upon the Syrenthian Brotherhood Knights of Darkness. Most Dissident Faction members were on the ground, but some were in the air. Those that flew were an easy target for the Syrenthian Brotherhood Knights of Darkness. The two opposing groups of ground forces clashed. Many of the Dissident Faction members were met with laser fire. Some of them carried long staves. They were successful in impaling a couple of the Syrenthian Brotherhood Knights of Darkness members. Once other members saw they were being stabbed by the Dissident Faction, they literally began to pound the Dissident Faction member's faces with their gloved fists. The beatings continued. Objects were thrown at the incoming forces. With so many people in close proximity, the Syrenthian Brotherhood Knights of Darkness slung their laser rifles over their shoulders and began using their laser pistols. The bloody altercation lasted for some time. As more bodies fell to the ground from both sides, the diminished numbers who remained standing became easy targets. Soon, every Dissident Faction member that was outside attacking the Syrenthian Brotherhood Knights of Darkness was down. The twelve remaining members of the Syrenthian Brotherhood Knights of Darkness walked among the bodies that littered the street. The Humolfan Command officers soon caught up to the group and landed on the ground, retracting their wings. The Humolfan Command officers began the process of clearing the fortress structures, one at a time. Within a relatively short time, they only had stronghold number nine and ten yet to clear. Suddenly, a woman came out from the destruction of stronghold number ten. It was Gramer Moss, leader of the Dissident Faction. She held a very large laser cannon in her hands and limped out of the rubble. The muzzle of her weapon was pointed to the ground. She was disoriented and looked around at the destruction of the strongholds. Gramer noticed that stronghold number nine was left undamaged. All of the dead bodies that littered the street came into full view as she rounded a corner. A dozen laser rifles were pointed at her as she slowly limped forward. Her left wing was broken and hung low, scraping against the ground as she limped along. In her condition, the weight of the large laser cannon she held was too great for her to even lift it up. Her arms and legs trembled as she dropped the weapon to the ground. She continued walking a few more steps before collapsing to her knees. She looked up at the forces pointing their rifles at her. A surge of lightning flashed across the gray sky as a storm began to approach.

"Shoot me. Please, just kill me," Gramer Moss said as blood dripped from her mouth.

She looked up at all of them and noticed they were staring at a new person who had emerged from stronghold number nine. The forces of Operation Reprisal weren't sure why they were told by Yilran Taw not to destroy that particular structure. A young Humolfan man emerged from stronghold number nine. They did not shoot at him. He was also injured, but it could not have been from them since they did not fire on stronghold number nine. He walked over to Gramer Moss and looked down at her.

"Inatharr? What are you doing?" Gramer asked. Blood sprayed out of her mouth as she spoke.

"I believed in your cause. I tried to fit in. Apparently, my background mattered to the Dissident Faction. I wasn't good enough for your movement. Your members attacked me because of who I am. I just wanted to be a part of something. But it didn't matter. I've seen your shit for long enough and I don't want to be a part of it anymore,"

Inatharr said.

A new figure, dressed in a blue military uniform, appeared from the medium-sized, sleek ship, *Sharlexx*. He soared through the air toward the group.

Gramer Moss looked up at Inatharr. "Who *are* you?" Gramer asked him.

The figure landed on the ground near Gramer Moss, his black wings retracting. She looked up at the new arrival.

"He's my son."

"Yilran Taw?"

"The Dissident Faction has been offered on multiple occasions to be left in isolation here on S3 since you did not want to assimilate with the rest of the galaxy. Nothing was good enough for you. Your organization killed innocent people, destroyed property, and tried to prevent us from repatriating back into galactic society for years and years. Every prospect we have found to advocate for us, the Dissident Faction has either killed or tried to kill. You have shed enough blood and the Dissident Faction is over!"

"I hate you!" Gramer screamed.

"The feeling is mutual," Yilran said.

Gramer Moss was on her knees in pain as she reached for a rifle in the hands of the dead body on the ground next to her. As she gripped the weapon, a Humolfan Command officer shot her in the head, the blue laser slicing through her brain. She slumped over dead.

"I'm sorry, Dad. I didn't know what I was getting into until I was in too deep," Inatharr said.

Yilran looked at his son. He could see that he had been severely beaten. "I love you, Inatharr."

One of the Dissident Faction members from stronghold number nine who had participated in beating Inatharr was lying on the ground nearby, badly wounded, but not dead. He leaned up from the ground with a laser pistol and shot Inatharr in the chest. Inatharr fell to the ground, clutching the hole in his chest. A storm of laser fire from the Humolfan Command officers completely destroyed the Dissident Faction member who shot him.

Yilran ran over to his son's side. He immediately saw the laser hole in his chest. Their eyes met in a heartbreaking moment.

"I love you too, Dad," Inatharr said as he breathed his last breath.

Inatharr's eyes remained open, staring up at the turbulent, gray clouds in the sky.

Yilran knelt over his son and began to sob heavily as he hugged him tight. Once again, lightning flashed across the gray sky. Suddenly, cold rain began to fall. In the soaking rain, Yilran held his lifeless son. Argenniss and the remaining Syrenthian Brotherhood Knights of Darkness members and Soltuss Yow and the Humolfan Command officers stood surrounding Yilran as he cried in the rain.

The Syrenthian Government armada exited lightspeed-plus and entered the Shardaa Sector. The Sharasp Tharrian Asteroid Mass had moved along its orbit and was completely out of their way when they arrived. The ten battleships traveled onward toward S3.

"Enable deflector shields. Gunners, stand by. I want the *Linerston, Truliniot, and Godspeed* to take out the ground laser cannon that was reported. Fighter pilots from all ten battleships, prepare your SG302s for launch on my mark," Admiral Lytria Foss commanded.

As S3 loomed ahead of them, the captains of the battleships took their assigned positions in orbit around S3. There was no sign of incoming fighter ships.

"Scan the planet and report," Admiral Lytria Foss told one of the personnel on the bridge of the *Syrenth.*

"I'm not reading any life forms, Admiral."

Lytria had a strange look on her face. "Put me through to Captain Arbin Xaanoss of the *Dignity.*"

"Right away, Admiral. Okay, you're connected."

"Captain Xaanoss. You and Braxton Stryderr did mention that you were attacked from forces on the planet of S3, did you not?"

"Yes. We were attacked. And now nothing…" Captain Arbin Xaanoss said.

"There are no life forms on the planet, Captain Xaanoss," Admiral Lytria Foss said.

"Would you like me to send in a team to check it out?" Captain Xaanoss asked.

"Affirmative, Captain," Admiral Foss said.

"I'll get a team down there right away."

As the entire fleet drifted in orbit, ready for battle, a single shuttle departed one of the docking bays on the *Dignity.* Braxton and several armed officers were aboard. The shuttle made its way through the gray clouds toward several structures in the distance. Braxton could see from the observation window that major destruction had occurred.

What the hell? he thought.

Once the shuttle landed, the armed officers exited with their laser rifles drawn. They scanned to the left and to the right. The only movement was a slight breeze that made its way along the street. Braxton walked along the street and inspected blood stains on the concrete, along with what appeared to be black feathers scattered about. Although it looked as if rain had washed some of the blood into streams of red in the open areas along the street, Braxton was able to decipher from the washed patterns that it was indeed blood. He entered each of the destroyed strongholds and one that was still intact. There were no bodies to be found.

He turned on his comm. "Something bad happened down here. The area has been cleared of bodies, but there is overwhelming evidence of a battle that took place here. Damaged structures, blood soaked streets, and odd feathers scattered about is what we are finding," Braxton said.

Odd feathers... Wait! Priscilla mentioned that Sierra had seen odd feather symbols, Braxton thought.

"This is some weird shit out here in the middle of a desolate region of space," Braxton said.

"Our scanners have confirmed the ground laser cannon that you told us about is totally destroyed," Admiral Foss said.

"Some of the markings painted on the structures indicate this place belonged to Dissident Faction," Braxton reported. "We are going to investigate further. I'll report back soon."

The team thoroughly checked the entire fortress again and found no explanation of what had taken place. Next to the destroyed fortress, a docking bay lay in ruins. There was only one ship under the rubble. It was totally flattened and unrecognizable. Farther out from the structures, Braxton and the team found a destroyed power station and what appeared to have been a weapons factory. After walking along a bit farther, Braxton stopped and looked in the distance at the flat grasslands and rocky areas as a breeze blew toward them. Suddenly, a metal clank noise came from behind them. The officers swirled around with their laser rifles drawn. One of the stronghold doors had fallen off its hinges from the gust of wind and landed on the concrete.

They each relaxed a bit.

"Admiral, there's nothing here but the remains of death and destruction. We are heading back up to the fleet to convene," Braxton said.

"Roger that," Admiral Foss said.

Braxton scanned the destruction one last time with a quick glance and headed for the shuttle with his team.

Captain Arbin Xaanoss and Braxton Stryderr of the *Dignity* met with Admiral Lytria Foss and Captain Roth Sirron of the *Syrenth*. They met in a conference room aboard the *Syrenth*.

"When we came to the Shardaa Sector looking for Sierra Shalinsky, we were attacked by forces from S3, including fighter ships and that ground laser cannon. It appears that someone else cleaned up the aggressors for us. But whom?" Braxton asked.

"That is a good question. There is something here that does not meet the eye," Captain Xaanoss said.

"Dennon Cobalt did mention that it seemed as if two different forces were against each other out here," Braxton said.

"This elusiveness has the entire fleet on edge. They were all told to relax for the moment," Admiral Foss said.

The comm sounded. "Captain Sirron, we are receiving an urgent message from an approaching ship," the officer said.

"Put it through!" Captain Roth Sirron said.

"This is Sierra Shalinsky aboard the *Sharlexx*. I am approaching to meet with you. Please do not fire on this ship. It looks like a Syrenthian Government armada from my vantage point. Is that correct?"

Braxton reached over to the comm. "*Sierra! Sierra!* This is Braxton. We've been searching for you for so long. What are you doing out here in the Shardaa Sector? Are you currently in distress?"

"Braxton! Oh my, it is so good to hear your voice. I am no longer in distress as I was when I sent the emergency distress signal out a while ago. Oh, do I have a lot of stuff to discuss with you all. Can we land on one of your battleships?"

"Yes. Land in starboard docking bay of the *Syrenth*. We'll meet you down there. Are you alone?" Braxton asked.

"No. I have Yilran Taw with me. He is the leader of the Humolfan

Government."
    "The *what* Government?" Braxton questioned.

CHAPTER ELEVEN

THE *SHARLEXX* LANDED in the starboard docking bay of the *Syrenth*. Sierra and Yilran stepped out into the docking bay. Sierra was familiar with large space vessels, like the *Deliverance* hospital ship with her job at Galactic Emergency Medical Services. Yilran, however, had never seen a spaceship that large before. The ship was much larger than the Humolfan Command ship, *Wings of Shardaa*. He found himself looking up at the beams high above the floor and to the catwalk that crossed over to a control platform. Several humans walked down a metal stairway from the platform toward the docking bay floor. Admiral Lytria Foss, Captain Roth Sirron, Captain Arbin Xaanoss, and Braxton Stryderr approached Sierra and Yilran. It wasn't until they reached half the distance across the floor that they all halted in their tracks. The confusion expressed on their faces was very evident. They slowly proceeded forward with caution.

"Are those wings?" Admiral Foss finally asked.

"They are," Yilran said.

"But…" It was all that Captain Xaanoss could manage.

"What species are you?" Captain Sirron asked.

"My name is Yilran Taw. My species is Humolfan. We live in the Shardaa Sector. I am the leader of the Humolfan Government."

Admiral Lytria Foss rested her hand on a pistol at her side. "So, you are the ones that attacked us?"

"Attacked you? No. If you were attacked, it would have been from the Dissident Faction. They have caused so much trouble throughout the years, it's unbelievable. We recently destroyed them. They stood in the way of our repatriation back into galactic society," Yilran said.

"So, the damage we discovered on S3 during our investigation was from you eliminating them?" Braxton asked.

"That is correct," Yilran said. "They were given many opportunities to stay isolated if they chose to, but they tried to stop us from going back into the rest of the galaxy."

"Repatriation? You mean, your species was originally from somewhere else in the Syrenthian Galaxy?" Admiral Foss asked. She relaxed her hand away from the pistol.

"Can we all sit down and go over the details?" Sierra asked.

"Yes. Let's head up to the conference room and you can explain everything in detail," Captain Roth Sirron said.

"By the way, Yilran, this is Braxton Stryderr, an investigator for the Syrenthian Government and a good friend of mine. And since I'm not familiar with the rest of you, I'll let you all introduce yourselves," Sierra said.

"I'm Admiral Lytria Foss."

"My name is Captain Roth Sirron of this battleship, *Syrenth*."

"I am Captain Arbin Xaanoss of the *Dignity*."

"It's nice to meet you all," Yilran said.

Sierra and Yilran were led up the steps. Admiral Lytria Foss walked behind them, as a precautionary measure. They were led through a series of corridors to the conference room.

"I am amazed at the size of this ship. As we approached, I noticed the battleships in your armada are all the same class. This fleet is very impressive," Yilran said.

"Thank you," Admiral Foss said. "Here we are. It's that last door on the right."

The door swiftly slid aside and they all stepped into the conference room. Yilran adjusted his wings as he sat down.

"Sierra, you have been missing for eight months or more. The Syrenthian Government has looked for you, Priscilla and I have looked for you, your parents have looked for you, your fellow EMTs at GEMS have looked for you, and your bandmates from Maranadda have looked for you. You do realize you have a lot of people worried sick over you, right?" Braxton asked.

The expression on Sierra's face was one of sadness, caring, and thankfulness all wrapped together. A few tears began to flow down her cheeks.

"It means a great deal to me that you all care for me that much. You see, I was in a coma for seven of those months. I only recently woke. That is when I sent out the distress signal. That is before I knew what I was involved with. But now that I know the truth of what really happened…it has changed my life forever," Sierra said.

"If you were in a coma, who took care of you? And where were you? The distress signal came from S2," Braxton said.

"The distress signal did originate from S2. After I awoke from my coma, I was on the run from S6. I later discovered that when the Humolfan scout sought me out on Red Jacket after the Maranadda concert, I had fallen and hit my head on the concrete. I was brought to S6 to be cared for. They sought me out to advocate for their species. I was also attacked by the Dissident Faction on a couple of occasions, once on S2 and again on Shardia. That second assault almost killed me, but Yilran here saved my life," Sierra said, smiling at Yilran.

"Shardia?" Captain Xaanoss inquired.

"It is the seventh planet in the Shardaa Star System. That is where my government palace is located within the city of Naantress," Yilran said.

"So, there are more than six planets in the system?" Admiral Foss asked.

"Yes," Yilran said.

"So, when you spoke of repatriation, what exactly were you referring to?" Admiral Foss asked.

"Us Humolfans are the product of relationships between humans and Xenolfans from one thousand years ago…back when Xenolfans had wings and could breed with humans. But we were forced into isolation in the Shardaa Sector by Siiteper Affelum," Yilran said.

"How many of you are there?" Captain Sirron asked.

"Seventeen million," Yilran said.

"We came to the Shardaa Sector looking for you earlier, Sierra, and came across something called the Grave of Mothers on S4. Can you explain what that is all about?" Braxton asked.

"I'll let Yilran explain everything," Sierra said. "But he recently lost his son, so bare with him as he is a bit emotional right now."

Yilran sighed. "It all started a thousand years ago…"

During their long meeting in the conference room aboard the *Syrenth*, the officers of the Syrenthian Government fleet were astonished. Sierra explained to them her plan to advocate for the Humolfans before they mixed back in with galactic society. She told them her plans to have the entire Humolfan population tested for STIs and treated, if necessary, so any potential infections were not re-introduced to the STI-free population of the galaxy. Yilran Taw mentioned that he was going to have a speech with his people to prepare them for the upcoming repatriation. He would require his people to go through the STI testing process. Yilran mentioned that he was going to have a large number of history books from the atheneum mass printed and distributed to the rest of the galaxy in order to give them the truth about the Humolfans. He said the idea was a suggestion of Sierra and her friend Estrus. It was explained that some Humolfans planned to move from the Shardaa Sector, but most considered it their home. The Syrenthian Government officials realized this new freedom for the Humolfans to travel outside the Shardaa Sector was a very significant event for them, which they had literally waited centuries to achieve. They also realized that humans and Xenolfans would be able to discover new worlds in the Shardaa Sector as well. In the meeting, they discussed how the strange occurrences that have been associated with the Shardaa Sector over the years would need to be explained as being caused by the Dissident Faction. Admiral Lytria Foss decided it was best for the fleet to travel back to Exandra with all the information and call for an emergency council with the Syrenthian Government leader, Edward Sirlain, and the Xenolfan Government leader, Phensiarr Charseaa. Yilran Taw also planned to be in contact with the other two governments regarding a smooth repatriation. They would then be prepared for Sierra's advocating.

"So, I see that you are quite taken to Yilran," Estrus said.

"Oh, Estrus… He is the best man I've ever met. It's really sad about his son," Sierra said.

"Yes, it is. But I am also pleased that the Dissident Faction has been eradicated from the galaxy. After what they did to my mom, I have no sympathy for any of them," Estrus said.

"I don't blame you. Yes, Yilran is quite something," Sierra said. She stared off into the distance with a smile.

Estrus noticed Sierra's expression. "Did you two…?"

"Oh, I wanted to, believe me. He wants to wait a little longer."

"Ha! What a tease," Estrus said, laughing.

"The anticipation gets me wet all the time. We are dating. We talked about my advocating strategy at great length before I left Shardia."

"Nice."

"So, do you have all your things packed? I'm not sure when we'll be back here on S6," Sierra said.

"I have everything I'll need," Estrus said.

"Hey, bring some Ginger Alquinola."

"No! You've had enough of that stuff."

They both laughed. Estrus held a large duffel bag in her hand. She looked down at her dog, Thepsi. He tilted his fluffy head and looked at Estrus with what appeared to be tears in his eyes. She set the bag down and kneeled on the floor.

"Oh Thepsi… You look so sad and so adorable at the same time. Mommy's going away for a little while, but don't you worry. I'll be back as soon as I can. Soltuss is going to come here and take care of you every day. Don't you worry about that, little guy. I'm going to miss you. Mommy loves you. Give me a kiss."

Thepsi licked her face a few times and she gave the dog a long hug. She stood up, grabbed her bag, and they left her quarters.

"I never asked you where in the Shardaa Sector dogs come from," Sierra said as they walked along the corridor toward the docking bay.

"There are no dogs naturally here in the Shardaa Sector. Narris, who is one of the Syrenthian Brotherhood Knights of Darkness, brought Thepsi back here to me from Enax Port, I believe. We do have other indigenous animals, however…some of which we use as sources of meat. I'm so glad Narris survived Operation Reprisal. Many of the Syrenthian Brotherhood Knights of Darkness members did not," Estrus said.

After they entered the docking bay, Soltuss Yow met them near the *Aileron*. Estrus's ship looked cleaned up for the long voyage, the overhead illuminators reflecting from its polished surface.

"Well, Soltuss, we are off to do some advocating. I trust you will take good care of Thepsi for me," Estrus said.

"I am head of the Humolfan Command. I'm sure a little dog isn't going to be a problem."

Images of Thepsi getting into pretty much everything popped into Estrus's head.

"I hope not," Estrus said.

"I got this," Soltuss said. "I'll even pet him for you."

"Thank you, Soltuss," Estrus said.

"Good luck and safe travels."

"Thanks," Estrus said.

"Bye," Sierra said.

They entered the *Aileron* and prepared for launch. The ship was facing the docking bay exit. As Sierra sat there staring out the observation window at the beautiful mountains in the distance, she could not help but think of the mission that she was about to embark on. How would the rest of the galaxy react to these new people? Would they be receptive or would they reject them? The *Aileron* launched and Sierra was pushed back in her seat.

"Here we go! So, where is our first stop?" Estrus asked.

The ship flew past the majestic mountains and ascended through the blue sky toward space.

"Our first stop will be one of our largest human sex clinics that I helped to establish. They are all over the Syrenthian Galaxy for both humans and Xenolfans. I need to talk to Dr. Givinis to see how we can coordinate all seventeen million Humolfans to get testing for sexually transmitted infections. One of the reasons I helped set up these clinics across the galaxy was to eliminate STIs from the galaxy by having all of our population get testing and treatment at the same time through a scheduled program that saw everyone. It took some time, but we did it. Now, the galaxy is STI-free. I spoke with Yilran Taw regarding this as being one of the conditions for me to advocate. The Humolfans must all be checked for STIs and treated, if necessary, so the rest of the galaxy is protected."

"That sounds like a big undertaking," Estrus said.

"I'm sure it will be much easier than what we've already done," Sierra said. "So, let me tell you what other purpose the sex clinics serve. I think you're going to like this."

Estrus made an adjustment on the control panel and the ship changed to lightspeed-plus.

"Why is that?" Estrus asked.

"The Syrenthian Government and the Xenolfan Government both finally recognized the importance of sexual release as medically healthy and necessary. So, the other purpose the sex clinics serve is to help humans and Xenolfans release their sexual tension with manual and oral stimulation," Sierra said.

"Seriously? Wow! That sounds exciting. You know how sexual I am. How has that worked for both species?" Estrus asked.

"It has been very successful. Some people have high sex drives and others have no other companions to help them sexually," Sierra said. "All the medical costs are covered by the respective governments."

"Okay, Sierra, now I'm getting aroused."

"They can certainly accommodate your problem."

"What about my appearance?"

"That's why we are arriving early, before they open for appointments."

The *Aileron* landed at a space station located in the Galeva Krove Star System. Other than the station itself, there wasn't much in the system, except a few small planetoids and a planet that shared the same name. The planet, Galeva Krove, had a ring of frozen ice and rock around it. The station itself was one of the largest sex clinics in the Syrenthian Galaxy. The facility was also the administration building for all the sex clinics. The docking bay was large enough to accommodate many ships for the various clients. Estrus had nothing to disguise her Humolfan appearance as they exited the ship. She was nervous as they walked across the bay toward the offices. She tried to pull her wings together slightly, but realized it didn't make much difference. Besides, with the difference in skin tone, there was no hiding that she was different. As they approached the office entrance, Sierra noticed the anxiety that began to overwhelm Estrus.

"Estrus, you need to relax. People will get over the initial shock eventually. If the Humolfans are going to mix in with the rest of the galaxy, you are all going to have to be comfortable with yourselves and not give a shit what other people think," Sierra said.

"You're right, Sierra."

"Are you ready?"

Estrus took a deep breath. "Yes."

They entered the clinic. Since they had arrived before any clients, the waiting room was empty. They walked up to the front desk. The human woman who sat there looked up at the two of them and then move back in her chair about a half meter as she gasped.

"Hi. I need to speak with Dr. Givinis immediately," Sierra said.

"What are you?" the receptionist asked.

"I am a Humolfan," Estrus said.

"It's a long story. I'm sure you will be filled in with all the details soon enough. If you could get Dr. Givinis…" Sierra said.

"Yes, right away," the receptionist said.

She reached over to the comm with a shaky hand.

"Let her know Sierra Shalinsky is here to see her."

The receptionist's jaw dropped when she realized it was Sierra Shalinsky. "Dr. Givinis. Umm, *the* Sierra Shalinsky is here to see you. And she has a…guest with her." She turned to the two of them. "She'll be right out."

They both sat down in the waiting room. Soon, a door opened to reveal an older female human doctor. When the doctor walked out into the waiting room to greet them, she also looked shocked at seeing Estrus.

"Hi, Dr. Givinis. It's been a long time. I would like you to meet Estrus. She is a Humolfan," Sierra said.

"A *what?*" Dr. Givinis asked.

"A Humolfan. The Humolfan species is a crossbreed between humans and Xenolfans," Sierra said.

"But…humans and Xenolfans cannot breed together," Dr. Givinis said.

"It's a long story," Sierra said.

"How about we go into my office to discuss it?"

An hour later, Dr. Givinis knew the entire story and was taken aback by the new information.

"Well, Estrus, it sure is an honor to meet my very first Humolfan," Dr. Givinis said. She shook Estrus's gray hand.

"Okay, moving on to other things that I came here to discuss with you…" Sierra said.

"Well, I'm very happy that you have been found and are safe, Sierra. Whether you know it or not, you are very popular in the galaxy. Many of us have been very concerned about you. I still remember when we met during your push for these sex clinics. You are a hero in our community," Dr. Givinis said.

"Thank you. I need to be tested for STIs, as I have had sex with two Humolfans, Estrus being one of them. Since their entire population has not been tested, it is a precautionary measure. Estrus should be tested as well. And we need to discuss how we are going to schedule their entire population to be tested," Sierra said.

"Okay. We can certainly test you both for STIs. Assuming there are no new infections within their species that we are not aware of, we have you covered. So, how many people are we talking about?" Dr. Givinis asked.

"Seventeen million," Estrus said.

Dr. Givinis did a few calculations on the computer and looked up at them. "It will take about two and a half months with two shifts of ten doctors at over ten thousand of our larger clinics and four patients per hour. We have done this before on a larger scale with humans and Xenolfans. So, since this will be an immediate need, let me get all of the schedules and logistics in place so we will be ready for it."

"With everything that has been established with a galaxy free from STIs, I felt this is a necessary first step in the Humolfan repatriation," Sierra said.

"Definitely. We can also have additional doctors available to check for any other, non-sexual, diseases. So, are you two ready for your tests?" Dr. Givinis asked.

"Yes," Sierra said.

"I also want to do another test to see if Humolfans can breed with humans and Xenolfans. I'll have the nurse do that one as well and inform you of the results when I get them back," Dr. Givinis said.

"Okay. Also, assuming the STI test results are fine, we are both interested in receiving sexual release," Sierra said.

Estrus gave Sierra a look of concern.

"I assume until there is a public announcement, you want to keep a low profile. We certainly can do it, but if we are to fit you both in before any of the clients arrive, we'll need to put you together with the nurse," Dr. Givinis said.

"Actually, I think that will work out quite nice," Sierra said. She smiled at Estrus.

"The nurse today is a Xenolfan named Versi"

"Since when are Xenolfans at human sex clinics?" Sierra asked.

"Oh, a few months ago, we had a ruling that opened the human and Xenolfan clinics to each other for clients and workers. Phensiarr Charseaa actually suggested it. You know, we have needed a leader like her running the Xenolfan Government on Olf Teruda for a long, long time," Dr. Givinis said.

"That's incredible news. I'm happy to hear it," Sierra said.

"Well, let's get you both tested. Let me have a brief meeting with my staff so they know what to expect…including the receptionist. I'll be right back," Dr. Givinis said.

A short time later, the doctor returned to her office where Sierra and Estrus waited.

"Okay, they now have a brief understanding of what's going on. Right this way," Dr. Givinis said.

They both followed the doctor out of her office and down a corridor to a room on the right.

"Good luck with everything, Sierra. We will be ready for the Humolfan STI testing soon. Assuming your test results are negative, enjoy your time with the nurse," Dr. Givinis said.

"Take care, Dr. Givinis," Sierra said.

As the door slid aside, they walked into the patient room. It was a larger room with two exam tables. A Xenolfan nurse turned toward them as they entered. Although Dr. Givinis had briefly mentioned Estrus and the Humolfans, seeing Estrus in person was quite interesting for the nurse.

"Hi. My name is Versi. It is a pleasure to meet both of you. Sierra, I've heard so much about your work. And Estrus, this is a historic moment. When the Humolfans are publicly announced, I want to hear the speech. It sounds like there is so much to learn," Versi said.

"Thank you," Sierra said.

"So, let me get your testing done," Versi said. "First, I will do the breeding test."

Versi took some blood samples from Estrus and ran them through a machine. She then grabbed a device and held it up to each of their upper arms. The results were displayed.

"Dr. Givinis will contact you on the results of the breeding test. You are both negative for all known STIs," Versi said.

"Good. That's nice to know," Estrus said.

"Now that we have the testing out of the way, I understand we are doing a double arrangement with both of you at the same time so you can leave before our first appointments arrive," Versi said.

"That is correct," Sierra said.

"Okay. I'll have you both remove your clothes and relax on the exam tables. Will this be manual or oral?" Versi asked.

"Definitely oral," Sierra said.

Sierra and Estrus removed their clothing and set the items on the counter. Versi started with Sierra by gently rubbing her bluish-gray hands along Sierra's tan thighs and gently stroking Sierra's labia with both thumbs. Sierra needed to be touched so badly.

"Cool feathers tattoo," Versi said.

"Thanks. Estrus has one just like it," Sierra said.

As Versi stroked Sierra's pussy with her bluish-gray Xenolfan fingers, the sensations sent through Sierra were incredible. Versi leaned in and began to lick at Sierra's wetness, her long tongue thrusting against Sierra's clit. Sierra caressed her own beautiful, tan breasts. From the second exam table, Estrus watched with pure excitement. Versi swirled her long tongue around Sierra's pussy with quick, repetitive motions. Sierra pointed her toes in the air and moaned loudly. Versi looked up at Sierra with her sapphire eyes. Sierra looked down at Versi and closed her eyes. As she reached a slight orgasm, she pushed her pussy upward from the table.

"Mmm… That was nice," Sierra said.

"Thank you," Versi said.

"By the way, I will need some contraceptives while I'm here. I've been off from them for many months."

"I will hook you up with some before you leave," Versi said.

Versi stood up, grabbed a towel, and wiped her face. She then moved over to Estrus and took a long look at this new species. Estrus's black wings were gently tucked under her back.

"Indeed you do have the exact same tattoo. Is there a story behind this?" Versi asked.

"Every Humolfan woman has a Feathers of Shardaa tattoo. It is a coming-of-age ritual for the females of my people. Sierra was inked in order to honor my people," Estrus said.

"I see. Well, I'm honored to be the first nurse at the sex clinics to pleasure a Humolfan. I see Humolfans also have reuleaux triangular genitalia. This is so exciting!" Versi said.

"One in thirty-five thousand Humolfans have human-like genitalia. So, there are about five hundred of us that are not like this, about half of that being female. Hey, do all Xenolfans have long tongues, like yours?" Estrus asked.

"Yes, we do. The women even more so... We all make high-pitched, reverberating moans during orgasm as well," Versi said.

Estrus recalled Sierra telling her about their high-pitched moans when they were in her quarters back on S6. Versi gently rubbed Estrus's gray pussy. Her touch felt so very nice.

"I'm not used to the wings. Let me know if you need to adjust yourself to a more comfortable position," Versi said.

"I'm fine," Estrus said, breathing heavily. "I've never seen a Xenolfan pussy before. Do you mind?"

"We have a no-touch policy, but I suppose I can show you for educational purposes," Versi said.

Versi slid her pants down and pulled up on the top of her bluish-gray vulva. Estrus saw the similar reuleaux triangular vagina and immediately felt a pleasant connection between the two species. After pulling her pants back up, Versi slowly went down on Estrus and sucked along the gray labia folds. It was like her own bluish-gray pussy, except a nice warm gray color. Versi found it quite exciting to eat the pussy of this new species. She found her job as a sex clinic nurse to be very satisfying. As Versi concentrated her long tongue against Estrus's clitoris, Estrus slowly gyrated her hips. Versi looked up at the large, gray boobs and saw Estrus smiling back at her. A kindred bond could be felt between them as Versi looked into the familiar sapphire eyes and at the familiar white hair. She looked away and concentrated on performing cunnilingus. Moving her head side to side, Versi added pressure with her tongue.

"Oh, that feels so good. Yes, right there. Right there! Ohhh!" Estrus moaned as an orgasm gripped her entire body.

Versi stood up and, once again, wiped her mouth on the towel.

"You two can freshen up in the bathroom and then get dressed," Versi said.

When Sierra and Estrus were finished, the nurse went into the back bathroom, washed her face, and used a minty solution to wash her mouth. When she returned to the patient room, Sierra and Estrus were almost finished getting dressed.

"This was very exciting for me, ladies. Thank you for this opportunity to serve," Versi said.

"It was exciting for us as well," Estrus said.

After Versi gave Sierra her contraceptives, they left the patient room and followed Versi toward the exit.

"Come again," Versi said.

Sierra and Estrus met Dr. Givinis in the waiting area.

"I saw the STI test results. By the moans coming from the patient room, I take it you found everything satisfying," Dr. Givinis said.

"We did," Sierra said.

"Yes! It is so nice that you offer that type of service for those who need it," Estrus said.

"We will be ready for the influx of Humolfan patients," Dr. Givinis said.

"Good luck with everything. Now, I need to go arrange a press conference," Sierra said.

"Good luck with that as well," Dr. Givinis said. "I will get back with you on the results of the breeding blood test when it is finished. You can be confident that none of my staff will reveal the existence of Humolfans until after we publicly hear it from you. I've spoken with them about that as well."

After their farewell, Sierra and Estrus left the office and returned to the *Aileron*. Sierra took one of the monthly contraceptive pills that she received. In the occasion she had sex with a human male, she would be all set. Just as the *Aileron* exited the docking bay, two ships landed for the first appointments of the day.

"That was close. We got in your ship just in time. We want to have the conference before a bunch of random people begin to see a species they don't understand," Sierra said.

"Definitely," Estrus said. "So, the services at the sex clinics are pretty satisfying."

"Yeah…" Sierra hesitated. "For some reason, I just wasn't feeling it this time."

"Your mind is on Yilran," Estrus said.

"Perhaps…"

"Oh Sierra, it's so nice to see you. We were hoping to hear from you soon. The Syrenthian Government and the Xenolfan Government recently had an emergency council meeting regarding the Humolfan repatriation and both our governments are prepared to stand with you for your advocating. You have lead on this, so just let me know what you need and I'll get right on it," Braxton said.

Sierra and Estrus took a seat at the conference room table. Braxton Stryderr sat with them in the administration building on Exandra.

"Okay. What I would like to do is hold a public press conference and give a speech that advocates for the Humolfan people. I will have Estrus with me and we can explain everything and how it will be implemented. I need Edward Sirlain and Phensiarr Charseaa at the conference so the people of the Syrenthian Galaxy know this is serious and there should be no discrimination toward the Humolfans. They've been through enough over the years. I want nothing more than this to be a smooth process," Sierra said.

"We will have your back," Braxton said.

"So, let's schedule my advocating speech on Olf Teruda next week and make an announcement for the press conference. I choose Olf Teruda because that is where this all began one thousand years ago," Sierra said.

"That's an excellent idea, Sierra," Estrus said.

"I will contact Phensiarr Charseaa right away. Do you have a speech ready?" Braxton asked.

Sierra thought back to how long it took her to prepare her sexual freedom speech. She did not have that kind of time.

"Not exactly. I'll just improvise," Sierra said. "Estrus will help me out."

"Well…good luck. I'll see you on Olf Teruda in a week," Braxton said.

Sierra and Estrus exited the *Aileron* and were greeted by a welcoming party. The humidity on Olf Teruda was tremendous. Both Sierra and Estrus found it a bit uncomfortable.

"You must be Sierra Shalinsky. And this is Estrus, I presume?" the dignitary asked.

The Xenolfan man looked at this new Humolfan with curiosity. The large, black wings certainly peaked his interest.

"That is correct," Sierra said.

"I will take you to see Phensiarr Charseaa, our Xenolfan

Government leader. She has been expecting you," the dignitary said.

He led them toward the entrance of the government palace. As they walked along, Estrus turned toward the beautiful mountains and waterfalls in the distance. She saw the natural arches of stone that bridged the gap across the tallest waterfall.

That's beautiful, Estrus thought.

Upon entering the palace, the dignitary led them up the curved, stone stairway, across the mezzanine, and to Phensiarr Charseaa's office. The government leader sat at her large desk as they entered. Her long, white hair was eloquently styled.

"Welcome to Olf Teruda. Braxton Stryderr from the Syrenthian Government said you would be coming and explained everything to me. This is quite an honor. Not only do I get to meet the famous Sierra Shalinsky, but I also get to meet a very beautiful woman from the Humolfan species. It is a pleasure to meet you both. Please, have a seat," Phensiarr said.

Sierra and Estrus made themselves comfortable in a couple of chairs in front of the desk. Phensiarr stood from her desk and walked over to greet them. After Phensiarr returned to her desk, the dignitary left her office.

"An announcement went out last week for this event. We will be using our auditorium on the other side of the palace for the press conference tomorrow. I have been contacted by the press. There will be a lot of journalists here. Since this conference does affect the entire Syrenthian Galaxy, there will be attendees from Shar Nefalis, Aomium Swith, Ardellia, and Chelliss in the Industrial Sector, many casino owners from Salinarr Nevis, and people from Exandra, Red Jacket, Asparr Celtarious, Stilkoten Artibular, and several other planets as well. You two will certainly have the spot light," Phensiarr said.

"We appreciate your hospitality. Just so you know, some of what we will be saying tomorrow will come as a shock to the Xenolfan people, including yourself, with respect to Siiteper Affelum and the things he did," Estrus said.

Phensiarr's sapphire eyes looked from Sierra to Estrus. Her bluish-gray face had an expression of understanding on it.

"Estrus, I've seen things that our former leader, Aaranix Tuvelless, has done in the past in regard to interspecies relationships. Sierra Shalinsky here, along with Priscilla Stryderr—Braxton's wife—had gathered signatures from all across the galaxy to advocate for interspecies relationships and sexual freedom. All the petitions were condensed onto micro prints and given to Aaranix Tuvelless. Had they not been presented as micro prints, they all would not have fit in this office. Still, there were quite a few stacks of petitions. Aaranix Tuvelless wanted no part of that and ended up discarding them. They were ultimately destroyed. But I had seen them beforehand. I know how much work went into that effort. Aaranix has killed many people in his damn idealistic belief of some book called *Anathema Strain* that was written by Siiteper Affelum. It was a book that was destroyed in the archives of the lower levels. Truth is something that I believe in, Estrus. If what you two have to say tomorrow fixes a wrong and brings out the truth, then I'm all for it. I know we've had past Xenolfan leaders that were bad people. But we have also had many, many great leaders through the centuries as well. So, nothing you say will offend me," Phensiarr said.

"The Humolfan Government leader is Yilran Taw. He will be distributing copies of a history book of our people that will break it down into much greater detail than our speech will. And just so you know, us Humolfans have the original copy of *Anathema Strain*. It was swapped out from your archives for a copy many centuries ago. It is a hateful book full of lies about my people. That book and those lies are brought to light in our history book that will be distributed," Estrus said.

"What is the current status of Aaranix Tuvelless?" Sierra asked.

"He is scheduled to be terminated next week," Phensiarr said.

"Well, I would like to be there when that takes place. I want him to see with his own eyes the monsters that he was so afraid of and murdered so many innocent people over," Estrus said.

"It is open to the public. You are even permitted to speak, if you choose," Phensiarr said.

"Good," Estrus said.

The Olf Teruda morning sunlight brightened the guest room that Sierra stayed in. Estrus was in another guest room next to hers. Phensiarr Charseaa accommodated Sierra and Estrus with great palace hospitality. Sierra looked up from the comfortable bed toward the window. Removing her covers, she sat up on the edge of the bed, dressed in her panties and bra. She moved her long, black hair aside and walked over to the window. The tall waterfall could be seen in the distance. It drained into the beautiful blue pond. She saw a few other waterfalls across from the pond also empty into its clear depths. The other waterfalls dropped from a few different heights. The jungle surrounding the pond and palace was full of many shades of green foliage. Sierra was suddenly startled by a knock at the door. As she walked over to answer it, she could not help but think of Yilran Taw and his palace on Shardia. She cracked open the old, wooden door to see Estrus standing in the corridor.

"Can I come in?"

"Yes."

Sierra opened the door wider so Estrus could come in and then she shut it. Estrus was already dressed and ready for the day. She had brought in her bag from the ship and had put makeup on.

"Sorry to bother you, Sierra. I had a difficult time sleeping. Something is bothering me. Can I talk to you about it?"

"Of course. You look lovely, by the way."

Sierra quickly straightened up the bed covers so they could both sit down. They made themselves comfortable. Sierra noticed tears begin to flow down Estrus's gray cheeks. The black eye liner surrounding her sapphire eyes began to run slightly.

"What's wrong, Estrus?"

"I've been thinking about my mother. Today is going to be a historic moment and I wish she could have been here. She wanted to be a part of this repatriation so badly. I miss her so much, Sierra."

Estrus began to cry with heavy breathing. Sierra gave her a long hug. Estrus's tears dripped onto Sierra's bare shoulder and rolled down into her bra. Estrus tightened the hug and Sierra found herself smothered in the black feathers of Estrus's wing.

"I can't breathe," Sierra said.

Estrus pulled away and Sierra took a deep breath.

"Sorry. I didn't mean to suffocate you," Estrus said.

"That's quite all right," Sierra said.

Sierra wiped away the moisture of Estrus's tears from her boob.

"I'm sorry your mother could not be here. I would have loved to meet her. She will always be in your heart. In there, she will never leave you," Sierra said.

Sierra's words echoed through Estrus's mind.

"You're right, Sierra."

"You need to fix your eye liner. And I should get dressed. We have a long day ahead of us. Before we have this press conference, I need to let some very concerned people know that I'm all right, including my parents, my co-workers, my bandmates, and some friends. Perhaps I can find out where my ship is as well," Sierra said.

Sierra's comm sounded. It was Dr. Givinis from the sex clinic. Estrus listened in on the conversation. The doctor gave Sierra the breeding test results.

The Xenolfan Government palace auditorium was packed with journalists, businesspeople, citizens, and government officials from both the Syrenthian Government jurisdiction and the Xenolfan Government jurisdiction. The upper balcony was packed as well. Many journalists looked down from the balcony through their cameras. The galaxy was watching. Sierra and Estrus were both backstage with Edward Sirlain and Phensiarr Charseaa. Sierra and Estrus, the two women from different species, didn't have a written speech or script, but they had a story the galaxy needed to hear. The curtain opened and Phensiarr Charseaa walked from behind the stage curtain toward the podium microphone. The others were still hidden from the audience.

"Thank you all for attending this historic Humolfan Repatriation Conference here on Olf Teruda. We are about to re-introduce to you a species that is new to us, but has been around for a thousand years. A dark past will be revealed about the Xenolfan Government. I am not proud of this new information, but I am happy to be a good leader for my people. Now, Edward Sirlain has a few words he would like to add," Phensiarr said.

She stepped off to the side of the stage as Edward Sirlain appeared from behind the curtain.

"Thank you, Phensiarr Charseaa, for putting this Humolfan Repatriation Conference on here at the Xenolfan Government palace. Your hospitality is much appreciated. As most of you know, Sierra Shalinsky was missing for going on nine months. Many people were searching for her, including the Syrenthian Government. It appears Sierra has been very busy in a region of space that we all consider dark and desolate. She was recruited by a species unknown to you and I in order to advocate for them. Sierra has a gift for advocating for special causes. We are all very glad she has been found alive and well," Edward said.

There was a round of applause from the audience.

"I would like to introduce to you Sierra Shalinsky and Estrus, the Humolfan," Edward said.

Edward Sirlain joined Phensiarr Charseaa at the side of the stage. Sierra and Estrus walked from back stage and approached the microphone together. The audience gasped as they saw this new gray species with wings walk on stage with the tan human woman.

"Thank you all for coming," Sierra said. "I know discovering a new species can be a bit of a shock. I know that initial shock will diminish as we share the story of the Humolfan people. Before we get started, I would like to introduce myself for those of you who do not know me. My name is Sierra Shalinsky. Many of you know me as the driving force behind all of our sex clinics. Some of you know me as an advocate for sexual freedom between humans and Xenolfans, or as the vocalist for the symphonic metal band Maranadda. Some victims of tragedies may remember me as the Galactic Emergency Medical Technician that saved their life. No matter how you know me in all that I've done, I'm here to tell you that this very Humolfan Repatriation Conference may be the single most important thing that I've ever done. Not only am I here to introduce to you a new species, but I will continue to be there for their needs as we go forward.

"I want to give a shout out to my parents, Ralger and Cathin Shalinsky. I know you are both ecstatic that I'm alive. I know my co-workers, Sethain Absoneth and Rasmond Echeon, are so very grateful to have their Galactic EMT back. To my bandmates, Yosemite McFarlin, Arrian Trodder, Arvon Estivant, Sanarith Raastarr, and Kulu Avolium, I know you are all delighted to hear the good news of my return. To my friends, Shaslin and Vincent Macenburg, Braxton and Priscilla Stryderr—who are both here today—and Gathin and Eslarr, I know you are all overjoyed as well. Thank you all for caring for me and not totally giving up on me. You don't even know how much it means to me.

"So, without getting into specifics, I was recruited by Estrus here to advocate for their species. They knew from scouting the galaxy that I was good at advocating. Unfortunately, I had fallen and hit my head at the very beginning of this journey and I was in a coma for seven months. Estrus took care of me day after day in the hope that I would come out of it. She is someone who really cares. I've met some wonderful Humolfan people in my absence. One of those people is the Humolfan Government leader, Yilran Taw. He is a wonderful man and a great leader to his people. Like we have had our own struggles with conflict in the past, the Humolfans are not immune to that. They have had a struggle for a century with a group within their species that did not want to repatriate back into galactic society. They were offered isolation, but chose destruction and murder to those who thought different than them. They even tried to kill me twice. The Dissident Faction was recently destroyed and they no longer pose a threat to anyone.

"What we explain to you today is really just the surface of details. Very soon, a Humolfan history book will be distributed throughout the Syrenthian Galaxy that will go into much greater detail. We're going to take you back one thousand years to the time when Siiteper Affelum was leader of the Xenolfan Government. From this very palace, he commanded very horrible things to be done. I will let Estrus explain," Sierra said.

Estrus stepped up to the microphone.

"Hi. My name is Estrus. I am the Humolfan that recruited Sierra Shalinsky. We tried to recruit other potential advocates in the past, but each time we did, the Dissident Faction that Sierra mentioned would drive them away or worse. We are very thankful that Sierra has embraced our cause with such enthusiasm. So, as you all know, one thousand years ago, Xenolfans could fly. You Xenolfans were taught that you lost your wings due to microevolution. The truth is that it was never microevolution at all. Siiteper Affelum's hatred for the offspring of humans and Xenolfans was so great that he did genetic modifications on his own people so they would no longer be able to breed with humans. The truth is that the loss of Xenolfan wings one thousand years ago was an unintended side effect of Siiteper Affelum's genetic experimentation. He then had the Xenolfan history books blame it on microevolution. Yes, humans and Xenolfans were able to breed at one time. That is how us Humolfans came to be. But Siiteper hated the Humolfans because one of them killed his wife. He began a campaign of genocide that murdered all of the human and Xenolfan interspecies families. They rest in a cemetery on the planet S4 in the Shardaa Star System. For some unknown reason, he did not finish the genocide against the remaining Humolfan children and young adults.

He later wrote a book called *Anathema Strain* about how his wife was killed and in the book he expressed his hatred toward Humolfans. His disdain for us comes in the form of lies and misinformation for the reader to be deceived. The book was kept in the lower archives of this very palace. That is where Aaranix Tuvelless read it and formulated his recent opinion about humans and Xenolfans having relationships together. Of course, they could no longer breed together because of the experiments and genetic modifications Siiteper did on his own people. Only the sitting leader of the Xenolfan Government was permitted to read *Anathema Strain*. It was later destroyed when the pond outside of these walls flooded the lower archives. Little did anyone know that our very own Syrenthian Brotherhood Knights of Darkness took the original book out, and later replaced it with a copy. The book is now preserved in a temperature-controlled environment in our very large atheneum. Yes, the Syrenthian Brotherhood Knights of Darkness have always been our scouts that have performed critical missions for our species. They clip their wings and make other changes, dedicating their life to our cause. Siiteper guarded the Shardaa Sector with a battleship for many years so no one would go in or out. We had no ships and were stranded on S4 until two Xenolfans managed to elude the battleship and brought us supplies, Asparell coins, and a ship. Since they came in two ships, they were able to leave one ship for us and still get back home. Over the last one thousand years, we have developed our society and explored and settled most of the other planets in the Shardaa Star System. We are now about as advanced as the rest of the galaxy," Estrus said.

Standing together as a team at the podium, Sierra felt honored to have been chosen by the Humolfans. She leaned in toward the microphone.

"I have recently met with Dr. Givinis, administrator for the sex clinics across the Syrenthian Galaxy. Since we now live in an STI-free galaxy, I have initiated the task of the entire Humolfan population of seventeen million people to be tested for STIs so we remain a galaxy free from STIs. In my absence over the last several months, it looks like they have opened up the human and Xenolfan sex clinics to each species. This desegregation move is one that is a long time coming. Now, we will have three different species involved. There was a test done while we were at the sex clinic in the Galeva Krove Star System. The test results have revealed to us that humans can breed with

Humolfans and that Xenolfans can also breed with Humolfans. It has been determined that in just one generation, a current Xenolfan has the potential to have a child with wings, as their ancestors once had. The interspecies mix is something that will be profound," Sierra said.

Estrus leaned in toward the microphone.

"Just for the record, most of us don't plan on leaving our home in the Shardaa Sector. We simply want the freedom to leave and roam the galaxy like the humans and Xenolfans enjoy…a freedom that was taken from us one thousand years ago. It also means that human and Xenolfan tourism will become a real thing in the Shardaa Sector. Some of us may move outside the Shardaa Sector and some humans and Xenolfans may move into the Shardaa Sector. Freedom…it's a wonderful thing," Estrus said.

Sierra leaned in toward the podium.

"I have a message specifically for a human man named Dennon Cobalt. If you are listening to this conference, you were never a delusional space traveler. You were a chosen recruit to advocate for the Humolfans, but the evil Dissident Faction that did not want to repatriate stopped you. I was the Humolfans' next choice for an advocate. Ironically, I was also one of the Galactic EMTs that rescued you from S2 in the Shardaa Sector. So, I hope you can finally have some closure regarding that unexplained time in your life," Sierra said.

Estrus looked at Sierra for a moment. "I could not be more proud of this advocate for my people," Estrus said, wrapping her right wing around Sierra. "This incredible woman was so empathetic toward our people that she received a Feathers of Shardaa tattoo on her mons pubis. That is a ritual that is carried out by all Humolfan women when we come of age. That gesture that Sierra did means more to me than you could possibly know. You see, the Feathers of Shardaa symbol represents, with a broken feather, the sad loss of the Xenolfans' ability to fly. The unbroken feather represents our Humolfan wings. The symbol has deep meaning and is associated with the womb. A new species was born with wings, while an old species had theirs stripped away… The symbol can be found above caves, on carvings, with our tattoos, and on the gravestones of our foremothers."

Once again, Sierra leaned in.

"As mentioned earlier, you will all soon be able to see these truths and the Humolfan history in much greater detail when the history books are distributed. The Grave of Mothers on S4 is where Siiteper

Affelum carried out his genocide against human and Xenolfan mothers, many of which were pregnant with Humolfan child. But he also murdered the human and Xenolfan fathers by forcing them off a cliff to their deaths. Siiteper Affelum was a horrible man, as is Aaranix Tuvelless. I understand he is scheduled to be executed for his crimes on Shar Nefalis and Aamaress. In the book *Anathema Strain*, Siiteper Affelum had Aaranix Tuvelless believing humans and Xenolfans would create monsters. Siiteper was the monster. Humolfans are not monsters. There are good and bad people in every species. Humans, Xenolfans, and Humolfans all have choices in life that can determine which path they take. No one is perfect. And I'm thankful for redemption," Sierra said.

"There is one thing that us Humolfans have the ability to do that may startle some of you," Estrus said. "We have the ability to make people faint, using our eyes. This is generally used as a self defense mechanism. We still do not know how we have this ability. As far as our wings go, it would be no different than what you would have seen a thousand years ago with Xenolfans. Other than the late Dissident Faction, we are really a peaceful species. And the Dissident Faction has been destroyed. They caused so much destruction to the rest of us, their elimination was justified. They even killed my mother. She would have loved to be here in this very auditorium with us now. She wanted to meet humans and Xenolfans and begin new meaningful relationships with others on the outside of the Shardaa Sector. So, it is on her behalf that I say thanks to all of you for embracing us back into galactic society. Your understanding of our differences means so much. Bless you all."

"Edward Sirlain and Phensiarr Charseaa would like to conclude the Humolfan Repatriation Conference with a few words," Sierra said.

Sierra and Estrus stepped aside and Edward and Phensiarr returned to the microphone. Estrus quietly spoke with Sierra.

"That went well," Estrus whispered.

"Yeah, but my throat hurts where I had my surgery. After this is over, I'm going to go rest up in the guest room for a while," Sierra whispered back.

"Thank you, Sierra and Estrus. That was an incredible speech. There are a couple of things to note," Edward Sirlain said. "As you can expect, we will now have three governments in the Syrenthian Galaxy. The Syrenthian Government is relinquishing control of the Shardaa

Sector to the Humolfan Government. As we move forward, travel information to and from of that region of space will be released. With the mentioned Dissident Faction eliminated, no one should fear that area of space based on all of the mysterious things that have occurred over the years. It was all of the Dissident Faction's doing. The only thing to fear in that region of space is the Sharasp Tharrian Asteroid Mass and the large Shaeolian Black Hole. So, future Shardaa Sector travelers, beware of those. Space navigation will be updated in the coming days. There is even a planet in the Shardaa Star System called Shardia that we didn't even know existed…and it is the seat of the Humolfan Government. I am looking forward to meeting their leader, Yilran Taw, in person. We have already spoken to him and worked out some details of government interaction," Edward said.

Phensiarr Charseaa stepped up to the microphone.

"I am also looking forward to meeting Yilran Taw. As it goes with leaders throughout history, you get the good and the bad. We are not proud of the bad leaders, like Siiteper Affelum and Aaranix Tuvelless, but they were in power. We cannot erase that fact. We cannot eliminate a set number of years from our history. But we can learn from our past. The truth will always prevail. It might take a thousand years, but the truth always comes to light. Portraits of every leader the Xenolfan Government has ever had hang in a dark, private corridor near the lower levels of the palace. The portraits of Siiteper Affelum and Aaranix Tuvelless hang there among them. With this truth that has been brought to light, you may wonder if either portrait will come down. The answer is no. As I said, you cannot erase a set number of years. You must know what this monster looked like. You cannot have a gap in history, nor will there be a gap on that wall. It is strange how a few bad people can change the lives of so many good people. We must look forward and prevent people like Siiteper and Aaranix from ever coming to power again. Be diligent. Don't be deceived. Always protect your freedoms.

"There is no excuse for discrimination against someone who is different than ourselves. We had that problem one hundred years ago during the Syrenthian War. If anyone unjustly oppresses the Humolfans, then they will be punished with a treaty that Edward Sirlain and I have signed into law yesterday. The opposite is true as well. The treaty also has a provision built into it to protect humans and Xenolfans from Humolfans, if need be," Phensiarr said.

Edward moved toward the microphone.

"The scheduled STI testing for Humolfans will begin soon and occur over the next two and a half months, so expect some delays as all appointments are temporarily switched to third shift, while the first and second shifts will focus on the testing of the seventeen million Humolfans," Edward said.

Suddenly, a Xenolfan journalist lost his balance on the crowded balcony and began to fall. He caught the edge of the railing with his hand and held on for his life as he watched his camera drop to the floor far below and shatter into pieces. The balcony was so crowded that no one could reach down to help him. He could feel his grip slipping. Estrus saw the Xenolfan man dangling and leaped into the air, spreading her large, black wings out as she soared toward him at lightning speed. Just as his hand slipped off the rail and he fell, Estrus swooped up and caught him. She carried him safely to the floor below and then flew back to the stage. The audience became deathly quiet as they looked onward.

In an abrupt burst of emotion, the journalist cried, "Thank you! Thank you!"

Suddenly, the entire audience stood up and cheered for this new alien among them.

Chapter Twelve

Estrus landed the *Aileron* at the Maranadda studio on Red Jacket. Since the Humolfan Repatriation Conference had taken place, Estrus was free to roam the Syrenthian Galaxy wherever she wanted to go. The public was made aware.

"There's my ship!" Sierra said.

She looked out the observation window. Just as her bandmates had confirmed when she contacted them, her ship was still parked where she had left it at the Maranadda studio. Sierra recalled parking it there before her last big concert at the Civie Arena, before she was abducted by Estrus. Seeing the scorch mark on the starboard side of the *Tenebris,* she recalled being attacked by an odd drone spaceship when she was en route to Priscilla Stryderr's house on Exandra. She had destroyed that drone ship with the laser weapons that she had Flux Ship Mods install beforehand.

"That's the cool fighter ship that you were telling me about?" Estrus asked.

"Yes. It is an old fighter ship from the Syrenthian War. When I purchased it, it had been stripped from its weapons, but I recently had them installed again," Sierra said.

"So, this is where the band practices?" Estrus asked.

"Yup. Since I contacted them ahead of time, everyone should be here."

Estrus disabled the *Aileron's* engines and they stepped out onto the rusty colored ground. Trees and shrubs were scattered about. That area of Red Jacket was an oasis compared to the more barren, desolate desert areas. They entered the studio and heads turned.

"Sierra!" they all shouted simultaneously.

"Hi, guys! It's so nice to see all of you. I want you all to meet Estrus. She is the first Humolfan that you'll see," Sierra said.

They looked at the woman behind Sierra. The large, black wings caught their attention at first, then the gray skin, beautiful sapphire eyes, and long, white hair.

"Hi, Estrus. We all saw the Humolfan Repatriation Conference broadcast. It is a pleasure to meet you," Yosemite McFarlin said.

"It's nice to meet you all as well. I was actually at Sierra's last concert with you here on Red Jacket and I think Maranadda sounds awesome," Estrus said.

"I saw you save that journalist at the conference. It's awesome that you can really fly," Kulu Avolium said.

"Thank you. Xenolfans should be able to fly as well, but as you probably heard from the conference, Siiteper Affelum fucked that up," Estrus said.

"You were at our concert here?" Sanarith Raastarr asked.

"Yes, that is when I basically abducted Sierra to advocate for my people," Estrus said.

"That's fucked up!" Arvon Estivant said.

"I admit that it *was* fucked up, but it is the only way we knew how to have her advocate for our people. She was not mistreated under my care," Estrus said.

"Why didn't you contact us sooner? You had a lot of people worried sick over you," Yosemite said.

"She couldn't," Estrus said.

"I was in a coma for seven months. I fell and hit my head on the concrete. I contacted you as soon as I could. Estrus took care of me the entire time I was in a coma," Sierra said.

"I actually caused her to faint and she fell off the wooden crate in the warehouse of the arena after the concert. I failed to catch her in time as she fainted, so it is my fault she went into a coma in the first place. I apologize a million times over for that. I'm certainly glad she woke up and we are now good friends. I ask that you all forgive me too, if you would," Estrus said.

"Well, it looks like it all worked out. The main thing is that Sierra is okay," Arvon said.

"Aww. I love you guys," Sierra said.

"It's so nice to see you," Yosemite said.

"Oh, it is great to have you back," Arvon said.

"We've missed you so much," Sanarith said.

"Yes, we have," Kulu said.

"You should have heard the vocalist we just got rid of," Arrian Trodder said.

"What? You guys got a different vocalist?" Sierra asked.

"Well, we didn't know what happened to you. So, yeah…" Yosemite said.

"Okay. I get it. What was his or her name?" Sierra asked.

"Aymreth Rosenn. She is a female Xenolfan. She's a nice person, but she can't sing," Arrian said.

"Well, I hope it was a pleasant departure," Sierra said.

"Um…she did not take it very well," Arvon said.

"Well, I'd like to speak with her. I don't want any hard feelings," Sierra said.

"She lives here on Red Jacket. I'm sure Vincent and Shaslin can show you where," Arrian said.

Sierra smiled. "I'm sure they can. So, where are they?"

"They will be here shortly. They are running behind," Sanarith said.

"So, have you guys done many shows with Aymreth as vocalist? What do the fans think?"

"We had several shows that Shasta Varium scheduled for us. The fans hated Aymreth Rosenn as the new vocalist. We lost a lot of them. As our manager and booking agent, Shasta was not thrilled about that either," Yosemite said.

"Well, I'm back. But there was an incident and I almost died. I'm not talking about the coma. I was stabbed in the neck and the knife went into my throat. It missed my artery by millimeters. My throat gets sore if I talk too much, like at the conference. I haven't even tried to sing yet, but I think it may affect my vocals. I need more time to heal, so don't start planning concerts just yet," Sierra said.

"Who stabbed you?" Arvon asked.

"It was a group in the Shardaa Sector called the Dissident Faction. They did not want to repatriate back into galactic society with the rest of the Humolfans and would attack and murder any advocates that were chosen to help," Sierra said.

"They were all killed recently for the many terrible things they have done over the years," Estrus said.

"Well, I'm glad you are okay. We can hold off on booking any shows until you feel better. It's not like we have any scheduled right now anyway," Yosemite said.

The studio door opened and Vincent and Shaslin Macenburg walked in, followed by Aymreth Rosenn.

"Sierra!" Shaslin shouted.

"Hi, Shaslin! Hi, Vincent! I've missed you two," Sierra said.

Sierra gave them both a hug and kiss. As swinger partners in the Lifestyle, she knew them both very intimately. She recalled their last play time together at the casino hotel on Salinarr Nevis. The erotic memory made her smile.

"This is Estrus, the first Humolfan that you will meet," Sierra said.

"Hello," Estrus said.

"Wow! It is nice to meet you, Estrus," Vincent said.

"Yes, it's very nice to meet you," Shaslin said.

"Hi, Estrus," Aymreth said.

"It's nice to meet you all as well," Estrus said.

"Sierra, I heard the Superior Mountain Club acquired your land because of some abandonment clause in a law on Asparr Celtarious," Vincent said.

"Are you fucking joking?" Sierra asked.

"That's what I heard, but I don't know the details," Vincent said.

"The fucking Jinkins! I'm going to have to get to the bottom of that," Sierra said.

It became awkwardly quiet for a moment.

"So, I just wanted to stop by and say that I have no animosity toward any of you. Plus, when Vincent and Shaslin said Sierra was going to be here, I wanted to meet her," Aymreth said.

Sierra shook her bluish-gray hand. "It is a pleasure to meet you. I'm sorry things didn't work out with Maranadda. Perhaps after my throat heals, we can experiment with some duet vocals," Sierra said.

"Well, that would be awesome," Aymreth said.

"We appreciate you stopping by, Aymreth. We have no animosity toward you either," Yosemite said.

"What happened to your neck? Is that a scar?" Vincent asked.

"I just got through telling them that when I was in the Shardaa Sector, I was stabbed in the throat by some members of a terrorist organization called Dissident Faction," Sierra said.

"Well, I'm glad you're okay," Vincent said.

"Yes," Shaslin said.

"Hey, let's all go out to dinner. There is this new restaurant down the street from CJ Whitmann's Hardware & Supply Co. that has awesome food," Yosemite suggested.

"You must be talking about the new Copper Meadows restaurant. That sounds good," Aymreth said.

"Yes. I just need to run upstairs and grab my keys," Yosemite said.

"Speaking of CJ Whitmann, how is his son, Benjamin, doing?" Sierra asked.

Sierra was referring to a disabled boy they knew on Red Jacket whose dad owned the local hardware store.

"Benjamin Whitmann is doing great. He loves my new quad that finally arrived. We go out on the trails often," Yosemite said.

"And my kids, Aaron and Shanda, have taken Benjamin for rides on the quads as well. They have made a good friend with him. They are now used to helping him out of his wheelchair and onto the quad. In fact, we just invited Benjamin's mom and dad over for dinner last week. I tell you, Angie Whitmann is a good cook. She helped my wife, Misty, with dinner and it was amazing," Kulu said.

"You're making me hungry. Let's go," Vincent said.

"Are you okay with dinner, Estrus? I know you are excited to go out and explore the galaxy. I appreciate you bringing me here to my ship," Sierra said.

"Dinner sounds good. I will take off and do some exploring on my own after dinner," Estrus said.

"Are you sure you don't want me to be there advocating for you as you go out exploring the galaxy?" Sierra asked.

"I'll be fine," Estrus said.

"Okay. Well, I will give you some credits to use since Asparell coins are worth way too much to use for regular things on your journey," Sierra said.

"Good point. I didn't think of that," Estrus said.

"I'll stop home and get Misty and the kids," Kulu said.

"Yeah, and I'll stop home and see if Arcashia wants to go too," Sanarith said.

"Arrian, what about your girlfriend, Jackie, and your daughter, Sophie? Would they like to go as well?" Sierra asked.

Arrian looked at Sierra with a strange expression, his long, brown hair shifting to the side.

"You must have hit your head real hard when you went into a coma, if you're asking Jacquelyn Enelra to come. I thought you two hated each other," Arrian said.

"Well, let's just say what's happened to me over the last several months has me thinking about things a bit differently. Hell, I may even get along with my old boss, Madison Stephard… Okay, maybe not Madison," Sierra said.

They all laughed, knowing how much Sierra hated working for Madison as the director of her old Galactic Emergency Medical Services unit. She enjoyed working for Sethain Absoneth, the director of her new unit.

"I'll check with Jackie," Arrian said. "I'm sure her and Sophie would like to get out of the house. And Jackie might find the fact that you asked a bit meaningful to mend old differences."

The group headed out the studio door.

"Can we see you fly, Estrus?" Arvon asked.

"Guys, come on! Don't ask her to do that," Sierra said, shaking her head.

The group ate at Copper Meadows restaurant. After they finished their meals and caught up with some much needed socializing, Sierra told her bandmates that she would let them know when her throat and voice was better. Estrus parted ways, with plans to explore some interesting places in the Syrenthian Galaxy. After leaving the restaurant, Vincent and Shaslin Macenburg had an arousing conversation with Sierra outside the restaurant. They invited Sierra over to their house for some sexual play. They had played together with Sierra on many occasions in the past.

Sierra followed them home and landed the *Tenebris* next to their house. She somehow felt different about having sex with them this time. She couldn't quite figure out why. They entered the house and made themselves comfortable in the living room.

"It's been a while since we've all been together," Shaslin said.

"Too long," Vincent said.

Sierra sighed deeply.

"What's wrong?" Shaslin asked.

"I… I don't know. It's nothing against you guys, but I would just like to watch. I hope you don't mind," Sierra said.

"Well, we miss you, but we also respect you. You've been through a lot lately. So, it's all good. Don't worry about it and just enjoy the show," Vincent said.

"I will certainly enjoy the show," Sierra said.

Sierra made herself comfortable on the loveseat while Vincent and Shaslin undressed, their clothes landing on the floor. Shaslin positioned herself on the couch, lying on her back. Her pussy was fully visible on the edge of the couch with her legs spread open. Sierra smiled at the view. Vincent made himself comfortable with his knees on the soft carpeting. He leaned in and buried his mouth onto her pussy. With his mouth covering her labia, he slid his tongue in downward motions along her wet slit. With each thrust, his tongue brushed against her clit. The sensation sent surges of ecstasy to her very core. Vincent changed it up by tracing the tip of his tongue between each labia fold before plunging it into her hole. Her pussy spasmed with excitement and he could taste her luscious juice.

"Mmm," Vincent said.

"That feels so wonderful," Shaslin said.

He smiled up at her and continued to dance around her pussy with his tongue.

"It *looks* so wonderful," Sierra said.

Vincent made his way up to Shaslin's breasts. He caressed her left breast and surrounded her nipple with his mouth. He playfully swirled his tongue around it and lightly sucked. Moving to the right breast, he repeated the action. They kissed and then Vincent lay on the couch, his cock erect and ready to receive her mouth. Shaslin leaned over him and slid her lips over the tip of his cock. Sucking up and down, she sent erotic sensations through him. He moaned with delight. Shaslin slid her tongue up the bottom side of his shaft and flicked it against his frenulum before continuing to suck. She soon straddled him, grabbed his hard cock and guided it into her. She slowly slid down onto its intense heat. With easy motions, she gyrated her hips and ground down against the base of his rigid member, its full length deep inside of her. Shaslin faced Vincent and Sierra could see them fucking from behind.

Sierra reached her hand into her pants and began fingering her pussy, the tips of her fingers coming into contact with the warm, moist lips. The scene before Sierra aroused her immensely. Rubbing her fingers side to side across her clit felt very satisfying. Sierra continued to watch them fuck on the couch.

"I'm gonna come!" Vincent said.

Shaslin continued to grind down on his hard cock as it pulsated inside of her. She could feel the hot load burst in her depths. As Shaslin's pumping motion slowed, she pulled free from Vincent, the cum dripping out onto his stomach.

"Did you have an orgasm, honey?" Vincent asked.

"Yeah. It was a slight one, but that's okay," Shaslin said.

"Ahhh!" Sierra shouted.

Vincent and Shaslin looked over to the loveseat at Sierra fingering herself.

"Well, at least *she* had a deep orgasm," Shaslin said.

"Oh, that felt good. Watching you two was very arousing," Sierra said.

"Thanks," Vincent said.

"Are you sure nothing is wrong?" Shaslin asked.

"Yes. I just need to slow down or take a break from the swinger Lifestyle. I… I'm in love with someone," Sierra said.

"What? Sierra is in love? That's funny," Vincent said.

"Yeah, it is. I thought you were all about sexual freedom, bisexuality, and swinging. I'm in love with Vincent, but we still swing," Shaslin said.

"I know. I can't even explain my feelings. I haven't even had sex with him yet, but I'm just so attracted to him," Sierra said.

"Is it infatuation or something more?" Shaslin asked.

"I think it is infatuation, attraction, lust, and love all rolled into one. We've gone on dates and he treats me like a queen. I've toured his palace, I've had long and intimate conversations with him, I've comforted him when he lost his son. Whatever this is, it is very deep and meaningful to me and to him," Sierra said.

"He's a Humolfan?" Vincent asked.

"Yes. He mentioned that, unlike most Humolfans, he has a human cock, so that's a bonus. Not that there is anything wrong with reuleaux triangular cocks..." Sierra said.

"After we get cleaned up, you can tell us more about your new love," Shaslin said.

"Yes. I need to wash my hands too. You need to hear about the palace. It's so elegant and amazing," Sierra said.

Sierra approached the planet Stilkoten Artibular where her parents lived. It was a fairly large planet compared to her home planet of Asparr Celtarious. On the flight there, she tried singing some of her favorite Maranadda songs, but found that her tone was off and her throat hurt where she had been stabbed. She then hummed, but it was also met with pain.

That's not cool, she thought, rubbing her neck.

Stilkoten Artibular was also the planet where Sierra grew up as a child. As the *Tenebris* flew through the sky blue atmosphere, Sierra could see the alluring landscape of pine forests, lakes, and mountains. It was much like her home planet of Asparr Celtarious, but much more populated. Ralger and Cathin Shalinsky lived in a small town called Wolf Peak. Wolf Peak was located in a mountainous area. Not far from the mountains, a meadow transitioned into salt plains that littered the wide valley. The salt plains were decorated with clusters of pine islands and muskeg. It was a great natural wonder and included spectacular rock formations. White pine, black spruce, tamarack, and subalpine fir enveloped the area in various shades of green. In the distance, a river cut through the rock of the conifer forest, dropped over a gorgeous waterfall, and continued into the forest below. Near her parents' home, there was an enchanting view of a lake, surrounded by white pine trees. The mountains and white pines reflected from the surface of the calm, clear water. It reminded Sierra of her own Lake Serenity next to her home on Asparr Celtarious. The information she heard about the Superior Mountain Club taking her land was one more thing she had to deal with.

The Jinkins better not have messed with my property! Sierra thought.

Sierra landed the *Tenebris* outside of her parents' house. As she exited the old fighter ship, she looked around the area where she had played as a child, a plethora of nostalgic thoughts returning to her mind. Sierra's parents came running out of the house to greet her.

They were both in their sixties. Her father, Ralger, had brown hair. Like Sierra, her mother, Cathin, also had black hair, but mixed with a bit of gray.

"Mom! Dad!" Sierra greeted them.

"Sierra! Oh Sierra! We've missed you," Cathin cried.

"We've searched all over for you, Sierra. We didn't think we'd ever see you again," Ralger said.

Cathin and Ralger both hugged Sierra tight and rocked her side to side. They all started to cry.

"We love you so much, Sierra," Cathin said.

"I love you too. I'm so sorry I've been distant, even before my disappearance," Sierra said as they hugged.

Her parents pulled away and looked at her for a long moment, soaking in the blessing of her return. Sierra was thankful to still have them both in her life. Thoughts of the Grave of Mothers briefly crossed her mind.

"Like I said when I contacted you from Olf Teruda before the Humolfan Repatriation Conference, I was in a coma for seven months. I contacted you as soon as I had a chance. I'm so sorry you had to worry for so long," Sierra said.

"We're just happy you're alive," her father said.

Sierra wiped away the moisture from her face.

"How about we sit down inside and I will tell you all about my adventures? I can't wait to tell you about this man I met," Sierra offered.

"That sounds great," her mom said.

Sierra walked between them and put her arms around them both as they made their way toward the house.

Sierra Shalinsky was excited for the reunion at the Galactic Emergency Medical Services facility on Relistorr. She had disappeared from the galaxy months ago without a trace and her employer was left wondering what had happened. When her unit director, Sethain Absoneth, and her fellow Galactic EMT, Rasmond Echeon, found out she had gone missing, they both set out on a quest to search for her, like others close to her had done. When the search ended without success, they decided not to fill her position in their unit. It meant becoming a bit more efficient and doing a lot more work, but they managed. The fact that she was back and had contacted them before her recent Humolfan Repatriation Conference was such good news. Sethain Absoneth had looked forward to this GEMS reunion.

Awaiting clearance to land on Relistorr always tried Sierra's patience. Her previous clearance code to land on the secure planet had expired, so she had to go through the process of receiving a new one in order to land. After landing the *Tenebris*, Sierra headed for her office. Upon arriving to her office, she noticed it was just as she had left it. The janitors had kept it dust-free. She looked down at her EMT bag that lay on the floor next to her desk and smiled. It was nice to be back.

She met Sethain Absoneth and Rasmond Echeon in the conference room to catch up on things. She told them about her latest adventures and near-death experiences.

"We are so overjoyed that you're okay," Rasmond Echeon said.

Rasmond wore her long, brown hair in a ponytail. Sierra's unit director, Sethain Absoneth, had short, blond hair. They both wore GEMS uniforms with a spiral galaxy and heart logo embroidered into each shoulder.

"Yes. We've missed you here at GEMS. Even your old unit director, Madison Stephard, was asking about you," Sethain said.

"It's nice to be back. Before I actually begin work, however, there is something I need to deal with. I was told that my home on Asparr Celtarious has been acquired by the Superior Mountain Club, a group of people that I've had issues with for years. Once I get that straightened out, I can get back to work," Sierra said.

"That's totally understandable. Man, you certainly have been through some crazy shit lately," Sethain said.

Sierra sighed deeply. "Yes, but I'm hanging in there. Life seems to throw shit at me all the time. I don't know…it's getting old," Sierra said.

"Cheer up, Sierra. You're a strong person. Hey, did I tell you that GEMS was informed by the Syrenthian Government that—even though the Shardaa Sector is now officially recognized as Humolfan Government territory—we will still be servicing that region of space for our unit? I believe Edward Sirlain, Phensiarr Charseaa, and Yilran Taw had a recent communication together and are scheduled for an in-person meeting as well," Sethain said.

"Cool. Well, at least I won't be freaked out to travel there anymore. All the strange mysteries have been solved," Sierra said.

"So, you may have noticed everything in your office is still in order.

We've had them keep it clean for you," Rasmond said.

"I *did* notice that. Thank you."

The comm sounded in the conference room and an urgent message came through from the dispatch officer.

"Sethain, your unit has been directed by the GEMS incident commander, Elliss Millott, to begin a scheduled training exercise in the Shardaa Sector immediately. It will be on a planet in the Shardaa Star System called Shardia. Elliss Millott already has the hospital ship *Deliverance* waiting in Relistorr's orbit for your shuttle," the officer said.

"Thank you," Sethain said. He turned to Rasmond. "This should be interesting. It's too bad you aren't quite ready to join us, Sierra. You know more about that region than we do."

"I'm sure you'll do just fine. I really do need to get to Asparr Celtarious. Hey, do you know exactly what exercise they have coordinated with the Humolfans?" Sierra asked.

"Yes. The training exercise will be a rescue from someone falling through a hole in some bridge on Shardia. I think it is called the Ocean Port Bridge," Sethain said.

"Oh shit! I've actually been on that bridge. You need to be real careful of the holes in that bridge. You can fall right down to the concrete pylons in the ocean inlet. Also, you can get impaled on the rebar mesh poking out of the concrete. It's a very dangerous place," Sierra said.

"We will be lowered from the bridge on ropes to the bottom for this exercise. It sure didn't take long for them to set this training exercise up. The government leaders were just talking about it yesterday," Rasmond said.

"While we're out there, we will be taking a new class on Humolfan anatomy. Their anatomy is very similar to Xenolfan anatomy, but we will primarily be focusing on treating injured wings. None of us are familiar with a species that can fly, so it is all new," Sethain said.

"I should be there, but I can certainly learn that later. I have many sources to learn it from within the Humolfan population," Sierra said.

"Yeah. It's really special that they picked you to advocate for them. How does that make you feel?" Rasmond asked.

"Very important and humble," Sierra said.

"Well, we need to move out. Good luck on Asparr Celtarious," Sethain said.

"Thanks. You two be safe out there. I will see you both soon," Sierra said.

• • •

The flight to Asparr Celtarious was an anxious one. From what Maranadda's sound technician, Vincent Macenburg, had said, her property on Lake Serenity had been taken by the Superior Mountain Club. She tried to think of something else in order to ease her mind. Sierra reflected on the reunions she had had since she came out of the Shardaa Sector. For some reason, everything from before seemed like a totally different life. The coma she was in seemed like it changed her. She was trying to be who she had always been, but it just seemed foreign to her...almost as if her former self was a different person. Thoughts of Yilran Taw appeared in her mind. He was such a gentleman. Perhaps her feelings for him were causing the odd thought patterns of being a stranger to herself.

No. It can't be that I'm different. Maybe I'm just maturing. But that's like saying I wasn't mature before, and that's fucking nonsense, Sierra thought.

She came to the conclusion that the coma *did* actually change her psychologically somehow. Whatever the case was, Sierra certainly felt increasingly strange in the new universe she found herself in. Being the advocate for the Humolfans was something she was proud of. She wasn't even sure if her role as an advocate was finished or if there was more to do. She did offer to join Estrus on her adventures of exploring and discovering the many interesting things outside of the Shardaa Sector, but Estrus had declined her company. Was Sierra even needed in the role anymore? Many things played through Sierra's mind as she approached Asparr Celtarious. She longed to sleep in her own comfortable bed at her home on Lake Serenity. Whatever Vincent was talking about with regard to her property certainly had her on edge.

Flicking several switches on the dashboard of the *Tenebris,* she began to descend through the atmosphere of Asparr Celtarious. Soon, she saw Lake Serenity in the distance and her house. The nearby mountains and white pine trees reflected on the water. It was truly a beautiful place to live. Sierra loved it there. As she neared the house, she saw several things that didn't seem right.

Wait! What the hell? Who's ship is parked on my property. Where the hell are my adirondack chairs that were sitting by the lake? Who the fuck is on my deck? She thought.

She landed the *Tenebris* and exited the cockpit of the old fighter ship. Walking toward the house at a fast pace, she looked up at the man standing on the deck.

"Who the fuck are you? And why are you on my property? You're trespassing" Sierra shouted.

"This property belongs to the Superior Mountain Club. And I'm afraid it is you who is trespassing. You must be Sierra Shalinsky, the person that always had a problem with the Superior Mountain Club. Well, it just so happens that when you abandon property for more than six months on Asparr Celtarious, your property goes up for auction. So, this is no longer your property. It has been acquired by the Superior Mountain Club. The Jinkins committee has met with the local governance of Asparr Celtarious and purchased the land that you abandoned. We got the land for a great deal. You might say that it was a steal. The Superior Mountains are such a lovely backdrop across Lake Serenity, don't you think so?" the man sneered.

He took a long drink of ale from a bottle in his hand as he looked down at Sierra.

"I was in a coma for seven months. This is my fucking property and you need to leave before I remove you myself," Sierra said.

"Well, it looks like I'm just going to have to contact the local authorities," he said.

He disappeared from the deck into the house.

"Fucking Jinkins!"

She walked over to the door, but it was locked. Her key code no longer worked. She contemplated destroying the man's ship with the laser weapons that she had installed onto the *Tenebris*. She was furious.

How can they do this? she thought.

"Fucking Jinkins!" she shouted again. The sound echoed across the lake.

She went back to the *Tenebris* and climbed into the cockpit. Staring out the observation window at her house in disbelief, she felt numb. The words of her GEMS unit director echoed through her mind. He had encouraged her to cheer up and that she was a strong person. Sierra could not help but feel the total opposite in her current situation. With a surge of anger, she launched the *Tenebris* and quickly maneuvered around to fire her laser cannons at the ship in front of her house. Her thumb hovered over the red button. Before she could fire, two ships from the local authorities swooped down on either side of the *Tenebris.*

"We have a report that you are trespassing and threatening the property owner," the officer said over the comm.

"I am the owner of this property! That man is trespassing! What is wrong with you people?" Sierra asked.

"We are aware of a recent property ownership change due to abandonment. If you are the previous owner, I would suggest scheduling a meeting with the local governance office to file a grievance," the other officer said over the comm.

Sierra removed her thumb from the laser trigger switch.

"This isn't over!" Sierra shouted over the comm.

She changed trajectory and left the scene, heading toward the town of Nassathia. After seeing that Sierra had left the area, the authorities also left in a different direction. Nassathia was not far from Lake Serenity. Sierra flew around a small range of mountains and down into the town. Nassathia was surrounded by mountains. The small community, was very well kept. She landed the *Tenebris* next to the local governance office.

They better be open, Sierra thought.

After exiting her ship, she entered the building. A receptionist sat behind a glass window.

"May I help you?" the woman asked.

"I need to file a grievance. The Superior Mountain Club has acquired my property on Lake Serenity. How could you people let this happen?"

The receptionist could see Sierra was furious.

"Let me get my superior for you regarding this matter."

The woman left her seat and disappeared into the offices. She soon returned with a man that Sierra recognized as one of the members of the Jinkins committee of the Superior Mountain Club.

"I understand you want to file a grievance. What seems to be the problem?" the man asked.

You're fucking kidding me! Sierra thought.

"Your Superior Mountain Club has stolen my land!"

"I believe you are referring to the property on Lake Serenity. The property was abandoned for at least six months. According to our local ordinance, if a property is abandoned for at least six months, it goes up for auction. The Lake Serenity property was acquired by the Superior Mountain Club last month. I will get you the paperwork for your grievance; however, realistically speaking, the chances of getting it back are zero," the man said.

"There is a conflict of interest with you working in the local governance office and also being a part of the Jinkins committee of the Superior Mountain Club," Sierra said.

"Do you want the paperwork or not?" the man asked.

"Not if it's a waste of my time," she sneered. "But you know what? I will fill it out and I will appeal your decision directly to the Syrenthian Government on Exandra."

"You certainly may do that. Good luck. It has never successfully been done," the man said. "She'll get the paperwork for you. Have a nice day."

The man turned around and left the front office. The receptionist pulled the form up on the computer, printed it out, and handed Sierra the copy along with a pen. Sierra filled out the form and handed it back to the woman.

"We will contact you via comm with our decision in the next several days," the woman said.

The man walked back into the office and took the paperwork from the receptionist.

"Actually, I have time to review your grievance now," he said.

He took a pen and checked a box at the bottom of the form.

"I understand you advocated for the Humolfans. I watched the Humolfan Repatriation Conference broadcast. So, on this paper, you wrote down you were in a coma for seven months. It doesn't matter. Your grievance is denied," he said as he gave the form back to the receptionist.

Sierra did not reply. She turned around and exited the building.

"Fucking Jinkins!"

Sierra sat in her ship with the engines off, just staring out the observation window. She wanted to cry, but she was much too angry. Sierra sat for a long time wondering what to do. She so desperately wanted to just lay in her own bed and go to sleep. Since Braxton Stryderr worked for the Syrenthian Government, perhaps he could help her somehow. She lifted the ship from the surface of Asparr Celtarious and headed for Exandra.

Chapter Thirteen

Estrus felt privileged to be the first Humolfan to freely roam the galaxy. The Syrenthian Brotherhood Knights of Darkness were always in disguise. On her mission to abduct Sierra Shalinsky, she had to be in disguise. She recalled how uncomfortable she had been with her wings hidden in a large backpack. To be free with wings out and to just be herself put a smile on her face. There were so many sites she wanted to visit out in the Syrenthian Galaxy. If only her mother were still alive to see it… She was grateful that Sierra Shalinsky offered to be with her as an advocate, if necessary, but her exploration was something she wanted to do on her own. So far, from the places she had visited, she was received with a warm welcome. Estrus realized that everyone may not have seen the Humolfan Repatriation Conference that was broadcast. If she came across someone who was not aware of current events, she may frighten them. She was hoping that would not happen.

Her next stop was Enax Port. It was her understanding that her 38th great grandmother, Destiny—who was buried in the Grave of Mothers on S4—and her 38th great grandfather—who was in the pile of bones at the bottom of the cliff on S4—were both from Enax Port.

Estrus didn't know where on Enax Port they were from, but she still wanted to visit the planet to get a sense of connection with her ancestors. She also heard that Enax Port had a large swinger community and was home to some wild sex parties. So, she was not sure what to expect. Perhaps she would just grab a bite to eat and explore the planet a little.

That looks like a good place to eat, Estrus thought.

She set the *Aileron* down at an intoxication joint and restaurant called Aura's Delight. Upon entering the establishment, Estrus was greeted by the hostess. Estrus received the usual initial stares that she had come to expect as of late. There was something about the particular patrons of Aura's Delight that was a bit different than what she had experienced before. The stares had a lustful curiosity to them. She smiled at the other guests as she was led to her seat. There were both human and Xenolfan couples and singles in the intoxication join, some of which were in interspecies relationships.

A sexy human waitress, dressed in a very short, black skirt, stopped at her table with a menu.

"Wow! I saw the conference of you that was broadcast. It's an honor to meet you in person. It's really cool that you saved that guy who fell from the balcony," she said.

"Well, thank you," Estrus said.

"Don't mind the stares from these people. They're just curious. What can I get you to drink?"

"I suppose you don't happen to have any Ginger Alquinola, do you?" Estrus asked.

"Some *what?*"

"Oh, never mind. It's a Shardaa thing. I'll have an ale," Estrus said.

"Sure thing. I'll be back in a flash," the waitress said.

Estrus watched her sexy ass as she disappeared around a corner. She turned and scanned the room. As she looked around, the other patrons quickly turned away from staring at her.

This is a bit uncomfortable. I feel like a fresh piece of meat they want to devour, Estrus thought.

There was one Xenolfan woman who sat alone whose stare was actually not uncomfortable. Estrus smiled back at her. She had a beautiful bluish-gray face that was accentuated by long, sexy white curls. Her sapphire eyes told a story of their own. The Xenolfan's features reminded Estrus of her own self with her white hair and sapphire eyes. Estrus looked down at her gray skin and then back to the bluish-gray skin of the Xenolfan. Shifting her eyes toward the woman's back, Estrus wondered what the Xenolfans looked like back in the day when they had wings. Her 38th great grandmother had such wings. The Xenolfan woman stared back with such a curiosity that she tilted her head, amazed at the large, black wings. Moving her shoulders slightly in a circular motion where her wings would have been, the Xenolfan woman looked down at her drink, almost with a look of defeat. Seeing this reminded Estrus of exactly why the Feathers of Shardaa symbology was so representative of the brokenness of the Xenolfans. The Xenolfan woman looked back up and hesitated. She looked as if she was gathering courage for something.

Damn Siiteper Affelum! Estrus thought.

The waitress came back with her ale. The golden liquid foamed at the rim of the glass.

"Are you ready to order?" the waitress asked.

"Oh sorry. I haven't looked at the menu yet," Estrus said.

"Take your time. I'll be back."

The Xenolfan woman worked up enough courage and stood up from her table. The woman walked over and joined Estrus at her booth, sitting down in the seat across from her.

"Hi. My name is Sheena. Do you mind if I join you?" the woman asked.

"Hi, Sheena. I don't mind at all. My name is Estrus. I am a Humolfan. Did you happen to watch the Humolfan Repatriation Conference?"

"I did. It's awesome to meet you. When you explained about the Feathers of Shardaa symbol and what really happened to the wings of my people, I felt so sad and betrayed, even though it happened so long ago. The time between doesn't really matter. Whether it was a thousand years ago or just yesterday, it is still a tragedy that affects all Xenolfans. I'm happy that you have brought the truth out of the Shardaa Sector," Sheena said.

"Well said. Very soon, the Humolfan Government will distribute an accurate history book from the Shardaa Sector to the rest of the Syrenthian Galaxy that you will want to read. It explains everything that you could possibly wonder about regarding what had happened," Estrus said.

The waitress came back to take Estrus's order and saw that the

Xenolfan woman had joined her.

"I'm sorry. I still haven't looked at the menu. Sheena, what would you recommend from the menu?" Estrus asked.

"Oh, I like the Quillexx," Sheena said.

"Okay. I will go with her suggestion," Estrus told the waitress.

"Did you want to order as well, or do you want to get another drink?" the waitress asked Sheena.

"I'll have the Quillexx as well…and another drink," Sheena said.

The waitress took their orders, grabbed the menu from the table, and left.

"So, I stopped on Enax Port because my 38th great grandmother, Destiny, who was a Xenolfan, and my 38th great grandfather, who was a human, were from here. She must have moved here from Olf Teruda when she met him. I just thought if I stopped here, I would feel a connection to them somehow. I don't even know where on Enax Port they lived," Estrus said.

"I wonder if they lived in the ancient city of Nasatomia in the southern hemisphere," Sheena said. "It would have been the only city on Enax Port one thousand years ago. You should check that out."

"Really? Cool. Maybe you can show me where it's at," Estrus suggested.

"I would love to. So, Estrus, tell me a little about yourself."

"Well, I live on the planet S6 in the Shardaa Star System. The Shardaa Sector includes the Shardaa System, the Sharasp Tharrian Asteroid Mass, and the Shaeolian Black Hole, just so you know. Anyway, I work for the Humolfan Government there. I was selected as the new lead on searching for an advocate to repatriate my people. I am lucky enough to have had success in finding Sierra Shalinsky. I have a dog named Thepsi, who is actually from here on Enax Port. He was brought to me by a friend. Oh, and I'm single and bisexual," Estrus said.

Sheena smiled. "I'm also bisexual, so I think we're going to get along real well," Sheena said.

"I couldn't touch it, but I did see a Xenolfan vulva at the sex clinic that Sierra Shalinsky brought me to. I felt an immediate connection with Xenolfans because most of us Humolfan females also have reuleaux triangular vulvas."

"Really?" Sheena asked, getting excited. "Although us Xenolfans have been able to participate openly in the swinger community for only several months, I've heard about Sierra Shalinsky from when I first started attending the parties here. I guess she's a unicorn…and, from what I hear, a hot one at that. Sierra has some close friends that I know, Vincent and Shaslin Macenburg. Those two are hot. Mmm… Although I have not played with them, I want to. I really enjoy the play rooms at the parties. Watching others in action makes me so wet."

"I've actually met Vincent and Shaslin! Sierra has been in a coma for seven months."

"Yes… That would make sense why I've never seen her here."

The waitress brought their food and more drinks to the table. As they ate their meals, they had a great conversation and became acquainted with each other on a more intimate level. By the time they finished their meals, they were both very aroused with each other.

"Well, Sheena, I need to cool off. You're getting me pretty wet. Perhaps after you show me this ancient city of Nasatomia, we can satisfy our curiosities," Estrus said.

"I would like that very much," Sheena said.

Sheena felt a warm, arousing surge of excitement slowly progress right to her pussy. She found herself breathing heavily and had to force herself to calm down.

Estrus paid for both her own bill and Sheena's bill using the credits that Sierra had given her back on Red Jacket. Sheena was very appreciative of the gesture and expressed that appreciation by kissing her on the mouth. It turned into a passionate kiss, their two different skin tones adding to their excitement. Other patrons of Aura's Delight gazed at them with a bit of envy. Many of them would have wanted to be in Sheena's position.

As they left their seats and walked together toward the door, Estrus wrapped a black wing around Sheena.

The ancient city of Nasatomia was very well intact for being as old as it was. Although it was set aside as a memorial and no one lived there in their present day, the local governance maintained it regularly. Estrus flew the *Aileron* over the ancient city and peered down at the old buildings and structures. She wondered which area her 38th great grandparents were from. As she made several passes over the ancient city, Estrus realized the connection she was hoping for was not there. They were just old buildings and nothing more. She felt a much deeper connection at the Grave of Mothers on S4. With a heavy sigh, she flew the *Aileron* away from the ancient city.

"Well, thank you for showing me where Nasatomia was located. I guess I'm not exactly sure what I was expecting. I don't really feel anything special here regarding my ancestors," Estrus said.

"Well, at least you made an effort to visit the place and you will always have that," Sheena said.

"So, where shall we fly?" Estrus asked.

"How about my place?" Sheena suggested.

Estrus looked at Sheena and smiled.

"Show me the way, sexy."

Before Estrus even landed the *Aileron,* she was wet with anticipation. Sheena was fairly quiet during the flight to her house. After they landed and entered the house, Sheena quickly went into the bathroom to freshen up.

"I'll be right out. Make yourself comfortable," Sheena said.

Estrus stood in the living room, looking at the art on the walls. Most of the paintings were very erotic. Estrus could tell Sheena was very sexual. She walked over to the couch and sat down.

"I figured I would get a bit more comfortable," Sheena said from the doorway.

Estrus looked up and saw that Sheena was completely nude. Her bluish-gray breasts were very nice. Estrus studied her long thighs and followed them up to her smoothly shaved reuleaux triangular vulva.

"That does look a bit more comfortable. I should join you," Estrus said, smiling.

"You should definitely join me."

Estrus slipped out of her clothes, carefully working around her wings. Sheena looked at her gray body and noticed the Feathers of Shardaa tattoo above her pussy. The beautiful breasts and smooth labia turned Sheena on in ways she had not felt before. She felt a connection because of the same reuleaux triangular genital shape, the same long, white hair color—although Sheena's was curly—and the same sapphire eye color. But it was Estrus's sexy grayness that really made Sheena's pussy throb. She walked over, took Estrus's hand, and led her to the bedroom. It was there in the dim light that their lips met once again. Estrus could immediately feel the length of Sheena's long

Xenolfan tongue. The passionate kiss gave way to them both sucking each other's tits and rubbing them together as they stood at the foot of Sheena's bed. Sheena took the lead and gently grabbed Estrus by the waist and guided her to sit down on the edge of the bed. Estrus spread out her wings slightly on the bed and spread her legs for Sheena. As a Xenolfan woman, Sheena realized this was a very unique opportunity and she felt special to be having sex with a Humolfan. Sure, she had been with humans too, but the act that she found herself in at that moment was the most arousing situation that she had ever been in. As she went down between Estrus's legs, Sheena looked up into her sapphire eyes. She maintained the eye contact as her tongue glided between the folds of Estrus's pussy. Sheena delicately made her way along each labia and explored the grayish-pink lips. Moisture dripped from Estrus's pussy and Sheena licked it up, enjoying her taste. Sheena's eyes then shifted to the Feathers of Shardaa tattoo with its intricate details. Seeing the broken calamus that represented the loss of Xenolfan wings, she was briefly distracted as her mind shifted. When Estrus put both of her hands on top of Sheena's head, Sheena regained her concentration and began licking the Humolfan pussy with quick movements. Sheena latched onto Estrus's labia and gently sucked them into her mouth. When Sheena delicately played with Estrus's clit, Estrus felt as if little surges of electricity emitted from her pussy in every direction. Sheena glided her tongue downward and traced around the reuleaux triangular vaginal opening. She plunged her long tongue inside and it was met with a fair amount of arousal fluid. Sheena enjoyed the fragrant taste of Estrus's sweet juices as they flowed forth. Moans began to emit from Estrus as she shifted slightly on the bed. Her breathing became heavy and she began to pump her hips against Sheena's mouth. Her body quivered for a moment as her toes pointed outward in the air.

"Ahhh! Ahhh! Ahhh! Ahhh! Fuck!" Estrus exclaimed, breathing in deeply.

Sheena disengaged from Estrus's pussy and attempted to wipe the wetness from her mouth. She found that not only was her mouth still wet, but the back of her hand was as well.

"Your cum just gushed out. Mmm, that was nice," Sheena said.

"Your tongue is amazing, Sheena."

They kissed once again and Estrus could taste her own juices on Sheena's lips. The kiss lasted longer than the previous. They changed positions on the bed and Estrus gazed at the stunning bluish-gray body before her. She gently rubbed Sheena's thighs and made her way toward that beautiful blue pussy. Estrus put two of her own fingers into her mouth to moisten them. She took her middle and ring fingers that she had moistened and slid them into Sheena's vagina. She positioned her index finger on Sheena's right labia and her pinkie on Sheena's left labia. With her thumb, Estrus massaged Sheena's asscheek. Moving her hand around in gentle motions, Estrus planted her tongue on Sheena's clitoris and flicked side to side. Sheena experienced attention on every part of her pussy and felt as if she was going to melt with orgasmic bliss. Estrus continued to manipulate Sheena's pussy. Finally, she withdrew her hand and fully licked at the pussy with graceful strokes. Sheena's bluish-gray hips began to rotate and a reverberating purr began to emit from her mouth. Estrus looked up with curiosity, but continued to lick her pussy. Suddenly, the purr became a loud, reverberating scream that was deafening. Sheena's legs came together tight against Estrus's head and she pushed her pussy up into Estrus's face. Sheena held that position for a long moment and then relaxed. Estrus stood up from the edge of the bed and covered her ears.

"Damn! What the hell was that?" Estrus asked.

"I'm sorry. When us Xenolfans reach orgasm, we do that. You get used to it after a few times," Sheena said.

"So I've heard… I don't know…that was pretty loud," Estrus said.

Sheena giggled. "Here, lie down on the bed. I want to show you my favorite thing to do…scissoring," Sheena said.

Estrus complied and lay on the bed with her legs spread open. Sheena swung one leg over Estrus and positioned her pussy against Estrus's pussy. They could immediately feel the heat radiate from each other's vulvas. They began tribbing together. Sheena held one hand under Estrus's leg for better leverage. They both rocked their hips in unison, their labia and clits rubbing against each other. The creamy sounds and musky scent aroused them both further. Sheena looked down at her bluish-gray body intimately connecting with Estrus's warm gray body and saw their hot pussies joining. They closed their eyes for a long moment, savoring the ecstasy as they pumped their hips together. When Sheena opened her eyes again, she looked down at Estrus's large, gray tits bouncing in circular motions. They smiled at each other. As they built up to their second orgasms, they both began to grind their pussies against each other even harder. Tribbing was Sheena's absolute favorite sex position. Breathing heavily, they began to moan with cries of ultimate joy. Their moans alternated back and forth for a bit and as they approached orgasm, the moans were in sync with each other. Suddenly, they burst with screams as their pussies spasmed, dripping white cream. Sheena's loud, reverberating screech did not catch Estrus off guard the second time. Their cream mixed together as they continued tribbing for a few moments afterward, their climaxes slowly receding. As they pulled apart, their merged arousal fluid created a creamy strand that connected their vulvas until finally separating.

"Mmm," Estrus moaned. "Your favorite thing may just be my favorite thing now too."

Both exhausted, they lay there on the bed for a long time, embracing each other in silence. Sheena leaned forward and sat up on the edge of the bed. Estrus massaged Sheena's bluish-gray breasts from behind her and then began to explore the genetic bumps where wings had once been on the Xenolfan species. She felt around the surface of the two bumps that were located near her shoulder blades and softly stroked her fingers across them. Sheena looked back at Estrus, stared into her eyes for a long moment, and began to tear up.

"I'm sorry you cannot fly. If I could go back in time and somehow change it all, I would," Estrus said.

Sheena turned around to face Estrus and looked down at the Feathers of Shardaa tattoo. Estrus began to tear up as well. They held each other tight, their breasts pressing together.

"Thank you…for everything," Sheena said.

Estrus had one more day to kill as she waited to attend Aaranix Tuvelless's execution. She did not want to miss that event for anything. To Estrus, Aaranix was just a modern-day Siiteper Affelum.

One more day… she thought.

She decided to travel to Salinarr Nevis for that extra day. She had heard so much about the gaming planet littered with casinos that she looked forward to investigating it herself. As the *Aileron* flew toward the planet, the bright lights on the surface could be seen from the distance space. After passing through the planet's atmosphere, she found an empty spot in one of the many docking bays. As she disabled the ship's engines, silence filled the small bridge. An occasional hiss of vapor releasing from the ship's vents could be heard. She stood up from her chair and gazed at her reflection in the observation window. She was a bit nervous about being around a lot of non-Humolfans, but she was getting more comfortable with it. She smiled as her mind shifted to the recent sexual encounter with the Xenolfan woman named Sheena.

That was hot! And now for some casino fun, she thought.

After entering the long corridor that led to the entrance of several of the casinos, she noticed the usual stare from both humans and Xenolfans. Being the first Humolfan to roam free, undisguised, outside the Shardaa Sector had its frustrating moments, but Estrus didn't let it bother her. She walked past various casinos, including Blue Sapphire, Auracon's Game, and Phensiarr's Fortune. There was a small sign below Phensiarr's Fortune that said it was formerly called Aaranix's Gold. After making her way through Casino 21 and The Wolf's Den, she rested on a soft, brown leather bench in the corridor. She had never seen anything like the casinos before and was not sure what to make of all the machines and tables. Both humans and Xenolfans seemed to be having a great time playing them. She looked up at the casino across the corridor. It was called Golden Oasis. Beyond that was another one called The Ascent. Estrus wondered how much profit was made from the casinos. It must have been a great amount for them to have all the fine amenities each of them offered. She was still trying to wrap her head around how her Asparell coins were worth so much outside the Shardaa Sector. Estrus could only use the credits that Sierra had given her, unless she wanted to throw a lot of currency away. Back home, the Asparell coins were only worth a fraction of what they were out in the rest of the Syrenthian Galaxy. She thought about that for a moment.

What if I bet an Asparell coin at a table and then win? I would gain a lot of credits in return, Estrus thought.

Estrus stood up from the bench and made her way down the corridor. She passed the Lucky Stone and entered a casino called Lightyear's Treasure. Strolling over to one of the table games, she observed a game called Duet Array. She watched for a short time while the play continued. The dealer and other players looked up at her with a brief surprise and then focused back on their game. When the game finished, a seat opened up for the next game. Estrus sat down and joined the other players, carefully adjusting a wing on either side of the chair. The dealer was a Xenolfan male. Across from Estrus, sat a human male. A Xenolfan female sat to her right and two human females sat to her left. It was a game of chance and didn't require much strategy. It involved matching up a chosen icon on a digital display to a randomly selected icon. The game ended after five rounds. If no icons matched, the house would win. Unlike most other table games in the casino, Duet Array did not require the use of cheques, but simply used the player's actual credits. Estrus used some credits that Sierra had given her. Each player selected their icon and wagered the minimum of fifty credits. The dealer activated the first round. The display did not match any of the players' selected icons. The dealer took all 250 credits from the table for the house. Each player put another fifty credits on their wager squares. They all watched the display as the dealer activated the second round. The human female next to Estrus won the round. The dealer slid the 200 credits toward the winner. Since she won, she was able to choose the wager amount for the next round. The woman retrieved more credits and put 300 of them on her table square. The other players did the same. The dealer began the third round and the random icon displayed the same icon that the human male across from Estrus had selected.

"Awesome!" he exclaimed.

The dealer pushed all the credits from their designated wager squares on the table over toward the winner. Estrus watched as her credits slid away toward the winner, disappearing from her square. She frowned. For the next round, the winner wagered 2,000 credits. He carefully stacked them on the table's wager square in front of him.

"I'm out," the Xenolfan woman said.

"Me too," the human woman next to Estrus said.

They both continued to sit and watch the game. The remaining human female player looked at the stack of 2,000 credits in front of the man next to her. The woman wagered 2,000 credits to match his and stacked them on her table square. They all looked at Estrus. She pulled out an Asparell coin and slid it across the table toward the dealer.

"An Asparell coin? Well, there is something you don't see every day. Only the Syrenthian Brotherhood Knights of Darkness are known to use Asparell coins these days. Let me have the pit manager determine if the house can exchange this for credits," the dealer said.

He contacted the pit manager over a comm and asked the question.

A few minutes later, he received an answer.

"He said we can most definitely exchange it for two thousand credits," the dealer said.

He took the Asparell coin and gave Estrus the equivalent credits. She set all of them on her wager square. The dealer activated the fourth round. The icon that Estrus had picked was displayed on the screen.

"Yes!" Estrus said.

The dealer pushed the other two player's credits over toward Estrus. The pile in front of her was worth 6,000 credits, including her own credits. The fifth round was about to begin. For the fifth round, they each wagered the minimum of fifty credits. The dealer activated the round. None of the remaining players' icons hit. The dealer slid the 150 credits from the three remaining players toward himself for the house's win.

"Congratulations to our winners. Our lucky Humolfan friend has won 4,000 credits on that last round. That's pretty incredible for the Duel Array game," the dealer said.

Estrus took all of her credits and left the Duet Array table. She realized after her losses and the big win, she was 3,550 credits ahead. Except for Estrus and the Xenolfan woman, all the other players stayed for the next game.

"Normally, the pot does not get that high for Duet Array, so today must be your lucky day," the Xenolfan woman said to Estrus as they walked away from the table.

"It must be. Thanks," Estrus said.

"I watched the Humolfan Repatriation Conference and it's nice to meet a Humolfan in person," the Xenolfan woman said.

"Thanks. I'm sure you'll see more of us in the near future," Estrus said.

They parted ways and Estrus made her way toward the main corridor. As Estrus walked along, she noticed a casino called Sex Palace. There was an advertisement for carriage rides in a sex mall. She also noticed a sign that indicated the Sex Palace Theater had combined their Xenolfan and human sex shows into one since the forbidden xeno tryst law had been repealed. Since Phensiarr Charseaa became leader of the Xenolfan Government and overturned Aaranix Tuvelless's unjust law, many changes had swept through the Syrenthian Galaxy regarding interspecies relationships. Estrus's curiosity tugged at her to go into the Sex Palace, but not as strong as her hunger. She wanted to check out the interesting casino, but the night had flown by and she needed to eat and leave. She did not want to be late for the execution of Aaranix Tuvelless on Olf Teruda.

Estrus noticed a Syrenthian Brotherhood Knights of Darkness member make his way along the corridor in her direction. It was Narris!

"Hey, Narris!" she shouted over the background noise.

The man turned his head, saw Estrus, and grew a big smile. He made his way over to her through the crowd.

"Estrus! I can't believe you're here on Salinarr Nevis. I saw Sierra advocate for us at the Humolfan Repatriation Conference. Is she with you, or are you out here by yourself?" Narris asked.

"She asked if I wanted her to come with me on my galactic adventures and advocate for me, but I declined. Honestly, I have not had any real issues. There are just some surprised looks," Estrus said.

"Well, just be safe. Did you leave Thepsi all by himself?" Narris asked.

"*No!* I have Soltuss Yow taking care of my dog. And thank you again for bringing him to me. He's the cutest little guy ever. I even visited Enax Port where you found him," she said.

"If Soltuss Yow is watching him, he is in good hands," Narris said.

"What are you doing out here on Salinarr Nevis?" Estrus asked.

Narris leaned in and whispered into her ear. "Yilran Taw has me checking into currency pairing between credits and Asparell coinage. It seems there may be an issue with the exchange when we begin to financially interact with the outside galaxy because ours are worth much, much more than theirs."

"Tell me about it. I just traded an Asparell coin for two thousand credits in a table game," Estrus whispered back.

Narris gave her a look of concern. "Don't be causing problems before my research is done. Two thousand? Wow! Well, that right there helps me with part of my mission. Speaking of mission…this will probably be the last mission for the Syrenthian Brotherhood Knights of Darkness. We are a bit upset that during the Humolfan Repatriation Conference, we were mentioned as being Humolfans. While those of us who are left are still around, we will continue to serve and protect Humolfan Government interests, but this will be the end of us as a secret organization. There will no longer be a need for us

Humolfans to clip our wings and be in disguise. The repatriation has changed all that. If we had been kept a secret, it would have been different, but Yilran Taw wanted to be transparent about everything. So, hopefully we don't get attacked for being different than others. The remaining Syrenthian Brotherhood Knights of Darkness members will still protect, if needed, but any element of surprise is all but gone."

Estrus thought about what Narris said for a long moment and realized he was right.

"I'm sure everything will be fine," she said.

"I hope everything will be fine. Well, it was nice to run into you. It may be a smaller galaxy than I thought," Narris said.

"Yes. Well, good luck with your mission," Estrus said in a low voice.

Narris continued down the corridor and disappeared from view. Estrus began searching for a restaurant.

Sierra Shalinsky sat in the living room of Braxton and Priscilla Stryderr's house on Exandra discussing her interactions on Asparr Celtarious.

"I can't believe the Superior Mountain Club did that to you," Priscilla said.

"The fucking Jinkins all need to pay for what they did," Sierra said.

The fury in her voice was extreme. Priscilla tried to calm her down.

"Braxton will check with the Syrenthian Government to see if they can do something about it," Priscilla said.

"I will talk to some people and see what we can do for you. You need to relax. We'll figure this out," Braxton said.

"It's very difficult to relax when someone stole my property, my house, and all my possessions," Sierra said.

Priscilla sat next to her and gave her a hug. She looked deep into Sierra's eyes for a long moment.

"I know something that will relax you," Priscilla said.

Sierra smiled. "Oh, Priscilla Pussy Lips, you are a persuasive woman."

"I haven't heard that nickname in a very long time," Priscilla said.

Braxton kneeled on the floor between Sierra's legs and began to rub her thighs. With their history of threesomes, Sierra had no doubt they would relax her. She accepted their offer and let them calm her frustrations. Braxton gently rubbed the palm of his hand against her pussy through the fabric of her pants. The distinct outline of her labia became more prominent as he rubbed in circles. Her tense muscles began to relax as she focused on the pleasurable feeling Braxton was creating. Priscilla caressed Sierra's boobs through the cloth of her top, gently massaging them.

"Let's get these clothes off you so we can really relax you," Priscilla said.

Sierra stood from the couch and took her top off. Braxton helped with her pants. Soon, they were all nude, their clothes thrown about the living room. Braxton kissed Sierra passionately on the mouth and they both fell to the couch. He pulled away from the kiss and she looked up at him with her alluring blue eyes. The black eye liner she wore accentuated their beauty. As Braxton knelt back down and planted his mouth on her pink pussy lips, Priscilla sucked her plump tits, alternating between each.

"Mmm... Braxton, your tongue feels so good," Sierra said.

Priscilla stepped up on the couch, swung a leg over Sierra, and lowered her pussy onto Sierra's mouth. Sierra licked at the smooth, pink folds and then focused on Priscilla's clitoris.

"Oh Sierra. I've missed your tongue," Priscilla said.

After a short time, they changed positions and Sierra lay in front of Braxton on the couch. He spooned her and entered her pussy from behind as she held her leg up, exposing the full view of their genitals in action. With each pump of his cock, Sierra's boobs bounced in sync. Sierra looked back at Braxton and then down at his hot cock where it disappeared inside of her. For some reason, she was not getting into her usual erotic, sexual mood. Sure, it felt nice, but something was missing and she could not figure out why.

Priscilla knelt down on the floor in front of them and began to fucklick them. She started at Braxton's smooth balls and slid her tongue up his hard shaft where it disappeared inside of Sierra's pussy. Priscilla continued flicking her tongue along Sierra's warm pussy lips and focused her attention on the clit. As Braxton pounded her, Sierra felt the beginning of an orgasm. Priscilla's tongue felt so good on her clit. Braxton pulled his cock out and Priscilla sucked on his wet member before he inserted it back into Sierra.

The orgasm finally hit, but was certainly not an intense one. The sex did relax her, however. Braxton pulled out and then focused on his wife. Priscilla leaned over the couch and Braxton entered her from behind, sliding his wet cock deep into her. She felt the tip hit far inside of her and she closed her eyes. Expressing her pleasure with a series of continuous moans, she felt a ripple of excitement ebb and flow from her pussy. It became more intense with each occurrence until, finally, his throbbing cock brought a wave of pure rapture that cascaded throughout her whole body. Priscilla looked at Braxton as she felt his warm load eject into her. She closed her eyes for a long moment, soaking in the ecstasy. As Braxton pulled out, both he and Priscilla grunted from their sensitive genitals.

Sierra sat on the corner of the couch, watching them as they finished.

"That was a great view. I appreciate you two trying to relax me," Sierra said.

"Do you feel more relaxed now?" Braxton asked.

"Sex is always relaxing. But…I have to admit that I wasn't feeling it again. This is the third time this has happened to me. First, at the sex clinic, then watching Vincent and Shaslin, and now swinging with you two. This time, it just felt too mechanical. I'm just not into swinging right now, I guess," Sierra said.

"I'm sorry, Sierra. You have been through a lot," Braxton said.

"Actually, I'm in love for the first time in my life. I'm finding sex with others is not satisfying to me. I haven't even had sex with him yet," Sierra said.

"Wow. Is this Sierra we are talking to?" Braxton asked.

"Who is he?" Priscilla asked.

"His name is Yilran Taw. He is the leader of the Humolfan Government."

Braxton and Priscilla looked at each other.

"Wait! He's the one I met when we discovered you out in the Shardaa Sector. He landed his ship, *Sharlexx,* in the docking bay of the *Syrenth,*" Braxton said.

"Yup, that's him," Sierra said.

"Well, if you are in love and swinging isn't doing it for you, no one said you have to keep doing it. When you do have sex with this Yilran Taw, I'm sure it will be on a much deeper level of intimacy than with other sex partners that you've had. Perhaps that is a missing piece in your life. You know, Sierra, you are the only person we swing with, but there is nothing like your own mate." He looked at Priscilla and smiled. "And if we don't have sex with you anymore because you stop swinging, that will never change our friendship. You will always hold a special place in our hearts," Braxton said.

"Aww. You guys are going to make me cry," Sierra said.

The three of them stood up and gave each other naked hugs.

"Let me get cleaned up and I will head to the government building and speak with them regarding your property situation on Asparr Celtarious," Braxton said.

"Thanks," Sierra said.

"Well, we should go shopping while we wait for Braxton," Priscilla said.

"That sounds fun. Let's do it," Sierra said.

Several hours later, they all met back at Braxton and Priscilla's house.

"I'm afraid I have some bad news, Sierra. I've spoken with several other administrators and we reviewed the existing laws regarding Asparr Celtarious. I even spoke directly with Edward Sirlain. Apparently, the main Syrenthian Government cannot accept appeals for local governance affairs on Asparr Celtarious. Since they had a law on the books, that property can be auctioned off after being abandoned for at least six months and we have to respect that. And there is no situational circumstance that stops them from proceeding, including you being in a coma for seven months. I'm sorry. I tried. Perhaps you can try talking with the local governance again."

Sierra sat there in disbelief.

"No… They won't do anything. They don't give a shit about me. They only care about their fucking club. Fucking Jinkins! I hate them! They have been a thorn in my side ever since I purchased my property on Lake Serenity. They have caused trouble for me from day one," she said, taking a deep breath.

Silence filled the room

"I tried," Braxton said.

"Yes, and I appreciate it. I guess I'll have to find someplace else to live. Well, I need to go. I'm going to head back to the Shardaa Sector and see Yilran."

"Well, be safe and keep in touch. We are so glad you're all right and not missing anymore," Priscilla said.

"Thank you guys for everything. I'll see you around," Sierra said.

• • •

Estrus landed the *Aileron* on Olf Teruda at the landing pad of the prison. Being present for the execution of Aaranix Tuvelless was very important to her. Although the former Xenolfan leader committed some terrible crimes himself, Estrus somehow felt it was a proxy execution of sorts for Siiteper Affelum from one thousand years earlier.

It took some time for her to get through security due to lack of protocol for Humolfans. She was very cooperative and eventually found her way to the public area of the execution chamber. She hesitated before the gray doors and then pressed the button to enter. There were several people in the observation area, both Xenolfan and human. Some of them had papers in their hands. Estrus made her way to the front row and sat down. Noticing the black wings, the other observers recognized her from the Humolfan Repatriation Conference.

There was a large window in the observation room that revealed an empty execution chamber bed. The bed itself was made of a laser-absorbing material. A microphone and speaker were located on the wall next to the window. The white room was well illuminated. A large exhaust fan was built into the ceiling. A single door was located on the other side of the room. Above the bed was a laser grid array that would simultaneously slice the prisoner into many pieces, which would later be cremated. Because of instant cauterization, there was usually very little to no blood. It was Estrus's understanding that because the process was almost instantaneous, anesthesia was never given to the prisoner.

Within a short amount of time, Aaranix Tuvelless was led through the door and into the execution chamber by two heavily armed guards. He wore a white uniform that matched his white hair. A grave look could be seen on his bluish-gray, patterned face. They placed him on the bed and tied him down at his chest and legs, leaving his arms free. One of the guards pressed a lever and the bed tilted upward toward the observation room. As the two guards left, the prison warden entered the room. Although it had been read previously when he was arrested and again during his judgment, the prison warden read his sentence. The microphone and speaker system at the window was enabled.

"Aaranix Tuvelless, you are being executed for the murder of

Tellaris Whitestone from the Syrenthian Government, the mass murder from the missiloid attack on Aamaress, the mass murder from the bombing of the thermal cube factory on Shar Nefalis, and the mining and production of a compound of human poison called Toraanium on the planet Montoraania in the Montoraania Star System, which is the Syrenthian Government's territory. The observers of your execution will be given a chance to say a few words, if they choose. Do you have any last words?" the prison warden asked.

"I'm sorry. I'm sorry it had to come to that. I warned of the consequences of interspecies relationships between Xenolfans and humans. According to the book I read, *Anathema Strain,* written by Siiteper Affelum one thousand years ago, their unions will create monsters. I was only trying to prevent that," Aaranix Tuvelless said.

The prison warden looked toward the window. "Observers can now respond," he said.

In the observation room, a tall, beautiful Xenolfan woman stood up from her chair and made her way toward the microphone next to the window. Her long, white hair was draped in front of her.

"Aaranix, I'm sorry everything has come to this. I love you and I will miss you, as I have since you've been in here. Your other poly lovers aren't here because they don't want to see you go out this way. But I had to be with you. I love you," she said.

Tears formed in Aaranix's eyes. "I love you too, Malanaa," he said as he tapped his fist against his heart twice.

When Malanaa turned around and returned to her seat, the other visitors could see the tears flowing down her bluish-gray cheeks.

Another Xenolfan woman stood up from her chair and made her way toward the microphone. She had several scars on her face and neck that were a lighter shade of blue. One of her eyes could only open slightly. She walked with a limp and held a paper in her shaky hand to read from.

"Aaranix Tuvelless, you murdered my human partner when you attacked Aamaress. You permanently disfigured me and I will never be the same again. This execution will be too quick for what I wish on you," she said.

The Xenolfan woman returned to her seat and a human woman walked up to the microphone. She looked at Aaranix strapped to the angled bed.

"My name is Rheena Whitestone. You murdered my husband,

Tellaris Whitestone. You took from me my life partner and left me in devastation. You deserve to die!" she said.

Rheena Whitestone made her way back to her seat as a human man stood up and made his way to the window.

"Aaranix, my name is Bradford Smith. I'm the owner of the thermal cube factory that you bombed on Shar Nefalis in the Industrial Sector. You murdered many of my employees who had worked for me for a great number of years. You weren't there to explain to their families that they weren't coming home from work that day. You trapped miners down in a shaft as well. I'm thankful the Galactic Emergency Medical Services were able to rescue them. Although we have rebuilt the factory, things will never be the same again because of you," he said.

He returned to his seat and no one else approached the microphone.

"Is there anyone else who would like to speak?" the prison warden asked through the speaker.

Estrus stood up, adjusted her wings, and walked over to the observation window. She noticed the expression on Aaranix's face at the sight of her. She looked at him for a long moment before speaking.

So, this is Aaranix Tuvelless, she thought.

"Aaranix Tuvelless, I was told that you are not kept up to date on current events in here. So, let me tell you about some recent events. My name is Estrus and I am a Humolfan. My species have been in isolation for a thousand years in the Shardaa Sector. We are the offspring from the union of Xenolfans and humans. We are the very monsters that you are so afraid of. Do I really look like a monster to you? The truth is, Aaranix, that we are not monsters at all. Sure we have good and bad people, just like the Xenolfans and the humans do, but whatever you were afraid of is unfounded. Let me tell you a little bit about your precious Siiteper Affelum. His wife was killed by a Humolfan. So, he decided to commit genocide on all interspecies families. He took them to the Shardaa Star System on S4 and killed them all. That is where the Grave of Mothers is located. For some reason, he did not kill the remaining Humolfans and left them banished in a desolate region of the galaxy. He hated my people. The book you read, *Anathema Strain,* was written by him to show his hatred toward us. We are not monsters. *He* was the monster. And you are just like him. The copy of *Anathema Strain* that was destroyed in the Xenolfan Government palace archives was exactly that…a copy. My people have the original book preserved in an atheneum on Shardia. We secretly seized the book hundreds of years ago and replaced it with a copy. It's nothing more than a hate book. And Xenolfans didn't lose their wings to microevolution. They lost them as a side effect to Siiteper Affelum's experimentation and genetic manipulation of Xenolfans to prevent interspecies breeding. He had history books changed to accommodate his lie. The real history of what happened will soon be in the hands of everyone in the Syrenthian Galaxy. So, I am really what you were afraid of," Estrus said.

She expanded her wings out and up high and then retracted them back to her sides.

"I tell you what, Aaranix Tuvelless, I can make it possible for you to feel no pain when the laser grid array hits you. Do you trust me?" Estrus asked.

After a long moment, Aaranix nodded an affirmative as tears of regret flowed from his sapphire eyes and rolled down his bluish-gray, patterned face. He had nothing to lose at that point. Estrus sat down and the prison warden lowered the bed back to its horizontal position. The prison warden left the room. When Estrus saw the laser grid array above the bed activate, she looked at Aaranix with glowing eyes. He immediately fell into a state of unconsciousness. The laser grid array instantly sliced him into many cauterized squares. Smoke rose from the table and the exhaust fan pulled the cloud out of the room. The window was then darkened to obscure the people in the observation room from seeing any further. Estrus stood and turned toward the exit. She followed the other observers out of the room.

"Why did I make him feel no pain?" Estrus asked herself quietly.

Because I'm not a monster, she thought, answering her own question.

CHAPTER FOURTEEN

YILRAN LOOKED UP from his office desk as the palace butler entered.

"Hi, Thomas," Yilran said.

"Yilran, you have a visitor," Thomas said.

"Is Sierra back?" he asked excitedly.

"Ah, no. It is…Arrvia," Thomas said.

"Oh. Thank you."

Yilran stood up from the desk and followed the butler out of the office. He made his way down the curved, wooden steps and to the front door. Yilran hesitated for a moment before opening the electronic door.

"Arrvia! What brings you here? I haven't seen you since Inatharr's funeral," Yilran said.

"Can I come in?" she asked.

"Yes, of course," Yilran said.

He stepped aside and she entered into the great room. As the door shut, the butler stopped next to them.

"Would either of you like a refreshment?"

"I will not be staying long," Arrvia said.

"No, thank you, Thomas," Yilran said.

Thomas left the great room. Arrvia looked around the room and then back to Yilran.

"I miss my son and I blame you for his death," Arrvia said.

She began to cry and Yilran could see pain and anger flow to the surface as her gray face darkened. She flared her wings slightly.

"I made—"

"You made a fucking mess!" she shouted, cutting him off. "You killed our son!"

Tears dripped from her eyes as she breathed heavily.

"No, I did not kill Inatharr. How dare you accuse me of that! I made sure the stronghold he was in was not attacked. It was specifically left alone during the attack. His fellow Dissident Faction members beat the shit out of him, but he came out of the stronghold alive. I saw it with my own eyes when I arrived on S3," Yilran said.

"He contacted me when your forces attacked. He was scared for his life. Then our connection went dead," she cried.

"Arrvia, we took out the power plant and their communications ended. He came out of the stronghold and walked toward me. It was one of his own people that shot him. Arrvia, I held him in my arms as he died. He told me he was sorry and that he loved me," Yilran said.

Yilran too began to cry.

"I'm sorry. I didn't know that. I miss my son," Arrvia said.

"I should have explained to you earlier what had happened. I miss him too. I did everything I could to get him out of there alive. Neither of us are responsible for Inatharr getting himself into that situation. But I tried… I tried…" Yilran said, sighing.

Yilran looked across the room at the picture of their son that sat on the fireplace mantel.

"I've been holding all of this in since the funeral while I saw you working on the repatriation. It just seemed like you didn't care," Arrvia said.

"Arrvia, I do care. Inatharr is always in my thoughts," he said.

"I'm sorry I accused you of that. I should be leaving now," she said.

She made her way back to the door and it opened.

"Arrvia…take care of yourself," Yilran said.

She turned back toward him and nodded an affirmative. As she left, a single black feather fell out of her wing and landed on the great room floor. When the door closed, Yilran leaned his back against it, covering his face with both hands. He took a deep breath and sighed. Removing his hands from his face, he looked down at Arrvia's feather and picked it up. Yilran walked over to the stone fireplace mantel and set the feather next to the picture of their son.

On her return flight to Shardia, Sierra tried to sing once again, but found that her voice was not the same as it was before she was assaulted by the Dissident Faction. During the entire trip from Exandra to Shardia, she kept trying to calm herself. She thought singing would help as it had in the past.

Gazing out the observation window, Sierra enjoyed the beautiful constellation of stars near Shardia, referred to as Blue Space. The light blue colored space was a phenomenon that stretched as far as Aamaress. Most of the space in the Shardaa Sector was very dark, however. She noticed a small asteroid in the path of the *Tenebris*. It must have been a straggler from the orbit of the Sharasp Tharrian Asteroid Mass. Sierra's old, black fighter ship with its tapered and swept delta wings was modified with some very nice laser cannons. She quickly fired her lasers at the small asteroid and destroyed the threat.

Soon, Sierra passed the moon of Sharsia and arrived on the beautiful blue and green planet of Shardia. She gazed out across the ocean as she lowered the *Tenebris* onto a landing pad at the Humolfan Government palace. Once again, her own home being taken from her occupied her mind.

How could the Superior Mountain Club do this? Sierra thought.

Sierra dismissed the thought. She exited the ship and strolled along the stone walkway and up a few steps, stopping at the front door of the palace. After sounding the chime, she waited, looking around the palace grounds.

What a beautiful day it is in the city of Naantress, she thought.

Sunlight brightened the green grass and surrounding trees. A blue butterfly flew toward her and landed on the red leaves of a nearby shrub.

An intercom sounded next to the door. "May I help you?" the butler asked.

"Hello. It's Sierra Shalinsky. I'm here to see Yilran," she said.

"One moment," Thomas said.

The butler made his way back up to Yilran's office. Yilran was looking over a treaty and realized the Humolfans owned more territory in the Syrenthian Galaxy than the Xenolfans did. He looked up from the papers on his desk as Thomas approached again.

"Hi, Thomas," Yilran said.

"Yilran, you have another visitor," Thomas said.

"Are you joking? How am I ever going to get this foreign government treaty looked over? Who is it this time?" he asked.

"It's Sierra Shalinsky, sir," Thomas said.

Yilran stood up from his desk in surprise. He left the office toward the mezzanine and jumped off, expanding his wings. Yilran soared down to the front door, just missing the chandelier. Thomas looked down over the railing in amazement. Yilran opened the door and Sierra turned toward him. Their eyes met and they both smiled. Yilran stepped out and kissed her passionately on the lips.

"Seeing you makes my heart sing," Yilran said.

Sierra took a deep breath and smiled once again.

"I've missed you, Yilran," she said.

"Please, come in," he said.

They stepped into the palace great room and the door automatically slid shut behind them. After they made themselves comfortable on the couch, Thomas stopped next to them.

"Refreshments?" he asked.

"I'll have a Ginger Alquinola, if you have one," Sierra said.

"We do. And for you, Yilran?"

"I'll have the same," Yilran said.

"Were you able to see the Humolfan Repatriation Conference?" Sierra asked.

"Unlike comm signals, we normally aren't able to see low-level broadcasts from that far away, but a signal booster made it possible for us to see the conference. So, I was able to see it. You did a wonderful job advocating for us. Estrus was a great help as well. It was nice that she was able to save that man who fell from the balcony. I've been in contact with Edward Sirlain from the Syrenthian Government and Phensiarr Charseaa from the Xenolfan Government. We have worked out many details of government interaction. Some things were already put into place before the conference. I'm currently looking over a treaty that was drafted by them for our three governments to work together smoothly," Yilran said.

"Now that there's a choice for Humolfans to move from the Shardaa Sector to anywhere in the Syrenthian Galaxy, I wonder how many will take advantage of that. Also, I wonder how many others from the rest of the Syrenthian Galaxy will move here," Sierra said.

"In the treaty, there are limitations for either direction. But we certainly don't mind having Xenolfans and humans here. Like you said during the conference, if there are interspecies families with Humolfans, the next generation to come will have the ability to fly," Yilran said.

"Yes. It's profound," Sierra said.

"A little bit ago, Inatharr's mother stopped by, blaming me for our son's death. She is hurting badly. I explained what happened on S3. Now that she knows what happened, I hope she can finally have some closure," Yilran said.

"That whole thing is very sad," Sierra said.

"So, how have you been?" Yilran asked.

Sierra didn't speak for a moment as she tried to figure out how to tell Yilran about her predicament.

"Well, I have been terrible," Sierra finally said.

"What's wrong?"

"When I was in a coma, the Superior Mountain Club on Asparr Celtarious acquired my property. They took my home and all my possessions. The local governance has a rule that if a property is abandoned for at least six months, it can be auctioned off. I filed a grievance, but was immediately turned down by someone who is actually a part of the Superior Mountain Club," Sierra said.

"That's terrible. So, everything you own is unavailable to you and now you have nowhere to live?"

"That's correct. I can ask my parents if I can stay with them for a while until I find another place. They live on Stilkoten Artibular where I grew up. It's a beautiful planet," Sierra said.

Yilran looked up for a moment and stared at the chandelier.

"Would you like to stay here in the palace on Shardia? I have plenty of guest rooms," Yilran said.

Sierra looked at him and contemplated his offer. "Okay…if you don't mind. I would really appreciate that. Since my unit in the Galactic Emergency Medical Services covers this region of space, at least I won't have far to travel for my job."

"Well, that's a bonus. While you were gone, GEMS actually did a training exercise on the Ocean Port Bridge. That went really well. Hey, let's go upstairs and you can pick out a room," Yilran said.

As they stood up, Thomas returned with two bottles of Ginger Alquinola. Yilran took the bottles from the tray and handed one of them to Sierra.

"Thank you, Thomas. Sierra will be staying in the palace. We are going upstairs so she can pick out a guest room," Yilran said.

"I see. Well, I will be sure to make housekeeping aware of that," Thomas said.

Sierra took a drink of her Ginger Alquinola.

"Mmm. I love this stuff," she said.

"It is very good," Yilran said, taking a drink of his own.

They made their way up the curved, wooden stairs. Sierra looked around, once again, amazed at how elegant the palace was. After viewing several of the guest rooms on the third floor, she chose one of them at the end of the long corridor. It reminded Sierra of the guest room that she stayed in at the Xenolfan Government palace on Olf Teruda. Instead of a window view of a beautiful waterfall, Sierra had a window view of the beautiful blue ocean.

"There has been something on my mind that I would like to discuss with you, Yilran," Sierra said.

She sat on her new bed. Yilran leaned against the door frame, giving her his full attention.

"What is it?"

"I know we've discussed this briefly a couple of times during our dates, but I've come to a decision. I will be ending my involvement as a bisexual unicorn in the swinger Lifestyle. I know you are not interested in the Lifestyle. You know about my past and how sexual I've been. Swinger sex has become too mechanical for me and I've lost interest in it. Perhaps my disinterest in swinging is due to everything that I've been through since my coma. I don't really have an answer as to why I feel different now. My feelings are very different than they previously were. I've tried several times, but I'm just not feeling it. In giving up my promiscuity, will I miss it? Perhaps. Perhaps not. My sex drive has gone down considerably. But my Lifestyle friends will always be my friends, regardless if I no longer have sex with them."

"Communication is essential in a relationship. So, I appreciate your open discussion on the matter. I certainly hope that, when the time comes, I will fill that void in your life."

"Yilran, I have no doubt."

"Perhaps monogamy is where your treasure lies."

Monogamy… Sierra contemplated.

"I believe monogamy is *exactly* where my treasure lies," Sierra said.

Estrus landed the *Aileron* in the docking bay on S6. She was so glad to be home. Stepping out of the ship, she met Soltuss Yow in the docking bay.

"Well, it's about time you're back," Soltuss said.

"I'm glad to be back. And how is my little Thepsi boy?"

"Your dog is spoiled," Soltuss said.

Estrus laughed. "Yes, he is," she said.

"It went well. He's a good boy and a little cutie," Soltuss said. "Hey, I watched the Humolfan Repatriation Conference. Sierra and you both did a great job."

"Thanks. I've already been checked, but starting next week all Humolfans will begin a two-and-a-half-month process of being checked and treated for any potential STIs. I was informed the sex clinics across the Syrenthian Galaxy are now prepared for us to begin," Estrus said.

"It is my understanding that next week, they will be distributing all the Humolfan history books throughout the Syrenthian Galaxy as well. People will finally know the truth in great detail," Soltuss said.

"That's awesome. Well, I'm going to go see my dog," Estrus said.

"I'm sure he will be excited to see you. It's nice to have you back, Estrus," Soltuss said.

Estrus made her way from the docking bay, down the corridor, and to her quarters. When she opened the door and Thepsi saw that it was her, he barked, leaped up onto her, and began licking her face with repeated kisses.

"Aww. I've missed you too, little guy. Don't you worry, mommy is home now."

Thepsi tilted his head and looked at her with the cutest little face.

After Narris reported back to Yilran Taw regarding his currency pairing mission on Salinarr Nevis, Yilran paced back and forth along a palace corridor. He knew the three governments would need to settle on a currency exchange in the near future. He knew it would need to take place in the next few weeks. Asparell coins were worth much more outside the Shardaa Sector than they should be, giving the Humolfans an unfair advantage. He knew that was going to change real soon. But there was something he needed to do before that happened. He put his finger to his chin in thought as he paced along the intricately decorated corridor. Suddenly, a sense of urgency overcame Yilran. He quickly sprinted to his office and activated the comm.

"Narris, I have another mission for you…"

On many occasions over the next several weeks, Yilran had taken Sierra out on dinner dates at some of the finest restaurants on Shardia. On their latest date, Sierra found herself at an elegant restaurant named Abbostyl. They served her an amazing pasta with marinara sauce. A glass of red wine sat next to her plate. Yilran had ordered the same dish. He had a glass of white wine. Sierra wore a light blue dress with artistic patterns woven into the fabric. The low-cut top section accentuated her breasts. The design had a reuleaux triangular cut-out in the lower abdomen region with three wing cut-outs on either side. The cut-out section revealed her Feathers of Shardaa tattoo perfectly. Yilran had purchased the dress for her a few days earlier. When she tried the dress on that day and Yilran saw that she had received the Feathers of Shardaa tattoo, his connection with her became even more special. She looked absolutely stunning in the dress and it brought out her beautiful blue eyes. Earrings, made from beautiful light blue sapphire, hung from Sierra's ears on long, dangling chains. They too complemented her eyes.

Suddenly, Yilran stood up from his chair, walked over to Sierra, and knelt down on one knee. He held a small box in one hand and opened it. Displayed before Sierra was a beautiful gold engagement ring with a large center diamond, two medium diamonds, symmetrically located on each side, and a series of smaller diamonds that wrapped down the curved sides. It was truly beautiful.

"Sierra Shalinsky, will you marry me?" Yilran asked.

The shock on her face was priceless as her jaw dropped. She was suddenly filled with tears. Other guests in the restaurant began to notice the proposal.

"Yes! Yes, Yilran Taw, I would love to marry you!" Sierra said.

He took the engagement ring and slid it onto her finger. He had worked diligently over the past few days to get her ring size and find the most beautiful ring he could. They both stood up and hugged each other tight. The other restaurant guests began clapping for their leader and his new love. Smiling, Sierra stepped back and looked at the ring on her finger as it sparkled in the light.

"Yilran, you never cease to amaze me," she said.

Her happiness was very evident with her beautiful smile. Yilran felt her love deep in his core and he emitted an aura of joy. They both sat back down to finish their meals.

"So, do you like the ring?"

"I love the ring. I love the way it wraps around. It is absolutely beautiful, Yilran."

"With everything settling down, we can focus on a wedding date and have time to prepare for an excellent ceremony."

"Yes," she said.

As Sierra lay in her bed, she stared at the patterns in the ceiling design of the guest room. With each passing day, she felt more comfortable in her new room. She could not believe she was engaged. Sierra realized she was engaged and they hadn't even had sex yet. Many thoughts went through her mind. She looked at the sparkling ring on her finger. Perhaps the love she found with Yilran was what she had been looking for her whole life. She looked around her room. Everything from the patterns on the ceiling to the fabric of the curtains was so beautiful. She looked at the dresser and then to the end of the bed. As comfortable as her new bed was, she really did miss her bed on Asparr Celtarious. Thinking about that situation again was just going to piss her off.

Fucking Jinkins! she thought.

Sierra sat up on the side of the bed and looked at herself in the mirror. Other than the decision to become monogamous, there was another decision she had recently made. She no longer had the desire to be the vocalist for Maranadda. Symphonic metal would always be in her heart, but after the knife in her throat, her singing did not sound the same. It actually hurt the nerves along her neck. She planned on breaking the news to her bandmates in person. She also planned on working with Aymreth Rosenn so that Aymreth could be a better vocalist for the band. She knew her throat would feel a bit painful to train Aymreth, but it would only be temporary. Sierra was able to hear some of Aymreth's vocals and thought she was very good. She just needed a few pointers. Under the circumstances, Sierra hoped the fans would understand. But she was not going to hold her breath. Maranadda fans have not been so understanding in the past, like the time at the Silver Star Concert Hall on Salinarr Nevis. Many fans had started a riot because Sierra was not there to sing at the beginning of the show. What a disaster that was.

Sierra's thoughts then shifted to her work. She had been back to work at the Galactic Emergency Medical Services on Relistorr for a week. She enjoyed working with Sethain and Rasmond. They had both congratulated her on her engagement. Her unit had already been on a run to rescue several space travelers in a disabled ship.

She stood up from the bed and walked over to the window. Sierra looked down at the palace gardens below as the evening settled in. She peered at the beautiful blue ocean beyond, sunlight reflecting off the water. Sierra had never imagined she would be living in an absolutely luxurious palace and be engaged to the leader of a government. Sierra also realized that, after the wedding, she did not need to work for GEMS anymore.

Hmm...

She planned to speak with Yilran about that in the morning.

The morning light brightened the guest rooms on the third floor of the Humolfan Government palace. Sierra awoke and quickly got dressed. After freshening up in the side bathroom, she left her bedroom and made her way down to the great room where Yilran sat. He was usually up early, relaxing in the great room before starting his daily routine.

"Good morning," Sierra said.

"Hey, Sierra," he returned.

"Once we are married, should I continue to work at GEMS?"

"You won't need to. Financially speaking, everything you could possibly want will be provided. It's just a matter of wanting to for the sake of helping others. It is up to you," Yilran said.

Sierra smiled. "Well, I think I will continue to work for GEMS. I do like helping people. But I've decided to leave Maranadda. My voice isn't the same anymore. I used to sing so beautiful, before my assault. All of my Maranadda albums are at my home on Asparr Celtarious. I need to collect all of them again so I can listen to them here in the palace. I would love to show you how I used to sound," Sierra said.

"Yes. Let's get those albums. I would love to hear every song. But to me, your every word sounds beautiful," Yilran said.

"Thanks. Speaking of Maranadda…I need to travel to Red Jacket and give them the news. They will just have to keep Aymreth Rosenn as vocalist," Sierra said.

"Okay. Well, good luck, Sierra. I need to take care of some infrastructure matters for the Ocean Port Bridge. Now that the Dissident Faction is gone, we will be rebuilding that bridge and the nearby buildings. I plan to make a memorial along the shore as dedication to those who have died from the attack, which includes Estrus's mother," Yilran said.

"That sounds like a wonderful gesture," Sierra said.

She stood up from the chair, kissed Yilran on the lips, and headed toward the door.

Sierra and Aymreth walked into the Maranadda studio on Red Jacket. The entire band was there. They all looked up in surprise.

"Sierra… Aymreth?" Yosemite McFarlin said in surprise.

"Hey, guys. I have an announcement. I—"

"Is that a fucking ring on your finger?" Arvon Estivant asked.

"Yes, Arvon. You're my favorite drummer in the entire galaxy and I know you won't like it, but I'm engaged to Yilran Taw," Sierra said.

"Well, there goes my chance to be with you," Arvon said, jokingly.

"Hey, what ever happened to your girlfriend, Rosheil?" Sierra asked.

"You know… It was just a fling," Arvon said.

"Congratulations on the engagement," Yosemite said.

The others followed with the same statement.

"Thank you all. Well, I have an announcement. I've been working with Aymreth to help train her voice. She's not a bad vocalist. She just needed to use her diaphragm more instead of straining her voice. We also worked on sustaining her soprano notes. With more training, she will be an excellent replacement for me," Sierra said.

"Replacement?" Arrian Trodder questioned.

"Yes. After I was stabbed in the throat, my voice is not the same. It actually hurts to sing. Sharp pains shoot through my neck when I try. I'm not even sure if I was a good trainer because of the pain," Sierra said.

"You did just fine," Aymreth Rosenn said. "The advice and training you showed me will help me become a better vocalist."

"We can practice a song here shortly and you can show us an example," Kulu Avolium said.

"Sure. I do need to continue the training, however. But I think you are going to like the improvement already," Aymreth said.

"Well, we understand your decision and the situation that you're in, Sierra. I'm sorry that happened to you," Sanarith Raastarr said.

"Thank you, Sanarith. Don't worry, guys, I will be around following Maranadda. Tell Shasta Varium that I'm sorry. I just can't physically sing anymore. And look…the fans will always get upset if a vocalist changes. You guys know that. You'll lose some and you'll gain some. It is what it is. Let everyone know that Sierra Shalinsky officially endorses Aymreth Rosenn. I'll try to come up with a public statement and send it to you when I get a chance," Sierra said.

"We'll let Shasta know. And welcome back, Aymreth," Yosemite said.

"Thanks. Shasta has been a very understanding manager. I think everyone will be pleasantly surprised with my new sound," Aymreth said.

"Hey, are there extra copies of all our albums around here? I lost everything I owned on Asparr Celtarious and I need copies of our albums again," Sierra said.

"Yeah, we do. I'll grab them for you," Yosemite said, leaving the studio.

"When you guys see Vincent, let him know that he heard correctly about my property on Asparr Celtarious. My house on Lake Serenity and all my possessions now belong to the fucking Superior Mountain Club," Sierra said.

"I'm sorry, Sierra," Arvon said.

"That sucks. Can you do anything about it?" Kulu asked.

"I've tried. But I live in a palace now, so I guess it doesn't matter. I still hate those fucking Jinkins, though," Sierra said.

Yosemite McFarlin returned to the studio with all the Maranadda albums in his hand. He walked over to where Sierra stood and handed her the discs.

"Here they are. You now have Esoteric, Novels, Discord, and the new album, Surefire, for your collection. Since we already had the recordings finished, we released Surefire a couple of months ago. In fact, after that concert at Civie Arena, we were having a discussion about the recording process we had finished and when to release it," Yosemite said.

"Thank you, Yosemite. I can't wait to hear my vocals on the new album," Sierra said.

"Oh, you're welcome. You sound angelic on the album. Your vocals absolutely shine," Yosemite said.

Sierra smiled.

"So, Aymreth, which song would you like to practice?" Kulu asked.

"Let's do Red Jacket," Aymreth said.

"Okay," Kulu replied.

Kulu turned on his keyboards, Yosemite and Sanarith grabbed their guitars, Arrian grabbed his bass, Arvon sat on the throne of his drum set and grabbed his sticks, and Aymreth stood in front of her microphone. Since Vincent wasn't there to adjust the soundboard, its current settings would have to do. Sierra stood off to the side of the studio, ready to listen to Aymreth's newly trained voice.

The song Red Jacket began with crisp, clean guitars and soon transitioned into a heavy, distorted, thrash sound. The double bass provided by Arvon was thunderous. Suddenly, the keyboards were added in for a beautiful, melodic sound that fit the song nicely. When Aymreth began to sing, they all immediately heard a much deeper and more powerful voice than they had previously heard with her. They all had surprised looks on their faces. Even on the vocal parts that required a sustained note, Aymreth did better than she had ever done before. When the song ended, they all clapped.

"Wow, Aymreth, that was excellent!" Kulu said.

"What a difference!" Yosemite said.

"Thank you guys. The techniques that Sierra showed me were very enlightening," Aymreth said.

"I am totally impressed," Sierra said. "You guys will be ready for concerts again in no time," Sierra said.

Suddenly, Sierra's comm beeped and she answered. The band watched Sierra and waited for her to finish up the conversation and end the transmission.

"I just received a message from my unit director at GEMS. I need to leave for an emergency run that we received. It was nice to hear you guys play again. Aymreth, you sound great. Maranadda will do well. I have to go. Thank you for the albums. Oh, and you are all invited to my wedding. I'll let you know when it is as soon as I know," Sierra said as she hurried out the door.

"I want you both to know that I don't plan to leave GEMS after I'm married," Sierra said.

"Even if you're the wife of such a wealthy man? We noticed the palace when we were doing training on the Ocean Port Bridge in Naantress. It is very beautiful," Rasmond Echeon said.

"I assumed you would be leaving GEMS at some point," Sethain Absoneth said.

"Actually, I don't plan to leave," Sierra said.

"Well, we will understand if you change your mind, but it is nice to have you on our team," Sethain said.

"It's nice to feel wanted and needed. It's nice to use my Galactic EMT skills and have a team who cares about me as a person and the work that I perform. Working under your leadership, I don't feel like a plug-in module or an insurance policy in case shit doesn't work out with someone else. I'm treated with value and respect in this unit and that makes all the difference in the galaxy. You don't marginalize me, like my other unit director did," Sierra said in a heartfelt moment.

Sethain Absoneth looked back from the front of the shuttle toward Sierra. He sat at the controls of the medical shuttle as it left the docking bay of the large *Deliverance* hospital ship.

"Your words hold great meaning for me. Your value to this unit is priceless, Sierra. We certainly missed you when you disappeared. I want to thank you for your service and all that you do for GEMS. If you stay, it would truly be a blessing," Sethain said.

"Thank you," Sierra said.

The three of them gazed out the observation window of the medical shuttle. Galactic Emergency Medical Services had received a message regarding a Humolfan being assaulted on Salinarr Nevis. As more and more Humolfans were cleared from the STI testing, many of them were exploring their newfound freedom in the Syrenthian Galaxy. Unfortunately, there were a few incidents where humans and

Xenolfans had attacked the Humolfans out of fear and prejudice for them being different. Since there were new laws against it, and also laws against Humolfans attacking humans or Xenolfans in an opposite scenario, it did help thwart most issues.

"I cannot understand why people have to be total Jinkins! The report says the Humolfan was just having fun at the casino. She didn't have a problem with anyone," Sierra said.

"Yeah, well…assholes will be assholes, no matter the species," Rasmond Echeon said.

"So, this new data we received on the vitals for Humolfans will be helpful. It's not only helpful for our jobs as Galactic Emergency Medical Technicians, but I also have Humolfan friends. So, knowing their numbers is nice. The numbers are very close to the Xenolfan vitals," Sierra said.

"Yup. But we don't have any Humolfan blood on the medical shuttle and we don't have an adequate blood supply for Humolfans on the *Deliverance* yet. That is coming soon because they are asking for donations during the STI testing at the sex clinics," Rasmond said.

Rasmond put her long, brown hair in a ponytail and checked her EMT bag for supplies. Sethain looked toward the back of the shuttle from the pilot's seat.

"We'll be landing shortly. You may want to buckle in," Sethain said.

Sierra and Rasmond fastened their seat belts in the back of the shuttle. As the medical shuttle approached Salinarr Nevis, Sierra gazed at the countless casinos in the distance. Ship traffic was fairly heavy. Sethain maneuvered the medical shuttle toward the coordinates they were given for the run. As the unit director, he wanted to be sure they were as efficient as possible. Getting the location wrong could potentially cost someone their life.

He settled the shuttle down on the concrete next to an older section of buildings. The older casinos were a bit run down compared to some of the newer ones. After exiting the shuttle, the GEMS team made their way toward a small crowd that had gathered near a tunnel that connected two outside areas through one of the older casinos. The Xenolfan authorities stood near the tunnel with laser rifles drawn. Two of the officers held a human in their gloved hands.

"They finally caught the piece of shit," a human woman yelled from the crowd.

"Don't think you can come to Salinarr Nevis and do that shit," a

Xenolfan man said from the crowd.

"Stabbing one of our new Humolfan friends in the back from inside the tunnel? I hope you get what you deserve, idiot!" a Xenolfan woman shouted.

"I hope they make a good example of you to deter other idiots," a human man yelled.

Oh, they will, Sierra thought.

The people gathered were very much against anyone causing issues with casino guests from any species. They were not particularly fond of the man's prejudice actions. The Xenolfan authorities hauled the man away in handcuffs.

Sierra saw the young Humolfan female lying on the ground, covered in blood. Her wings were damaged very badly. One section of her left wing was torn and bent at an odd angle. Black feathers were scattered about the concrete. She looked up at Sierra with teary eyes.

"What's your name, sweetie?" Sierra asked.

The Humolfan's jaw quivered as she tried to speak, but nothing came out. Sierra felt her gray skin. It was cold. For being hot and humid on Salinarr Nevis, the sensation against Sierra's fingers was strange. She knew the Humolfan woman was not doing well. Sethain set the transfer board down next to the woman. Rasmond discovered the source of the blood that covered the woman. There was a small wound near her back, next to the damaged wing. Rasmond looked over to a metal staff on the ground not far from where they were. Blood covered the tip of it.

"Did the man they just took away stab you in the back with that staff over there?" Rasmond asked the young woman.

She shook her head in an affirmative motion as tears flowed down her gray cheeks. Her short, white hair was streaked with red blood. The woman looked over toward the staff and closed her eyes for a long moment.

Lifting the back of the woman's shirt, Sierra cleaned the wound and put a large bandage over the area. Her vitals were slightly off from where the new Humolfan data showed they should be.

"Let's get her on the transfer board and back to the medical shuttle. The doctors need to find out how deep this is and if any internal organs are affected," Sethain said.

They carefully lifted her onto the transfer board. Sierra gently held the hanging section of her left wing as they stood up and carried her toward the medical shuttle. Rasmond looked back and saw one of the Xenolfan officers pick up the staff and walk in the same direction they had brought the criminal who attacked the Humolfan woman. As they carried her, another Humolfan flew through the air and landed near the building. She came running toward them.

"Shaania! Shaania! What happened? I heard a Humolfan was attacked and I feared the worst," the woman said.

The Humolfan woman on the transfer board turned her head toward the new arrival and managed a slight smile.

"Do you know her?" Rasmond asked the new arrival.

"Yes. She's my sister. Is she going to be okay? It looks really bad," she said.

"We need to get her in the medical shuttle and get her up to the *Deliverance* for examination right away," Sethain said.

"So, you are her sister? What is your name?" Sierra asked.

"My name is Lydia. My sister is Shaania. We just wanted to come here and have fun. This is awful!" she said.

"Yes, it is awful. Whenever anyone is assaulted from someone else, no matter the species, it is a tragedy," Sierra said. She felt her own neck where the blade had gone in.

"Your sister has lost some blood. We only have a limited amount of Humolfan blood on the *Deliverance* hospital ship, but they may have enough," Rasmond said.

"I'd be honored to give some of mine, if she needs it," Lydia said.

"We may just need it. It's nice that Humolfans only have one blood type, like the Xenolfans. It looks like you get to see inside a huge medical ship," Sierra said.

They reached the medical shuttle and entered. After moving Shaania to a bed and strapping her in for the liftoff, they all fastened their seat belts. Sethain engaged the engines and they lifted from the surface of Salinarr Nevis.

"I guess I'll have to come back for my ship later," Lydia said.

She looked over at Sierra and Rasmond.

"Your ship will be fine. I can bring you back down to get it and you can park it in one of the docking bays, *if* we end up needing to travel to the Naantress Hospital on Shardia," Sierra said.

Lydia's look at Sierra was a surprise. "You're familiar with Naantress Hospital?" she asked.

"Yes. Yilran Taw brought me there when I was assaulted by the

Dissident Faction," Sierra said.

Lydia's expression of awe was very evident on her face. She tried to stand up and realized her seat belt was still fastened.

"You can remove that now. We are in space above Salinarr Nevis," Sierra said.

Lydia removed the seat belt and walked over to shake Sierra's hand.

"You are Sierra Shalinsky, our Humolfan advocator!" Lydia said.

"Yes. That's me."

"I'm sorry for what the Dissident Faction did to you. Do you hate us Humolfans now?" Lydia asked.

Sierra looked at the concerned expression on the woman's gray face.

"Humans, Xenolfans, and Humolfans need to learn to get along with each other and with themselves. There is no room for prejudice. No, I don't hate Humolfans anymore than you should hate humans for what happened to your sister. In fact, I'm in love with Yilran Taw. We're engaged!" Sierra said.

The look on Lydia's face was priceless as she gazed at Sierra's ring.

"That's awesome," came a weak voice from the bed.

They all looked over to Shaania. Sierra and Rasmond unfastened their seat belts and went over to where the woman lay on the bed. Rasmond removed the safety straps and looked at the bandage where the wound was located. The bandage seemed to be holding well.

"How are you feeling?" Lydia asked.

"It hurts where the man jabbed me with that metal thing. He kept hitting my wings with it and telling me I wasn't welcomed there," Shaania said.

Sierra looked into Shaania's beautiful sapphire eyes. "Don't you ever believe that for one second. You are welcome anywhere in the Syrenthian Galaxy," she said.

"We're approaching the *Deliverance* docking bay," Sethain announced.

"You just hang tight. You are going to see some of the best doctors in the galaxy in a few minutes. We did a recent training exercise on Shardia. Some of those doctors met with Humolfan doctors and they learned many things from each other," Rasmond said.

Sethain settled the medical shuttle in the docking bay. They quickly disconnected the stretcher bed and rolled it toward the triage center. Lydia looked high up in the ceiling to where the metal beams connected. She had the urge to fly up there and immediately dismissed the thought. From the stretcher, Shaania followed her sister's gaze and smiled.

"I know what you're thinking, Lydia," Shaania said.

Lydia smiled back at her sister.

Sierra, Sethain, Rasmond, and Lydia waited in a lounge for an answer from the doctors. Lydia was pacing back and forth as the three Galactic EMTs sat in the lounge chairs. Sierra wondered if the *Deliverance* was going to need to travel to Shardia for an emergency surgery, in case Shaania's injury was beyond their scope.

"This hospital ship is very impressive. We don't have anything like this in the Shardaa Sector," Lydia said.

"Well, GEMS services the Shardaa Sector, so the Humolfans really do have the *Deliverance* when needed," Rasmond said.

They all looked up at the door as one of the doctors walked into the lounge.

"Is my sister okay?" Lydia asked.

"You can ask her yourself," the doctor said.

He stepped aside as Shaania entered the lounge. Her left wing was wrapped with a brace.

"I'm fine…just a little sore for now," Shaania said.

"She has a broken wing. It will take a couple of months to heal. None of her internal organs were damaged from the puncture wound. She's lucky it wasn't worse," the doctor said.

"Thank you," Sethain said.

"I highly recommend that she see a Humolfan doctor as soon as possible. We may be trained in Humolfan anatomy and medicine now, but it will be best for her to see a regular Humolfan doctor as soon as possible," the doctor said.

Sierra looked up at the doctor as he left the lounge and then she looked at Shaania and smiled.

Using my gifts to help others is such a rewarding and fulfilling experience. I will always be grateful to help across the Syrenthian Galaxy through GEMS as a Galactic EMT, even after I become the rich wife of Yilran Taw, Sierra thought.

Chapter Fifteen

When Sierra arrived late at the government palace on Shardia, Yilran was waiting up for her in the great room. He stood up from his chair and met Sierra near the stairs. Yilran hugged her tight, wrapping a black, feathery wing around her. She looked up into his sapphire eyes.

"When I heard about the urgent GEMS run, I was worried about you," Yilran said.

Sierra kissed him and felt the warmth of his lips. The tips of their tongues delicately pressed together, playfully dancing around. Yilran lightly tugged at her lips with his. The kiss was long and affectionate. The passion Sierra felt was very powerful. She closed her eyes and melted into his arms.

"I don't want you to worry about me," she whispered.

"I know, my love. I will do my best not to worry when you respond to galactic emergencies," Yilran said.

They stared into each other's eyes.

"My desire for you has yet to be quenched. I want you so badly, Yilran," Sierra said.

"Will you move into my bedroom tonight?" he asked.

Sierra's heart skipped a beat as she thought about the guest room that she was currently staying in. She smiled.

"Yes!"

Yilran looked at her for a long moment.

"Sierra?" he asked.

"Yeah?"

"I would love to do the mating ritual with you now."

"But…I can't fly."

"Trust me. I will hold you tight as I fly high up into the open space above the great room. Thomas has retired for the evening, so we are alone," Yilran said.

"I want you to make love to me, Yilran."

Although clothes could be removed either before or after the mating ritual flight, they both began to undress immediately. As each article dropped to the floor, they both became very aroused. Standing before Sierra was the sexiest man she had ever seen. Yilran's long, white hair lay against his gray chest. His sapphire eyes were captivating. Sierra's eyes shifted downward, across his firm abs toward his hanging, gray cock. She studied his member with a smile. Just as he had previously described, he had a gray, human-looking penis. And it was a nice one. Sierra continued smiling as Yilran fluttered his black wings. Yilran adored Sierra's black hair and blue eyes. He admired her nice-sized, tan breasts. His eyes were drawn to her Feathers of Shardaa tattoo as he inspected the intricate details of each feather. Looking down farther, Yilran saw Sierra's smoothly shaved vulva. It was much different than the reuleaux triangular vulvas that he had seen on Humolfan women. This human vulva, with its beautiful, tan outer labia and its luscious, pink inner labia was very alluring. He suddenly felt his cock begin to swell. Looking back up at her blue eyes, he smiled. A pulse of ecstasy shot straight to her pussy as she stared into his eyes.

Yilran picked Sierra up with his strong arms and spread his wings outward. Sierra held onto him tight as he lifted from the floor and slowly flew upward toward the high ceiling. He was sure to keep away from the chandelier as he began to slowly fly around in a small, circular pattern. Normally, during the Humolfan mating ritual, the couple would circle each other in flight and then come together as they land, wrapping their wings around each other. Since Sierra had no wings as a human, Yilran had to compensate. As he lowered back down toward the floor and landed, he wrapped his wings around Sierra's back and she was pushed up against him. She could immediately feel the warmth of his body against hers. The surge of emotions she felt earlier intensified. They stayed in that position for a long moment before Yilran retracted his wings.

Sierra felt very special to have participated in a love ritual that was never intended for humans. The love that Yilran showed for her was incredible. They put their arms around each other and kissed once more. She felt surreal, as if she was dreaming, but when she opened her eyes during the passionate kiss, it was as real as could be. Yilran felt a rush of excitement flow through his body. His cock stood firm as he softly spoke into her ear. The arousing whispers were barely audible, but Sierra was able to decipher them.

"I love your warm embrace," he whispered.

Sierra's revealing eyes hinted of a lustful desire. Their bodies seemed to melt together in the long embrace. Yilran's passionate kisses made their way under her jaw and down her neck. He gave particular attention to the scar on her neck. Moving farther down, Yilran gently caressed her breasts.

"These are like divine fruit," he said.

Yilran kissed them with a sensual desire and sucked at her nipples. Sierra closed her eyes and tilted her head back, enjoying the sensation. Surges of pleasure traveled from her nipples straight to her pussy. Yilran alternated between each breast and kissed along their sides.

"Your kisses feel so nice on my tits," she said.

Yilran continued as he gently squeezed and caressed them.

"Let's go onto the soft rug in front of the fireplace," Yilran said.

Yilran took Sierra's hand and led her across the room. As they made themselves comfortable on the soft, white rug, Sierra glanced down and noticed his blissful rise. The rigid member was certainly a nice sight. She smiled in anticipation of the pleasure to come. As her arousal intensified, she could feel her juices begin to flow. Sierra lay down and Yilran stroked his hands lightly across her ribs. He kissed the Feathers of Shardaa tattoo on her mons pubis. The intricate details from the artist were visibly noticeable. The shadowing of the feathers was perfect against her tan skin. He kissed downward toward the succulent essence of her human pussy. The sexual experience with a different species was such an incredible feeling to Yilran that he seemed to be floating on clouds. As he delicately licked along the luscious folds of Sierra's labia, he closed his eyes and immersed himself into the experience. He playfully licked between each fold with the graceful motions of his tongue. Sierra moaned with such a beautiful voice.

"Ahhh," she sang.

Yilran enjoyed the sweet sound of her voice. He mildly sucked on her clitoris and pushed his tongue down against it repeatedly. Sierra squirmed slightly on the rug, her legs spreading farther apart. He explored inside of her vagina and was greeted with creamy, white arousal fluid. The musky taste of her secretions sent a pulse of pleasure directly to his cock. Yilran flicked his tongue along the moist lips and enjoyed the pleasant taste.

"Your sweet nectar is delicious," he said.

Waves of ecstasy rippled through her as Yilran continued to perform cunnilingus. Breathing heavily, Sierra grabbed the soft white rug on either side with clenched fists.

"Ohhh! Ahhh, that feels so good. Please don't stop!"

As Yilran continued, the cascading wave of orgasms flowed through her until they reached what felt like a free fall drop. Sierra felt as if she had drifted off the edge of a waterfall and plunged into the depths of a wet canyon. Suddenly, an extreme crash of pleasure exploded and the sensation carried on for a long time as every nerve in her body quivered. Cum flowed from her pussy. Yilran's tongue danced along the white, creamy drips. He finished eating her by sucking her labia into his mouth and slowly pulling away. Their wet form finally slid away from his mouth. Sierra's breaths were quick and shallow.

"That was the most powerful and relaxing orgasm that I've ever had," Sierra said, swallowing hard.

"Oh Sierra…you are delicious!"

"Lie down, Yilran."

They switched places on the rug and Yilran made himself comfortable. Sierra grinned at him and moved in between his legs. She blew warm breaths along his rigid shaft. Sierra knew from the heat radiating from his cock that it was going to feel absolutely wonderful inside of her. She kissed very lightly along his length, enjoying the taste. She slowly wrapped her mouth around the head of his human-looking cock and delicately began to suck. Yilran felt warm ripples of pleasure as Sierra thrust her tongue along his shaft. Gliding her lips against the underside, she made her way down to his balls. Gently cupping them in her hand, she licked at the smoothly-shaved surface. Sierra carefully massaged their soft form. Wrapping her hand around the shaft, she slowly stroked up and down in a rhythmic motion. She soon inserted the hard cock back into her mouth and continued to suck.

"Ohhh! Sierra, that's so nice. Ahhh!"

Sierra could feel the throbbing sensation in her mouth as he groaned. The intense feeling of her warm mouth made Yilran melt. He had never experienced fellatio so wonderfully performed. As Sierra moved her mouth down on his shaft, she extended her tongue out beyond her bottom lip and enveloped the entire underside of his cock down to his balls. Yilran could feel his swollen member pulsate in her mouth. Sierra tasted his pre-cum as she sucked at the tip.

"Oh fuck!" he shouted, breathing heavily.

Sierra pulled away and Yilran took a deep breath and slowly exhaled.

"You have a very nice cock," she said.

He stared at her with a dreamy smile. "Thanks," he managed to say.

Once again, they exchanged places on the white rug and Sierra lay on her back with her legs spread. Yilran knelt before her and took a moment to admire her beautiful, tan body. Soaking in the alluring figure before him, he leaned forward and put an arm on either side of her. He slowly penetrated Sierra, gently sliding into an incredibly warm and creamy place. Yilran leaned forward on his elbows and slowly pushed inward, inserting his cock all the way into Sierra. It was as if his human-like cock was in its rightful home, its proper place to be. He no longer regretted being different than other Humolfan men. It was the most wonderful feeling in the universe. As Yilran slowly pumped Sierra's pussy, a rush of amazing waves rippled through him to his very core. In the depths of her inner place, he felt an erotic sensation, slowly raging to the surface. Ecstatic moans continuously emitted from Sierra's lips. Her heavy breath was in harmony with the natural fucking motions. Being filled with Yilran brought Sierra an even deeper intimacy with him. The exciting sensation was on another level that she had never felt with any other partner.

"Would you like to lean over the chair so I can come in from behind?" Yilran asked.

"Yes," she replied.

Yilran withdrew his cock, leaving Sierra with an empty feeling. Her pussy spasms screamed for his return. She stood up and leaned over one of the chairs that sat near the fireplace. She placed both hands across the chair to the arm on the other side and pushed her ass in the air. Yilran moved in behind Sierra and, once again, slid his hard shaft deep into her pussy. They both felt the warm ripples emanate through their bodies as they fucked. He held her hips as he pushed into her soft, pink heaven. Sierra squeezed her pelvic muscles against his thrusting cock.

"Ahhh!" he groaned.

His pace quickened as he slapped hard against her asscheeks. Sounds of the repeated wet collisions filled the room. Sierra could feel Yilran's balls brush up against her clit with each forward motion. Sierra's tits swayed back and forth underneath her to the rhythm of his love. She turned back and smiled at him, an ambiance of warm, romantic bliss overcoming her. Sierra put her head back down and pushed back hard onto his thrusting cock. The aura of bliss suddenly became that familiar cascading wave of orgasmic pleasure she had felt earlier when Yilran ate her, but this time it was much more intense. Yilran also felt an unstoppable climax approaching. Sierra closed her eyes and rode the epic wave until it exploded into a rapture of pure wetness. Yilran burst inside of her and they both screamed with pleasure as they came simultaneously. He thrust several more times before pulling out of her hot pussy. The thirst of their pent-up sexual tension was finally quenched. They both made their way back over to the white rug and lay down, embracing each other. The calm relief of their afterglow felt very dreamy. They fell asleep.

Sierra never dreamed that she would be planning a wedding, let alone her own wedding. She strolled down the Humolfan government palace corridor at a quick pace, ribbon decorations in each hand. She made her way to a hall toward the back of the palace. Passing Thomas, she turned around.

"Do you know if the candles arrived from off-world?" she asked.

"They did, Sierra. I just put them in the hall," Thomas said.

"Thank you," Sierra said.

She continued at a quick pace down the corridor. Soon, she arrived in the hall. It was a very large room with a high, domed ceiling. A carpet of brilliant blue decorated the floor with eloquent gold patterns woven into the fabric. Sierra set the ribbons down on one of the many tables that filled the hall. She noticed Estrus walk into the room from another doorway.

"Hey, we have the cake scheduled to be made in the next couple of days. The cake decorator is one of the best on Shardia," Estrus said.

"Good. It seems like everything is coming together perfectly. The invitations were sent out a few weeks ago. I've already received most responses. I picked up my dress yesterday. You're going to help me with my hair before the wedding, right?" Sierra asked.

"Of course. You will look fantastic," Estrus said.

One of the housekeepers walked up to where Sierra and Estrus stood. She handed Sierra a menu.

"This is what the chef came up with for the dinner menu. He wants to know if you approve," she said.

Sierra looked over the menu and opened it. Browsing through the items, she was quite impressed. She handed it back to the housekeeper.

"Let him know that it's perfect," Sierra said.

"Okay. Thanks," the housekeeper said, walking away.

"Well, in several days, you will be Sierra Shalinsky-Taw. Are you getting nervous?" Estrus asked.

Sierra smiled as they walked toward a cooler of fresh flowers that sat along the back wall.

"Maybe a little nervous. Wouldn't you be? But this is so exciting. Estrus, I've never felt so happy in my life." Sierra stopped and turned toward Estrus. "This may sound strange, but thank you for choosing me to advocate for the Humolfans. I don't think I would have ever been this happy if I hadn't met Yilran." She hesitated for a moment. "Do you think if I was never assaulted by the Dissident Faction that I would have never met Yilran?"

"No! You were chosen as our advocate. He would have met you eventually. But I am glad he was there that night when you were assaulted," Estrus said.

Estrus looked at the scar on Sierra's neck. They continued onward toward the cooler.

"I want to show you these flowers I chose for my bouquet," Sierra said.

She opened the cooler and picked several different flowers from their respective holders.

"I like the display of colors you've chosen for your wedding. Your bouquet is going to be very appealing," Estrus said.

Sierra held flowers of fuchsia and yellow in her hands.

"There will also be hints of green in the bouquet," Sierra said.

She smelled the fresh flowers and put them back into the cooler.

"Who is putting the bouquet together?" Estrus asked.

"Thomas. He is really good with flowers. The fuchsia flower is the same type that Yilran brought to me when I was in the hospital," Sierra said.

Sierra and Estrus looked up as Yilran walked into the hall with a Syrenthian Brotherhood Knights of Darkness member. They made their way toward the cooler where the two women stood.

"Sierra, I don't believe you've met Narris," Yilran said.

"I don't believe I have. I've seen members of the Syrenthian Brotherhood Knights of Darkness before, but I've never actually been introduced to one. It is a pleasure to meet you, Narris," Sierra said.

"It's nice to finally meet you as well," Narris said.

"Hi, Narris," Estrus said.

"Hi, Estrus," Narris said.

"Narris is the one I told you about that brought me my dog, Thepsi. I saw him on Salinarr Nevis just before the execution of Aaranix Tuvelless," Estrus said.

"Yes. I remember you mentioning Narris when I met your dog. Estrus, you never told me how the execution went," Sierra said.

"As you could imagine, it was bittersweet. For some, it was closure, for others, loss. It will never bring back the victims," Estrus said. "I actually made him faint just before the execution so that he would not feel any pain."

"Wow! That was…noble of you," Sierra said.

"I would agree, Estrus, that was very noble of you to make him faint before the execution," Yilran said.

"Sierra, I have a question. Aaranix Tuvelless and the other male Xenolfans have patterns on their faces, but none of the females do. It is not something that was passed on to the Humolfan species. Why do Xenolfan males have patterns on their faces?" Estrus asked.

"I think it's just part of their genetics. I have no idea," Sierra said.

"So, the reason why I'm here, Sierra, is because I have a surprise for you," Yilran said.

"A surprise?" Sierra questioned.

"Yes. I've been working with Narris on the currency exchange that we settled on between our Asparell coins and the credits used by the Syrenthian Government and the Xenolfan Government. It is now at a much more fair rate of exchange with those governments than it had been. So, Estrus, your Asparell coin is no longer worth two thousand credits at the casinos," Yilran said.

"Well, shit," Estrus said.

"I didn't think you would like that," Narris said.

"Before the effective date of the new currency exchange, I had Narris make a very large purchase for me. When the Asparell coins were still worth a lot, I purchased a pre-wedding gift for you, Sierra," Yilran said.

"A pre-wedding gift? But I didn't get anything for you. I didn't even know that was a thing," Sierra said.

"That's fine. It's not necessary to get me a pre-wedding gift. But I could not pass up the opportunity to get this gift for you, Sierra. And I would like to present it to you now," Yilran said.

"Okay. Do you have it with you?" Sierra asked.

Yilran and Narris laughed. Sierra and Estrus gave them strange looks.

"No, I don't have it with me. You see, it would not fit in this room. In fact, it would not even fit on Shardia," Yilran said. "Narris, show Sierra my gift."

Narris pulled a hologram device from the pocket of his black leather jacket. He held it up in his hand and activated it. A miniature display of a planet appeared on the hologram.

"That's my home world of Asparr Celtarious. Do you mean that you got my property back on Lake Serenity?" Sierra asked. Her eyes lit up with excitement.

"Well, not exactly. You see, I purchased the entire planet from the Syrenthian Government. Asparr Celtarious is now Humolfan territory. But it's actually all yours," Yilran said.

Sierra's jaw dropped. "The entire planet? What about the Superior Mountain Club?"

"Gone. They've been evicted and made to leave immediately. You now own all of the Superior Mountains. The other citizens on the planet were given more time and a choice to become Humolfan Government citizens or move. So, if any of them choose to stay, there will still be some people there. But no member of the Superior

Mountain Club remains...even the one that worked for the local governance in the town of Nassathia," Yilran said.

"I...I don't know what to say. This is a total shock. Thank you, Yilran. I love you so much," Sierra said.

She gave Yilran a hug. Narris disabled the hologram and returned the device to his pocket.

"We can use the property as a vacation home. Would you like to check out your house on Lake Serenity to be sure they didn't violate it too much?" Yilran asked.

"You bet I would. Those Jinkins! When do we leave?"

"Right now," Yilran said.

Arriving on Asparr Celtarious was very strange to Sierra. One quarter of the population had already moved. Those who remained, were now Humolfan Government citizens. Of course, there were both humans and Xenolfans that remained, but they would soon share the planet with Humolfan residents. When Sierra, Yilran, Estrus, and Narris stepped out of Yilran's ship, *Sharlexx,* they all took a deep breath of the fresh air. They gazed across Lake Serenity toward the Superior Mountains.

"It's beautiful, isn't it?" Sierra said, breaking the silence.

They all agreed.

"It's breathtaking," Estrus said.

"So, those Superior Mountains across the lake are now your property. The Superior Mountain Club is no longer here, so any of their structures can be demolished, if you want. The other citizens that have chosen to stay are far from Lake Serenity, so there is some very nice privacy here," Yilran said.

"This will make a great vacation getaway," Sierra said.

"And a nice getaway, it is," Estrus said.

"Well, I need to see how badly my house has been violated," Sierra said, walking toward the door.

The house had a rustic look to it. Large, round, natural stone siding decorated the front. The remainder of the house was decorated with slate blue siding. A large, spacious deck could be seen off the second floor, overlooking Lake Serenity. Like she had done previously, Sierra tried to unlock the door with her usual electronic code, but it still would not open.

"I didn't think it would work. The cunts changed the lock code! I found that out when I came here last time and saw that Jinkins on my deck," Sierra said.

"I can use an override device that Yilran has on the ship. I'll be right back," Narris said.

He walked back toward the *Sharlexx*.

"Ah! That's where my adirondack chairs are," Sierra said, looking up on the deck.

Yilran and Estrus followed her gaze. Two blue adirondack chairs sat on the deck.

"Where should they be?" Estrus asked.

"I had them setting on the flat, brown stone slab next to the water. That's where I would sit and enjoy the beautiful reflection of the mountains on the water. I just hope they didn't fuck up any of my shit."

Narris returned with a lock override device in his hand. He joined the others near the entrance to the house. After flicking a couple of switches, he slowly turned a dial until something inside the door lock clicked. Sierra tried the door and it opened.

"Nice work, Narris," Yilran said.

"No problem. I'll just return this and be right back," Narris said.

"I'm going to reset this to my old code right now," Sierra said.

She pressed a few buttons on the lock and reset it to her old code.

"This is nice!" Estrus said.

Narris returned and joined them as they walked through the kitchen and into the living room. Sierra looked upstairs at the open bedroom that overlooked the living room. She immediately went up the stairs to find the bed nicely made with her small blanket folded across exactly as she had left it.

That's a relief, Sierra thought.

"I don't think anyone has slept in my bed," she said.

Sierra took a quick look in the upstairs bathroom and found a couple of things out of place. She walked from her bedroom out onto the deck and grabbed the two chairs. She brought them back down the stairs with her.

"Here, let me help you with those. I'll put them out by the stone slab you mentioned that overlooks Lake Serenity," Yilran said.

He took the chairs from Sierra and headed out the door. She looked around the living room and straightened up a couple of items. She noticed her comm messages were full.

"Wow. I can just imagine what I have for messages," Sierra said. "I'll check those in a minute."

Sierra continued to inspect her house. Her office seemed to be intact. She arranged a few items in her downstairs bathroom, next to the hot tub. Yilran returned from putting the two adirondack chairs out by the lake. The kitchen had the most things noticeably displaced. Sierra took a few minutes to put things back in order. She hesitated before opening the refrigerator.

"I'm not sure if I want to look in here. It's going on ten months since I've looked in here last," Sierra said.

"There may be blue and green flavor crystals," Estrus said.

"Eww! I hope not. I usually didn't keep a lot of items on hand because I was always on the run for GEMS and Maranadda. Here goes…" Sierra said.

She opened the refrigerator.

"Oh wow!" Narris said.

"That is stock full of ale!" Yilran said.

"Well, I didn't put it there, but I'll have some. You guys want an ale?" Sierra asked.

They all gave an affirmative answer. Sierra passed a bottle to each of them. They opened their bottles and put the caps on the kitchen table.

"Mmm. Not bad," Narris said.

"I need to check my messages," Sierra said.

They followed Sierra as she walked back into the living room. After taking a long drink of her ale, she activated the comm messages.

"Hi, Sierra. This is Sethain. You haven't been to work in the last couple of days. Rasmond and I are starting to get worried about you. Contact us at GEMS HQ on Relistorr when you get this message."

"Sierra, Yosemite here. We have not heard from you. After the concert at the Civie Arena, you just disappeared. Your ship is at the studio. I'm not sure what's going on. You've missed the last several practices. The guys in the band are getting a little pissed. Please, return my message."

"Arvon here. Sierra, I'm troubled… Are you in any danger? I don't know." The drunk, slurred speech came from Maranadda's drummer, Arvon Estivant.

"This is Priscilla. What is going on with you? I haven't heard from you in a while. Braxton and I miss you. Let me know when you get this message."

"Sierra, this is Yosemite again. Did you quit the band? It would be nice if you could at least let us know so we can find a replacement."

"Sierra, this is your mother. We are worried sick about you. I don't know what's going on, but we've contacted your employer, Galactic Emergency Medical Services, and they haven't heard from you either. Please, contact us."

"Sierra, this is Shaslin. Vincent and I are very concerned about you. We miss you and we are worried that something may have happened. The guys in the band are worried too. They have some concerts to play and have had to find a replacement vocalist in order to continue. We're all worried about you. If something is bothering you, let us know. We can work it out."

"I'm not sure if this is the correct contact information. Sierra, this is Garrious. We met in the cave on the snowy planet of Aamaress. I just wanted to tell you that I'm sorry I lied to you and I'm sorry for flying the missiloid into Winterfest. I am scheduled for execution tomorrow here on Exandra. I never had a chance to go back to my home world of Olf Teruda and apologize to my people. I know Aaranix Tuvelless is scheduled for execution there in the near future. The officials here said I could contact you with an apology. Sierra, you opened up my eyes to the truth about interspecies relationships. Please forgive me. Even though the time I spent with you was short, it had great meaning for me. Goodbye, Sierra."

"Hi, Sierra. This is Eslarr. It has come to our attention that you've been missing for a while. It's like you just disappeared from the galaxy. You've done so much for Gathin and I and we care about your well-being. If you get this message, please contact us and let us know you're okay."

"Sierra, you've been missing for months. Your mother and I are worried sick. If you get this message, please, please let us know. We've joined in searches for you. Braxton Stryderr from the Syrenthian Government has been searching for you throughout the Syrenthian Galaxy. Your bandmates in Maranadda have searched for you. Your work friends at GEMS have searched for you. There are a lot of people who care about you. We won't give up hope. We just want you to be all right. We love you, Sierra."

"This message is for Sierra Shalinsky. This is the local governance in the town of Nassathia. It has been brought to our attention that you have abandoned your property on Lake Serenity for at least six months. Asparr Celtarious local governance law dictates that the property is now eligible for auction. There is already one bid for the property from the Superior Mountain Club. It is recommended that you contact us as soon as possible. The property transfer is scheduled for next week."

Sierra sat down on the slate blue chaise lounge chair next to the comm, staring at the floor. She was suddenly overcome with emotions as tears filled her eyes.

"I didn't realize how many people really care about me."

"Apparently, you have a lot of friends and family that care very deeply for you, Sierra," Yilran said. "I know you've already been in contact with all of them, but I'm looking forward to meeting each of them at the wedding."

Sierra and Yilran's wedding ceremony was located outside on the immaculate grounds of the Humolfan Government palace on Shardia. The grounds were landscaped very well. Red shrubs grew at various locations along the palace parameter. The red leaves added contrast to the nice shade of green the lawn provided. The impressive lawn overlooked a breathtaking view of the vast, blue ocean. Faint sounds of the beautiful blue water could be heard splashing against the rocky cliffs below. The damaged Ocean Port Bridge was visible in the far distance. It was a beautiful, warm day in Naantress. The sky was a brilliant blue. Other than an occasional light breeze, the air was calm.

As guests began to arrive, they were routed through the palace hall and encouraged to take a complementary copy of the Humolfan history books that were available. The small gift to the guests told an accurate history of what had really happened one thousand years before. The books had also been successfully distributed throughout the Syrenthian Galaxy and given to educational institutions as well. Beyond the area of stacked books, guests passed a memorial that was set up for Yilran's late son, Inatharr Taw. The memorial featured his picture, lit candles, and memorabilia from Inatharr's life. Beyond the memorial, doors were opened to the outside palace grounds. Chairs for the ceremony were set up on either side of a white carpeted aisle that rested upon the green lawn. The carpeted aisle led toward a pavilion where a Humolfan gentleman stood, ready to officiate the wedding. The seats began to fill up quickly as guests arrived.

Gathin and Eslarr had arrived from Aamaress. Sitting next to them were Max and Mauve, two of the workers whom Sierra knew from The Avalanche Resort on Aamaress. All members of Maranadda were present. Sierra's wedding is something they would not have missed for anything in the galaxy. Yosemite McFarlin sat next to the aisle. Arvon Estivant sat next to Yosemite, followed by Arrian Trodder and his daughter, Sophie Enelra. Arrian's girlfriend, Jacquelyn Enelra, sat on the other side of their daughter. Next to Jackie was Kulu and Misty Avolium. Both of their children were going to be in the wedding party, so they were very excited. Sanarith and Arcashia Raastarr sat next to Misty. Toward the other end of the row, the new vocalist, Aymreth Rosenn, sat next to Maranadda's manager and booking agent, Shasta Varium. Across the aisle from the members of Maranadda, sat some of Sierra's old co-workers from her previous unit at the Galactic Emergency Medical Services. Alex, Aurora, Blaze, and Rachel did not want to miss out on Sierra's big day. Yosemite turned around and looked toward the rows behind him as members arrived from other bands that had supported Maranadda in the past. Members of Enchanted Resonance and Frozen Solstice took seats behind the members of Maranadda. All of the members of both bands knew Sierra and appreciated the invitation to the wedding.

An usher led the distinguished guests of the other galactic governments toward the front. They were escorted to the second row of seats on the left, behind the seats that were reserved for Sierra's parents. The Syrenthian Government leader, Edward Sirlain, looked very sharp in an elegant burgundy suit with his long, grayish-blond hair in its usual ponytail. The leader of the Xenolfan Government, Phensiarr Charseaa, also looked very classy in her stylish brown outfit. Since Yilran Taw of the Humolfan Government was getting married, he thought it would only be appropriate to invite the leaders of the other two galactic governments.

When it became apparent that all the guests had arrived, classical music began to play from a small orchestra that sat off to the side of the guests. The harmony playing from the orchestra had slight hints of heavier tones in the string and percussion sections while having lighter tones in the woodwind and brass sections. The usher walked Sierra's mother, Cathin Shalinsky, down the aisle toward the front row. Cathin moved over one seat to make room for her husband, Ralger Shalinsky.

Like he had done with all the other guests, the usher handed Cathin a wedding program. After seating her, the usher returned to the palace door of the hall. Since Yilran's parents had both passed years before, the two seats on the right front were left empty to honor them.

Yilran Taw appeared at the doors exiting the hall. He wore a stately, gray suit. Yilran's long, white hair rested at the front of his suit. His wings were immaculately groomed. He was escorted down the aisle toward the pavilion. As he walked along the aisle, he noticed his butler, Thomas, in the audience. He also noticed Soltuss Yow, head of Humolfan Command and Argenniss, leader of the Syrenthian Brotherhood Knights of Darkness. Reaching the pavilion at the front of the aisle, he stood next to the officiating officer.

The wedding party began to walk down the aisle. Narris was the best man. He wore a light gray suit. It was slightly lighter than Yilran's, distinguishing the groom from the other gentlemen in the wedding party. Narris walked down the aisle with the matron of honor, Priscilla Stryderr. Priscilla wore an impressive fuchsia dress and carried a small bouquet of fuchsia and yellow flowers. Next came the groomsmen and bridesmaids. The first couple was Braxton Stryderr and Shaslin Macenburg. Like the best man, the groomsmen wore the same style of light gray suits. Likewise, the bridesmaids wore the same style of fuchsia dresses. Braxton and Shaslin were followed by Vincent Macenburg and Rasmond Echeon. Next came Sethain Absoneth and Estrus. Reaching the end of the aisle, the pairs split up and fanned out along the front of the pavilion. After a short delay, the ring bearer, Aaron Avolium, strode down the aisle, carrying a silk pillow with the couple's rings attached. Following Aaron was his sister, the flower girl. Shanda Avolium proceeded down the aisle, spreading fuchsia and yellow flower pedals from the white basket that she carried. Kulu and Misty smiled with pride at their children and were honored that Sierra had asked them to be in the wedding. The colorful pedals made a beautiful bed for the bride to walk upon.

Once the children took their positions at the front of the pavilion, the orchestra began to play the wedding march. Sierra appeared in the doorway, holding her father's arm as they exited the hall. She wore a stunning, white corset wedding dress that was accentuated with sparkling sequin embellishments. Crisscrossed laces decorated the back of the bodice section. Along the train, off-white brocade patterns were visible. Sierra did not wear a veil. Estrus had styled Sierra's black hair very eloquently. It was braided in several locations along each temple. With the front length pulled back in a wavy style, she looked absolutely spectacular. Sierra was a bit nervous as she began to walk down the white, carpeted aisle with her father. She held a larger floral bouquet of fuchsia and yellow flowers. Hints of green were distributed throughout the bouquet. Stepping in time with the musical cadence, Sierra looked at the crowd on both sides of the aisle. She noticed Aurora sitting in the crowd. What a memorable time they had together. She then noticed Yttursal sitting in the crowd. Yttursal smiled at Sierra as she walked by, remembering their time together. Sierra turned toward the other side of the aisle and noticed Remywian Yort, the bartender from Volum. She was surprised by Remywian's attendance, as she did not expect her favorite bartender at her wedding. He was certainly welcomed, but it was unexpected. As Sierra and her father proceeded down the aisle, she caught a glimpse of Mazniriatt, the tattoo artist. He winked at her as they marched past. When they reached the front of the pavilion, her father kissed her cheek and sat down next to her mother in the front row. Sierra looked at her wedding party and realized she had slept with the majority of them. She certainly enjoyed her newfound monogamy, however. She stepped forward next to Yilran and smiled at her groom. The music for the wedding march stopped and Sierra, Yilran, and the officiating officer stepped up onto the pavilion. The pavilion was decorated with fuchsia and yellow ribbons and flowers. The bride and groom turned toward the officiating officer.

The guests looked onward as Sierra and Yilran began to recite their vows. The wedding photographer, as well as many guests, took pictures of the ceremony.

Yilran began first. "I, Yilran Taw, do solemnly declare that I take to myself and acknowledge you, Sierra Shalinsky, as my wife. I accept your faults and your strengths, as you do mine. I trust in your judgment. I'm proud of you. I have faith in your character. I believe in you. I promise that I will love you and maintain you. I love you and your boundless beauty and I will never forsake you. You are my best friend. You are my soulmate. You are my sexy lover. Our flame burns forever bright, illuminating life. I love you Sierra, my beautiful bride. I do. I do."

Sierra smiled at her groom.

"Before I recite my vows, I just want to say thank you for the pre-wedding gift of the entire planet of Asparr Celtarious." Sierra cleared her throat. "I, Sierra Shalinsky, do solemnly declare that I take to myself and acknowledge you, Yilran Taw, as my husband. I accept your faults and your strengths, as you do mine. I voluntarily give up my former self to give you my all…not because I have to, but because I choose to. I promise to be your pillar of support, no matter what life brings and I will never forsake you. You are the best thing that has ever happened to me. Our story is one of love, romance, and passion. Our story is one of commitment and compromise. It is a wonderful tale, a symphony of love, and a beautiful canvas of art."

Yilran returned the smile as the ceremony continued. Aaron stepped forward on his cue to present the wedding rings that rested upon the silk pillow. Sierra and Yilran exchanged rings. Sierra put Yilran's ring onto his finger first. Sierra had temporarily put her engagement ring on her right hand for the ceremony. Once Yilran had slid her wedding ring on, he moved the engagement ring from her right hand back to her left hand. The two rings twisted into place, connecting perfectly into a locked position. They both turned back toward the officiating officer. After a few more words of inspiration, Sierra and Yilran each took a lit candle and they held them next to a larger, unlit candle. After the third candle was lit, they blew out the candles they held and returned them to their respective holders. The unity candle represented the two of them coming together as one and had great significance for their commitment to each other.

"You may now kiss the bride," the officiating officer announced.

The crowd looked onward with anticipation. Sierra and Yilran looked into each other's eyes for a long moment and then their lips slowly came together in a long, passionate kiss. Their tongues merged together with a blissful expression of their love. Pulling away, Sierra rested her head on Yilran's shoulder and they hugged tight. Yilran wrapped his black wings around Sierra for a brief time.

"It is my pleasure to introduce Yilran and Sierra Taw," the officiating officer said.

The crowd clapped and cheered as Sierra and Yilran walked back down the aisle toward the palace entrance to the hall. The orchestra resumed the music as the bride and groom were followed by the wedding party back toward the palace. Sierra and Yilran greeted their guests as the guests made their way into the hall. Sierra was repeatedly complimented on how beautiful she looked in her wedding dress. She felt very flattered.

Soon, the entire wedding party posed for wedding pictures that were taken at various locations around the palace and outside on the palace grounds. After the wedding party was finished with pictures, they returned to the palace hall. The reception immediately followed. Each table was decorated with a fuchsia and yellow centerpiece, which looked fabulous. Sierra and Yilran mingled with their guests for a long time, making sure not to miss anyone. An announcement was made by the palace chef and each of the tables began to receive their food. The aroma was mouthwatering. The wedding party took their seats at the head table. A certain aura of joy filled the hall as everyone enjoyed their meals and each other's fellowship. Soon, Narris stood up to make a speech. The conversation died down and he reached for the microphone.

"Thank you all for attending the wedding of Sierra and Yilran. My name is Narris, and as the best man, I am honored to say a few words about the groom. I've known Yilran for most of my life. We grew up together. When we were older and Yilran took his rightful place as leader of the Humolfan Government, I dedicated my life to the Syrenthian Brotherhood Knights of Darkness. It gave me pride to know I could go outside the Shardaa Sector on missions to help my best friend with government issues. We all wanted to repatriate and Yilran was finally going to be the leader to make that happen. We first had to defeat the Dissident Faction with Operation Reprisal. The timing had to be just right. It really was the only way to free ourselves from isolation. For many generations, literally a century, they have thwarted our efforts. Unfortunately, Yilran's only son died in the process. Our hearts have bled with you, my friend," he said, turning toward Yilran. "Yilran was a lonely man for a long time…until he met Sierra Shalinsky. The Dissident Faction assaulted her and almost killed her, but Yilran saved her life. It's as if fate had intervened and created something so profound, the likes of which has never occurred in the Syrenthian Galaxy. A human and a Humolfan in love… The fact that we are no longer isolated to the Shardaa Sector has opened up the possibilities for interspecies relationships involving any combination of the three species in this galaxy. I am so proud of Sierra and Yilran. And I look forward to the day when I get to see their children running through the palace. That is to never take away from Yilran's late son, Inatharr. I'm sure any future children would love to hear about their brother when he was a child. Yes, Yilran has had a lot of weight on his shoulders recently. But what a fantastic job he's done with the repatriation, the government treaties, and the currency exchange. You know what my favorite thing is? He loves his bride so much that he acquired an entire planet for her because she had lost her property. It has added to the Humolfan Government territory. Yilran Taw has learned a great deal about leadership from his late father and he has done an amazing job. Let's toast to our beloved Humolfan Government leader. We love you, Yilran."

Everyone raised their drinks in the air. Narris put the microphone into its holder and sat back down as the guests cheered and consumed their drinks.

"Thank you, Narris," Yilran said.

Priscilla Stryderr stood up and took the microphone from the stand.

"Hello. Welcome to this wonderful wedding reception. My name is Priscilla Stryderr. It has been a pleasure to meet Yilran. I've known Sierra for a long time and I've never seen her this happy. Sierra is a strong woman with a kind heart. She is responsible for helping establish the important sex clinics throughout the Syrenthian Galaxy. Sierra and I have worked on numerous projects together over the years. We've both written articles on sexual health. We've worked very hard together as we diligently collected signatures on petitions across the Syrenthian Galaxy in our fight for sexual freedom. We stood up to the leadership of Aaranix Tuvelless and advocated for interspecies relationships. Sierra was a warrior in that realm. She had attended many events, even before I was involved. Her sexual freedom speech was phenomenal. Sierra is such a fascinating woman. Not only did she advocate for interspecies relationships between humans and Xenolfans, but she is also the former vocalist for the symphonic metal band Maranadda. And she is employed by the Galactic Emergency Medical Services as a first responder, helping others out during galactic disasters. When she went missing for months, I was devastated, as were all who care for her. When she was finally discovered, it was such a blessing and a relief. Sierra has been an enjoyable friend on many fronts and I will always cherish our memories and our friendship. I appreciate being her matron of honor. And I look forward to what the future holds for Sierra and Yilran."

Priscilla set the microphone down and returned to her chair.

"Oh Priscilla, that was awesome. Thank you," Sierra said.

Once again, the guests cheered and clinked their glasses until the bride and groom kissed. The palace staff began to clear the tables as the guests finished their meals. Sierra and Yilran stood from the head table and walked over toward a side table with a large cake on it. The three-tier cake was very elegant and featured fuchsia and yellow frosting designs on a white background. The two of them carefully cut the cake and fed each other a piece. They smiled at each other and kissed. Each of the wedding guests were served cake as the palace staff distributed it to all the tables. The delightful lemon raspberry flavor was enjoyed by all.

Sierra and Yilran visited the table where Gathin and Eslarr sat.

"So, where are you two lovebirds going for your honeymoon?" Eslarr asked.

"Actually, we plan to visit The Avalanche Resort on Aamaress for the first half of our honeymoon," Sierra said.

Eslarr's sapphire eyes lit up and a smile spread across her bluish-gray face.

"We would be delighted to host your honeymoon on Aamaress!" she said, twirling her long, white hair.

"We're looking forward to spending some time in a cozy cabin, snowmobiling, and skiing. Yilran has never seen snow, so I think he will enjoy it very much," Sierra said.

"You never know, you may see a new side to me if I can just relax for once," Yilran said.

They laughed.

"You deserve to have some relaxation, Yilran. I'm sure Gathin and Eslarr will be wonderful hosts," Sierra said.

"So, if Aamaress is only the first half of your honeymoon, where will the second half take place?" Gathin asked.

"The second half of our honeymoon will be on Asparr Celtarious, at the quiet and peaceful house on Lake Serenity. I'm sure both locations will provide a very romantic atmosphere," Yilran said.

Sierra looked at Yilran. "I'm immersed in a dreamy love world with you. I would not trade our passion for anything in the galaxy," she said.

Yilran smiled. "I love you, Sierra."

As the reception continued, music and dancing began to fill the hall. The small orchestra had moved inside the hall and provided a variety of music in classical form. Arvon walked over to the table where they sat.

"Sierra, may I have this dance?" Arvon asked.

"Yes, you may," Sierra said.

They headed toward the dance floor. Special dances that involved the bride and the groom were the highlight of the evening, especially when Yilran lifted Sierra up into his strong arms and flew around the hall, dancing on air. After the dances, the bride and groom sat and opened their gifts while the guests observed. They received many nice gifts from their families and friends. The time spent with those who cared about them most was truly invigorating. As the guests continued to socialize, great conversations were made. Current affairs were discussed. Nostalgic feelings were awakened. Old memories were reminisced. Sierra sat with Yilran and looked around the palace hall at all the activity taking place at each table and she smiled. To be surrounded with all that love made Sierra's heart sing.

Six years later…

Sierra found herself on the lawn of the palace grounds, in the same exact spot she had stood during her wedding ceremony. It was a gorgeous, warm day, like it had been six years earlier. The sky was, once again, a brilliant blue. The beautiful ocean could be seen in the distance with the familiar sound of splashing waves against the rocky cliffs below. In the distance, traffic could be seen crossing the new Ocean Port Bridge. Shortly after the wedding, the bridge had been rebuilt, connecting two important points on Shardia. A memorial park was made near the bridge to honor all of those who had died that day when the Dissident Faction attacked. Estrus's mother was listed among the names on the memorial. A lot of improvements had taken place since Sierra's wedding. One of those improvements stood in front of her.

"Mommy, I wish you could fly with me."

The cutest little girl stood on the lawn in front of Sierra. She had black hair, like Sierra's. Her eyes were sapphire blue, and her skin was a blend of tan and gray. She adjusted her little black wings as she lifted from the palace grounds.

"I know, Yilerra. I wish I could fly with you too. It is a bit difficult for me to teach you how to fly from the ground. When your father gets home, he will be able to show you some aerial techniques that will help. But you are doing great, sweetie," Sierra said.

Yilerra flew up and around her mother in circles, flapping her wings gracefully. She was the first child born between a human and a Humolfan. Others followed, including between Xenolfans and Humolfans. A new Feathers of Shardaa tattoo was designed by tattoo artist Mazniriatt with a display of multiple unbroken feathers fanned out. Once the new interspecies females were of age and if they chose to receive the new design, it would be ready.

"Mommy, watch this," Yilerra said, flying up high and swooping down.

"That's great. Spread your wings a little farther when you swoop down like that, sweetie."

"I can't wait to show grandpa and grandma!"

As Sierra watched Yilerra fly above her, she was so proud of her daughter. She reflected on memories of her pregnancy. It had been such a wonderful feeling, knowing that her precious baby was growing inside of her. The sensations Sierra had felt against her ribs when Yilerra would move around inside her womb were priceless. Sierra found herself immersed in nostalgic memories as she stared into the distance. She shook her head and looked up at Yilerra. Her daughter was very close to the airspace above the ocean cliff, which made Sierra nervous.

"Yilerra, you're getting too close to the edge of the ocean. Fly over this way," Sierra said.

"Mommy, look what I can do," Yilerra said.

The little girl flew up high and then swooped down over the cliff and out of sight.

"Yilerra!" Sierra screamed.

She ran toward the edge of the green lawn where it ended at a fence. "Yilerra! Yilerra!"

Sierra panicked as she looked over the cliff at the watery rocks far below. She noticed Yilerra swooping down and arcing back up far out over the ocean. Sierra held the metal fence tight as her heart raced with fear for her daughter's safety.

I wish I could fly! she thought.

Yilerra flew over the water and soared high up into the sky. She made her way back to the palace grounds and landed next to her mother.

"Wasn't that cool, Mom?"

Sierra knelt down next to her daughter in tears.

"Oh honey, you scared mommy half to death. Never do that again without your father here," Sierra said.

"Okay, mommy. I'm sorry I made you cry."

Sierra hugged her daughter tight and then looked into her sapphire eyes. "I love you *so* much, Yilerra."

"I love you too, Mommy."

Appendices

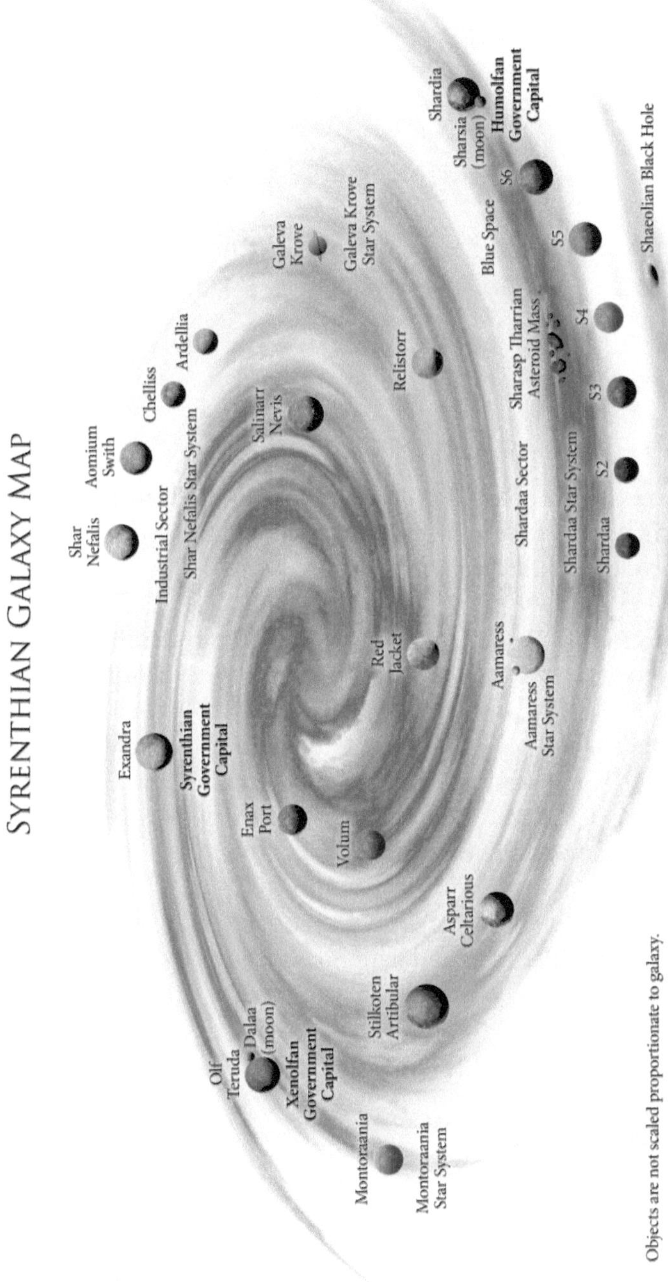

SYRENTHIAN GALAXY MAP
Shar Nefalis
Aomium Swith
Chelliss
Ardellia
Industrial Sector
Shar Nefalis Star System
Galeva Krove
Galeva Krove Star System
Salinarr Nevis
Relistorr
Shardia
Sharsia (moon)
Humolfan Government Capital
S6
Blue Space
S5
Sharasp Tharrian Asteroid Mass
S4
Shardaa Sector
S3
Shardaa Star System
S2
Shardaa
Shaeolian Black Hole
Exandra
Syrenthian Government Capital
Enax Port
Volum
Red Jacket
Aamaress
Aamaress Star System
Asparr Celtarious
Stilkoten Artibular
Olf Teruda
Dalaa (moon)
Xenolfan Government Capital
Montoraania
Montoraania Star System
Objects are not scaled proportionate to galaxy.

Terminology Glossary

Chapter references are where the term first appears in the novel.
(Some terms may contain slight spoilers.)

A

Aamaress - (Chapter 3) A snow planet located in the Aamaress Star System, within the Syrenthian Government's territory. Aamaress was the location of The Avalanche Resort.

Aamaress Star System - (Chapter 5) A star system in the Syrenthian Galaxy, within the Syrenthian Government's territory.

Aaranix's Gold - (Chapter 13) A casino on the planet Salinarr Nevis. Aaranix's Gold had a name change to Phensiarr's Fortune when Phensiarr Charseaa replaced Aaranix Tuvelless as leader of the Xenolfan Government.

Aarria - (Chapter 1) She was a Humolfan who lived on the planet S4. Aarria had white hair and sapphire eyes that glowed. She also had large, black wings. Aarria was the partner of Athenarr.

Abbostyl - (Chapter 14) An elegant restaurant on the planet Shardia.

Absoneth, Sethain - (Chapter 3) He was a unit director and Galactic Emergency Medical Technician for Galactic Emergency Medical Services. Sethain had short, blond hair.

Affelum, Myreness - (Chapter 1) She was a Xenolfan who had lived in the Xenolfan Government palace with her husband Siiteper on the planet Olf Teruda one thousand years earlier. Myreness had long, white hair and sapphire eyes. She also had large, black wings.

Affelum, Siiteper - (Chapter 1) He was a Xenolfan who had lived in the Xenolfan Government palace on the planet Olf Teruda. Siiteper had been the leader of the Xenolfan Government one thousand years earlier. He was the author of the book *Anathema Strain*. Siiteper had long, white hair and sapphire eyes. He also had large, black wings.

Aileron - (Chapter 4) A spaceship owned by Estrus.

Albriggs, Dr. - (Chapter 1) He was a Xenolfan scientist. Dr. Albriggs worked for the Xenolfan Government. He had white hair and sapphire eyes. Dr. Albriggs also had large, black wings.

Alex - (Chapter 2) He was a Galactic Emergency Medical Technician for Galactic Emergency Medical Services. Alex had brown hair.

Anathema Strain - (Chapter 1) A book written by Siiteper Affelum who was an ancient leader of the Xenolfan Government. *Anathema Strain* warned about a host of problems caused by relationships between Xenolfans and humans.

Aomium Swith - (Chapter 1) A planet located in the Shar Nefalis Star System, within the Syrenthian Government's territory. Aomium Swith was part of the Industrial Sector and was the planet that gave the Industrial Sector its name from the large industrial empire that was first developed there.

Ardellia - (Chapter 11) A planet located in the Shar Nefalis Star System, within the Syrenthian Government's territory. Ardellia was part of the Industrial Sector.

Argenniss - (Chapter 10) He was a Humolfan. Argenniss was the leader of the Syrenthian Brotherhood Knights of Darkness.

Argonn, Dr. - (Chapter 1) He was a Xenolfan scientist. Dr. Argonn worked for the Xenolfan Government. He had white hair and sapphire eyes. Dr. Argonn also had large, black wings.

Arrkid, Dr. - (Chapter 1) He was a Xenolfan military doctor. Dr. Arrkid worked for the Xenolfan Government. He had white hair and sapphire eyes. Dr. Arrkid also had large, black wings.

Arrvia - (Chapter 9) She was a Humolfan who lived on the planet Shardia. Arrvia had white hair and sapphire eyes that glowed. She also had large, black wings. Arrvia was the mother of Inatharr Taw.

Ascent, The - (Chapter 13) A casino on the planet Salinarr Nevis.

Asparell coin - (Chapter 1) Coins that had been used in ancient times and were worth about 2000 credits each. There was only one group of people who currently used Asparell coins in the galaxy, the Syrenthian Brotherhood Knights of Darkness.

Asparr Celtarious - (Chapter 1) A planet within the Syrenthian Government's territory.

Athenarr - (Chapter 1) He was a Humolfan who lived on the planet S4. Athenarr had white hair and sapphire eyes that glowed. He also had large, black wings. Athenarr was the partner of Aarria.

Aura's Delight - (Chapter 13) An intoxication joint and restaurant on the planet Enax Port.

Auracon's Game - (Chapter 13) A casino on the planet Salinarr Nevis.

Aurora - (Chapter 15) She was a Galactic Emergency Medical Technician for Galactic Emergency Medical Services. Aurora had blond hair and brown eyes.

Avalanche Resort, The - (Chapter 3) A resort on the snow planet Aamaress.

Avolium, Aaron - (Chapter 12) He lived on the planet Red Jacket. Aaron had blond hair. He was the son of Misty and Kulu Avolium.

Avolium, Kulu - (Chapter 3) He lived on the planet Red Jacket. Kulu was the keyboardist for the band Maranadda. He had long, blond hair.

Kulu was the husband of Misty Avolium and the father of Aaron and Shanda Avolium.

Avolium, Misty - (Chapter 12) She lived on the planet Red Jacket. Misty had long, blond hair. She was the wife of Kulu Avolium and the mother of Aaron and Shanda Avolium.

Avolium, Shanda - (Chapter 12) She lived on the planet Red Jacket. Shanda had blond hair. She was the daughter of Misty and Kulu Avolium.

B

Bapbs - (Chapter 1) He was a Xenolfan. Bapbs, along with Rodes, was involved in a last stand against the Xenolfan Government's genocide campaign. He had white hair and sapphire eyes. Bapbs also had large, black wings.

Bapbs & Rodes Last Stand - (Chapter 5) An area on the planet S4 where a Xenolfan named Bapbs and a human named Rodes took a last stand against the Xenolfan Government's genocide campaign.

Blaze - (Chapter 15) He was a Galactic Emergency Medical Technician for Galactic Emergency Medical Services. Blaze had brown hair.

Blue Sapphire - (Chapter 13) A casino on the planet Salinarr Nevis.

Blue Space - (Chapter 5) An area of light blue colored space that was a phenomenon that stretched from Shardia to Aamaress.

Blue Star - (Chapter 9) A Syrenthian Government battleship. The *Blue Star* was one of ten battleships in the fleet that responded to an attack in the Shardaa Sector.

C

Casino 21 - (Chapter 13) A casino on the planet Salinarr Nevis.

Celestial - (Chapter 9) A Syrenthian Government battleship. The

Celestial was one of ten battleships in the fleet that responded to an attack in the Shardaa Sector.

Charseaa, Phensiarr - (Chapter 3) She was a Xenolfan who lived in the Xenolfan Government palace on the planet Olf Teruda. Phensiarr was the leader of the Xenolfan Government. She had long, white hair and sapphire eyes.

Chelliss - (Chapter 11) A planet located in the Shar Nefalis Star System, within the Syrenthian Government's territory. Chelliss was part of the Industrial Sector.

Civie Arena - (Chapter 12) A venue on the planet Red Jacket.

CJ Whitmann's Hardware & Supply Co. - (Chapter 12) An old hardware store on the planet Red Jacket that was owned by CJ Whitmann.

Cliven - (Chapter 1) He was a Xenolfan who lived on the planet Salinarr Nevis almost one thousand years before casinos were built there. Cliven had white hair and sapphire eyes. He also had large, black wings. Cliven was friends with Tarrias.

Cobalt, Dennon - (Chapter 2) He worked for the marketing department of the StellularNav Corporation. Dennon was previously rescued from the Shardaa Sector by Galactic Emergency Medical Services. He was asked by the Syrenthian Government to help in their investigation to find Sierra Shalinsky in the Shardaa Sector. Dennon had black hair.

comm - (Chapter 1) A communicator device that had multiple functions.

Copper Meadows - (Chapter 12) A restaurant on the planet Red Jacket.

Correthell, Dr. - (Chapter 1) He was a Xenolfan military doctor. Dr. Correthell worked for the Xenolfan Government. He had white hair and sapphire eyes. Dr. Correthell also had large, black wings.

D

Dalaa (military base) - (Chapter 1) A Xenolfan Government military base located on the satellite Dalaa.

Dalaa (satellite) - (Chapter 1) The single satellite of the planet Olf Teruda. Dalaa was the location of a Xenolfan Government military base of the same name.

Darrian, Commander - (Chapter 1) He was a Xenolfan. Darrian was a commander in the Xenolfan Government military. He had white hair and sapphire eyes. Darrian also had large, black wings.

Deliverance - (Chapter 8) A large hospital spaceship owned by Galactic Emergency Medical Services. The *Deliverance* had multiple levels and numerous facilities. A state-of-the-art surgical center was one of its many features. The ship was continually staffed by a multitude of doctors, surgeons, nurses, therapists, and emergency personnel. Most staff worked in shifts, but others worked on an on-call basis. Part of the emergency services division had some military personnel in the mix, as well as a salvage unit.

Deltarr - (Chapter 8) A Xenolfan Government battleship. The *Deltarr* was destroyed in a battle at Olf Teruda during the New Syrenthian War.

Destiny - (Chapter 5) She was a Humolfan. Destiny had white hair and sapphire eyes that glowed. She also had large, black wings. Destiny was the 38th great grandmother of Estrus.

Dignity - (Chapter 8) A Syrenthian Government battleship under the leadership of Captain Arbin Xaanoss. The *Dignity* was one of ten battleships in the fleet that responded to an attack in the Shardaa Sector.

Discord - (Chapter 14) Maranadda's third album.

Dissident Faction - (Chapter 2) An organized group of Humolfans that separated from the rest of the species and lived on the planet S3.

The Dissident Faction did not want to repatriate back into galactic society and fought the other Humolfans who were attempting to repatriate.

Duet Array - (Chapter 13) A table game of chance that didn't require much strategy. It involved matching up a chosen icon on a digital display to a randomly selected icon. The game ended after five rounds. If no icons matched, the house would win.

E

Echeon, Rasmond - (Chapter 3) She was a Galactic Emergency Medical Technician for Galactic Emergency Medical Services. Rasmond had long, brown hair.

Enax Port - (Chapter 1) A planet within the Syrenthian Government's territory.

Enchanted Resonance - (Chapter 15) A symphonic metal band.

Enelra, Jacquelyn "Jackie" - (Chapter 12) She lived on the planet Red Jacket. Jacquelyn was the girlfriend of Aarian Trodder and the mother of Sophie Enelra. She had long, brown hair.

Enelra, Sophie - (Chapter 12) She lived on the planet Red Jacket. Sophie was the daughter of Jacquelyn Enelra and Aarian Trodder.

Eslarr - (Chapter 6) She was a Xenolfan who lived in the town of New Winterfest on the planet Aamaress. Eslarr and her husband, Gathin, were managers at The Avalanche Resort in New Winterfest. She had long, white hair and sapphire eyes.

Esoteric - (Chapter 14) Maranadda's first album.

Estivant, Arvon - (Chapter 3) He lived on the planet Red Jacket. Arvon was the drummer for the band Maranadda. He had long, brown hair, tattoos, and piercings.

Estrus - (Chapter 2) She was a Humolfan who lived on the planet S6.

Estrus was an officer in the Humolfan Command. She was responsible for locating an advocate for the Humolfans. Estrus had long, white hair and sapphire eyes that glowed. Estrus also had large, black wings and a Feathers of Shardaa tattoo on her lower abdomen. She owned a dog named Thepsi and a spaceship named *Aileron*.

Exandra - (Chapter 1) A planet that was the seat of the Syrenthian Government.

F

Feathers of Shardaa - (Chapter 4) It was a symbol with great significance to the Humolfans. In the early centuries of the Humolfans being exiled to the Shardaa Sector, they would inscribe Feathers of Shardaa symbols above caves, on mountain rock walls, and on gravestones. The feather that leaned to the left represented the Humolfans ability to fly, while the broken feather on the right represented the Xenolfans being stripped of their ability to fly. When Humolfan females reached a certain age, they would receive a Feathers of Shardaa tattoo on their mons pubis.

Flux Ship Mods - (Chapter 12) A company that specialized in modifying spaceships.

Foss, Admiral Lytria - (Chapter 9) She was the admiral of a Syrenthian Government fleet of ten battleships that were bound for an operation in the Shardaa Sector. Lytria was stationed aboard the battleship *Syrenth* during the operation.

Frozen Solstice - (Chapter 15) A symphonic metal band.

G

Galactic Emergency Medical Services (GEMS) - (Chapter 2) An emergency medical services company serving the entire Syrenthian Galaxy with headquarters on the planet Relistorr.

Galactic Emergency Medical Technician (Galactic EMT) - (Chapter 2) A specially-trained medical professional and generally a first responder during galactic disasters and crisis.

Galeva Krove - (Chapter 11) A planet located in the Galeva Krove Star System, within the Syrenthian Government's territory. Galeva Krove had a ring of frozen ice and rock around it.

Galeva Krove Star System - (Chapter 11) A star system in the Syrenthian Galaxy, within the Syrenthian Government's territory.

Garrious - (Chapter 4) He was a Xenolfan who lived on the planet Olf Teruda. Garrious was a Xenolfan military officer who accepted a missiloid suicide mission. He had long, white hair and sapphire eyes. Garrious was scheduled for execution on the planet Exandra for his crime of flying a missiloid into the Aamaress town of Winterfest.

Gathin - (Chapter 6) He lived in the town of New Winterfest on the planet Aamaress. Gathin and his wife, Eslarr, were managers at The Avalanche Resort in New Winterfest. He had shoulder-length, brown hair. Gathin had a wolf tattoo on his left side.

Ginger Alquinola - (Chapter 4) A carbonated alcoholic beverage with a considerable amount of effervescence. The ginger content was very spicy and it had a hint of lemon.

Givinis, Dr. - (Chapter 11) She was the senior doctor and administrator at the main sex clinic space station in the Galeva Krove Star System.

Godspeed - (Chapter 8) A Syrenthian Government battleship. The *Godspeed* was one of ten battleships in the fleet that responded to an attack in the Shardaa Sector.

Golden Oasis - (Chapter 13) A casino on the planet Salinarr Nevis.

Graluss, Dr. - (Chapter 7) He was a Humolfan doctor on the planet Shardia. Dr. Graluss helped with Sierra Shalinsky while she was in a coma. He had white hair and sapphire eyes that glowed.

Grave of Mothers - (Chapter 1) A cemetery on the planet S4 where

Siiteper Affelum of the Xenolfan Government committed genocide against interspecies families. The mothers were killed in a field and the fathers were forced off a cliff at the edge of the field where they fell to their deaths. The children were left to bury their mothers.

GrayMar - (Chapter 8) A Syrenthian Government battleship. The *GaryMar* was one of five Syrenthian Government battleships that was involved in a battle at Olf Teruda during the New Syrenthian War. It sustained minimal damage. The *GrayMar* was also one of ten battleships in the fleet that responded to an attack in the Shardaa Sector.

H

Humolfan - (Chapter 1) One of the three known intelligent species in the Syrenthian Galaxy, other than humans and Xenolfans. Humolfans had white hair, sapphire eyes that glowed, and gray skin. They also had large, black wings and the ability to fly.

Humolfan Command - (Chapter 2) The military arm of the Humolfan Government.

Humolfan Government - (Chapter 5) A government within the Syrenthian Galaxy that had Humolfan citizens. The seat of the government was on the planet Shardia.

Humolfan Repatriation Conference - (Chapter 11) A conference to prepare for the repatriation of Humolfans back into galactic society after their one thousand-year exile. It was led by Sierra Shalinsky and Estrus.

I

Industrial Sector - (Chapter 8) A sector in the Syrenthian Government's territory that included the entire Shar Nefalis Star System with the planets Shar Nefalis, Aomium Swith, Chelliss, and Ardellia. Manufacturing, mining, and other productive facilities were abundant on all four planets.

intoxication joint - (Chapter 7) A drinking establishment.

J

Jareen - (Chapter 3) She was a secretary at the Syrenthian Government building on the planet Exandra.

Jinkins (committee) - (Chapter 3) A committee comprised of members of the Superior Mountain Club on the planet Asparr Celtarious. The Jinkins committee made decisions regarding many aspects of the Superior Mountain Club property.

Jinkins (insult) - (Chapter 3) An insult used by Sierra Shalinsky that derived from her discord with the Jinkins committee of the Superior Mountain Club on her home planet Asparr Celtarious. Sierra owned adjacent property across Lake Serenity from the Superior Mountain Club. She defined the insult of Jinkins as meaning idiot.

L

Lake Serenity - (Chapter 3) A lake on the planet Asparr Celtarious that was surrounded by white pine trees. Lake Serenity sat below the Superior Mountains.

Leerial - (Chapter 1) He was a Humolfan with pilot skills. Leerial had gray skin and sapphire eyes that glowed. He also had large, black wings.

lightspeed-plus - (Chapter 1) A general term used to reference spaceship speeds beyond that of light.

Lightyear's Treasure - (Chapter 13) A casino on the planet Salinarr Nevis.

Linerston - (Chapter 8) A Syrenthian Government battleship. The *Linerston* was one of ten battleships in the fleet that responded to an attack in the Shardaa Sector.

Lucky Stone - (Chapter 13) A casino on the planet Salinarr Nevis.

Lydia - (Chapter 14) She was a Humolfan. Lydia had white hair and sapphire eyes that glowed. She also had large, black wings. Lydia was the sister of Shaania.

M

Macenburg, Shaslin - (Chapter 3) She lived on the planet Red Jacket. Shaslin had long, brown hair. She was the wife of Vincent Macenburg.

Macenburg, Vincent - (Chapter 3) He lived on the planet Red Jacket. Vincent was the sound technician for the band Maranadda. He had long, brown hair. Vincent was the husband of Shaslin Macenburg.

Mainter, Iisherth - (Chapter 1) She human who lived on the planet Olf Teruda as a widow. Iisherth had been in an interspecies relationship with a Xenolfan man who had died in a mining incident. She was the mother of the Humolfan, Jerex Mainter.

Mainter, Jerex - (Chapter 1) He was a Humolfan who lived on the planet Olf Teruda. Jerex had white hair and sapphire eyes that glowed. He also had large, black wings. Jerex was the son of Iisherth Mainter. He was good friends with Marsull.

Malanaa - (Chapter 13) She a Xenolfan who lived on the planet Olf Teruda. Malanaa had long, white hair and sapphire eyes. She was one of the many polyamorous lovers of Xenolfan Government leader Aaranix Tuvelless.

Maranadda - (Chapter 2) A popular symphonic metal band whose home planet was Red Jacket. Maranadda had an original lineup of Sierra Shalinsky on vocals, Yosemite McFarlin on guitars, Sanarith Raastarr on guitars, Arrian Trodder on bass, Kulu Avolium on keyboards, and Arvon Estivant on drums. When their vocalist went missing, she was replaced with Aymreth Rosenn. Their manager and booking agent was Shasta Varium and their sound technician was Vincent Macenburg.

Marsull - (Chapter 1) He was a Humolfan who lived on the planet Olf Teruda. Marsull had white hair and sapphire eyes that glowed. He also had large, black wings. Marsull was good friends with Jerex Mainter.

Mauve - (Chapter 6) She was a host at The Avalanche Resort on the planet Aamaress. Mauve had blond hair. She was the girlfriend of Max.

Max - (Chapter 6) He was a host at The Avalanche Resort on the planet Aamaress. Max had brown hair. He was the boyfriend of Mauve.

Mazniriatt - (Chapter 4) He was a Humolfan who lived on the planet Shardia. Mazniriatt was the owner of a tattoo shop on Shardia. He was a gifted tattoo artist and was known for his Feathers of Shardaa tattoo. Mazniriatt had short, spiky, white hair and sapphire eyes that glowed. He also had large, black wings.

McFarlin, Yosemite - (Chapter 3) He lived on the planet Red Jacket. Yosemite was one of the guitarists for the band Maranadda. He owned the house and studio where the band practiced. Yosemite owned several all-terrain vehicles that the band used on Red Jacket trails. He had short, spiky, brown hair.

Millott, Elliss - (Chapter 12) He was the incident commander for Galactic Emergency Medical Services. Elliss had gray hair.

missiloid - (Chapter 4) A type of weapon used by the Xenolfan Government against humans durning the Syrenthian War. A missiloid was also used by the Xenolfan Government 100 years later to attack the planet Aamaress, which contributed to the brief New Syrenthian War. The weapons were made from a small asteroid mounted with a cockpit and an ion engine that controlled its direction. Missiloids had no additional weapons and only served the purpose of a suicide mission of mass destruction on a planet.

Montoraania - (Chapter 13) A planet located in the Montoraania Star System, within the Syrenthian Government's territory. Montoraania was known for its compound Toraanium, which was toxic only to humans.

Montoraania Star System - (Chapter 13) A star system in the

Syrenthian Galaxy, within the Syrenthian Government's territory.

Moss, Gramer - (Chapter 4) She was a Humolfan who lived on the planet S3. Gramer was the leader of the Dissident Faction. She had long, white hair and sapphire eyes that glowed. Gramer also had large, black wings.

Motevell, Whitney - (Chapter 5) She was a Humolfan. Whitney was the head librarian at the atheneum in the city of Naantress on the planet Shardia. She had long, white hair and sapphire eyes that glowed. Whitney also had large, black wings.

N

Naantress - (Chapter 5) A large city on the planet Shardia.

Naantress Hospital - (Chapter 9) A hospital in the city of Naantress on the planet Shardia.

Narris - (Chapter 11) He was a Humolfan. Narris was a member of the Syrenthian Brotherhood Knights of Darkness.

Nasatomia - (Chapter 13) An ancient city in the southern hemisphere on the planet Enax Port.

Nassathia - (Chapter 12) A town on the planet Asparr Celtarious.

Nast, Captain - (Chapter 1) He was a Xenolfan captain in the Xenolfan Government military. Nast was the captain of the battleship *Olf Maximus*.

Neothuss - (Chapter 1) A Xenolfan Government battleship that secretly guarded the Shardaa Sector during the time of Siiteper Affelum as leader, although that was Syrenthian Government territory.

New Syrenthian War - (Chapter 8) A brief war between the Xenolfan Government and the Syrenthian Government. The New Syrenthian War included a space battle at Olf Teruda and a Syrenthian Government presence in space at Salinarr Nevis.

New Winterfest - (Chapter 6) A town in the Northern Territories on the planet Aamaress. New Winterfest was the result of the town of Winterfest being rebuilt after it had been destroyed by a missiloid attack.

New Winterfest Memorial Lodge - (Chapter 6) It was located in the town of New Winterfest in the Northern Territories on the planet Aamaress. New Winterfest Memorial Lodge was part of The Avalanche Resort. It was dedicated to all who those who lost their lives during the missiloid attack on the former town of Winterfest.

Northern Territories - (Chapter 6) A remote northern area on the planet Aamaress that included the town of Winterfest.

Novels - (Chapter 14) Maranadda's second album.

O

Ocean Port Bridge - (Chapter 5) A bridge on the planet Shardia that connected the city of Naantress to smaller city across an ocean inlet. The Ocean Port Bridge was destroyed by the Dissident Faction.

Oldstaff - (Chapter 8) A Xenolfan Government battleship. The *Oldstaff* was involved in the New Syrenthian War and took extremely heavy damage at a battle at Olf Teruda.

Olf Maximus - (Chapter 1) A Xenolfan Government battleship under the leadership of Captain Nast.

Olf Teruda - (Chapter 1) A paradise planet that was the seat of the Xenolfan Government.

Operation Reprisal - (Chapter 10) A military operation by the Humolfan Government using both Humolfan Command and the Syrenthian Brotherhood Knights of Darkness to eliminate the Dissident Faction.

P

Parker - (Chapter 3) He was the senior officer of the Communications Department for the Syrenthian Government on the planet Exandra.

Patriot - (Chapter 8) A Syrenthian Government battleship. The *Patriot* was one of ten battleships in the fleet that responded to an attack in the Shardaa Sector.

Phensiarr's Fortune - (Chapter 13) A casino on the planet Salinarr Nevis. Phensiarr's Fortune was formerly called Aaranix's Gold, but the name was changed to Phensiarr's Fortune when Phensiarr Charseaa replaced Aaranix Tuvelless as leader of the Xenolfan Government.

Priscilla Pussy Lips - (Chapter 13) A Nickname given to Priscilla Stryderr by Sierra Shalinsky.

Q

Quillexx - (Chapter 1) A popular meat from the planet Olf Teruda.

R

Raastarr, Arcashia - (Chapter 12) She lived on the planet Red Jacket. Arcashia had long, blond hair. She was the wife of Sanarith Raastarr.

Raastarr, Sanarith - (Chapter 3) He lived on the planet Red Jacket. Sanarith was one of the guitarists for the band Maranadda. He was bald. Sanarith was the husband of Arcashia Raastarr.

Rachel - (Chapter 15) She was a Galactic Emergency Medical Technician for Galactic Emergency Medical Services. Rachel had brown hair.

Railler, Captain Linex - (Chapter 8) He worked for Galactic Emergency Medical Services and was the captain of the hospital ship *Deliverance*.

Red Jacket (planet) - (Chapter 1) A planet within the Syrenthian

Government's territory. It had once been the location of a large copper mining industry.

Red Jacket (song) - (Chapter 14) A song by Maranadda from their first album, Esoteric. Red Jacket was a song about the copper mining history on the planet Red Jacket.

Relistorr - (Chapter 12) A planet within the Syrenthian Government's territory. Relistorr was the headquarters of Galactic Emergency Medical Services. The planet was extremely secure and only medical and other emergency personnel had access to and from its surface.

Riggs, Misner - (Chapter 1) He had lived on the planet Exandra. Misner had been the leader of the Syrenthian Government one thousand years earlier.

Rodes - (Chapter 1) He, along with Bapbs, was involved in a last stand against the Xenolfan Government's genocide campaign.

Rosenn, Aymreth - (Chapter 3) She was a Xenolfan who lived on the planet Red Jacket. Aymreth was the new vocalist for the band Maranadda. She had long, white hair and sapphire eyes.

Rosheil - (Chapter 14) She was a girlfriend of Arvon Estivant.

S

S2 - (Chapter 1) A desolate planet located in the Shardaa Star System, within the Syrenthian Government's territory and later officially within the Humolfan Government's territory. S2 was part of the Shardaa Sector. It had an atmosphere of air.

S3 - (Chapter 1) A planet located in the Shardaa Star System, within the Syrenthian Government's territory and later officially within the Humolfan Government's territory. S3 was part of the Shardaa Sector.

S4 - (Chapter 1) A planet located in the Shardaa Star System, within the Syrenthian Government's territory and later officially within the Humolfan Government's territory. S4 was part of the Shardaa Sector.

S5 - (Chapter 1) A planet located in the Shardaa Star System, within the Syrenthian Government's territory and later officially within the Humolfan Government's territory. S5 was part of the Shardaa Sector.

S6 - (Chapter 1) A planet located in the Shardaa Star System, within the Syrenthian Government's territory and later officially within the Humolfan Government's territory. S6 was part of the Shardaa Sector.

Salinarr Nevis - (Chapter 1) A planet within the Xenolfan Government's territory. Salinarr Nevis was filled with casinos across its surface. Years before, the human-controlled Syrenthian Government and the Xenolfan Government agreed that gaming facilities could be developed on the planet Salinarr Nevis to help the Xenolfans compensate for the previous damages done from the old Syrenthian War.

Sanctuary Star - (Chapter 8) A Syrenthian Government battleship. The *Sanctuary Star* was one of five Syrenthian Government battleships that was involved in a battle at Olf Teruda during the New Syrenthian War. It sustained minimal damage. The *Sanctuary Star* was also one of ten battleships in the fleet that responded to an attack in the Shardaa Sector.

Sevis - (Chapter 4) A sweet carbonated beverage.

Sex Palace - (Chapter 13) A casino on the planet Salinarr Nevis. Sex Palace featured sex-themed games, the Sex Palace Theater, and an adjacent shopping sex mall.

Sex Palace Theater - (Chapter 13) A theater within the Sex Palace casino that featured live sex performances of both humans and Xenolfans

SG302 - (Chapter 8) A Syrenthian Government military fighter ship.

Shaania - (Chapter 14) She was a Humolfan. Shaania had white hair and sapphire eyes that glowed. She also had large, black wings. Shaania was the sister of Lydia.

Shaeolian Black Hole - (Chapter 1) A black hole space object located in the Shardaa Sector, near the Shardaa Star System.

Shalinsky, Cathin - (Chapter 3) She lived on the planet Stilkoten Artibular. Cathin had black hair. She was the wife of Ralger Shalinsky and the mother of Sierra Shalinsky-Taw.

Shalinsky, Ralger - (Chapter 3) He lived on the planet Stilkoten Artibular. Ralger had brown hair. He was the husband of Cathin Shalinsky and the father of Sierra Shalinsky-Taw.

Shalinsky-Taw, Sierra - (Chapter 2) She lived on the planet Asparr Celtarious and later Shardia. Sierra was a Galactic Emergency Medical Technician for Galactic Emergency Medical Services. She was the former vocalist for the band Maranadda. Sierra had been an advocate for sexual freedom between humans and Xenolfans and an advocate for the Humolfan repatriation. She had long, black hair and blue eyes. Sierra owned a spaceship named *Tenebris*. Sierra was best friends with Priscilla Stryderr. She was the wife of Yilran Taw and the mother of Yilerra Taw.

Shar Nefalis - (Chapter 3) A planet located in the Shar Nefalis Star System, within the Syrenthian Government's territory. Shar Nefalis was part of the Industrial Sector.

Shar Nefalis Star System - (Chapter 8) A star system in the Syrenthian Galaxy, within the Syrenthian Government's territory.

Sharasp Tharrian Asteroid Mass - (Chapter 1) A small asteroid mass located in the Shardaa Sector, near the outer region of the Shardaa Star System.

Shardaa - (Chapter 1) A desolate planet located in the Shardaa Star System, within the Syrenthian Government's territory and later officially within the Humolfan Government's territory. Shardaa was part of the Shardaa Sector. It did not have an atmosphere.

Shardaa Sector - (Chapter 1) A sector in the Syrenthian Government's territory and later officially within the Humolfan Government's territory that included the entire Shardaa Star System with the planets Shardaa, S2, S3, S4, S5, and S6 as well as other celestial objects.

Shardaa Star System - (Chapter 1) A star system in the Syrenthian Galaxy, within the Syrenthian Government's territory and later officially within the Humolfan Government's territory.

Shardia - (Chapter 4) A planet located in the Shardaa Star System that was the seat of the Humolfan Government. Shardia was part of the Shardaa Sector.

Sharell - (Chapter 1) She was an officer in the Syrenthian Government. Sharell was part of the crew who helped rescue Tarrias.

Sharlexx - (Chapter 10) A medium-sized, sleek spaceship owned by Yilran Taw of the Humolfan Government.

Sharsia - (Chapter 5) The single satellite of the planet Shardia.

Sheena - (Chapter 3) She was a Xenolfan woman who lived on the planet Enax Port. Sheena had long, curly, white hair and sapphire eyes.

Silver Star Concert Hall - (Chapter 14) A venue on the planet Salinarr Nevis.

Sirlain, Edward - (Chapter 3) He lived on the planet Exandra. Edward was the leader of the Syrenthian Government. He had long, grayish-blond hair.

Sirron, Captain Roth - (Chapter 10) He was a captain in the Syrenthian Government military. Roth was the captain of the battleship *Syrenth*.

Smith, Bradford - (Chapter 13) He was the owner of a thermal cube factory and mine on the planet Shar Nefalis. Bradford had gray hair.

StellularNav Corporation - (Chapter 8) A company that manufactured parts for the Syrenthian Government SG302 fighter ships.

Stephard, Madison - (Chapter 12) She was a unit director and Galactic Emergency Medical Technician for Galactic Emergency Medical Services. Madison had long, curly, red hair.

Stilkoten Artibular - (Chapter 11) A fairly large planet within the Syrenthian Government's territory.

Stormy - (Chapter 6) He was a wolfdog owned by The Avalanche Resort.

Stratuss, Dr. - (Chapter 1) He was a top Xenolfan scientist. Dr. Stratuss worked for the Xenolfan Government. He had white hair and sapphire eyes. Dr. Stratuss also had large, black wings.

Stryderr, Braxton - (Chapter 2) He lived on the planet Exandra. Braxton was a Syrenthian Government investigator and administration official. He had short, brown and gray hair. Braxton was the husband of Priscilla Stryderr.

Stryderr, Priscilla - (Chapter 2) She lived on the planet Exandra. Priscilla worked in the health care industry at a hospital on the planet Exandra. She had been an advocate for sexual freedom between humans and Xenolfans. Priscilla had long, blond hair. She was best friends with Sierra Shalinsky.

Superior Mountain Club - (Chapter 3) An exclusive club located in the Superior Mountains on the planet Asparr Celtarious. The club was run by the Jinkins committee. Members of the club acquired a large amount of property in the Superior Mountains. They were known to be snobs, hypocrites, and rude to others on the planet.

Superior Mountains - (Chapter 12) A mountainous region in the northern territory on the planet Asparr Celtarious.

Surefire - (Chapter 14) Maranadda's fourth album.

Syrenth - (Chapter 8) A Syrenthian Government battleship under the leadership of Captain Roth Sirron. The *Syrenth* was one of ten battleships in the fleet that responded to an attack in the Shardaa Sector.

Syrenthian Brotherhood Knights of Darkness - (Chapter 4) A mysterious group of people in the Syrenthian Galaxy who were known to be badasses and not to be messed with. The group were the only ones in the Syrenthian Galaxy to still use Asparell coins. The members were Humolfans who dedicated their life to the group, dying their hair black, wearing special contacts to conceal their sapphire eyes that glowed, tanning their skin, and clipping their wings.

Syrenthian Galaxy - (Chapter 1) A galaxy controlled by three governments. The Syrenthian Government was home to humans who controlled most of the galaxy. The Xenolfan Government was home to Xenolfans who controlled the planets Olf Teruda and Salinarr Nevis. The Humolfan Government was home to Humolfans who controlled all of the Shardaa Sector.

Syrenthian Government - (Chapter 1) A government within the Syrenthian Galaxy that had mostly human citizens; however, there were some Xenolfans who lived in Syrenthian Government territory. The seat of the government was on the planet Exandra.

Syrenthian War - (Chapter 4) A war that took place about one hundred years earlier. The Syrenthian War was fought between the Xenolfans and the humans. The humans had become aggressive against the aliens for unjust causes. When the Xenolfans started to fight back, it turned into a terrible galactic war. In retaliation, the Xenolfans had used controlled asteroids, dubbed missiloids, to assault human-occupied planets.

T

Tales of Shardaa - (Chapter 7) A song by Maranadda from their first album, Esoteric. Tales of Shardaa was a song about an uncharted, desolate, and mysterious region of the Syrenthian Galaxy called the Shardaa Sector.

Tanorra - (Chapter 3) She was a communications technician for the Syrenthian Government.

Tarrias - (Chapter 1) He was a Xenolfan. Tarrias was an officer in the

Xenolfan Government military. He had white hair and sapphire eyes.
Tarrias also had large, black wings. He was friends with Cliven.

Taw, Inatharr - (Chapter 9) He was a Humolfan who lived on the
planet S3. Inatharr was a member of the Dissident Faction. He had
white hair and sapphire eyes that glowed. Inatharr also had large,
black wings. He was the sone of Yilran Taw and Arrvia.

Taw, Yilerra - (Chapter 15) She was the first human and Humolfan
mix who lived on the planet Shardia. Yilerra had black hair and
sapphire blue eyes. She also had little, black wings. Yilerra was the
daughter of Yilran Taw and Sierra Shalinsky-Taw.

Taw, Yilran - (Chapter 5) He was a Humolfan who lived on the planet
Shardia. Yilran was the leader of the Humolfan Government. He had
long, white hair and sapphire eyes that glowed. He also had large,
black wings. Yilran was the husband of Sierra Shalinsky-Taw and the
father of Yilerra Taw. He owned a spaceship named *Sharlexx.*

Tenebris - (Chapter 2) A spaceship owned by Sierra Shalinsky. The
Tenebris was about one hundred years old and was once a fighter ship
in the Syrenthian War.

Thepsi - (Chapter 4) He was a little dog with white, brown, and black
fur, and brown eyes. Thepsi was owned by Estrus.

thermal cube - (Chapter 13) A device that was designed to warm up
an area in cold weather. Thermal cubes contained an element that
heated up when activated and cooled back down when deactivated by
its electronic circuit.

Thomas - (Chapter 14) He was a Humolfan who lived in the Humolfan
Government palace on the planet Shardia. Thomas worked for Yilran
Taw as the palace butler. He had white hair and sapphire eyes that
glowed. Thomas also had large, black wings.

Ticrisuda Powersports - (Chapter 3) A company on the planet Shar
Nefalis, in the Industrial Sector, owned by Garnell Meshtief. Ticrisuda
Powersports manufactured snowmobiles, all-terrain vehicles, and

other recreational sport vehicles.

Toraanium - (Chapter 13) A compound found on the planet Montoraania that was toxic to humans.

Tovels - (Chapter 1) He was a Humolfan who lived on the planet S4. Tovels had white hair and sapphire eyes that glowed. He also had large, black wings.

Trodder, Arrian - (Chapter 3) He lived on the planet Red Jacket. Arrian was the bass player for the band Maranadda. He had long, brown hair. Arrian was the boyfriend of Jacquelyn Enelra and the father of Sophie Enelra.

Truliniot - (Chapter 8) A Syrenthian Government battleship. The *Truliniot* was one of ten battleships in the fleet that responded to an attack in the Shardaa Sector.

Tuvelless, Aaranix - (Chapter 3) He was a Xenolfan and the former leader of the Xenolfan Government. Aaranix was forced to step down and later arrested and put into prison on Olf Teruda for several crimes that required the death penalty. He had long, white hair and sapphire eyes

V

Varium, Shasta - (Chapter 12) She was the manager and booking agent for the band Maranadda.

Versi - (Chapter 11) She was a Xenolfan nurse who worked at the main sex clinic on a space station in the Galeva Krove Star System. Versi had white hair and sapphire eyes.

Volum - (Chapter 7) A planet within the Syrenthian Government's territory.

W

Whitestone, Rheena - (Chapter 13) She was the widow of Tellaris Whitestone.

Whitestone, Tellaris - (Chapter 13) He had been a Syrenthian Government investigator. Tellaris had grayish-white hair. He was the late husband of Rheena Whitestone.

Whitmann, Angie - (Chapter 12) She lived on the planet Red Jacket. Angie was the wife of CJ Whitmann and the mother of Benjamin Whitmann.

Whitmann, Benjamin - (Chapter 12) He lived on the planet Red Jacket. Benjamin was a disabled young boy who enjoyed watching the ATVs race along the trails. He had brown hair. Benjamin was the son of CJ and Angie Whitmann.

Whitmann, CJ - (Chapter 12) He lived on the planet Red Jacket. CJ owned a hardware store on Red Jacket named CJ Whitmann's Hardware & Supply Co. He had gray hair. CJ was the husband of Angie Whitmann and the father of Benjamin Whitmann.

Wings of Shardaa - (Chapter 10) A Humolfan Government battleship under the leadership of Soltuss Yow. The *Wings of Shardaa* was the only battleship in the Humolfan Command.

Winterfest - (Chapter 4) A town in the Northern Territories on the planet Aamaress that was destroyed by a missiloid attack.

Wolf Peak - (Chapter 12) A small town on the planet Stilkoten Artibular.

Wolf's Den, The - (Chapter 13) A casino on the planet Salinarr Nevis.

X

Xaanoss, Captain Arbin - (Chapter 8) He was a captain in the Syrenthian Government military. Arbin was the captain of the battleship *Dignity.*

Xenolfan - (Chapter 1) One of the three known intelligent species in the Syrenthian Galaxy, other than humans and Humolfans. Xenolfans had white hair, sapphire eyes, and bluish-gray skin. Male Xenolfans had a patterned face. One thousand years earlier, the species had large, black wings.

Xenolfan Government - (Chapter 1) A government within the Syrenthian Galaxy that had Xenolfan citizens. The seat of the government was on the planet Olf Teruda.

Y

Yort, Remywian - (Chapter 4) He was a bartender at the Eccentric Elixir intoxication joint and cafe on the planet Volum. Remywian had gray hair.

Yow, Soltuss - (Chapter 2) She was a Humolfan. Soltuss was the head of the Humolfan Command military on the planet S6. She had long, white hair and sapphire eyes that glowed. Soltuss also had large, black wings.

Yttursal - (Chapter 15) She was a Xenolfan. Yttursal had long, white hair and sapphire eyes.

A NOTE FROM THE AUTHOR

Thank you for your interest in this WymerNovels title. If you enjoyed this novel, consider helping other readers discover it by leaving a review online. If you have any questions, please contact me at www.WymerNovels.com.

—Troy D. Wymer

Novelist Bio

Troy D. Wymer is a science fiction space opera novelist from Michigan, US. He started writing in 1984, but it wasn't until 2016 that he formed the WymerNovels imprint and began to publish novels. Troy enjoys reading, writing, and listening to various subgenres of metal music.